Huckleberry Dreaming

Huckleberry Dreaming

BROOKLYN BEAUMONT

The manufacturer's authorised representative in the EU
for product safety is Authorised Rep Compliance Ltd,
71 Lower Baggot Street, Dublin D02 P593 Ireland (www.arccompliance.com)

Troubador Publishing Ltd
Unit E2 Airfield Business Park,
Harrison Road, Market Harborough,
Leicestershire. LE16 7UL
Tel: 0116 2792299
Email: books@troubador.co.uk
Web: www.troubador.co.uk

ISBN 978 1836283 560

British Library Cataloguing in Publication Data.
A catalogue record for this book is available from the British Library.

Printed and bound in Great Britain by 4edge Limited
Typeset in 11pt Minion Pro by Troubador Publishing Ltd, Leicester, UK

Cover illustration by Kit Turner

For Steven

Prologue

"Step inside the machine."

The accents were Eastern European, the same as I'd heard in those artsy movies with subtitles—the ones Lucy used to take me to at The Apex on Saturday afternoons. But the words were spoken so coldly, I didn't know if I could trust them. I mean, I couldn't even see them, and I had no idea what the machine was, or what it would do to me.

"I... I don't wanna."

"It's important. We can't stress that enough. You have no idea."

A chink of light seeped through a crack somewhere, but still there were no faces. All I could see was a grid of little golden boxes gleaming in front of me, so I reached out, swiveling one about ninety degrees about the y-axis. And then they were whispering to each other behind my back.

"He made a move?"

"Yes, I can confirm that."

"A rotation?"

"Yes. No translation, though."

"Which box?"

"It will be cataloged, of course."

"For the copy?"

"Yes. But ask him one more time. We can avoid the copy if he agrees."

"Step inside the machine, Carney."

Part of me wanted to go along with it, just to find out what the hell the machine was supposed to do, and why they wanted me inside it so badly. But I was a six-year-old kid with a serious bout of the jitters, and I guess I was pretty stubborn, even at that age. "I wanna go home."

They spoke to me firmly and formally, as if I were an adult, almost like they had no concept of what it was like to be a child. "We can't make you go inside. We can only assure you of the importance of your decision. Please, think carefully. And remember that you have moved a box. That can only be undone if you enter the machine. We're opening the door for you now, Carney Caldwell. Once the bells stop ringing, take seven steps forward, and you'll be inside. Let the glory be yours."

There was a clang—a metal door sliding open, and I felt a rush of warm air sweep past my face. Then a chiming started, like the toll of an old grandfather clock. But in the end, I chose not to trust them. I turned in the opposite direction and bolted into the dark, as fast as I could manage, my limbs actually moving under the sheets.

In the morning, I asked Lucy if she knew anything about a machine guarded by Eastern European folk, and she laughed.

"You've been dreamin', Smoky." And, as if to drive the point home, she slipped The Everly Brothers' 'All I Have to Do is Dream' onto the gramophone turntable. "This was your ma's favorite," she told me, smiling as the stylus made contact. "It was top of the charts the week you were born."

"But how d'you know there's no machine?"

She was swaying just a little, in time to the music. "Ain't no one from Europe left," she said, a hint of sadness in her eyes. "They were all wiped out durin' the Leptotronic War."

"None of 'em came to Nunus?"

"No, none of 'em."

I guess the dream stayed at the back of my mind all the while I was growing up. I remember feeling like I'd let those people down by running away. But it didn't really bother me a great deal—at least, not until I was eighteen years old and about to graduate high school.

That was when everything changed—when the dream came back to haunt me.

1

The Arrest

The blue lights are like a mist now, and inside that foggy mess, the heads of paramedics bob up and down, not fast, not slow, but methodical, precise. And then a dolphin leaps out from the middle of it all, flicks its tail, and lands with a splash in a puddle of those little pink pills.

The paramedics don't seem to notice. "Can you hear us? Give us a sign."

I glance up at Akkasom—full, but sleeping in a downy quilt of cloud, the air swirling, cold inside my lungs. They're not doing CPR. Or are they? It's so hard to figure out what's real. I mean, I know there's no damn dolphin, but what the hell is going on here?

I'm flung over the hood of a Lincoln Continental, someone frisking me. Yeah, I'm pretty sure that's happening. Then a dude strolls down the alley with a radio, stopping in his tracks for the free sideshow, and suddenly The Platters' 'Only You' becomes a part of it all—a musical rubber stamp that validates the irony, the pathos.

"Move along," the cops say. "Nothin' to see here. Nothin' at all."

The sirens get real loud, almost deafening, but I'm so lucid at this point, I can see every zit on the teen cop's face.

"You're under arrest on suspicion of assault."

I reckon it must be his first time busting someone, the way he stammers toward the end as he reads me my Mirandas. Then the other two shove me in the back of the squad car, and 'Fraidy-Cat is forced to sit there at the side of me, squirming, twisting his hands, watching, like he's expecting me to jump him or something.

"Dunno what happened back there," I tell him, just wanting to get back to the alley so's I can make sure my buddy's okay. Then it all gets too much, and I start bawling. "I'm a pacifist, man. Always have been… Only just graduated high school last summer."

He looks at me like I'm some kind of screwball, and who can blame him? Everyone on the planet is a pacifist after the horrors of the Leptotronic War. It's written into our goddamn DNA. And to make matters worse, my right knuckles are throbbing something fierce, blood all over the seat.

"Please. You gotta turn around. He's my best buddy. He needs me."

"Sorry," 'Fraidy-Cat says. "You've been arrested. You do know what that means?"

The journey seems to take forever. It's as if each second is holding back, forcing me to grapple my way through it, slowly, painfully, before I reach the next, my nerves shredded to dust. And when they finally usher me into the precinct, it's hard to focus—to take anything in. There's the constant blare of phones, the clackety-clack of typewriters, a baffled-looking cop behind a sliding glass window, filling in forms, pressing buzzers, multitasking the hell out of everything.

"You wanna call your attorney before we take you for questioning?" he asks.

"Ain't got no attorney. Can't afford one, neither."

"Then we'll get Trellaman to sit in with you."

I'm escorted into room five: the interrogation suite, where a sixty-something plain-clothes cop sits waiting, another guy hovering round him like a tetchy old wasp.

"Sit down, please, Carney. I'm D.I. Langley and this is Mr. Trellaman, your brief."

"Look. I know the sheriff. He's a friend a' the family."

"He ain't here. And just 'cause you know Bewick, don't mean you can go around beatin' folks up and get away with it. You wanna tell us why you did it—why you knocked a member of your own gang unconscious?"

Langley reeks of stale sweat and cigarettes, and there are wrinkles all over his face—real deep-seated, like tree bark. Maybe there's a notch there for every perp he's squeezed a confession out of. As for Trellaman, you'd be forgiven for thinking they offered the job to the first bum they found out on the streets.

"It's all so damn hazy. It's like I was stoned, but I didn't take much—not enough to get into that kinda state. All I know is... I'm drownin' in guilt. And not just 'cause a' what went down in the alley. I got this weird thing where I blame myself for everythin'—for the way the world is. It's this dumb dream I had as a kid. You wouldn't understand."

D.I. Tree-Bark scowls, the creases in his skin multiplying tenfold. "A dream?"

"I know it sounds crazy. But it's like I shoulda done what they wanted, but I didn't. I made the wrong choice, and I can't stop thinkin' about it—"

Langley cuts me off sharp. "Stick to the incident, Carney. We don't need your goddamn life story. Anyway, we got a call from the medical center while they were bringin' you in, and I'm sorry to tell you it's not good news. The victim's in a coma, so the charge is aggravated assault now. You're lookin' at fifteen years minimum if you're found guilty, and let's face it, you were caught at the scene with blood all over your knuckles. So, the sooner you figure out what happened and tell us, the better."

I guess it had to go one way or the other. When folk get taken out, they either come around or they don't. I want to run into the middle of the nearest field and just howl at the moons—howl until my throat bursts.

"Hey, slow it down there, bud. We ain't established nothin' yet." Trellaman plonks a stick of Beemans into his mouth. "Bail's out the question for aggravated assault," he tells me, shaking his head. "And that's the law, Carney. Applies across the whole a' Cassaforta." He grins, patting me on the shoulder, the gum lodged between his teeth. "But you only just graduated high school last summer. I'll see if I can pull some strings." It's obvious he's bullshitting from the cheapness of his suit. The only strings a sidewinder like that can pull are his bootlaces.

Langley takes out a pad, slides a pen from the side of his ear. "Whenever you're ready, Carney, you can make a statement—in your own words."

"Okay, but I need a cigarette. I mean, this is my best buddy we're talking about. *My best buddy.*"

"Sure." Trellaman pulls a box of Lucky Strikes from his jacket pocket, hands me a smoke, then holds out his lighter, the words Dakota whispered last spring almost floating in the air, like a gateway to the past—a beautiful but unreachable vortex: *It's nice when someone offers you a light. It's like keepin' a promise. Makes you feel you matter in some small way.*

I draw on the cigarette, my hands still trembling, wisps of smoke blotting out their faces. If I squint a bit, I can kid myself that they're not really here at all. "My gang, the Arch Angels, they were my world. I grew up with them: Earl, Taylor, Booker,

4

and then Dakota. It was pretty much plain sailin'. I mean, the five of us were happy as pigs in mud—never so much as frowned at each other, I swear. Well, that's how it seemed, till Marshall Bexley showed up. After that, things were never quite the same. One afternoon, when we were down at the creek, Taylor lost it with Earl for no damn reason. I guess that was when it all kicked off—when the whole godforsaken nightmare started to unfold."

2

A History Lesson

t was our senior year at Santa Sasoonia High, and we'd finished with Earth history. Bren-Dougal was on to Banunus and all the stuff about the Dillingers now.

"So, it was Walter Dillinger, the older brother, who came up with LIDSOC," he told us. "It stands for 'leptotronic inter-dimensional space-ordered curvature'. A bit of a mouthful, I know, but the key point here is that, for mankind, it was the gateway to the stars." Bren-Dougal swung his arms about so much when he talked, you couldn't help but giggle. He was like some big old windmill, sails turning like crazy in the middle of a storm.

Taylor Pumble stuck his hand up. "Where'd the idea come from, sir?" he said.

I was never quite sure if Windy knew about the game. I mean, it wasn't hard to figure out the pattern. Taylor would ask a question, Windy would answer, and Earl Hunter would come out with some smart remark. Then I'd score him based on the kind of reaction he got. If the class ended up rolling on the floor, or if Windy joined in, there'd be extra points, and that happened a lot because Earl could pretty much wring a laugh out of any old thing. I guess you could say he was the ultimate class clown—one of those guys who just oozed charisma from every pore in his body.

"Ah, good question. According to some sources, the real breakthrough came in 2150 when Walter was a researcher at Cornell. His group was attending a conference near Ithaca Falls. It's a bit like Newton and the apple, I guess. They say Dillinger bit into a slice of prize-winning watermelon, but it crumbled in his hand. He was just staring down at the pieces for the longest time, totally lost in thought. Then, all of a sudden, he took to his heels— ran all the way back to the hotel without a word to anyone."

"He was desperate for the john, alright."

Everyone bar the dweebs at the front fell into a state of near hysteria. It was the voice Earl was putting on—the one that sounded like Jimmy Cagney on helium. Windy screwed his face up for a while, then chuckled plain enough to score Earl a nice fat bonus.

"No, Earl," Windy said, once the noise reached a manageable level. "Walter was desperate to get his ideas down on paper, although no one knows for sure whether the melon thing is true." He paused by the board with the chalk still in his hand, a faraway look in his eye. "Those leptotronic spaceships came to be, though, and Earth was plunged into a new age. Telescopes constructed using LIDSOC technology made observation of the remotest galaxies possible. And that was how Alpin Dillinger discovered the Dolon system, and the remarkable Earth-like planet that we live on today."

"When did all this happen?" Booker Pachello was scribbling down everything Windy was saying. She was hell-bent on getting to college to study space science come the fall, but she didn't sit with the dweebs, no siree. Booker was what I like to call 'Arch Angel to the core': a wild, fast-talking, quick-witted beatnik with a real taste for hard liquor. But I'm not implying here that we all had the same personality. I mean, Taylor was hot-headed as an air balloon, Earl was so laid-back he was practically floating, and Dakota, Taylor's girlfriend of nearly three years, was deep as the Mariana Trench, but I'll come back to that later.

"I was just getting to the dates, Brooke," Windy said, forcing Booker to cringe. It always rattled her when folk used her real name. "The first lepto ships were designed in 2156, the prototypes were completed in the early 2160s, and the Dolon exploration program commenced in 2173." He chalked the dates on the board next to his LIDSOC diagrams. "Now, the ships didn't reach their destinations by breaking light speed," he explained. "That's just impossible. They did it by bending the space around them, with the effect that distances were reduced by a factor of almost a trillion. However, unfortunately, the new technology also introduced the leptotronic bomb. An almighty flash of super-stretched gravitons devastated the entire Earth in 2176. It was the darkest time in history for mankind. Their only hope of survival was to go elsewhere."

"Don't get all 'melon-choly', sir."

Windy tried to shush everyone. "Cool it with the melon jokes, Earl," he said.

Earl could easily have snatched a ten for that one, maybe even gotten something extra for getting Windy all stirred up, but gags made off the cuff didn't count in the game.

"Of course, Banunus wasn't always so Earth-like," Windy went on. "A lot of work took place to change the gravity, and the axis and period of rotation to mimic Earth seasons and time—to make them align precisely. Flora and fauna were brought across, too—spores, seeds, and DNA samples from every known Earth species. The conservationists wouldn't have it any other way.

"Now, in terms of dates, the preparatory work and the full colonization were completed by 2190, but only the Magnatellan continent was populated. Migration to Cassaforta didn't happen until 2217. You see, the Dillingers were brilliant scientists, but lousy governors who failed to appease Gilbert Gowder and the pacifist rebels. In the early twenty-third century, Gowder and his followers—those who feared the bomb—had shunned anything to do with modern technology, fleeing the cities to seek complete separation on the uninhabited Cassaforta continent over four thousand miles away."

Earl shrugged. "When life throws ya melons…"

The class were busting a gut, and even Windy was trying his darndest to stifle a grin. "I'll throw something at you if you don't quit," he said, finally giving in and letting his smile take over.

"Yeah, put a LIDSOC in it," Booker said, pretending to scowl. "Some of us are tryin' to listen."

Windy didn't fuss too much if we goofed around, but the noise must have filtered through to Principal Thackery's office, because he breezed into the classroom without even knocking on the door. He glared at the chalkboard and whispered, "Too much modern science, Mr. Bren-Dougal. Too many details. You know the cut-off dates. You know the rules."

"Sorry, Mr. Thackery."

"Please, wipe the diagrams. Wipe them immediately."

After school, Earl and I trekked along the dust path that led to the cornfield surrounding the creek. The sky was turquoise, and Dol was peeking out behind the ulu trees, playing a cheeky game of hide-and-go-seek with the last few wisps of cirrus cloud.

"Thackery sure had a bee in his bonnet this afternoon. Dunno what all the fuss was about."

"Well, you know how jittery folk get when it comes to shit like that." Earl pushed a loose strand of his quiff back into place.

He liked to keep it neat, heaping on a ton of Brylcreem in the mornings just to mold it into shape, and you could guarantee there'd always be a comb sticking out the back pocket of his jeans.

We crossed the hillock, passed the faded metal sign that read, 'Danger—Pettiworn Rapids', and then strolled single file between the corn beds, jackets tied round our waists. The smallest of breezes was making the tassels nod, and in the distance, puddles of last night's rainwater rippled and quivered.

"Just thinkin' 'bout the time we first stumbled on the creek, all them years back."

"Yeah, second grade, after softball practice," Earl said, swishing a long branch out across the cornstalks. "Place ain't changed much."

We made our way down to the clearing where the towering boon-rocks had all but crumbled away, and you could get right down to the rapids. Then, without saying anything, we began scooping up pebbles, sorting out the flattest, and skimming them out across the water, one after the other, as looth birds chirped at us from up in the ulus. The old tire was still there, tied to what we called the hunchback tree. The first time we came here, it was the start of summer—so hot we could have fried our dinner on the sidewalk. We ended up staying until Dol went down, we were just so caught up in the fun of swinging into the river on the tire to cool off. And the following day, we couldn't wait for classes to be out, so's we could do it all over again. After that, hotfooting it to the creek just became a regular thing.

Earl chuckled. "We musta been a right pain in the ass when we were kids. Always buggin' our folks for inner tubes."

He knelt down, gathering up more skimmers, and I thought back to those glorious days when, sopping wet and pumped full of adrenaline, I'd be tossed around in an old tractor inner tube as it bounced ever closer to the boonstone jutting out over the mini waterfall. The trick was to work up enough speed and hit it right on the sweet spot, so's you'd glide out as far as you could before landing in the splash-pool at the bottom. Only then could you score the perfect arch. That was pretty much how we got our gang name: the Arch Angels, forever emblazoned on the back of our matching Maya-blue baseball jackets.

I spun a piece of flint level with the jetty, but it wasn't flat enough and only made a couple of jumps. "Say, major bummer about Windy droppin' that term paper on us. How we s'posed to write five thousand words on the mass colonization?"

A train of pebbles glided from Earl's hand, each one rolling gracefully over the skin of the water, and it occurred to me that the guy was as much a part of the creek as the swirling eddies, the grand old ulus, and the giant boon-crags that loomed on the horizon whenever you gazed north toward Hap Town.

"I think it's interestin'. Read some stuff that time Hobart stuck me in detention," he said, as if it was something that didn't happen too often. The truth was, he'd had more detentions than any other kid in school—more demerits as well, although school stuff didn't seem to bother him that much. He quit skimming and lit two Dime Chimes, passing one over to me. "They reckon old Walt felt guilty about the Leptotronic War, but there was no time to mope. He had to lead the people to the new promised land, along with his bro, of course. Alpin wanted scientists to go, but Walt thought it should be pacifists only. In the end, it was both." He stood up, tall and straight, then went into his best Windy, arms flailing about all over the place. "The colonists built magnificent cities in Magnatella—the most technologically advanced metropolises mankind has ever seen. No windmills, though, the goddamn geeks."

"You got him down to a tee, Early-Bird."

"Your turn."

We chased about the riverbank, sniggering and dragging on the smokes, our arms flying about in all directions. Earl was getting into the skit big time, telling how you could migrate from Cassaforta to Magnatella but never vice versa. He was so creased up, he could hardly get the words out. Then he tripped on a boonstone and, even though he could have saved himself, went skidding into the river just for the hell of it. I mean, it wasn't dangerously deep or anything like that, but it was wide and real fast-moving, so you needed your wits about you.

"We all know the continents are separated by the mighty Disian Ocean," he hollered once he'd surfaced, arms still whirling like crazy.

It was hard not to be just as wild and reckless whenever he was around, so I jumped in after him, the cold snatching the breath clean from my lungs. Then, after we'd splashed around for a while, we swam out to the old wooden jetty and hauled ourselves up on top of it.

"Man. That was just like the old days. Can't believe we did that." I felt the roots of the jetty wheeze and give a little as it took our weight. "Y' know, Earl, at some point, we quit with all the tube racin'. Does that mean we grew up?"

"Nah," Earl said. "Creek just turned into somethin' else is all." I guess he meant it was more of a place to chill out, smoke, and get howling drunk without anyone having to know too much about it. He pulled a soggy Dimer from his jacket pocket and tossed it over the side. "Anyway, remember, Caldwell: if this thing collapses before summer's out, you owe me fifty bucks."

We lay there in the sunlight for a while, just shivering and looking up at the sky, and then we started sniggering all over again.

Not long after, still splayed out on the jetty, we caught sight of Taylor and Dakota rambling through the overgrown grasses of Beau Lily Fields, Marshall Bexley tagging along behind them. Earl groaned.

"Face it," I said, totally knowing which buttons to push. "He's an Arch Angel. I mean, Taylor's been knockin' round with him since the start a' fall."

"I guess." Earl folded his arms and let out a long sigh. "Maybe that makes him one of us. Don't mean we have to like the grouchy old son of a gun, though."

Apart from Taylor, none of us were particularly fond of Marshall Bexley. He was gruff, rarely said anything agreeable, and seemed to think he was some sort of hood, just because he went around in a black PU jacket that had more zippers than anyone could ever hope to need. And sometimes he just plain made stuff up, like when he told us his uncle invented bubblegum. I mean, who does that?

"Got nothin' against guys from the Ambinas," I said. "But Marsh? He's somethin' else."

Dakota was waving a shiny glass bottle at us, and I could just about make out the Grimley's Diamond Cut Bourbon label. "See what I got," she was hollering. "This ain't any old tonsil paint. It's class, and I'm willin' to share."

The offer was just too tempting. "Bring it on," I called back. "I dare ya."

Without dithering, Dakota paddled in, waded over to us, and then scrambled up onto the jetty next to me. She handed me the bottle, and I chuckled, rubbing at it.

"Maybe there's a genie inside."

"You never know. Give it a good ole shine and see what comes out." She glanced sideways at me, and I lowered my gaze. It wasn't easy meeting those piercing baby-blues. They had a habit not only of reaching into the depths of your soul, but also plucking it out, kicking its ass, and stuffing it right back in there.

I downed a quick shot of Diamond Cut, feeling the warmth of it ripple down my throat as clouds of little spearflies hovered and hummed by the bulrushes. Dakota smiled, pulling a bobby pin from her jacket pocket and then pushing it through the mini beehive that all the girls her age were wearing.

"You two still fightin' over that gal at the record store?" she said, snatching the Grimley's from me and taking another gulp. She acted tough like that most of the time, but I reckoned it was all just to compensate for being kind of fragile. I mean, she did a darn good job of pretending to be 'Arch Angel to the core', but there was an awkwardness about her sometimes, a kind of painful introspection that put her ill at ease. She was taken away from her real folks seven years ago, on account of their neglect, and I guess the whole business must have weighed heavy on her soul.

"Ah, sweet Mackenzie Mulhoone," Earl said, fluttering his eyelashes. "She's like an Egyptian goddess."

I nodded, eyes wide. "We're both still soft on Kenzie, but we agreed to let it slide. Wouldn't be fair on the other. Get this, though. Her bro told us she's baseball crazy; used to carry round a cardboard cut-out of Kirby Henshaw when she was a kid." Even though Henshaw was the star pitcher for the Grade Glennings Gazelles, and I'd got more than a dozen baseball cards with his face on, it had been hard for me to love him since hearing that. It was the green-eyed monster, plain and simple.

Taylor was busy shimmying up the hunchback tree, the rest of us still yakking, idly watching as he scuttled out onto the long branch overhanging the creek. As usual, Earl couldn't resist pulling a stunt. He yelled out so loud, a bunch of jackrabbits bolted into the cornfield, and it spooked Taylor so bad he lost his balance and went toppling in. Earl and Taylor were always carrying on that way: winding each other up, pretending to scrap, dancing round each other like a pair of mighty brown bears. We were all whistling and howling, expecting the same old sketch to unfold, but as soon as Taylor's head poked up out the water, I knew it was never going to happen. He stomped over to us, churning up the silt, eyes like daggers stabbing into Earl's.

"What's the matter, Pumble? Ruin ya hairdo?"

"Shut it, Hunter. I'm warnin' ya. I ain't in the mood." He prodded Earl hard in the eye with his index finger, and it struck me as odd, because it just wasn't like Taylor to get so bent out of shape with his buddies. I mean, folks in authority were one thing—they could have him brooding and cussing like there was no tomorrow, but he never lost it with the Arch Angels.

"Hey! What the hell was that for?"

Earl didn't say anything else, but I was pretty sure he was thinking the same as me: that Taylor's crankiness probably had something to do with Marshall Bexley. I glanced over at the cluster of boulders skirting the bank in a rough horseshoe shape. Marshall sat alone there, leant against the largest, not even bothering to watch. He pulled an ebby from his boot, scraped a match against the rock, and lit up, blowing out long trails of fern-colored smoke. Then he took a swill from a dark brown liquor bottle, wiping his lips with the sleeve of his jacket.

Don't get me wrong; I didn't hate the guy. Hailey's Town was pretty much a place where no one hated anyone. At least, I thought so then. I just didn't get why Taylor wanted to hang out with him, and why it was accepted that he was an Arch Angel when he plainly didn't fit the mold.

3

The Interview

guess I'm clinging to the past because the only future I can see is a cell in some stinking poke hole, those pesky uninvited thoughts stuck in my head for the rest of eternity:

Shoulda gone into the machine.

Why'd you spin that goddamn box? Who knows what you changed by doin' that?

This world is just a copy, and it's all your fault.

Yeah, I can definitely see it happening. I've been in the slammer a week now, and the damn dream won't stop scrolling through my skull. Even in those rare moments when I manage to shake it, I just end up mulling ad infinitum over that final scene in the alley with the little pink pills, the flashing blue lights, the sirens. But I'm no nearer figuring out what went down that night than I was at the start. Maybe it's dumb of me to try; I'm like a dog in a crate, constantly chasing its tail.

I shuffle my cards for the thousandth time, stretch myself out on the rusty old slab of metal that passes for a seat, my soul

16

a sinking boulder, drowning me in the bitterness of what little I remember.

"...Carney Caldwell..."

The sheriff's whiskery rasp drifts down the corridor. I didn't catch the rest, but the name sounds kind of odd now—as if he's talking about some guy who never even existed. There are footsteps and then he's out in the passageway, keys jangling against bars—echoes that make my stomach churn. I gaze down at my hand, almost retching when I catch sight of the bruises spread across the knuckles. I can't bear to look, so I focus on Bewick instead—the big felt campaign hat he never seems to take off. Maybe his hair's gotten so white and wispy, he thinks it's best left be.

"Carney, this is Weinberg," he says, as a much younger man squeezes into the cell.

I've seen the guy before behind the counter in the radio store at the top of Swicken Street, but I barely know him, and I've no idea why he's here. I size him up, guessing he must be in his late thirties. He's clean-shaven, dressed in a lily-white store coat, and he's so damn reedy he's having to stoop.

"We oughta just grab one a' the interview rooms," Bewick says, red-faced because Weinberg can hardly move. "More space, don't y' know."

I'm glad to be out the cooler for a while, even though it's room five we end up in.

"Lucy's still at my place," the sheriff tells me. "And it's probably best she stays there till we figure out what to do."

It's my cue to thank him, but the words are wedged in my throat, strangled before I can get them out. My mouth is dry, I'm sweating like an ailing pig, and my hands are shaking something crazy. I need to pull myself together.

Bewick is scratching at his graying beard and sideburns. "Me 'n' Luce go way back," he says, grinning as he turns to Weinberg.

17

"She was one a' my poker game buddies, back in the day... before I took up office, before she had the stroke."

Thinking back, I must have been about four or five the first time he came over to Captain's Way. I can still see the pair of them hunched over the dining room table with the cards all fanned out, Lucy rattling the chips and saying, "You stay good 'n' quiet now, Smoky. Me an' Uncle Boo got a game to play." Of course, he wasn't my real uncle, but I remember how I was hiding under the table, and he snuck me a lemon popsicle, ruffled my hair, and whispered, "Heads up, son." Then he smiled at me all lopsided, and I knew from the gleam in his eye why Lucy liked him so much. It must be pretty awkward for him: the grandson of one of his oldest buddies turning out to be some sort of juvenile delinquent.

I figure it's best to change the subject. "How's the patient?" The image of a dying baby bird hits me—one too young for feathers. There are pimples on the skin as it trembles, draws its last breath. Is my voice really that shaky, that weak?

"Still blacked out." Uncle Boo lays a hand on my shoulder. "We'll let you know, son, soon as there's any change." The rumble of his voice is oddly soothing, and he smiles that same old smile with only one side of his mouth turned up, the way he used to all those years ago when he was winning at poker. "And stop starin' at them bruises, y' hear me?"

"Can't help it. They're takin' forever to fade." I gape at the wall instead, dark damp patches sprawled across the paintwork—a dirty great map of someplace no one wants to go. "But I can'ta done what they're sayin'. Ain't in my nature."

Weinberg clears his throat. "Okay, Carney," he says, in an accent I've never heard before. He taps his metal-frame glasses tight against his nose, smooths a hand over his dark, slicked-back hair. "Why don't we start at the beginning? I know it was your gran'ma, Lucy, who raised you, but what can you tell me about your folks?"

I'm guessing this is the first in a lightning round of crass personal questions, but I don't get why he's asking; the sheriff knows my family history inside out.

"Nothin' much about my mom. She came down with consumption, died not long after I was born. Sheriff'll tell you. All I know is stuff I got from Lucy: that she was called Dolly, taught piano, liked to go hikin' in the Bolars."

"And your father? His name was Chase, I gather."

"Pop was a ditch banger for the gas corps, but it's just a bunch of hazy memories. He passed away from a heart attack before I even turned three." The words are spilling out my mouth right enough, but the sound is far-off—like someone else is saying them. "Don't see myself as an orphan, though: Lucy's always been there, and my brother Leyland, well, he's seven years older than me."

Hang on a minute... the penny's dropped. Weinberg must moonlight as a shrink, and this is all just part of some fancy psychological test. I mean, I must have seen more than a dozen movies where the analyst starts with, "Tell me about your mom."

Weinberg and Bewick are eyeing each other, and it looks kind of shifty.

"A word," Weinberg says, and they leave me sitting there alone, time moving on in prickly silences, my breath slow and easy. It's so quiet now, I can hear my watch tick—the gold, dual-akka-phase one that Lucy gave me when I turned fifteen. I cast my mind back to the moment when I opened the small steel-blue box and first glimpsed its face: the twin dials glimmering in the afternoon sunlight, Akkasine showing a waxing quarter phase and Akkasom a plump and shiny full moon. Lucy's words ring out in my head as clear as the day she uttered them: *Look up at the sky tonight, Carney. You'll see just how beautifully it works.* She meant the watch was super accurate, but she was probably hinting at the glory of the celestial movements up above as well.

I've thought about it a lot over the years, because it was the last time she said anything that made any kind of sense.

They're back now, seated again, and the radio guy is staring at me, the rhythm of his voice synced wholly with the tat-a-tat of the akka-dial watch.

"Carney, you should know that…"

I'm scrunched in a ball on the cold concrete floor, a thudding pain soaring through my temples. My eyelids flicker open every now and then, giving me mirage-like glimpses of human shapes—distorted heads that gaze down at me, whispering and wiggling as I float in and out of consciousness.

4

Aspirations

THE PRESENT

It's been about three hours since I came around, and it's already dark outside. I'm in a medical bed in a tiny room with a narrow horizontal window so high up you can't see through it. The stretched-out shadows of tree branches dance across the pane, warped by a mesh of dusty iron bars.

"You hit your head on the floor, goddamn it," Bewick told me, soon after I woke. He wouldn't say why I dropped, just that they couldn't risk it happening again.

I reach up to my forehead, trace the contours of an olive-sized bump before a fully fledged flashback knocks the stuffing right out of me. There's the skinny guy leaning in close, fingers locked together, ice-blue eyes drilling into mine. But his voice—whatever it was he was trying to tell me—is somehow lost, swallowed up in the hugeness of the moment. There's only a name, dangling at the back of my subconscious, like some murky, half-remembered dream: *Harvey Wilder*.

A medic comes in and forces a shot into my arm without even

talking to me—not that I mind; whatever was in that syringe has my eyelids fluttering like moths in a twin moon, and it's not long before all notion of the crime is shunted away to a part of my brain that's so far out of reach it doesn't seem to matter. It's as if the whole shebang just wafted up and out through the crisscross window, weedy Weinberg and gracious Uncle Boo included.

All I can think about now is the creek, and a warm smile starts to sneak across my lips.

THE PAST

We sat under the rocks, passing round what was left of the Grimley's, all the while serenaded by a mellow twittering from up in the pines. Gale birds were swooping against an indigo sky, and Dol was melting into its fiery pit, pink streaks radiating out like the limbs of a giant pinwheel.

I was casually watching the colors shimmer off the water when Booker and Dakota came tramping up the slope, arms laden with beer bottles and packets of Dime Chimes. Dakota's folks owned a liquor store on the corner of Parapine Street, and that gave her a free pass for whatever she wanted, even though she was officially too young to buy most of it. Her old man turned a blind eye as long as she didn't go too crazy and paid for whatever she took, and that was never a problem because she worked pumping gas every other weekend at the station out near Caters Mead. She'd even saved up for a used Hudson Hornet that was so damn slick you just wanted to drool.

Our clothes had dried out, but it was getting mighty chilly, so we lit the kindling we'd gathered in the center of the boonstones—old sticks, branch pieces, and dead leaves—and once the flames took hold, we gathered round the fire, helping ourselves to the booze and cigarettes.

"I wonder what Magnatella's really like," Dakota said, trying to sound as much like Doris Day as she could manage. "No one ever talks much about the cities."

"Ain't nothin' like Hailey's Town, that's for sure. If you stayed here, you'd just end up fixin' cars, waitin' tables, or baggin' groceries." Booker had a cute husky voice and a real faint lisp, but she always came off sounding super smart.

"Reckon that's how they want it," Earl said, narrowing his eyes. "Anyone with a half-decent brain gets packed off to the cities, 'cause town folk don't want change; they're scared of it."

Dakota sighed, wistful as ever. "I bet Magnatella's beautiful. I can just imagine the capital: full of big silvery skyscrapers, floatin' cars, and chirpy little servin' bots trundlin' about everywhere."

"You really think they got cars that float?" I was struggling a bit with my words because the beer and the Grimley's were taking a hold, and everything was turning kind of foggy. That was just the way with the chaser, I guess. It seemed to dull every sense, rock me pretty damn close to the point of slumber, but at the same time, I'd feel like a Thunderbird suddenly roaring into gear—so much bolder, smarter, wilder.

"Sure. Why call 'em groundies over here if that ain't the case?" Dakota's voice was pretty much the opposite of Booker's: smooth as silk. It always gave me goosebumps.

"Don't believe in them flyin' car fables," Booker said, trying not to sound too high and mighty about it. "There's a lot a' stuff you hear about Magnatella, like the medicine bein' so good, folks live well beyond three hundred. You gotta take it all with a pinch a' salt."

"How come Buddy Holly's lived so long, then?" I pointed out. "Been churnin' out hit after hit for decades." We'd had the same bull session a thousand times before but, like Buddy himself, it never grew old.

Booker was fishing in her jeans pocket for a matchbox, an

unlit Virginia Slim hanging from her lips. "Guess I'll find out soon enough," she said, grinning. "I'm applyin' to a college in Amchuda to study space science. Won't be long before I'm crossin' that big blue sea."

"Unless you flunk out." Taylor blocked his face with his arms, fully expecting to be cuffed round the ears, and then we watched as the two of them acted out a kind of slapstick struggle that ended with Taylor's unconditional surrender.

"Don't push my buttons, potato brain." Booker settled herself back down, finally lighting the Slim. "Anyway, if anyone's gonna bomb…"

"Well, that's just how I roll," Taylor said, a twinkle in his eye. "Hooky's my thing." He was always slinking off, especially on Wednesday afternoons when The Apex ran old martial-arts reels.

"You better write and give us the 411 once you get there," Dakota said to Booker, folding her arms tight across her knees. I guess it rattled her that she was younger than the rest of us and had a whole other year to wait.

Booker wound a lock of her thick jet-black hair round her index finger. "Don't worry, Kota. I'll write you soon as I get there—if sendin' mail to Cassaforta's allowed, that is."

"I'm goin' to college too," I said. "Wanna be a writer, so I guess I'll take literature." I rolled my sleeve up and ran my fingers over the white-tailed eagle etched onto my inner right wrist—an everlasting memento of my devotion to my gang. It was Earl who set the blueprint: an Earth bird of our choosing, flaunting a full wingspan with the letters 'AA' inked in yellow in the middle of the body. When the rest of us got them, aged fifteen, Kota had to hitch all the way to Hap Town, where folks didn't know she was underage. I guess she didn't feel like a bona fide gang member until she could show off her brand-new Inca dove. "I'll be just like him once summer's out," I went on, still poking at the eagle. "Take flight from here. I'm thinkin' of the Nellic Islands, 'cause it ain't part a' Magnatella. Leyland says you can come back from there anytime you want."

"Yeah, but nellies ain't proper degrees; that's what my old man told me. Reckons they're second-rate." Dakota's eyes were burning into my soul again.

Taylor foraged through the pile of freshly chilled beers and pulled out a bottle of Wild Bandit. "I'm probably gonna be one a' those dudes who just bums around... you know... a drifter, just roamin' from town to town, never quite settlin' anywhere." He cracked the lid off the bottle. "But I'll move on to more wholesome pursuits when I'm good 'n' ready."

Earl laughed so hard he spat out a mouthful of ale. "What 'wholesome pursuits' might they be?" he managed to ask between gasps for breath.

"Dunno yet. Maybe I'll train to be one a' them knife-wieldin' ninjas." Taylor grinned and rose to his feet, acting out some half-hearted karate moves that had us all beating the ground with our fists in sheer amusement. Even Marshall was sniggering.

"I'd stick to the knittin' club if I were you," Earl told him after he'd calmed down some.

"Cut the gas, knucklehead. You ain't seen me with my kunai knives." Taylor was kidding, of course: weapons of any kind were out-and-out banned in Cassaforta.

"Oh yeah? What d' ya do with 'em? Peel potatoes?"

"You shut y' trap." Taylor sat back down and took a long quaff of ale, while Earl stoked the fire with a gnarly branch that had fallen from one of the ulus. The embers glowed and some of them broke free, whirling in circles for a while until they glided off into the darkness like a swarm of tiny fireflies.

"Well, my old man wants me to go to engineering school," Earl said after a while. "He reckons I'm smart. But if I am, it has nothin' to do with porin' over books and learnin' facts by rote. I just wanna stay here, fix bikes for a livin.'" Earl was never happier than when he was tinkering about with motorcycles, stripping out any part movable and putting it all back together. His folks bought him a Douglas Appaloosa on his sixteenth birthday, and it didn't take him long to have it all souped up with a Zoziniah X41B engine. He'd won every local drag race since, thanks to that little piece of wizardry.

Dakota edged closer and offered him a Dime Chime. "Come on, Earl," she said. "Most kids dream about the cities. And they say Elvis Presley lives in Magnatella somewhere. Hell, that's reason enough to wanna go. 'Sides, don't you ever feel trapped here?"

Earl shook his head. "Not the least bit. Some folks are cut out for a city life, but I ain't one of 'em. I belong here in Hailey's. It's a culture, a way of bein'. I like that it never changes. Kids've been wearin' the same kinda clothes for as long as this town's been here, and in ten years, twenty years, they'll still be wearin' 'em, and they'll still be cruisin' round Javapod in the same old groundies. Man, I love this place. I've no great yearnin' for anythin' else." He was talking so plain and so passionate I felt it almost as a living thing—a spark of bliss that was wholly captured by the reflection of the flames dancing wildly in his eyes. He lit the Dimer. "Anyways, don't you think it's all a bit strange and suspicious that no one ever comes back from Magnatella—not even to visit?"

"I'll bet there's no colleges there at all," Marshall cut in with a kind of sardonic grin. "If you ask me, it's all just a ploy to get you over there, so's they can brainwash you, do all kinds of experiments on you, then dump your corpse in the Disian Ocean once they're done."

Booker scowled at him. "You're such a jerk, Marshall. Leptotronics is outlawed over here. No one's allowed to know anythin' about it. That's all it is."

He ignored her, stubbing out his smoke on the boulder behind him, straightening the taupe-brown fedora he always wore. Then he turned to Earl. "Another thing that bugs me: it's guaranteed your old man'll never see you again if you go away to college, so why's he so keen to see the back a' ya? I mean, I can understand mine wantin' rid, but you? Ain't you s'posed to be the golden boy round here?"

Earl just shrugged, totally unfazed by it all. "Guess he just wants me to do well, be the best I can. What you plannin' after graduation, anyways? You musta thought about it."

Marshall snorted, as if the notion of graduating was something totally ridiculous to him, and then he turned, staring into the heart of the fire like he was spellbound. "Kids like me don't get to college," he muttered, eyes narrowed, as the twisting flames crackled and popped. "For a start, I'm from the wrong side a' the tracks. And for another, I already got me a pretty challengin' career just dodgin' the law."

Maybe I was too loaded to take it all in, but I thought I saw something in his gaze then. His stance reeked of arrogance, and he was smirking like he'd just cleaned up at Shannon's Casino, but the swagger seemed to be tangled up with another feeling that I couldn't quite pin down. Was he scared about something?

Before anyone could ask any questions, Taylor launched into a drunken snicker, slapping Marshall hard on the back. "You and ya hokey yarns. You almost had us fooled, bud."

Marshall's hand was gripping the liquor bottle real tight. He glowered at Taylor, lips pursed as if he was about to spit blood, but when he spoke, he didn't sound mad at all. "Don't try 'n' cover up what we got goin' on here, Pumble."

He finished downing the liquor, then hurled the empty bottle at the shadowy rocks on the other side of the creek. We sat there, still as anything, the shattering sound echoing northward between the rock tors a couple of times, and then there was a silence that clung to the air like a tick on hot, itchy skin.

I prodded at the bonfire with a stick. "Dare we ask what all this is about?"

"Wouldn't wanna ruin the peace," Marshall muttered, staring down sullenly at his boots.

"It's too peaceful. We gotta get ourselves over to Javapod. Go see some action or somethin'." Taylor reached for another beer, but it seemed to me like his hand was shaking.

"Come on, Tayles," I said. "Arch Angels don't judge."

Taylor took a long breath, then nodded slowly. "Alright, Caldwell; we got a stash," he said, "over at Marshall's place. Come see, if you want."

I gazed at the darkening creek, Dol quivering on the surface, the colors dazzling my eyes so bad I was forced to close them. It was mighty strong stuff in those bottles, alright.

THE PRESENT
Tuesday, January 20ᵗʰ, 2325

Hushed voices out in the corridor drag me out of sleep. It's the small hours, I'm parched as hell, and all I can do is scratch at the pillows as memories of the felony come creeping back. Goddamn shot must have worn off altogether. Maybe they'll give me a double dose next time when they see how bad I am.

I slip out of bed, scooting over to the door so's I can hear what the janitors are muttering about.

"Can't help but pity him. Poor wretch lives in a fantasy world. Don't even know who he is, or why he's really here." The male one sounds kinder, like he thinks of this headbanger as a person, not just some commodity he has to deal with.

"No clue what he's done, neither. That's why the room gotta

be guarded night and day." The woman is either in her nineties or smokes like a chimney, judging from the voice.

"Is he dangerous?"

"I'll say. Don't like cleanin' in that room—the way he looks at you with them big, mournful eyes."

"Heard he ain't got no folks. That's why no one comes to visit."

The thought of some screwball lurking down the hallway scares the crap out of me. They'd better keep his goddamn door locked tight. I don't want some knife-wielding maniac wandering into my room at half past three in the morning.

I shuffle back to bed, my fingers gliding over the bump. It doesn't seem to have shrunk, and I still have no clue why I keeled over yesterday, or what that lanky guy was talking about. All I remember is the frost in his eyes, the gentle tick of the akka-dial watch as his lips formed silent words.

Harvey Wilder. There's that name again. Why that name?

I grab three more hours, wake up mumbling something about splitting myself in two, as a medic shakes me by the arm.

"Time for your meds, Mr. Caldwell." It's the same guy as before. He looks like he never bothers to wash his hair. You'd think they would make him, working in a bone factory like this. It's just not sanitary. Maybe he can tell me about the crank, though.

"Look. Is it safe in here?"

"How do you mean?" He flicks his long blond bangs out of his eyes.

"That guy down the corridor, the weirdo. He don't attack folk or nothin'?"

"Just relax. Roll your sleeve up for me, please." He raises the syringe, sucks up the juice from the vial, and then taps twice at the barrel.

"Ain't you gonna answer my question?"

"Dr. Weinberg'll be here later this afternoon. He's the one dealin' with your case. He'll answer all your questions just as soon as he gets here, and then you can start your treatment." The medic draws out the word 'all' like you might if you were talking to a bunch of preschoolers.

"Treatment? For what?"

5

Maple Road

THE PRESENT

'm at the creek again, but everything's mixed up. The branches of the hunchback tree are all bound together with thin metallic strings, and Taylor's up there, plucking them like a harp, sending out the most beautiful sounds you can imagine. Dol is beating down on me, and I'm trudging through the water, all sluggish, as if the sweep of the harp somehow has a hold on time—like those sweet, crystalline notes can grab it by the reins, slow it so far down it's almost at a standstill.

Taylor rakes the strings, making a chord so heart-rending time gets a major kick up the ass, and I stumble out onto the bank, cradling something in my arms as if it were a child. Night has come and the sky is black, save for a sliver of light from a fingernail Akkasine hanging low in the sky. And underneath, a giant pyre rages away beside the boulders as I'm dragged toward it, all the while clutching the sodden bundle to my chest.

Fireworks explode above me—huge neon chrysanthemums bursting into life. It's so loud, I cover my ears, the bundle slipping from my grasp, revealing itself as a crumpled, soaking-wet Arch Angels baseball jacket. I knew all along what was coming, but the shock and pain of seeing it slams an icicle through my heart, the coldness spreading through the rest of my body and down the banks, forcing the creek to scrunch into a frozen stretch of whiteness. And then faceless forms grab me by the wrists and ankles, swinging me endlessly, back and forth, back and forth. They won't stop; they're holding me so tight I can't wrench free. It's making me feel dizzy and sick…

"Help me!"

I sit bolt upright, hands snatching at the mattress, as the drab little room slowly comes into focus: the matte gray walls, the iron lattice in front of the window, and scrawny Dr. Weinberg lurking at the foot of the bed, a look of deep concern etched onto his brow. I'm too groggy to tell if it's for real.

"Ah, Carney, you're back from your slumbers." He smiles at me, but then his eyebrows knit together like a pair of hairy caterpillars. "I'm sorry about the bump to your forehead. I should have broken things to you more gently."

"What things?"

"You don't remember?" He rubs at his chin, seems thoughtful for a while, then snaps his briefcase open, pulling out an official-looking navy-blue binder. He inches closer, as if I'm some wild animal he's been charged with taming. "I doubt you've heard of it, but I'm trained in a relatively new technique called distraction therapy. It's where you listen to a story, and it stops you from dwelling on your own problems so much."

If it's a wild animal he's after, I'll damn well give him one. "Are you crazy?! You oughta be helpin' me figure out what's goin' on around here! What the hell did you tell me down at the precinct that made me slump on the floor like that?"

"Calm down, Carney. I know distraction therapy sounds a little off the wall, but why don't we give it a try? The stories are supposed to be relatable to your own experiences. The one I've chosen for you is about a boy called Doran. Granted, he's a fair bit younger than you, and he's from Banunus City, which you probably know is the capital of Magnatella, but I really think the story will help you."

It's like handing out Pepto-Bismol for a burst appendix, and he's acting so much like a shrink it makes me want to heave. But I've got nothing to lose, so I just nod at him and try not to catch his eye. He perches on the edge of the bed and opens the binder.

DORAN'S STORY

Amber Blake, head of the Maple Road Children's Home, heard a particularly loud knock one morning in the late summer of 2307. She swung open the orphanage's big yellow double doors to find Henna Juniper, the social worker for the Calahadra district, waiting patiently on the porch, a small wicker basket clutched in her hand. And when Amber peered inside, she saw a tiny baby tucked up beside a plush, crimson-colored toy: a smiling octopus that was just about the same size as the infant's head.

"Oh, my!"

"I know. Ain't he just as cute as a button?"

Amber showed Henna into the main office so that she could set the basket down on the camelback sofa. "How old is he?"

"Only four months," Henna told her. "Poor little fella's got no kin. And he's been in foster care most of that time, waiting for City Hall to get their act together. But I finally got the paperwork through this morning. They want to place him here with you."

"He'll be more than welcome," Amber said, smiling at the gentle cooing noises the infant was making. "What's his name?"

"They've been calling him Doran. Word means 'stranger', so I'm told. But there's no family name."

"Don't worry, Henna, we'll fix that right away." Amber scooped the gurgling, sable-haired child into her arms and carried him through to the staffroom at the back. Then, as soon as everyone was done with clucking over the little boy and asking countless questions, she invited them to make a shortlist of names.

Shellina Crawford, the head nursery teacher, was the first to make a suggestion. "What about Bayard? It was my maternal grandfather's name. It describes a man of great courage and honor."

"Doran Bayard—that's his name." Amber swayed the boy slowly back and forth in her arms. "It's like it was meant to be."

You might say Doran had been unlucky coming into the world with no kinfolk, but fate certainly cut him some slack the day it entrusted him to the care of the splendid Maple Road facility. Indeed, as his early years rolled by, materialistically, he lacked for nothing. Amber and Shellina both doted on the child, gifting him with toys, clothes, and books as if he were one of their own. And they would always make time for him, reading aloud his favorite stories before bedtime, playing games with him both indoors and out, or just being there to listen whenever he wanted to talk. Amber also saw to it that Doran was allocated the turreted room on the fourth floor of the building, because it faced out onto the apple orchard at the back. It was the smallest room of all, but the view of the trees was spectacular.

Despite their efforts to provide a happy, stable, and supportive environment, Amber and Shellina couldn't help but worry about Doran because he was so painfully shy, finding it difficult to communicate with the other children, all of whom were older.

"Aside from you and me, the only one he seems interested in talking to is that octopus," Amber would say, whenever the topic came up.

However, when the four-year-old son of a farmer arrived at the orphanage in January 2311, all their fears were cast aside.

"Do you like Spider-Man?" Quin Oakley whispered to Doran, while Amber was busy with the admissions paperwork.

"Yeah. I like how he uses his webs to climb up skies."

After that, no one could stop their constant chattering. Almost immediately, Quin moved onto the top floor with Doran, the single bed was swapped for a bunk, and the two became inseparable. Doran, for his part, loved being half of a double act, and Amber and Shellina would often joke that the two of them were joined at the hip. When school was out, the boys would sit in the apple trees for hours, just jabbering away, playing cards, or catching the sun. They'd explore the deserted wooden barns in the large meadow adjacent to the garden, pretending to be all manner of things: bartenders, hotel keepers, pirates, or cavemen. Sometimes they'd even imagine they were athletes, leaping from roof to roof without a care in the world.

The young Doran very much enjoyed the schooling he received at the home, and he was already excelling in English and the arts by the time he reached just seven years old. He was especially fond of the poetry classes that took place in the hexagonal-shaped conservatory every summer, and he proved himself highly adept at learning verses by heart and reciting them to the other students. When it came to the boy's own compositions, both poetry and prose, Mr. Fredrick always made sure to give him plenty of encouragement.

"Your writing shows a maturity way beyond your years," he would say, Doran smiling contentedly as the sun shone through the conservatory's skylight, warming his skin, projecting a comforting cobalt halo around the hologram screen.

Oftentimes, the tutor would take the class to the capital's illustrious Palderboon region, located at the very heart of the city, to attend theater productions, music recitals, and ballet performances. They would visit museums, art galleries, and observatories, participate in specially arranged science lectures and educational film screenings. Doran and Quin were particularly fond of the museum trips. They would tire themselves out, trekking through every floor, scrutinizing each exhibit in turn, whether it was a twenty-second-century colonization painting, a Pleasian fiber sculpture, or a holographic demonstration of leptotronic polarization. And when, at last, it was time to pile into the floaty to sail home, the boys would struggle just to keep their eyelids from closing.

In 2319, when Doran was approaching his twelfth year, an event occurred that was to change his fortunes, and not for the better. In early April, Quin Oakley's father turned up at the orphanage after serving an eight-year stint in jail for tax fraud. He told Amber he wanted to take Quin back to his farm cottage in Myndalthrapy Mone, a small farming community in the Dolands, some three hundred miles southeast of Banunus City. Although he held a criminal record, the man was still Quin's legal guardian, so regaining custody was only a matter of filling out the necessary forms. Thus, it was not long before the Oakleys were strolling side by side down Maple Road in matching green jackets, Quin's suitcases hovering obediently behind them.

It was a Saturday when they departed, and Doran watched them from the big bay window in the music room, his hands pressed hard against the ledge, his face wrapped in soft blue-and-yellow light where Dol was striking the antique stained glass. He stared for a while at the stone Dillinger heads that had always guarded the gateposts, the words Quin had told him echoing back through time.

"That's wiskadon stone. You can tell by the sheen. Comes all the way from Ostrapoctinus."

"Where's that?"

"It's the fourth moon of Dilius. Gramps was a miner on one of the lepto ships. That's how I know so much about it."

Once Quin was well and truly out of sight, Doran puffed dismally up the spiral staircase to the bunk room, flung the door open, and stepped gingerly inside, afraid of what he might find there. It was like looking at a different room. All Quin's possessions had been taken away and the cleaning staff had already stripped his mattress bare. Everything appeared so strange, so desolate and hollow, Doran had to turn away. The pain of it was practically choking the life out of him, forcing the walls of his chest to swell with a hot and feverish panic. In desperation, he scurried away, galloping down the stairs, heading straight for the orchard outside.

There was a stiff breeze, and the boughs of the apple trees were rocking a little, the green buds of their spring leaves just starting to poke through. But Doran found no comfort in seeing them, because the trunks, the branches, the entire garden was teeming with memories of moments lost forever. Frantically, he sprinted down to the rear wall and scooted over it, just as he had countless times before, always with Quin in tow. But when he landed on the other side in front of the familiar row of disused barns, he was so alarmed by the change in their character, he began to shake. He darted over to the first and rammed his shoulder hard against its big oak door, the smell of wet rot greeting him as he entered.

This was no longer the precious playhouse he remembered. It was a dilapidated old relic, dark and damp, full of shadows and musty old cobwebs stretching all the way from the floor to the rafters. He edged past them anxiously, shuddering as they tangled with his clothing, brushing them quickly away. Then his eyes settled on the oval glass table around which he and Quin had spent so many contented hours. Quin's dog-eared rummy deck was strewn across it, along with a scattered assortment of books, comics, and baseball cards.

It's become a museum, he thought to himself. *It's caught in a time warp.* And so, he gathered all the items together and fled from there.

Oddly, the boy was soon covered in mildewy spiderwebs once more, stooping over the exact same spot, arranging each article just where he had found it. *Can't have it all barren and empty-looking like the bunk room.*

Three days of intense indecision passed. On Sunday, Doran had visited the barn no less than six times, repeatedly removing the items and depositing them in the big fake treasure chest in the corner of the attic room, only to return so that he could restore them to their original positions on the table. After school on Monday, he went back again, retrieved everything, and stuffed it all into a worn-out pillowcase that he shoved beneath the bunk beds. On Tuesday, at lunchtime, he brought it all back to the tumbledown outhouse, only to salvage everything again in the evening, just before supper. On Wednesday morning, Doran was absent from all his classes and none of the teachers could find him.

THE PRESENT

"Sounds like Doran was losin' the plot." I slide my knees up to my chest and lean on them with my chin.

"Indeed, Carney, yes, indeed." Weinberg straightens his glasses and then gets up off the bed.

"But what does all this hokum have to do with me? I mean, how's it supposed to help?"

"The story's meant to get you thinking about other things," he tells me, tipping his head to one side. "But as I said, I chose it because it's relatable as well. And the more relatable it is, the more distracting it becomes for you. I believe you experienced something quite similar?"

"What? That's nuts. You're way off base there."

I gaze up at the window, where hazy streaks of light are toying with the dust particles swirling through the air. Magpies are chattering away outside, and there's the far-off drone of a hedge trimmer that makes me think of summer. Weinberg is staring at me, but he's all clammed up, like he's waiting for me to say something else.

"Guess your tale was good for somethin'. I know there's flyin' cars in the cities now. You said they got into a floaty. That was a flyin' car, right?" I'm not even sure why I tossed him a bone. Maybe the sound of that trimmer got me all mellowed out.

"It's just a story, Carney," he says. "Don't go jumping to conclusions." He jams the report, or whatever it is, back into his briefcase and turns away, chin raised in the air.

"Look. About that screwball down the corridor. He can't get in here, can he? Only, I heard the janitors talkin'."

There's a clumsy silence as Weinberg fiddles with the clasp on the bag, and then, when it's closed, he mumbles, "Don't worry; he won't bother you. You're perfectly safe in here." He starts for the door, but before he gets to it, he glances over his shoulder at me. "We'll continue tomorrow, same time."

He probably thinks I'm done talking; he's almost out in the passageway.

"Dr. Weinberg?" I'm sounding clear and focused now, maybe for the first time since they ran me in. "Who the hell are you?"

6

Ashman Court

THE PAST

"Sure is colder now," Dakota said, zipping her jacket up tight as we made our way through the parking lot at the back of Ashman Court. The clouds had drifted south, the sky was like a mighty pincushion, and a dusty half-moon had tucked itself just above the horizon, bathing the apartment blocks in a kind of strange silvery light.

"Ain't never been to the Ambinas before," I said, gazing up at the reams of washing dangling from balconies everywhere, but I wasn't watching my step and ended up blundering into a trash can.

"Shush," Earl said, as the lid went clanging to the ground, and all the dogs within a half-mile radius yapped in unison.

"You shush," I told him, and then Booker stumbled into one as well, and we all started shushing the hell out of each other, sniggering like ten-year-olds hyped up on sugar.

Once we got into the lobby, Marshall snapped the door shut.

"What we doin' here again?" Dakota pulled the rags of a roll-up from her lips and tossed it onto the concrete, killing the glow with the toe of her boot.

"Just fetchin' a little somethin," Taylor said, grinning. Then he turned to Dakota, eyebrows raised. "Better be quiet now we're inside. Don't want Marshall's old man gettin' wind of anythin."

Dakota shrugged, her breath swirling about in the cold as if it was the ghost of her trampled Dimer. "Gotcha, bud."

We followed Marshall up a shabby metal staircase lit only by moonbeams glimmering through the skylight. And when we passed directly under them, the shadows from an overgrown wood fern fell onto each of our faces in turn, making them look all fragmented and creepy.

"Am I the only one gettin' spooked here?"

"Don't be such a wuss, Caldwell." Marshall led us up to the fifth floor, then stood outside his apartment, fumbling for the keys. "You lot wait here."

"So, who's up for this?" Taylor seemed pumped as hell. He was pacing the corridor like an expectant father barred from the delivery room.

"We've all done notch before," Booker told him, folding her arms as if it was no big deal.

"This ain't notch and it ain't for the faint-hearted neither," Taylor said. Then he realized he was talking too loud and lowered his voice. "I'm tellin' ya. This is some serious shit."

Back on the lot, we climbed into Marshall's rusting Dodge Crusader—all six of us: Marsh and Tayles in the front and the rest of us in the back. It was a real squeeze, but no one griped about it. Once we were in, Marshall fired her up and she made an urgent popping sound before slowly shuddering to life. Then he flicked the light on and snatched at the radio.

"Aw, man. 'Somethin's Gotten Hold of My Heart," Booker said. "Turn it up, Marsh."

"You like Gene Pitney?"

"Hell, yeah. This is his best one yet. Only came out last week. Gonna buy it, soon as I get my allowance."

"This'll be right up your street, then." Marshall opened up the brown paper bag he'd just fetched, and everyone peered over, eager to see what was inside. I was in the back, but I could just about make out a cluster of organic-looking cubes about the same size as a poker dice but wrapped in long, trailing leaves. Marshall placed one on his tongue, waited a couple of seconds, and then swallowed it down. "They're called rush crinkles. Little devils only grow on Lapilert."

"That's in the Pugnax system," Taylor told us, prouder than a dog with two tails. "Makes 'em super rare." He grabbed the bag from Marshall, downed one, and then lobbed the bundle onto Booker's lap. "What d' ya say, Pachello?"

Booker pulled one into two pieces, dropping the other half back inside the bag. "Nothin's happenin', Pumble," she said, once she'd swallowed it.

"Takes a while," Taylor said. "Couple of hours, maybe, but it'll be worth it in the end. You'll see." He fished one out and reached over to Dakota in the back. "Your turn now, angel cakes."

"Well, ain't you the sweetheart." Dakota leaned over, taking the plant from his fingers with her teeth. "Tastes kinda sugary, but it's like there's aniseed in there somewhere, too." She licked her lips.

"Just think of it as one of your five a day," Taylor said, with a bullish grin. "Guess you're next, Early-Bird."

Earl reached into the bag. "Where'd you get this stuff?" he asked, scowling, and it sounded so harsh, Taylor winced.

"What are you, a fifty-year-old cop or somethin'?"

Earl lifted one up to the light and squinted at it. "I've heard about these. You remember that guy from Hap Town I used to race with before I got the Zoziniah? Called himself 'The Rooster.'"

"You mean Rufus Lester—that big guy who played

quarterback for Farla Blane High?" I lit up another Dimer. "Long time since I seen him around."

"Yeah, that's the one. He was into this thing big time," Earl said, holding the plant at arm's length. "Told me about some real bad trips—how they kinda screwed with his mind." He dropped the crinkle back in the bag, telling Taylor, "I'm gonna pass. Some a' the guys on the circuit reckoned Rufus ended up in that nuthouse out past Sorley Ridge—the one with the big watchtower."

"You're makin' it up," Marshall said sourly. "You're a goddamn square is all."

Taylor chuckled. "If you turn down one a' these babies, you belong in a nuthouse. Your loss, anyway. What about you, Caldwell? You up for a rush?"

"Always." I cleared my throat and dipped my hand into the packet. The plant felt like a powdery gummy bear, all soft and squidgy. "Hell," I said, "what harm can a little candy do?" I munched it like a marshmallow, thinking all the while about those shitty PSA film reels we had to sit through in middle school—polyester puppets preaching the perils and pitfalls of popping pills. Jesse Know was the main one—a collie dog. I knew Earl was really the cool one, but I didn't say he was right. I guess I just didn't want Marsh and Tayles scowling at me and calling me a square.

We pulled out from the lot and then Marshall stepped hard on the gas, jerking the wheel so quick the motor skidded, the stench of hot burning rubber wafting through the windows, gravel flying everywhere. He hung a left down a dimly lit side street, the Dodge juddering and rattling so loud it was like it just couldn't wait to get past the turnpike and be within shooting range of the bustling streets of Javapod.

7

The Runaway

Weinberg's sitting on the bed again, that same old ring binder tucked under his arm, 'N. W. Radios' stitched in bottle green across the top-left pocket of his whiter-than-white store coat. He gapes at me for a while, his eyes like a couple of Brach's Ice Blue Mint Coolers.

"Okay, Carney," he says, smacking his hands together. "We're going to continue with the story, if that's alright with you."

They stuck another needle in my arm just before he got here, and I'm not mincing words. "Naw, I'm done with it."

"Come now. Don't be discouraged. You haven't really given it a chance yet, have you?"

It's hard to sound hacked off when you're slurring your speech; you can't put any kind of feeling into it. I guess I'll just have to spell it out for him. "Don't wanna. You can shove your mindless story."

Weinberg doesn't react at all—just sits there for a while, still as an old millpond. Then he opens the file, turns a few pages, and looks up at me. "There's nothing mindless about it," he says. "Nothing nefarious either. I've hand-picked the therapy. Tailored it to your unique… situation."

"Alright. I get how it works. You make up fish tales about some nutty Magnatellan kid. I listen to 'em, and at some point, I cave—admit I'm a fruit loop just like he is. But it ain't gonna wash with me, Dr. Weinberg; I'm sane as you are. I know what's real and what ain't." Okay, there's the whole fixation with those Eastern Europeans and that machine I never got to see, but it doesn't make me a crackpot. He wouldn't know about that anyway, unless Langley told him.

Weinberg smiles, as if my words have amused him in some way. "Careful what you say, Carney. Reality can be such a… dangerous idea." He pats me on the arm, tilting his head like a parrot. "Anyway, that's not what this is about. I can assure you of that."

I'm searching his eyes. There's got to be poison prowling about in there somewhere, but if there is, I'm struggling to find it. And once I get past all that ice, a hint of something else hits me—a side of him he maybe likes to play down. Yeah, there's empathy in there alright. It could be the guy's nothing but an old softy after all.

He glances down at my Angels ink, probably just to break off all the eyeballing. "Nice artwork," he says. "Where did you get that?"

"Ziggy's. But I ain't gonna look at the damn thing, okay?"

"Fair enough." Weinberg goes back to the binder, pulling out three sheets.

DORAN'S STORY

Doran could not be found on that wet and windy Wednesday morning because he'd come up with a plan to soothe his troubled mind: he would return everything to Quin—the comics, the books, the cards, even a broken model Goshawk that he'd found tossed aside under the bunk bed. Thus, on the Tuesday evening he snuck into the library and downloaded a map of the Greater Banunus City Province onto a pair of holo-spectacles. He packed them neatly inside his rucksack along with Quin's things, a blanket, some spare clothes, a toothbrush, a torch, a hairbrush, the crimson octopus, and some food scraps that he swiped from the kitchen after the chef went home. Then, planning on a good night's rest before his long journey, he tiptoed up to the bunk room and crawled beneath the bedclothes, making sure to savor their warmth and security because, come the morning, he would be leaving all that behind.

It was twelve minutes past nine, and with lights out at eight, the house had already sunk into quiet mode, but Doran was too excited and too fretful to sleep. So, listening just to the hum of the washing machine on the second floor, and to some faint burbled dialogue coming from the holo-vision in the staff lounge, he unzipped his backpack, pulled out the octopus and the holo-specs, and slipped the glasses on, turning the dial so that he could study the three-dimensional map.

"They're my ace in the hole," he whispered, imagining the octopus could hear him. "I can secretly follow the route, and if I look like I know where I'm going, folks won't ask any questions."

He sat the toy next to him on the pillow and exhaled deeply. The road ahead would be hard. It was just short of three hundred miles to Myndalthrapy Mone, and Quin had never mentioned the exact location of the Oakley farm, so he'd have to work it out by piecing together the odd snippets of information he'd picked up over the years. He remembered sitting in one of the apple trees the third spring after Quin came, Quin reminiscing as they sipped ice-cold lemonade and played a silly game of flinging their flip-flops out across the lawn.

"There was a museum about deserts—pretty old and run-down, but it was magical to me," Quin had told him. "I guess it was 'cause Gramps always took me." He'd laughed, then. "There was a statue of a Regarafian doster dog at the front of the parking lot. I used to climb on it sometimes with a kid called Logan, but he fell off once and broke his kneecap. Gramps said we couldn't do it anymore after that."

"Didn't your pa ever take you?"

"No, but he used to play baseball with me every Saturday, down at the woods in Bindorn Hollows."

Doran set his airphone alarm to go off at six in the morning, and when the shrillness of its chime roused him from slumber, he dressed quickly, fastened his backpack, and slunk down the staircase for the last time, careful to avoid all the squeaky patches. Once down, he unlocked the French windows in the big day room, stepped out into the freshness of the dawn, and scurried over the wet grass, shimmying up the wall when he got to the bottom. Then he stood on top of it, affording himself a quiet moment to bid farewell to the splendor of the massive Maple Road building.

Dol was rising in the east just behind the summerhouse—a blurry, yellow-crested head peering gradually farther over the horizon, dousing the drizzled sky in fiery streaks of vibrant reds and pinks. He gazed up at the mesh of tiny threadlike sky-lanes where floaties were hurtling people across the stratosphere at mind-boggling speeds. Then, just as he was about to turn, a host of sunbeams came searing over the darkness of the summerhouse roof. And one of them was bouncing off the pane of his bedroom window, painting it gold. Doran took it as a sign that he should hurry back inside and forget about the Oakley farm, but then he thought he saw the dancing shape of a doster dog etched in the rosiness of the clouds and immediately accepted that as the definitive prophecy—one that eclipsed all others. He plucked the holo-spectacles out of his pocket, wiped the lenses on his jacket sleeve, and carefully flicked them on.

By twilight, Doran had made it as far as Dactyleonbar, one of the many college districts in the city, and he was in good spirits because it was at least three miles further south than he'd planned on reaching. However, his clothes were damp from the driving rain, he was tired (not only from walking, but from having to battle the gusts that had been tearing in from the east all morning), and several blisters were biting away at his toes and heels. Luckily, while he could still walk, he passed a small sports stadium and noticed there were no lights on inside the buildings. The field was part of the district's Lanila College campus, and Doran managed to smash a window in one of the locker rooms and crawl inside. There, he found a medical kit with enough Band-Aids to cushion the sores, and he was able to shower, change into some dry clothing, and polish off some of the rations without being disturbed. Then, too exhausted to be afraid, he wrapped the blanket around his shoulders and bedded down for the night in the darkness.

He set off again at first light, following a grassy trail that led from the edge of the campus grounds to a pleasant, wooded area with a wide bridle path running parallel to a small, stony stream. The rain had stopped, the winds had died down, and Dol's balmy rays were already piercing the canopy, percolating deep into his skin, revitalizing him. He kept to the track, marching briskly to avoid suspicion, shunning any kind of eye contact with the early-morning dog walkers who passed him by. Having studied the map, he knew the stream ran about ten miles further south, and would eventually become the River Orthoboon, which would lead him to the Pablon Estate. Everyone in the city had heard of the place, because it was so close to the space port that the windows of the houses were known to rattle whenever the great lepto ships took off and landed.

His goal had been to make it to Pablon by one o'clock in the afternoon, but shortly after midday, he felt hunger growling away in his belly and so he settled himself down on a wrought-iron bench by the side of the river. He pulled off his shoes, peeled off his socks, and changed the dressings on his blisters before helping himself to the pistachios he'd been saving as a special treat. Then he leaned his rucksack at the side of the bench, balancing the plush octopus on top of it to act as a pillow. If he took a half-hour nap, he reasoned, he could still be at the estate by one.

He didn't know how long he'd been asleep, but the sound of a bike bell and his head slamming hard against the bench woke him instantly. He sat up, and when his eyes gained focus he made out two youths, perhaps fifteen or sixteen, cycling off into the distance along the dirt path. They were tossing his backpack to and fro between them, all the while laughing and jeering.

THE PRESENT

"Now I feel sorry for the little dude. Can't believe those assholes fleeced him like that… and while he was sleepin' an' all."

"They didn't get the octopus," Weinberg says. "It fell to the ground, and they left it there." He shuffles over to the window, unhooks the wooden rod, and uses it to pull the pane back an inch or two. "Anything you want to ask me?"

"Yeah: why set the story in Magnatella, and why'd you know so much about the goddamn place?" I'm reading his face for clues I might be pushing things too far, but all I can make out is a kind of detached wistfulness.

"I have my instructions," he tells me, sighing like he wishes it wasn't the case. "And when we get to the end, you'll understand. You just have to trust me on that. Do you think that's possible, Carney?"

I guess Weinberg's okay. It's just hard to picture him as an ordinary guy: someone who goes out for groceries, mows the lawn on Sundays.

"I could give it a shot."

He smiles, kind of humble-looking. "Good. Tomorrow, I'll bring you a radio. And you can call me Nils if you want; I really don't mind."

A radio is probably the last thing I need right now, so I turn him down flat. It's not just that I feel unworthy. It's more to do with the crafty way music has of raking through the past, rubbing salt into bleeding wounds that you know can never heal.

The salesman reaches into his store-coat pocket and pulls out a packet of forty Oakwood Milds still wrapped in cellophane. "Okay, here, take these, then," he says, tossing them onto the bed. "You must be climbing the walls in here, and this is the least I can do."

After he's gone, I peer out into the corridor. There's a lardy cop on the far right, squashed into a chair, busy leafing through *The Hailey's Town Gazette*. I guess the room nearest him is where they're keeping that screwball, and just thinking about him gives me a weird kind of feeling—like maybe he holds the key to everything that's going on around here. I drag my bed across to the window in my room, balance on the headboard, but I still can't see out. There's nothing to do but light up an Oakwood Mild and wait, but it's half past ten in the evening when I'm finally blessed with the sound of Lardy's rubber soles squeaking across the tiles. I knew his bladder couldn't hold out forever. I slip out into the corridor, skulk up to the crank's door, then push down hard on the handle, only to find the damn thing locked.

"Get back to your room." A stringy cop grabs me by the arms from behind, shoving me forward.

"But I gotta talk to the crackpot."

I'm frog-marched back to my bed, Stringy yelling, "Xenon 90, please", and minutes later, a medic appears with a syringe.

"Roll up his sleeve."

Xenon 90 must be the stuff they're pumping me full of—the dope that helps me wind down. It always seems to set me off wallowing in the past, either purely for nostalgia's sake, or because I'm still trying to piece together the events that led to getting banged up in the first place.

Ten minutes in, and my brain has landed on Earl putting tighty-whities on the school's life-size Gilbert Gowder statue when we were in freshman year. We broke into the grounds and snuck into the quadrangle just after midnight, and I remember how I was sweating bullets keeping watch for him. He had to cut the underpants open, then sew them up again because Gilbert's legs were fixed to the base. Then he stuck them down with industrial-strength glue, so's they'd be real hard to peel off, and every day after, in the run-up to the holidays, he added another item of clothing, welding it down firmly with the gloop. As you'd expect, Thackery was mad as a hornet, and made no bones about suspending whoever was responsible. He even called a special assembly where he dubbed it 'a crime against the morals of Cassaforta', and offered a reward of sixty bandols for information. Of course, Earl couldn't resist sticking his hand up and saying, "It was me, sir. Can I have the sixty sheets?"

But as I'm recalling each gut-busting detail, something really odd happens. There's another kid standing next to me in the assembly hall. I sneak a look at him, but double vision takes hold, and the rest of the students blur into the background. For a while, it's just me and this other kid—all flaxen curls and Buddy Holly specs, first two of him, then one, then two again. I don't recognize him at all. He holds out his hand for me to shake.

"My name's Harvey Wilder," he says, "but you can call me Wallbanger if you want; everyone does."

He winks at me like it's some great secret—like I'm the only one allowed to know who he is. But there's something behind his impish grin and the gleam in his eye—a kind of double-edged sword, on the one hand pulling you in with a promise of trust, an assurance that he's been round the block a few times and knows how to take care of you. But at the same time, I can't help thinking he'll ram the damn blade straight through my heart the moment my back's turned.

When the shot finally wears off, it's about two in the morning, and I can't get that kid and the sword out of my head. It feels like a false memory or something. I never knew anyone called Harvey Wilder.

8

Javapod Street

THE PAST

The noise hit us from several blocks away—hoods and hipsters milling around on the sidewalks outside the bars, jive halls, and coffee shops, all of them acting out, knocking back ale, and hollering. It was always buzzing on a Friday night in downtown Hailey's. The whole place just seemed to come alive, like someone went around sprinkling a weird kind of electrical charge into the air that made all the kids act crazy.

Marshall pulled over at the top of Main Street as I peered out the back window, sleek, open-top groundies whizzing past us by the score, each one loaded with pumped-up heps. Horns were blaring as kids played musical cars, hopping eagerly out of one set of wheels and into the next, snatches of scrambled rock 'n' roll weaving together into a kind of patchwork soundtrack that seemed to sum up perfectly the joy of being a teenage kid in Hailey's Town.

"Gonna park further down," Marsh mumbled, so we bailed out, crossed at the junction, and joined the throng.

The Dodge made three more circuits of the block, Marshall sounding the horn each time he passed us. Then, when he overtook us a fourth time, Taylor leapt up onto the hood, slithering in through the open window, cat-burglar style, before they hurtled away at full throttle, only to pull up sharp when they got to the tailback at the lights. Hailey's seemed so damn happening that, with every step, I caught myself thinking about Earl's little speech down at the creek. I reckoned the guy had it figured just right. Nothing came close to the vibe of Javapod after Dol went down.

We were getting seriously jostled by the sea of kids making their way to The Apex, so Booker linked arms with Dakota for reinforcement. "Take it we're headed for Buddy's Deck?"

Earl beamed, marching a whole lot faster. "Where else? I'm just itchin' for some a' that Dutch spice." That was a code name for coffee laced with liquor—a secret specialty served up by Tamzin, the owner. It made the place a haven for every minor in Hailey's, and if you were to ask them, they'd probably say it rocked harder than any other joint in town.

Dakota always liked to nab a table in the booths at the side where the lights were dimmed. She said it was like being in a train carriage, and the puffy red seats looked like they'd been ripped straight out the back of a Chevy Bel Air. But once we got inside, Taylor was waiting for us by the door.

"No booths free tonight, Kotes," he said. "It's packed as hell, but Marsh's keepin' a table up front."

Once we claimed our spot, I felt a light tap on the shoulder and turned to see a familiar face. He was dressed in overalls, traces of dark oil smudged across his cheeks.

"Hey, Alpin-Joe, how's it goin'? Kepple's keepin' ya busy?" I swung an arm up to shake him by the hand.

"Leyland's finished for the day, but I'm workin' late," AJ said. He scraped a chair up and sat down next to me, the smell of engine oil and grease mingling with the rich scent of roasted coffee. "Just came by for a nightcap to keep me goin'."

"I'm guessin' that's Dutch spice."

AJ smiled back at me and took a rather cautious sip. He looked agreeable enough, but I couldn't help thinking his grin was forced and there was something about the way he kept twiddling his fingers. "To be honest, I was hopin' I'd find y'all in here," he said, after a while. He stared across at Taylor, and then Marshall leaned in over the table so that his nose was just a couple of inches from AJ's.

"Well? What's the word?"

"He stopped by the garage 'bout an hour ago," Alpin-Joe said. "He's lookin' for ya. Wants the money or the stuff back— one or the other. That's what he told me."

"We ain't conjurors." Marshall puffed away on another ebby and shook his head. "Goddamn lamebrain. He'll just have to cut his losses."

"You don't know shit about it." AJ was talking real quiet, but harsh enough to stir up a real sense of urgency. "This is Shap Ranton we're dealin' with. Man, you're off your head if you think he's just gonna forget about it. He's been inside three times. He's runnin' the biggest racket this side a' the Disian Ocean. And as for his cronies, you know as well as I do, they're total screwballs. They do anythin' he tells 'em; that's what's so damn scary."

His words were swimming in my brain like hot, sticky treacle, but Marshall seemed cool as ever. Come to think of it, I'd never seen him lose his rag over anything, except maybe earlier at the creek when he ended up smashing the liquor bottle, but I wasn't sure if that was just an act. Alpin-Joe was rattled, that much was clear, but Marshall just waved it away.

"No one's gonna step on our toes tonight. Just leave old Ranton to me."

"A wolf don't fear no barkin' dog," AJ said. "And you'd do as well to remember." There was an awkward silence while he supped his drink, then he shunted his chair back, eyes still fixed on Marshall. "You be careful, okay?" I watched as he pushed his stocky frame past a group of teenaged ear hustlers and weaved his way out, disappearing into the noise and bustle outside.

"Jeez, Marsh," I said, all wide-eyed. "You got a death wish or somethin'? I mean, for Pete's sake. Why get involved in shit like that?"

"Don't be so dumb, Caldwell. Those crinkles didn't fall off no holiday tree." Taylor was getting real twitchy now. I could tell because he would clutch at the back of his neck whenever he got like that.

Earl stood up and shrugged, his palms facing upward. "I'm gonna fetch the drinks," he said. "And when I get back, you two'd better have somethin' figured." He frowned, and there was a pained expression on his face. "If not, then… that's the end of us hangin' out." He crouched down low, voice all hushed. "We're decent folk in this gang. We don't pander to hoods like Ranton. If that's what you wanna do, then… you'll have to step down."

Taylor got to his feet, gritted his teeth, and grabbed Earl by the jacket collar. "You lousy hypocrite," he yelled. "You do notch smokes and hard liquor. You sat there in the Dodge while we took it, and you did jack shit. Who the hell do you think you are, anyway? This ain't your gang. You ain't in charge of us."

The whole of Buddy's was gawking, but Earl didn't struggle or say anything. There was just a baffled sadness in his eyes, like a puppy that can't work out what it's done wrong.

"Let him be, Tayles," I said quietly. "Kingpins is trouble, and we don't want it."

Taylor looked me in the eye for a few seconds, then slumped back down in his seat, head buried in his hands. I guess I was like the anchor to his willful sea of recklessness; I could always rein him in when things got heated.

Dakota tried to put an arm round him, but he shook her away, and she lost it big time after that. "Of all the nerve, Earl Hunter, thinkin' you can just kick folk out when it suits you. Tayles got as much right as you to be an Angel." She nodded in Marshall's direction, and I could see the pupils of her eyes getting smaller in the heat of everything. "It's probably all down to doom boy over there anyway."

Marshall scowled. "Get ya facts straight before ya go shootin' ya mouth off," he said. "Me 'n' Pumble were in this together—blood brothers, fifty-fifty split." He glanced over at Earl. "Don't give a cuss about the gang neither, so you can take a hike."

"We know that, right enough," Booker said. "You never bothered with the tattoo. Hell, you don't even dress like an Arch Angel."

"Hardly surprisin', is it? Who'd wanna look like you?" Marshall slouched back against the wall, smirking to himself before dragging on the weed again, green smoke wafting everywhere.

"Just crawl back into your swamp." Booker was scrunching her face up, the same way she always did when she was nettled by something. Her hackles were so far up I thought she'd pull him clean across the table.

"Calm down, Books," I said. "I'm goin' over to the bar. What do y'all want? It's all on me—peace offerin'."

Earl turned to Taylor, who was still hanging his head. "Look, Tayles," he said, much softer. "Arch Angels don't deal. Ain't sayin' it 'cause I think I'm in charge or any shit like that. It's just the way things are. Ain't what this gang's about." He smiled graciously at Kota and then strolled over to Tamzin in the jive hall, where the snail-shaped jukebox was blasting out Neil Sedaka's 'Oh! Carol' at maximum volume.

After the first round of Dutch spice, Booker and Earl went out the back to shoot some pool, but the rest of us sat it out. I guess we were dead beat, what with all the antics down at the creek, and then everyone locking horns like that. I slurped another mouthful of Dutch spice, all the while staring into the mug. It smelled of vanilla ice cream and you could taste the fire in it. But the most fun thing was watching the little brown bubbles rise up out of it and float off gracefully into the air. I thought it would be pretty cool to reach out and grab one, but then I realized it was just the rush kicking in, and I felt kind of dumb. I guess it must have been working its magic on all of us because Marsh and Tayles seemed much more chilled, and Dakota was resting with her boots on the table, her head leaned tight against Taylor's shoulder as she stared, goggle-eyed, at the mock-up gold discs and photos mounted on the wall.

"Buddy Holly, Eddie Cochran, Chuck Berry, Elvis Presley, Little Richard, Jerry Lee Lewis," she said, pointing to each one in turn, then frowning. "All the hottest stars."

"You okay, Kota?"

She giggled. "Just happy to be here."

Marshall offered me a green ebby. "That Earl cracks me up," he said. "Makes out like he's wacky as hell, but he's probably the most level-headed guy I know."

I slipped a smoke from the tin, a giddy smile plastered on my lips. "Broke the mold with that one," I said, ferreting in my pocket for a lighter, but I'd only taken a couple of drags when I noticed the color drain suddenly from Kota's cheeks. I followed her gaze and, straight away, figured out what was wrong. A thick-featured man and five of his henchmen were striding toward us.

"Time's up, Bexley. You ain't weaselin' yer way outta this one." Ranton's eyes were sunken, his nose was lopsided, and his teeth were mostly black and broken. But the things that really made my skin crawl were the scars: a thick streak that ran from his jawline all the way up to his cheekbone, and a knotted burn mark next to his eyelid that made it droop. "Ya got three choices: hand over the merchandise, cough up the gowder, or come with us." His voice was a kind of strangled scratch, grating on me like long fingernails scraped across a slate board.

I looked over at Marshall, expecting to catch a glint of that fear again, but somehow it was gone. He was scowling at Ranton, eyes wild as a marauding prairie dog. It was like the rush had dragged the dread right out of him, swapping it for a kind of foolhardy pluck. And there was no sign of an answer coming anytime soon. Taylor was sitting there, white as a sheet, and Dakota seemed totally out of it one minute, like a deer caught in headlights the next. For a grim moment, I thought the mob would beat up on us right there and then.

"You can take the Dodge," Marshall muttered eventually, offhand as anything. "She's fast once she gets goin'. And she don't guzzle much gas neither."

Ranton shook his head, smirking just enough to show off all that bad dental hygiene. "That old rust bucket? You gotta be yankin' my chain! On y' feet! All a' ya!"

They marched us out of Buddy's, a few yards down the street, and into the back of a plain black Chevy panel truck. The doors were banged shut and locked tight, and then the driver goosed it, the tires squealing noisily from the curb.

"Where they takin' us, Tayles?"

"Your guess is as good as mine, bud."

9

Domino

There are three token taps on the door, and then Weinberg strolls in, catching sight of the flower-patterned easy chair that the orderlies wheeled in earlier this morning. He draws it up beside the bed, then slips a freshly typed manuscript from his briefcase. Despite promising to trust him—a gut feeling that he's on my side—his vagueness is needling me big time. I need answers, and his distraction therapy bullshit isn't giving them.

"What's Xenon 90?"

Weinberg's eyes shift sideways a few times before latching onto mine. "Just something to help you relax," he says, a flat smile on his lips that makes me wonder why he bothered.

"Relax or hallucinate?"

"What do you mean?" He starts fiddling with his tie, as if I've got him all skittish.

"Who's Harvey Wilder?" I'm slowly realizing you have to bug the hell out of Weinberg if you want to get anywhere.

"I have absolutely no idea. Look, Carney, I don't have much time today. We need to press on with the story."

DORAN'S STORY

"We lost everything, buddy." Doran was talking to his octopus again. "I'm not giving up, though. Okay, the cards and comics are gone, but it won't stop me getting to the Oakley farm. I'll find Quin even if it means having to steal."

He zipped the toy into the lining of his hood to keep it safe. His plan was to return to Dactyleonbar, download another map from the college library, then double back to Cartow Boulevard because, passing through it the previous day, he'd noticed an abundance of street markets, inns, and stores. The place had been so vibrant, so full of bustling students and shoppers, he reasoned it would be easy to slip into a store unseen and take whatever he needed.

Doran arrived at the top of the boulevard a little after seven in the evening, but it was much quieter than before, and most of the stores were already closed, so he thought he'd stake out an old-fashioned late-night food mart where the street joined with Tinpan Square. He sat on a bench near the water fountain, fixing his eyes on the door.

After a while, he worked out that there was only one man at the checkout desk and, when the shop floor was empty, the guy would retire out the back, relying on the doorbell to alert him to folk entering. But there was a delay of about fifteen seconds between its ringing and his getting into position. Maybe that was enough time to wrap a sock around the clapper.

Doran tried to come up with a plan, but his stomach was complaining, and half a dozen gray gabble birds were flapping, flocking, and pecking about near his feet, filling him with apprehension. Then he spotted a young girl, perhaps thirteen or fourteen years old, marching up to the storefront, ash-brown hair tied in bunches under a Banunus City Bobcats cap. She shoved the door open with the full weight of her shoulder, and that was Doran's cue to start counting the seconds. But before he got to thirty, he saw her burst out with her backpack still unzipped in her arms, the storekeeper haring after her. It was the perfect chance for Doran to strike, because the store was completely unattended.

He jumped up, glancing first at the doorway and then back down the boulevard where the man was giving chase. You will, no doubt, recall his difficulty with making choices, but on this occasion he did not falter. Something deep within him, a strange compulsion for which he had no name, told him that he should follow the girl. Perhaps it was a quality in her features or a subtlety in her rhythms of movement that drew him to her, but he had no time to rationalize, so he started down the street in pursuit of her and, ravenous and tired as he was, felt a peculiar strength in his legs that seemed to come from nowhere. In a matter of minutes, he was so close he was forced to drop his pace. The merchant had reached the bottom of the winding strip, and was panting heavily, intently scanning the area for signs of the girl. Doran did his best to look casual, deliberately mingling with the clusters of students, revelers, and trundling service bots, but at the same time keeping fully alert for movement.

The man darted so fast down an alleyway, Doran almost missed it. He sidled over, peering cautiously round the corner. The girl was already more than halfway up an eight-foot wall, and the storekeeper was swiping at her rucksack, eventually tugging at it so hard that she slipped, toppling backward onto the ground, landing clumsily on her side.

The man closed in on her. "You'll pay now, you lousy, good-for-nothing thief."

"Stick it where the sun don't shine!" The girl kicked up at him and caught him on the chin, springing to her feet in the same swift motion. She turned to flee again, but the storekeeper grabbed her by the arm, drawing a wooden baton from his apron and raising it above her head.

Instinctively, Doran yelled out, "Hey!", and the merchant swiveled, the baton still hovering in the air.

Of course, the girl seized her chance, biting the man so hard on the finger, he had no choice but to drop the weapon. And then, before Doran could even think about what to do next, she'd fled back up the street, the man tearing after her.

Doran followed and, even though he was becoming breathless, managed to call out, "Stop! There's a whole gang of them looting the store! Forget about this one."

The man halted, leaning forward with his hands on his thighs. "How do I know you're not one of them?" he said, wheezing, looking Doran up and down suspiciously. However, he must have decided to believe him, because before too long he'd turned on his heels and was sprinting away into the distance.

Doran trudged back up the boulevard, giving the delicatessen windows a wide berth because it was more than seven hours since he'd scoffed the pistachios. He would not be able to steal from the minimart now, but he knew the sacrifice had been worth it. He'd saved the girl from the clutches of that horrible man, and the thought of it made the burden of his journey seem that much lighter. He imagined recounting the tale to Quin as they rambled through sun-drenched wheatfields on the way to Bindorn Hollows, Quin's eyes round as saucers, Dol nestled just above the snow-capped peaks of the rugged Doland Mountains. Smiling a little at the notion of it all, he passed a backstreet packed with deserted market stands, each one draped in a stripy blue-and-white tarpaulin, and it occurred to him that some of the produce might have fallen onto the road. It was a long shot, but he lumbered into the street anyway, carefully checking the stalls and gutters for stray fruits or vegetables, straining to see in the dimness.

He was nearly at the end when a sudden flapping of canvas made him jump, then a head poked out through the gap, and someone half-shouted, half-whispered, "Hey! Over here!"

Doran approached the stall tentatively from the front side. He could make out the slender figure of a girl hunched on a tabletop in the far corner, her face swathed in shadow, but even in the darkness he recognized her and again felt the tug of a sort of primordial calling—one that told him he was standing exactly where he was supposed to be. I guess for Doran the scene must have seemed altogether dreamlike. He stood there gaping, hesitating, afraid to speak in case the vision might suddenly fade.

"What's wrong with you? I don't bite," the girl said at last.

An uncomfortable silence passed in which she glared at him so fiercely, Doran could only shuffle his feet, but then she broke into a grin, snickering quietly to herself.

"Guess that was a bad choice of words. You saw me bite that guy on the finger, didn't you? That was self-defense, mind. You get that, don't you?" She glanced down at the table for a while and then regarded him sullenly as she chewed on a piece of gum. "Anyway, thanks for looking out for me back there."

He found it curiously difficult to bring forth words, because none of them seemed adequate. The soulfulness of those huge dark eyes conjured up an empathy in him that was felt almost as an orchestral movement—the kind that used to mesmerize him during theater trips to the Palderboon region. It got him thinking about those gut-wrenching moments when the violins would throw out a chord that forced him to gasp out loud with nameless emotions—ones he barely understood. But when the girl spoke to him and then broke into laughter, it was somehow, beautifully, at odds with those minor chords, like the violins had suddenly been smacked into rattling out a cheeky Irish jig that had everybody up and dancing in the aisles, oblivious to anything but the simple, unassuming joy of being alive. The juxtaposition of it was knocking him for six. He'd never met anyone who made him feel that way before.

It was hunger more than anything that finally squeezed the voice out of him. He mumbled something along the lines of, "Have you still got the food?", but on hearing how ill-mannered it sounded, he quickly added, "It's just that I'm a runaway and I've had nothing to eat since lunchtime."

The girl opened the haversack, laying out a loaf of bread, three oranges, two apples, a bottle of soda, and six candy bars. "What can I get you?"

Doran took some faltering steps toward her and stared at the plunder on offer, his mouth watering. "I'll take the candy."

She pressed one of the bars into his palm, and he tore into the wrapper at once, devouring the contents with just a couple of frantic bites, not really caring how primitive he was coming across.

"Sheesh, you sure were hungry. What's your name, anyway?" A rather grubby-looking hand was extended in Doran's direction. "I'm Domino."

The boy took her hand, but instead of shaking it as he had been taught at Maple Road, he just held it for the briefest of moments and then, silently, he let it go.

THE PRESENT

"So, this is where it starts to get mushy." I'm rubbernecking, trying to figure out what's written on the page, but Weinberg rolls the report into a tight tube and stuffs it at the side of the armchair.

He leans forward slightly, a half-smile teetering on his lips. "What's the problem, Carney? Don't you like romantic stories?"

"You're goin' all psychologist on me again. Don't do that."

"Haven't you ever been in love?"

"Lay off, will ya? I don't wanna talk about it."

After the session, I loiter by the door, Weinberg disappearing down the walkway. Lardy's chair is empty, so there's no time to lose. Running full pelt, I gatecrash the weirdo's room, my hand outstretched for the handle, when, right on cue, Stringy accosts me, calling for more Xenon 90.

"Why you doin' this? I just wanna talk to the guy!"

This time, the memory is the open-air dance that Taylor tried to organize on the top of Cobone Hill, four years ago. His crazy schemes always seemed to crash and burn, and this was a classic case. Despite weeks of planning, it rained like a monsoon, no one showed up, and the fuzz somehow got wind of it, storming into the marquee as if they were on some kind of top-secret sting operation—and all just to bust the kid for trading without a license. Of course, Taylor got all riled up, but I managed to talk them out of carting him off to jail. And the night wasn't a total write-off because Booker found a mudslide and we took turns hurling ourselves down it on our bellies. I can still hear Taylor yelling out, "Stick it to the man!" as he glided on down, an earful of rockabilly blaring out, full whack, over the hilltops.

But as I'm coming to the end of my second run, I notice that kid again, sliding down the track behind me, everyone else turning fuzzy.

"Why you here, Harvey? This is my memory, and you ain't a part of it."

"Maybe not," the kid calls as he passes me on the left-hand bend. "But I'm a part of you. And *he* is too, the other one. You've just forgotten, that's all."

10

The Rush

THE PAST

The back of the Chevy was awful dark, there were no seats or windows, and it was cut off from the cab, so we couldn't see who was driving or where we were going. The only sounds were the grinding rumble of the engine and the restless breaths of Tayles and Kota, who were leant against the bulkhead, one each side of me. I dug into my jeans pocket, pulled out my lighter, and flicked it on. Then I groped my way over to the back doors, where Marshall was crouched with his arms wrapped round his shins. I tried the handle, but it wouldn't budge.

"Okay, if you got a smart idea, now's the time."

"Wouldn't mess with the lock," Marshall muttered. "Might get 'em even more fired up. Don't wanna make things worse."

"Worse? How can it be worse than this?" Dakota's voice was quavering. "You saw that big ugly guy comin' at us, wieldin' a kunai knife!"

"Kota, there was no knife," Taylor said. "It's just the rush takin' effect, that's all."

"Oh, glory. So, now I'm seein' things? Whatever happened to 'No one's gonna step on our toes tonight' and 'Leave old Ranton to me'? You're so full of shit, y' know, Marshall."

I let go of the lighter switch, and for a while there was just the silence, the blackness, the heady stench of gasoline. But then the colors came, and it felt like, somehow, without really knowing it, I'd spent my whole life just waiting for them. It was just a bunch of purple sheets at first, seeping through the sides of the van horizontally, all glossy and crystal-like. Then the ceiling started dripping canary-yellow paint, the drops floating about like plasma, melding with the purple. Blobs of red started swirling about, twists of blue, little bubbly things the color of pocketbook plants. And when I reached out to poke at one, I giggled because it was like someone had flipped a giant zero-G switch. I drifted up to the roof as graceful as a snowflake, passed right through it, and carried on up.

"I'm headin' for Akkasine—"

"Carney!" Someone was shaking me, and I was back in the van again.

"Hey! Spoilin' it—quit. Quit. Cur-wit." My mouth seemed too big for my jawbone, and it was making the words come out all wrong, but I had no control over them anyway, because the colors were running everything. They always had been, I just never realized it.

I gaped in awe, the colors molding into the blurry shape of Walter Dillinger. And on further inspection, I saw that he was munching away on a wedge of watermelon as he strapped us into the carts of a Ferris wheel: Marshall and Taylor in one carriage, Dakota and I in the other. Then it started spinning, slow at first, but eventually hurtling us through the air so fast, it was like being sucked into the eye of a grade-five hurricane. Garbled carnival music was ringing out underneath, and then the wagon was plunging, rattling down the tracks of a white-knuckle roller coaster. I threw my arms up in the air, cried out with joy as we swooped through an almost seamless curve.

"What's happenin' to him?"

"Caldwell? You okay, man?"

The cart seemed out of control, jerking us about so hard, so random, all I could do was grab onto the sides and hope for the best. And then we were shunting up to the top, the gears and pulleys making a kind of chiseled cranking sound. We waited for the drop but, with a jolt and a clunk, the wagon derailed, and Dakota and I were suddenly gliding through a blushing twilight sky. I dangled my arm over the side, my fingers grazing cotton-candy clouds as we sailed on by.

"What happened to the others?"

"Think they're down there." Dakota nodded at a field below us that was covered all over in poppies, and then she started chuckling. "Look at all the funny scarecrows runnin' round it. Never saw anythin' quite so hysterical."

We sniggered uncontrollably for a full five minutes, all the while watching them.

"Boy, Kotes," I said, dabbing at my eyes. "Wish we could land down there and join in all the fun."

Dakota quit laughing, and I noticed that her head was flat, like a lollipop. "We could never get to 'em," she said. "They're from a whole other dimension. And they ain't made of atoms, neither. We couldn't even touch 'em."

"What they made of, then?"

"Fog," she said, as if it was obvious. "The kind that gets stuck in yer brain when things get overcomplicated." Her eyes were twinkling, sending out silvery sparks that were speeding through the air like tiny shooting stars. I snatched at one, wanting to keep it forever as a memento, but before I could, she caught my hand and slowly pulled it to her, lacing her fingers around mine. "Look where we are now," she whispered.

We were out on the creek, floating downstream in a canoe made entirely from fluffy white cantaboon leaves, time passing so strangely, so slowly, it felt as though you could pack a lifetime of happiness into a single second. And all the while she was holding my hand, just gazing at the eagle ink.

"I got a white-tailed eagle, you got an Inca dove," I said, running my fingertips gently over her wrist. "But it's the same tattoo. We're just looking at it from slightly different angles."

Kota let go of my hand, stretched herself out on the downy leaves, and I suddenly twigged that all her thoughts were visible. I saw how much the scarecrows had moved her, went through it the exact same way. And I felt like I could squeeze a tune out of the blues harp just by thinking about it.

"Jeez. This is unreal. Can you see inside my head as well?"

"Sure can. Right now, you're just wantin' to get on that old jaw harp. Fancy yourself as the next Larry Adler, I reckon."

"Weird thing is, Kotes, it all feels so regular—like this is the way things are s'posed to be—I mean, us knowin' everythin' about each other." I lay back in the canoe, limp with bliss, Kota beside me, the sun yawning away in the sky, broad, high, and handsome. And it seemed to me that, before all this, I'd been irrelevant—just another human caught up in the struggle of life, someone fighting to make sense of a universe that couldn't be explained. But now, just by being here with Dakota, by sharing my consciousness with her, I'd become the universe. There was no need for words, not even for thought.

The boat rocked lightly from side to side, and Dakota slipped into the river like a silky baby seal. I leaned over the edge, fumbling about in the coldness. "Kota? Where are you?"

"... she had no part in the deal. Leave her out of it!"

Rough hands were grabbing at me now, shoving me forward. I glanced down to see my feet stumbling along a dark, stony path.

"Walk, damn you!"

"I'm tryin'…." Why was it so hard to put one foot in front of the other?

There was a bleak, misty sea full of soldiers treading water, desperately paddling with their arms and rifles to keep afloat. They were about fifty yards out, nearly two hundred of them, some huddled together for warmth and all of them shivering so bad it was making their teeth chatter. Fierce waves were churning up a swell, and black clouds, dense as anything, hovered in clumps about a foot from the surface.

On the horizon, I could just about make out an old weather-worn pirate ship nodding up and down, all eight of its sails fluttering madly against the rigging. It seemed to be an organic thing, wholly alive, its hull the shape of an enormous humpback whale, and the grunts were sculling out to it, calmly and gently now, like a bale of leatherback turtles determined to reach the breeding ground. As the troops swam and the fog rolled about between them, the bow of the ship creaked open, and a far-off voice called out to me, loud and sonorous.

"Stretch your wings skyward, eagle-boy."

I splashed out into the ocean, working my arms up and down, but when I peered over at them, a pair of huge tawny wings were beating steadily, clawed feet skimming water. And then, still pumping the wings like billy-o, I was airborne, the ground shrinking away, the air sweeping by so fast every particle of me felt charged and alive. After a few minutes of frantic flapping, I figured out how to soar. The tips of the feathers were seeking out hot pockets of rising air all on their own, so I relaxed the muscles, keeping the wings fully spread out. Then, still gliding nimbly on the currents, I circled the ship three times, dizzy from the buzz of it all, the plangent tones of the ship juddering through my bones once more.

"Come again, eagle-boy, when you need your answers. I'll be waitin'."

I thought about landing on a clunky old cannon on the port side, but before I could home in on it, everything vanished and there was nothing but whiteness, and when I moved my limbs, all I could see were thin black streaks wiggling up and down.

"I'm a goddamn line drawin'."

I tried to reach forward, but I was jammed tight, stuck inside the confines of a flat sheet of paper. I was panicking so bad I couldn't get my breath, but then there was a white-hot light pulling at me, almost peeling me from the page.

Leyland's voice came from behind, making me jump so hard I spun round without thinking. "Carney, get washed up. Food'll be ready soon."

Supper was simmering on the stove as I watched him from the kitchen table. He was bustling about in his Kepple's coveralls, stirring the pans, all the while smelling of grease and spray paint. And Lucy was lolling in the chair by the porch in a pair of giant army boots. I knew it was her, even though she only looked about twenty-five. She winked at me as the kettle whistled and the pendulum of Grandpa's old wooden retirement clock swung to and fro on the wall above the twin-tub. Then her eyes were shifting left to right, fully synchronized with the beat, and Leyland was talking but there was no sound coming out of his mouth. I reached up to my head, massaging it where I could feel something sharp jabbing at me.

Rusting lug nuts were coming into focus, scattered across a clay-tiled floor thick with dust and dirt. One of the metal brutes was wedged hard against my forehead, so I sat up, wincing as a red-hot pain stabbed through the top of my left thigh, my stomach muscles pulling like overstretched elastic. Taylor was dozing on an old tarpaulin a few yards away, so I staggered over and shook him.

"Taylor! Wake up, dude. Your lip's all busted."

He blinked and sat up groggily, rubbing at the back of his

neck, mouth open in a kind of muted yawn. "Jeez, Carney, where the hell are we?"

"Ain't got a clue. My head's throbbin' like crazy." I peered about in the dimness. The only light was from a row of grimy, smashed-up windows daubed all over in graffiti. "It's quart to six," I said, glancing at my watch. "Where'd the others get to, anyway?"

"Don't remember. We got out the van, and then… it's all a blur." Taylor looked down at the floor, kind of sheepish. "I got the rush. Man, I was maxed out on it."

"Same here." I held out my hand so's he could pull himself up, and just as he was getting to his feet, we spotted a message scrawled in dust under one of the grungy old windows.

A DESPERATE INTENTION.
A DOL DIMENSION.
A PLACE NO ONE CAN FIND ME.

11

The Stowaways

THE PRESENT
Friday, January 23rd, 2325

've taken to staring at an oblong patch on the wall where the paint is slightly darker than the rest. A picture must have hung there once upon a time, and I can't help wondering what it was and why they took it away. I guess they thought it was way too classy for a jailhouse kid like me, but in a way, it's better; I can imagine whatever I want there now.

Yesterday, just before they turned the lights out, I saw an eastern screech owl nestled in an old tree hollow. He was gazing at me, all tufted ears, stripes of white and rust on his body. Seeing him kind of gave me some reassurance that the world was the way it was by chance—that it had nothing to do with that dream about the machine and the Eastern Europeans. But when I woke up this morning, the owl was gone. All I see now in that illusory frame is an eighteen-year-old kid with his head buried in his hands, as if by covering his face he could rid himself of all weakness—purge himself by becoming a featureless nothing.

I hear the plod of Weinberg's brogues out in the corridor, and then he's in here, rifling through the papers in the briefcase again.

"Just get on with the story," I tell him, not caring at all how drained and demoralized my words come out.

DORAN'S STORY

"So, you're from Earth?" They were onto the bread and apples now, the two of them sitting side by side underneath the tarpaulin.

"Place called Miami." Domino scratched at the back of her baseball cap, then gave Doran a little sideways glance, her mouth still open—a gesture Doran just wanted to bottle and keep. "We stowed away to Banunus, me and my folks," she said. "It was an Interstellar Class B Racer, biggest freight ship I ever saw—the *Hephaestus Grandulus*. I was only six but, boy, I'll never forget that name."

"Stowed away? Why?" Doran bit into his apple, thinking how it tasted even sweeter than the ones from the orchard back at Maple Road.

"Don't you know your history? Planet was fully colonized by 2190. If you live on Earth, smuggling yourself onto a cargo ship is the only way to get here."

Doran watched as the girl twisted the cap off a soda bottle, then guzzled half of it down.

"We were desperate to leave," she went on, looking intently at the glass, as if the memories were somehow stuffed inside it. "Earth's nothing but a lawless wasteland—has been ever since the war. And we'd heard guns were banned here, that crime was rare, that people lived in peace with plenty to go around."

"Where's your kin now?" he asked.

Domino looked down at her hands and was quiet for a while. Then she sighed and smiled at the same time, and Doran thought about the violins again, the loneliness seeming to drop from his shoulders like a snake shedding an old and very ill-fitting skin. "They found us soon as we landed," she said. "Busted us on the spot. We were carted away to a detention center, where they kept us for three long weeks. I remember my pa saying, 'At least we know there's law and order here.' But the irony was that we were on the wrong side of it." She leaned back against the stand's wooden frame and, just for a moment, Doran caught a flash of fire in her eyes that he somehow sensed she'd made peace with long ago. "They were sent for trial, Ma and Pa, but I guess I was too young to be called. By some quirk of fate, I was left alone in the cell the whole time, and that was when I noticed they'd turned the cameras off. I got out through a vent high up in the wall—unscrewed it with my watch strap. Then I crawled through the air ducts, not knowing where the pipes would lead, or even what I'd do if I could get to the end. But somehow, I wound up in an old storeroom, and no one was around, so I triggered the fire alarm. Then, after everyone filed out onto the street, I just casually carried on walking. That was seven years ago. I've been a vagrant ever since."

"And you never found them—your folks, I mean?"

"I read about the trial in a holo-reel two days after. They were found guilty of something called 'interplanetary trespass with intent'. The law shipped 'em straight back to Earth—same day, I reckon. Guess the jury thought that was punishment enough." Domino shrugged, a slight tremor in her lip. And then she was massaging her temples, eyes shut wearily, as if she was steeling herself. "But let's hear some more about you," she said, much more brightly. She plucked another candy bar from the pack, slipping a big chunk of it into Doran's hand. "You told me you're an orphan."

"I ran away from the Maple Road Children's Home," he said, once he'd taken another gulp of soda. "That's in Calahadra."

"Why'd you run away? I mean, it can't be that bad; Calahadra's real upmarket."

Doran fiddled with the zipper on his jacket, aware of her eyes on him and how strangely intoxicating it felt. "Maple Road was the best place in the world," he told her, turning to meet her gaze. "Big old airy house with four stories and turrets at the top—apple orchard and a koi pond out the back, too. I couldn't stay there anymore, though, not without Quin."

They wandered away from the boulevard, Domino leading Doran toward the Matapetus Waterfront, which was full of little yachts and barges bobbing up and down in the cool, dusky air. Akkasine was dangling low in the west, and you could hear the slap of the sleepy water against the stone of the harbor walls, as steam puffed up from the pavements, disappearing into the sky in ghostlike wisps.

"I've strayed too far to go back to base tonight," Domino said. "But we can stay with Sergeant Humbucker. He moors *The Dreamcatcher* along the canal here, most of the time."

"*The Dreamcatcher?*"

"That's his barge."

"Will he mind us sleeping there?" the young boy asked, keen not to invite any further drama into his life that night.

"The Sergeant? No, of course not."

Doran could see that the thought of Sergeant Humbucker, whoever he was, made Domino smile, and that when she did, two beautiful, moon-shaped dimples appeared on her cheeks.

THE PRESENT

"Why you botherin' with all a' this? I mean, I get that you wanna give me other stuff to think about, but why'd you care enough to do it?"

Weinberg dips his head, then takes off his glasses, and I can't help noticing how much smaller his eyeballs look without them. "I'm a pacifist, Carney," he says. "I uphold all the things that I believe are good and true." He breathes on the eyepieces, then polishes them with the bottom of his store coat.

"Most would say the same, but they ain't roamin' round medical centers tellin' complicated fairy tales. Can't you go bug some other perp instead?"

He smiles in that enigmatic way of his, replacing the glasses. "Come now, it's not really that complicated. It's just the story of a boy with certain insecurities… a boy who loved a girl. Isn't that everyone's tale sooner or later?"

"You're changin' the subject."

"Right. I was talking about peace, and that starts as an inner state." He taps his fingers vaguely against the arm of the chair. "If you don't have it on the inside, how can it exist externally? I promote peace in all its forms, and that includes making sure there's justice in my town."

"But you sell radios."

My watch ticks softly in the silence, as if it's counting down to something big—something that's about to smack me in the face—and all the while, Weinberg's magnified eyeballs flit about like moths under a skylight.

"I'm not a salesman, Carney," he tells me. "And I'm not a psychologist, either. I'm the governor of Hailey's Town and, as you'll see, an important part of my job is uncovering the truth."

"And what might that truth be, Mr. Town Governor? Why don't you just spit it out and let me alone?" I'm bawling again, and then, in a moment of sheer craziness or pure genius, I snatch the briefcase from his grasp and hightail it down the corridor, dodging into the bathroom so's I can lock myself inside one of the cubicles. There's a little red book in the bag that looks like a diary. I snatch it out, opening a page randomly, my hands trembling as I take in the words.

I must be extremely careful about the order in which I reveal things to Carney, or his fragile mental state could suffer. On Sunday, I will tell him about Cassaforta, and how it was created artificially by the pacifist rebels to replicate 1950s America.

The door swings open before I can read any further. I swear I locked it. But when I peer out, there's no one there, just a message scribbled on the mirror, traced in steam, and it scares the bejesus out of me.

IT WASN'T JUST YOUR BEST BUD YOU DID IT TO.
—WALLBANGER

12

Aftermath

"What d'you s'pose it means?" Taylor bent down to get a closer look at the message. "Is it Kota's writin'?"

Dakota! I remembered the cantaboon boat, the sparkle in her eyes that I tried to catch hold of, and the perfect stillness out on the river, but the memories were peppered with shame and confusion. It was wrong to think of her that way, because she was Taylor's girlfriend. In any case, it was all just a crazy fantasy—the product of an overzealous mind and a rush crinkle.

A frown was forming on Taylor's brow, so I just mumbled, "Maybe Marshall's gone someplace to hide. Left this as a clue."

"Nah, Marsh always told me he'd make for Nefamincle if the heat got too much. And it's gonna be my first port a' call too, once I start out travelin'." Taylor moved away from the window. "Anyway, we oughta check this place out—make sure Ranton and his bunch of goddamn Neanderthals are gone."

We combed the warehouse, but apart from the message, there was no sign at all that anyone else had been there, so we found the main exit and stepped outside into the open.

"Think I know where we are now," I said, once I caught sight of the Longboon Highway. The road was a major haulage route that ran east all the way from Del Kirkosa to Grade Glennings, and the silo was part of a defunct industrial estate out near Harlone Welby.

Taylor ran a finger over his busted lip. "Yeah. Reckon it's about ten miles back to Hailey's."

We set out on the long trek home, Dol climbing sleepily behind us, a light rain pattering onto the asphalt, painting the sky with a kind of washed-out yellow hue.

"So, what d' ya reckon to the green lady?" Taylor said when we were a few miles down the road. "You dropped before I did. You were actin' pretty crazy in the van."

The question made me feel so awkward, it was hard to find words, and in the end, I answered without looking at him. "Earl was on about bad trips, but it wasn't like that for me. It was just like… weird shit happenin', over and over. I mean, different things, stuff that seemed impossible, but it all felt so goddamn real. I turned into an eagle at one point; I actually flew."

"It's an elixir for the soul, alright," Taylor said with a gutsy smile. "Marsh calls it huckleberry dreamin'." Then his face paled, and he looked quite solemn. "But Earl's right: bad trips happen sometimes, and that's what's worryin' me. Kota said she saw Ranton holdin' a knife in Buddy's. She coulda got the shurbs."

"That's a bad trip, right?"

Taylor nodded and stuffed his hands in his pockets. "I just… hope she's okay. Won't ever forgive myself if anythin' bad's happened."

"Kotes'll be alright," I told him. "She's pretty tough." Setting his mind at rest was the decent thing to do, even if a bunch of doubts were niggling away inside of me.

We pushed on further down the road, the open fields on both sides giving way to woodland—droopy wither trees and gnarly jackhawks. I spotted a clearing a few yards in where woodcutters had hacked everything down to a cluster of stumps, so we picked our way through the overgrown bushes and sat down opposite each other.

"My stomach feels like a bottomless pit. Feel kinda giddy too."

"Gets you that way once you come down," Taylor said. "Best eat somethin'. And a cig might help stop the shakes." He dug into his pockets and pulled out some Steringo mints and a box of smokes. "Guess you want the lowdown on all this Ranton shit. You probably figured we work for the asshole—me, Marsh, and AJ."

"Yeah, but why was he after you?"

Taylor stared at the ground, absently kicking a jack cone about with his boot. "The first few weeks it was just notch smokes and pinch, that kinda stuff. But then he trusted me and Marsh to take a whole load a' rush on the understandin' we'd sell 'em and pay him a week later. It all went south second night, though. Fuzz showed up when we were out hustlin' over on Fiddler's Row. We packed up quick as we could and hot-tailed it outta there in the Dodge, but they chased after us. Marshall gave 'em the slip for a while, but then we heard the sirens gettin' close, so he ditched the stash in a field over by the old Tundles line. Cops caught up to us and searched the car, so it was lucky we dumped it. Went back the next day, but it was useless. Goddamn fields all looked the same in the dark. Couldn't find the gear anywhere."

"And the ones we took?"

"A little sample we kept for ourselves. Ain't much of it left."

It was just gone nine in the morning when I finally got back to Captain's Way, slipped my key in the door, and quietly pushed it open. Leyland always slept in on Saturdays, so I figured I could risk fixing a sub and then sneak up the stairs. If I ran into him, I'd just tell him the Angels pulled an all-nighter.

Once I got into my room, I wrenched my boots off and sat on the edge of the bed, rubbing at my feet. I wolfed down the sub, then climbed under the covers, still shaking, feeling all the while that the place had changed, like I'd outgrown it somehow. I closed my eyes and lay still, tried to force my body to wind down, trusting that my mind would follow suit, but a million questions were swirling about up there, and I couldn't stop my thoughts from racing, so I trudged over to the window and drew the drapes back.

Hailey's Town looked drab and old, as if it was falling to bits, and no one cared. There was the old town hall building, the early-morning shadow of its tower stretching halfway across the square, the giant mouths of its archways gaping open underneath. Opposite, the concrete library block and the boxlike bowling alley were begging for someone to knock them down and start from scratch. But behind it all, the rounded Bolar Hills nuzzled sleepily against the skyline, trying to dress it all up as something pretty. They were covered in a lush carpet of purple from all the tashur flowers, and I remembered how, before the stroke, Lucy liked to sit in the back garden so she could paint them in watercolors, always just before twilight, to capture the moment when Dol would slip down behind them.

"When ya hear that wind singin' over from the Bolars," she used to say, "it stirs somethin' deep inside a' ya."

I listened to it whooping and whistling from over in the north, but the only thing stirring inside of me was a rising dread about what had happened to Dakota. Great gray clouds were skittering across the sky, and a blanket of fog was coming down, draping itself over the hills like some otherworldly burial shroud.

13

Sergeant Humbucker

THE PRESENT
Saturday, January 24th, 2325

I wake just after eleven, cranky as anything, the guilt about the felony coiled around me like some fat old boa constrictor. Last night's dreams were just words, bouncing between my neurons in a violent esoteric pinball game that seemed like it would never stop.

Weinberg, Wallbanger. Carney, Harvey. Weinberg, Wallbanger. Carney, Harvey.

I have no recollection of coming back to my room after the shock of seeing that message, and the diary is nowhere to be seen. Did I really snatch Weinberg's bag and go tearing down the corridor with it? The whole business feels kind of surreal now, like it never happened at all. But when the town governor gets here, half an hour later, he seems more cautious than normal, which makes me suspicious. He wheels the chair over very quietly, with a guarded, "Good morning, Carney."

Maybe it's time to put my grouchiness aside. "Look, sorry I read your diary, man."

Weinberg looks puzzled. "I think you've been dreaming," he says. "I don't keep a diary."

My head sinks into the pillow. "Then I'm stumped. Got no clue what's goin' on. I just want a trial, like any other guy. No crazy stories, no Xenon 90, no weird messages on mirrors."

He frowns, running his finger across his lips. "I don't know anything about that, but there will be a hearing," he tells me, folding his arms. "You see, there's a much bigger picture for us here, and we must get to the bottom of it. You'll understand when—"

"When we get to the end, yeah, I know. It's horsefeathers— about as much use as a chocolate teapot." I got the chocolate teapot thing off Lucy, but Weinberg's stories are worse because, ever since I first heard Lucy say it, I reckoned you could eat a chocolate teapot, so it wasn't completely useless. "Ain't no therapy under the sun can take away the kinda shame I feel."

It's a while before Weinberg says anything. All I can hear is the squeak of the springs as he fidgets in the chair. "Look, Carney. I'll make a deal with you," he says eventually. "If you promise to continue with the treatment, I guarantee you'll be closer to the truth than ever before. In fact, by the time we wrap up today, you'll know more than anyone else in the whole of Hailey's Town, bar me."

DORAN'S STORY

The Dreamcatcher was a great deal smaller and far shabbier than Doran had imagined. There were no streetlamps once they got past the marina, but even so, he could see quite plainly that the wood on the hull was rotting, and the paintwork was faded and peeling so badly in places it made the barge resemble a huge teal mosaic.

"This is it? This is where he lives?"

"I call it the Ship of Dreams sometimes," Domino said, winking at Doran as she stepped onto the bow. Then she rapped loudly at the cabin door, gesturing for him to come aboard.

She hadn't said much about the man he was about to meet, except that he was rather eccentric and had spent most of his working life at sea—first in the Magnatellan Navy, and then as a transcontinental navigator on the Disian cargo ships. Doran hung his head, gawking at his feet, but then a lantern on the port side flickered on, the door was unlatched and opened, and a sprightly man with pale blue eyes peered out at them. Doran placed him in his mid-fifties, but the pointed beard, raggedy mustache, and graying hair gave him the air of someone at least ten years older.

As soon as he recognized the girl, a beam worthy of the boldest Cheshire cat appeared on the sailor's face, and he took off his beret, making a low, sweeping bow. "Well, if it isn't my little Astronomy Dominé," he said, his voice a songlike trill. "Come inside, my dear, don't be shivering out there in the cold."

Domino motioned first toward Doran and then to Humbucker, saying, "This is my friend." Doran wasn't entirely sure who was being introduced to whom, but he smiled and nodded politely, and then The Sergeant led them down some creaky wooden steps into a galley area that carried the musky scent of burning jasmine. There, he lit a hob on the gas stove and set an old copper kettle on top of it. Then he patted a sofa tucked behind a table, where an Irish flute, skillfully carved from the finest rosewood, was resting.

"Please, make yourselves comfortable," he told them, as he returned to the stove and pulled some mugs from the cupboard above it. "The blankets are in the box underneath. Stay as long as you wish. My home is yours, as always."

"It's just for tonight, Sarge. In the morning, I'll take Doran to Nentoke to meet the Shadow Dwellers."

The galley was dark, save for a flicker of light from the hob and the glow of a tiny wood burner underneath the window, so Humbucker fetched a kerosene Kelly lamp and some matches, and laid them on the table. "I know you're used to the shadows, but here, take these."

"It's best when it's just the firelight," Domino said. "You'll probably laugh at this, Doran, but sometimes we spend hours just picking out shapes in the flames, and then we take turns making up stories about them... but we can light the lamp if you want."

"I'm easy." Doran didn't wish to impose when he'd only just made their acquaintance, and in any case, he was grateful just to be among friends, and to have somewhere warm and safe to sleep. He also declined when Humbucker offered them both a Ramrod cigar as he'd never smoked before and he was afraid of embarrassing himself in front of them, but Domino smiled, took one from the tin, and stashed it behind her ear.

"Have a cigar," she sniggered, and The Sergeant seemed curiously amused by the words. Doran was about to ask why, but the girl was talking again before he could get anything out. "Guess you're wondering why they call him The Sergeant when he's a sailor."

"Kind of, yeah. 'Captain' would be more fitting."

Humbucker was mixing up an exotic-looking herbal brew, filling the galley with a wonderful aroma that included chicory, ginger, freshly roasted walnuts, and fennel. "Oh, I never made captain. I was chief petty officer back when I was in the navy," he told Doran. "And there were no ranks on the Disian ships. But I suppose I'm captain of *The Dreamcatcher* now."

"It's his ancestors," Domino said, striking a match and rotating the cigar over the flame at a forty-five-degree angle. Then she puffed at it until the foot finally ignited. "They came from France hundreds of years ago—the D'Argents. Tell him, Sarge."

They sat around the table, making idle chat and sipping away at the hot, syrupy beverage that The Sergeant called *boisenbois*. And every so often, he would lapse into half-whispered French soliloquies, his voice waiflike, the sounds tripping off his tongue so gracefully they had Doran almost believing he was back in the summerhouse at Maple Road, listening to another one of Mr. Fredrick's poignant poetry recitals.

"*La lumière est vide sans l'obscurité. Seulement, quand on les voit comme on, peut les vibrations de son âme résonner en accord.*"

Doran didn't know what the words meant, but they seemed to be stirring something inside of him, although he wasn't sure what exactly. And when, at last, his eyes became fully attuned to the dark, he noticed a large, shaggy-looking raven snuggled on Humbucker's lap, its curved beak opening and closing contentedly as it emitted a kind of garbled clicking noise that sounded just like ice cubes plinking into a glass of water. "You've got a bird!" he called out excitedly. "He's beautiful."

Domino giggled again behind ribbons of smoke that smelled delicious to Doran—hints of bourbon and wet, tangy wood.

"Indeed," The Sergeant said, his eyes glowing like polished sapphires. "But Carina is a she, and she doesn't belong to me. It's more the other way around, if you catch my drift. Anyway, enough of us; tell me about yourself and how you came to be in the company of these three ragged rebels."

Doran cleared his throat. "Domino knows some of it already," he said, stuttering a little because he had become the sole focus of attention. "But I guess the floating suitcases would be a good place to start." He launched himself into the tale, and by the time he came to the boulevard chase and the meeting with Domino, the quiver in his voice had all but vanished. Finally, both proud and buoyed up by getting through to the end, he delivered his swan song. "I've come all this way, but I think it might be time to head back now. I've decided not to go to the Oakley farm after all."

"Oh, and why is that?" Humbucker asked, gently lifting Carina onto the table so that she could dip her beak into what was left of the *boisenbois*.

"Well, since Domino has no kin, she could come and live at Maple Road with me," Doran said, stammering again when he realized he should have discussed it with her first. He watched as the two of them exchanged prudent glances, his face flushing. He gazed down at the carpet, cursing himself for blurting it out like that. Why couldn't he have kept his thoughts to himself?

"Look, Doran. I'll level with you," Domino said, and Doran could see that she was trying to smile but finding it difficult. "If the Magnatellan authorities got hold of me, they'd most likely run a DNA test, match me to my family, and ship me back to Earth before you could say 'Walter Dillinger'. And even if they let me stay, there's no way I'd want to go to an orphanage." The boy looked a little crestfallen, so she softened her voice. "I'm happy living on the streets. I like that I'm not on their radar... that they'll never get to me." She was staring across at Humbucker, her eyes searching his as if some unspoken blueprint for the handling of delicate situations might be found there.

"You were smart to run away," Humbucker told Doran, with an assuring nod of the head, and then Domino placed her hand on top of the boy's, squeezing it tightly for a moment.

"You're twelve years old, right? In a year's time they woulda stuck an implant into your brain to keep you from ever leaving this continent."

THE PRESENT

My face probably has a weird screwed-up kind of look, as if I'm wincing. I guess it's because I heard Weinberg's words, but I just can't take them in. And then, when I see him sitting there in the chair, laid-back as hell with his chin balanced on his fist, time seems suspended in the air, like some great cosmic pause button has suddenly been pressed. It's a good few minutes before I can make any kind of sound at all.

"That's crazy. You're tellin' me they operate on you in Magnatella? Why did no one mention this before?"

"It can't have come as a total surprise," Weinberg says. "You must have gathered already that college is a one-way ticket. How did you think it was going to work?"

"Yeah, but... I can't believe... I mean, this is just plain wrong."

Weinberg is nodding his head, the same way I pictured the old salt in the story. "I'm not privy to the details of modern science," he tells me. "I'm a Cassaforta man. But I do know that it's quite a simple procedure. It's called a tagmesh, and it's completely painless. Maybe now you can understand why I'm taking these explanations so slowly."

14

Ambledon Avenue

THE PAST

My eyelids opened and I yawned, staring blearily at my akka-dial watch. It was just after three in the afternoon, so I slung my clothes on and sloped downstairs to the living room where Lucy and Leyland were playing fake Lucy poker, the cards all spread out on the gate-leg table. Leyland made the game up a few years ago, to hoodwink Lucy into thinking she was actually playing something, and he always saw to it that she won.

"It surfaces," he said, slowly breaking into a grin, and I was glad to see him so upbeat. It meant he didn't suspect anything.

"Yeah, sorry. Had a late one out with the Angels. Y' know what we're like."

He shook his head and tutted. "Teenagers. Wasn't like that in my day. What time d'you get in then, Mr. Rip Van Winkle?"

I put on a scatty smile and perched on the edge of the sofa. "It was after midnight. We rigged up a knockout pool game, an' it went on for hours. Had a skinful, too. That's why I slept in so late." I hated making stuff up like that, and it was getting me all hot and antsy, but I didn't want him giving me the third degree. How could I tell him I got stoned on a weird-looking plant, was kidnapped, fell in love with someone else's girlfriend, lost all trace of her, and had to mooch all the way home from Harlone Welby? When I thought about it like that, it sounded totally crazy, and I was all set to laugh out loud until Lucy opened her mouth.

"Comin' back," she stammered, twisting her face, neck, and shoulders in an effort to spit the words out. She rarely spoke, but that was probably one of her top three phrases along with, 'No, no, no' and 'Poker time.' Leyland and I had pretty much gotten used to her muddled ramblings, so mostly we just ignored her. But this time, something about the way she said it sent a shiver dancing down my spine. It was like she'd read my mind, and she was talking about Dakota. She was looking right at me too, and for a while our eyes were caught in a kind of hypnotizing lock that I couldn't pull away from—as if the bond we used to share had suddenly sputtered back to life. But then she just turned away and went back to sizing up the fake poker hand. I guess she must have written it off as a bad one, because she suddenly thrust the cards at me, her right arm slipping off the table, swinging idly by her side.

Leyland picked the cards up, then gently placed her arm back on the table. "We'll play some other time, Lu," he said. "I bet Carney's starvin'. What can I get you, Li'lbro?" He still called me that, even though I'd quit calling him Bigbro about six years ago.

"It's okay; I'm goin' over to Earl's. I'll get somethin' there."

"C'mon, man, how about an oatcake sub? You can watch while I fix it for you. There's somethin' we need to talk about anyways."

I thought he might rake me over the coals for staying out all night, but when we got into the kitchen, he just pulled a frying pan off the wall and started ferreting about in the cupboards.

"Lucy's only gonna get worse if she stays here," he told me. "Ain't movin' nowhere near as well as last year, and one a' these days she's gonna quit talkin' altogether. But they gotta have some kinda treatment over in Magnatella. I'd bet my last ban on it."

"Guess there's no way a' knowin'."

"I've been weighin' things up, Carney. It'll be a big change for us, but I've decided to apply to one a' them medical schools over in Banunus City. Once I've spent three years there, I can send for you and Luce, and maybe then she can get sorted. After all, they say Magnatellan medicine is cuttin'-edge stuff." He squeezed some bigdin oil into the pan, slapped a savory oatcake on top of it, and started slicing the bread.

Once I got Leyland off my back, I trudged out the house and down Captain's Way, my boots splashing up dirty streaks of water in the puddles left over from the morning showers. His words would have felt like a big deal any other time, but right now I was like an old mutt too busy to reach up and scratch a flea in his ear. I'd have to stay in Hailey's Town with Lucy, college would be put on hold, and I'd need to find work too, but the only thing that really seemed to matter was Dakota, and why she hadn't been there with us on the floor of the silo when we woke up.

It was after five when I got to Earl's. He was out the back with the Appaloosa part stripped down, oily tools, nuts, and bolts strewn everywhere as he fiddled about with the carburetor. Then he saw me striding along the patio and waved, so I grinned back at him, greeting his German shepherd, Bear, with a tickle at the back of the neck.

Earl gathered the parts up, shoved them into a toolbox, and ran a cloth over his hand. "Carney, glad you're okay, man," he said. "Wasn't sure where you guys ended up last night. I had to flag down a cab 'cause Booker took sick." He covered up the

'Loosa and led me over to the garage side door as it had started drizzling again.

Once inside, Earl flicked the kettle on. "You wanna coffee?"

"Wish I hadn't swallowed that rush," I told him as I drew up a chair. "Shap Ranton showed up and bundled us all into a goddamn truck. Can't say exactly what went down 'cause I started hallucinatin'. Think we got beat up at some point, but Marsh 'n' Kota took off. Dunno where Kota's got to." The words seemed to tumble out my mouth all at once, but it was good to know Earl was on the receiving end. I felt sure he'd know what to do.

Earl slid the mugs onto the table and put his feet up. "Jeez, no wonder it's all a blur—you copped a whole one. Booker only downed a half, and that was bad enough. She collapsed at the foot of the pool table. She was just lyin' there on the floor, totally blotto, just repeatin' the same thing over and over: 'You don't fool me, Elvis.' I practically had to carry her out to the cab."

"What happened when you got to The Willows?"

"Got her to bed without her folks findin' out, but it wasn't easy." He stirred his drink, raked his fingers through his hair, then looked up at the fluorescent light. "So, no sign of Kota?"

"Me 'n' Tayles woke up in an old silo out near Harlone Welby. There was a creepy rhyme scribbled in the dust—somethin' about a desperate intention and Dol and a dimension… and not wantin' to be found."

"Who wrote it?"

"Beats me. S'pose I coulda, but I don't remember."

Earl mulled it over for a while, tilting the mug and staring into it. Then he said, "The manic scribblin's of someone off their head ain't s'posed to make much sense. Although maybe the last part's about Marshall hidin' out someplace, scared to come back 'cause a' Ranton."

"That's what I thought, but Taylor reckoned he was headed for Nefamincle."

"It figures. Wouldn't mind if he stayed there permanent. Beats me why he had to get mixed up with them drug-dealin' slimeballs in the first place."

"Guess he must be kinda messed up."

Earl nodded, then folded his arms and sighed. "He's a loose cannon alright, what with all them dodgy deals and stuff. But I heard his old man has back trouble, can't work, and gives him a hard time. And it can't be easy for 'em, livin' in that rough neighborhood." He plonked his mug down onto the table. "Anyways, let's make some calls. Find out what's goin' on."

I followed Earl and Bear up the path and into the hallway through the back porch, and straight away felt calmed by the aura of his big old house. The gentle ticking of about five different clocks, the abiding smell of fresh-baked cookies, and the roar of the wood fire in the hearth made the place seem forever quaint and cozy.

Earl dialed Dakota's number but there was no answer, so he called Booker. "She's alright—just a bit groggy," he told me once he'd hung up. "She's goin' next door to see if Dakota's there. She'll call us back in ten."

When the phone rang again, I almost jumped out my skin. This time, "Got it" was all Earl said.

"Was Kota home?"

"Nope. No one there. Booker said to meet us in the alley at eight. Let me get changed, then we'll go see Tayles."

"No, Earl. I gotta drive round. I gotta find her. I'll borrow Leyland's truck—go to all the places she hangs out. I'll tell him you need parts for the 'Loosa."

"Sure," Earl said, clapping me on the shoulder. He could see how panicked I was acting. "Me 'n' Tayles'll come with ya."

15

The Shadow Dwellers

THE PRESENT
Sunday, January 25th, 2325

Thoughts of being sent to some godforsaken bootcamp have been weighing down on me ever since they first picked me up. On the one hand, it makes me want to gag, but there's also a perverse kind of comfort in knowing it's what I'm due. Things are more complicated now, though, because a rotting jail seems kind of glamorous when you compare it to the alternative: a bunch of manic Magnatellans sticking a—what is it Weinberg calls them?—a tagmesh into my brain. I guess it's one of those catch-22s that slowly drives you nuts if you spend too long mulling over it, but I can't seem to stop. I've tried staring at the patch on the wall and willing something eye-catching to appear, something that could set my mind onto other things, but it's just not working. I've conjured up moon-drenched mountain chateaus, rustic riverside cottages, and breathtaking beachscapes, but no matter how stunning I make them, they fade in less than a minute. In the end, I always come back to the same old thing: a charcoal of a grimy old penitentiary. It's cold, flat, and soulless, wound top to bottom in barbed wire, and patrolled by these freaky-looking Magnatellans, huge demon-like masks jarred over their heads. And the guy who drew it must have been lying on his back with his head touching the walls, because the angles are so warped it gives me vertigo.

When Weinberg pokes his head round the door, I'm loath to admit it, but I'm grateful. It means I can forget about the charcoal for a while.

He puts on a gritty smile. "How are you feeling?" he asks, as he makes his way over to the chair.

I scowl, and he gets right away that it was a dumb thing to say.

DORAN'S STORY

Doran remembered when he was three, before Quin came—the time he first wondered about Amber swishing her hands in the air and talking to herself. He'd come scurrying into the kitchen to show her his sketch of a ladybug.

"What are you doing, Amber?"

"Hang on a minute." Amber turned her back and carried on jabbering, so he waited until she laughed and said, "Alright, you take care now, Ma", clapped her hands, and spun back round to face him. "I was on the phone, Doran."

"But you weren't holding anything."

Amber knelt down, so that her eyes were level with his. "That's because I have the insight. You'll get it too, when you're older."

"But what does it mean, 'the insight'?"

"It's a gift," Amber said, "a wonderful thing. It's a phone, a holo-vision, and a computer all rolled into one. And you don't have to carry anything around with you. Everything appears right in front of your eyes, just like magic." She smiled at him, and pretended her fingers were a spider walking across his belly.

"They never called it a tagmesh back at Maple Road," he told Domino, as they lifted the blankets from the trunk and spread them out along the galley floor. "It was always just 'the insight'. And they acted like it was something to be proud of—a coming-of-age kind of deal."

Domino pulled off her baseball cap and plopped it onto Doran's head. "Stick with me, kid," she said, "and you'll be alright."

Not long after sunrise, Humbucker sailed *The Dreamcatcher* west from the harbor along the Pallindrolin Canal, Doran and Domino taking turns at the tiller as the engine chugged and rumbled behind them. Doran found the sounds quite soothing, and he was surprised at how fast the old barge could move, once it got into a rhythm. The highlights of the journey, however, were listening to the airy swirls of The Sergeant's flute playing, and watching Carina, balanced on the tiller, seesaw up and down in time to the music.

About forty minutes into the journey, The Sergeant cut the engine and began to moor the boat by the side of a quaint old public house with painted brickwork, creeping red ivy, and a gold-and-navy swing sign that bore the legend 'The Crescent Moons' at the top.

"Thanks for the ride, Sarge." Domino saluted Carina, then stepped down onto the towpath, Doran close behind her.

Humbucker called out something Doran didn't quite catch, something about stars turning black, and then Domino was waving, so the boy joined in with her, only lowering his arm when the narrowboat had completely spluttered out of sight.

"Come on." Domino tugged at Doran's shirtsleeve, but he lingered by the canal side, just staring at the water, thinking how it was the same color as the mint and kiwi smoothies that Shellina used to make, back at Maple Road.

"You took a real shine to the C-POD, huh?"

"*Sea Pod?* I thought it was called *The Dreamcatcher?*"

"No, C.P.O.D.—Chief Petty Officer D'Argent. I shoulda told ya; that's another one of his aliases."

"You're not short of a few, either. Why did he call you Astronomy Dominé?"

The girl smiled glibly, and her cheeks folded into the same curved little dimples that Doran had seen when she was down at the quay. "It's a song. Humbucker's got a thing about old-time Earth music, 'specially the Floyd."

"What's the Floyd?"

Domino clambered over the gate in front of the tavern's garden, weaving past a dozen or so picnic benches, all sprouting parasols. Then she reached into a hanging basket nailed to an outhouse, plucked a key from it, and unlocked the door. The building was so full of stacked-up beer barrels it was hard for Doran to move around comfortably, but once they got to the far end, Domino yanked open a broken old cellar door, where a flight of concrete steps wound so far down, all he could see was darkness.

"There's a hole in the wall down there," Domino told him. "You can get to Nentoke through the steam vents, but you gotta crawl some of the way." She opened her rucksack, pulled out a flashlight, and flicked it on.

"What exactly is Nentoke?"

They were descending the steps, Doran gripping the back of Domino's denim jacket because he didn't want to end up slipping.

"It's an abandoned tunnel system," Domino said. "They built a subway here when the planet was first colonized—a water drainage facility too, but the station collapsed about a hundred years ago during a Nune-quake, and it was never rebuilt."

Doran's back ached and his knees were sore after so much ducking and scrambling along the narrow metallic passageways, but eventually Domino led him through a crumbling brick wall, down one final shaft, and into the main complex. The tunnels down there were so vast and winding, he wondered how Domino could tell one from the other, especially with only a flashlight to guide her.

"I'd never remember the way on my own," he said.

When they reached the remains of the old subway station, Doran was struck by the quietness. All he could hear was dripping water, the scurry of rats across the tracks. Moss was growing over tiled walls, and by the light of the torch he could see ripped-out seats, faded posters, and a rusted old subway train half-buried in debris. Domino jumped down onto the track, walked forward a few yards, then shone the beam at a hole in the side of the tunnel where several bricks were missing. It was just about large enough for one person to pass through.

"This was Novaturrell Subway Station," she told him. "It's where the ruins join up with dolomite caves. We spend most of our time down here."

Doran wriggled through, high-pitched squeals echoing through the cave walls. The place was damp, dark, and smelled of rivers, but it was warm on account of being so far underground, and everything was lit by tea lights dotted along the ledges. As he gaped around, he made out three faces in the dimness, all of them staring at him.

"Okay, introductions," Domino said, nodding to each face in turn. "Catlow's our founder, she's seventeen, then we've got Scout, sixteen, and Barlin over there, he's fifteen—our resident music maestro. This is Doran. He's twelve—an orphan and a runaway."

Doran wasn't fond of awkward greetings, so he quickly changed the subject. "Is it bats I can hear?"

"Those are the turritella bats," Catlow told him. She was stirring a large pot of soup that was bubbling over an open fire, her face round and kind-looking, her garments—army pants and a turtleneck sweater—uniformly black. "Don't be scared," she said, pushing aside long strands of dark, straggly hair. "Listening to them helps me sleep at night."

"We bed down in the alcoves," Scout said, her voice much gentler than Catlow's, but Doran didn't understand what she meant, so he just stood there blankly. Scout smiled. She was just a slip of a girl, he thought—pale and freckled, fair hair cropped tight to her scalp. "They're horizontal luggage lockers down in the old station," she explained. "Just the right length for a bed. We ripped the doors off when we first came here." Then she was chuckling a little. "The noises from the pipes are the best. You can hear the water gurgling round them all night. Better than any lullaby, hands down."

"And none of you are tagmeshed?"

"Man, he cuts right to the chase." Barlin was buttering soda farls at the table, stacking them neatly on a plate, and at first Doran was a little taken aback by the remark. But then, much to his relief, the boy grinned quite cheekily. "I'm only messing with you. Truth is, we chose a life in hiding rather than have that damn thing inflicted on us. But every time we go out on the scrobble, we risk getting caught and tagged."

Domino winked at Doran. "Reckon you'd fit right in here," she said, and Doran felt his heart begin to swell. "We'll show you how to look after yourself. You'll get a crash course from all of us."

"Dom's the best Mexican Train hustler in the whole quadrant," Scout said, proudly draping an arm round the Earth girl's shoulder. "And she can outrun any of those tag-crazy Tome-Bots. As for me, I can show you some pretty neat card tricks. And Barlin, he's an expert at picking locks."

Barlin raised his voice in protest. "I play the mandolin as well." He offered Doran the bread platter, eyes glittering with enthusiasm. "I'll teach you if you like. You can go out busking with me in Tierramont Square, once you're good enough. There's some real wealthy folk pass by—suckers for a sweet tune, too."

Catlow carried the soup pan over to the table, gripping the handle firmly with a cloth. "Blending invisibly into the background when you're out scrobbling—that's my specialty," she said. Then she was ladling spicy pumpkin broth into little clay bowls, swirls of steam wiggling upward, and Doran suddenly realized how tight his belly was with hunger. "I'll get you up to speed," Catlow continued. "And as long as you're a Shadow Dweller, there'll always be someone covering your back. You can count on that."

Later that morning, they took Doran to the alcoves in the subway station, and as soon as he clapped eyes on them, a curious sense of belonging swept over him, affecting him so much, he found himself trembling. The way the recesses were stacked on top of each other reminded him of the bunk beds back at Maple Road, and everything seemed so safe and serene—as if the stillness and purity of the air down there was a giant shield protecting him from any kind of harm.

"We don't have much, but we have our freedom," Scout said, as they wound their way back through the labyrinth of old brick tunnels. "And that's the most valuable thing of all."

"Why do they tagmesh people?" Doran asked. "I know it's partly to stop them leaving Magnatella, but I don't get why folk have to be kept here."

Catlow placed her hands on her hips, and Doran could see that he'd touched a raw nerve. "Don't get me started on Tabath Dillinger-Tome. She's the goddamn Head of State, but she won't change a thing—insists the tagmesh's central to keeping the peace. She goes on and on about the Grand Models and how no one can argue with them. Beats me why we need politicians at all when the models make all the decisions."

"AI programs," Scout said, seeing that Doran was confused again. "They predict a 0.5 percent chance of war if everyone's tagmeshed. Scrap the meshing, and the number goes up to twenty-eight, or whatever the latest figure is."

Barlin nodded at Doran. "I take it you know about the Cassafortans, and how they're a bunch of paranoid technophobes? They don't want Magnatellans coming into their land with all their evil leptotronic science, and the tagmesh keeps 'em out."

"Reckon they think Magnatellans do nothing but fool around with leptotronic bombs all day," Domino added, her wry little smile adding just enough sparkle to keep Doran from fretting.

"So Magnatella puts wires in people's brains just 'cause Cassaforta wants it that way?"

"Magnatella wants it too." The quietness of Scout's voice made it all the more poignant. "It's no great secret that the tagmesh keeps tabs on people. The official line is it 'detects anomalous thoughts', although no one's really sure what that means. If you ask me, I think folks' brainwaves are hooked up to the Grand Models in some way. And if they even think about war, they get some kind of leptotronic shock."

"Why don't the people rise up?"

"They don't give a damn about the Cassaforta ban," Barlin said, laughing quietly. "They see the place as backward—a land in blissful ignorance of its own government's deception."

THE PRESENT

Weinberg closes the binder. "You see, Carney, Cassaforta is a sham," he says. "It's a fake world originally created by the pacifist leaders to instill what they considered 'old-time values and sensibilities' into the people. Gilbert Gowder was fascinated by American 1950s culture—had been ever since a visit to the theater at the tender age of seven, to see a movie called *Rock 'n' Roll Homage*. Of course, this was long before the Leptotronic War, but he began collecting memorabilia by the bucketload, and by the time he reached his twenties, he was already holding the era as an exemplar—a blueprint for how life should truly be lived. It's hardly surprising that, once he established himself in power, he molded Cassaforta to fit his vision. Essentially, he borrowed the culture—the ethos, the clothes, the cars, the movies, the songs—the simplicity of a time that was free from war but not bursting at the seams with technology overload or choking to death on excess and greed. All those wonderful tunes that you think are the latest to hit the airwaves—those by Chuck Berry, for example—they're actually antiquated recordings made on Earth more than 370 years ago.

"Cassaforta isn't a complete carbon copy of Earth's 1950s," he continues. "Many records from later decades are approved, as long as they sound reminiscent of that era. We must provide the semblance of new music, after all. Stephen Sanchez is a good example. His music truly sounds like it comes from the '50s, but he wasn't born until the year 2002.

"Another major difference is that there are no television sets, although it's foolish of me to mention it because you won't be familiar with that concept.

"The main point is that everything you hear and see in Cassaforta—movies, long-players, forty-fives, magazines, newspapers, photographs, books, technology—it's all subject to censorship by town governors—people like me. We ban, edit, change, delete, and water things down as we see fit. Anything with the potential to stir up violence and hatred, inspire revolutionary ideas, or even cause people to deviate slightly from the 'idyllic' norm is prohibited; that is, it simply doesn't exist in Cassaforta.

"So now you understand what it means to be a citizen of this planet. You have to be controlled in one form or another, either by censorship and a spurious existence in Cassaforta, or by a tagmesh that holds you hostage in Magnatella, which, in a way, is the price you pay for the truth, for living in reality."

He probably wonders why I'm laughing like a hobo hepped up on moonshine. Okay, hearing it from him is a bombshell, and it's immoral, corrupt, sickening, and all the rest of it, but somehow, I'm staring at a blank wall: no charcoal, no Magnatellans, no barbed wire—nothing. His words prove that the diary was real—that he lied to me about it. Does that mean Wallbanger is real, too?

"I don't understand why it amuses you, Carney, hearing these truths."

"Sorry, Nils. It's just… I dunno what to think or say no more. Hell, I don't even know what to feel. I wanted rid of a drawin' that wouldn't go away, but now…" I puff my cheeks out and shake my head. "I got nothin'."

Weinberg climbs out the chair, slowly paces up and down, and then stands under the window with his back to me. "It's been this way ever since Cassaforta began," he says, and I get the feeling it comes out much more apologetic than he intended.

16

Broughton Alley

THE PAST

The drizzle carried on into the early evening, slate-gray clouds churning overhead, thunder grumbling at the back of us all the while we were driving round. And by the time we'd given up the search and brought the truck back, the air was rich with the smell of petrichor, and a light fog had drifted down, making everything seem echoey and dank.

We cut across the scrapyard at the back of the park, arriving at the alley just after eight. The place was little more than a passageway between two strips of storefronts on Fiddler's Row, but it had always been prime stomping ground for the Arch Angels on account of being so narrow. You could sink as many pints as you wanted there without being seen by anyone.

Taylor stretched himself out on the wall like a listless alley cat, his back propped against the side of the phone booth. He was dragging on a Dime Chime to cover his edginess, and every now and then he'd pull his Gazelles cap off his head, smooth his hair out, and put it back on again. "Quit patrollin', Caldwell," he said, when he saw me pacing up and down right under his nose. "You're givin' me the jitters."

"Sorry, Tayles." I wriggled into one of the bench seats. "You get in trouble this mornin'?"

"Nah. My folks sleep like logs, and I always had a talent for stealth. Anyways, I got bigger problems than them. The Dodge ain't parked on Main Street no more; I checked. Marshall's probably halfway to Nefamincle by now, so the heat's all on us. Keep expectin' Ranton to show up any minute—take the money out of our hides."

"He woulda done it last night, if he was gonna," I said. "Maybe he did already, and we just don't recall. Sure feels like I've been a few rounds with someone twice my size... and don't forget your lip got busted."

"How could I? Still smarts somethin' chronic."

Earl appeared at the top of the alley, clasping three cones stuffed full of fries that he'd fetched from Dawn's Diner at the end of Fiddler's Row. He passed one up to Taylor, handed me mine, and then divvied out the salt sachets and wooden forks. "Don't sweat it," he said when he saw how blue we were looking. "If somethin'd happened, we'd know about it by now." He sat next to me, tore one of the sachets open, and then, on the spur of the moment, we started hurling salt at one another. "There's been a weather warnin', apparently," Earl told us after we'd run out of ammo. "Was on the radio in the diner. It's gonna be rainin' pitchforks."

Taylor glanced up, frowning just for a moment at the wildness of the sky. "Better eat up, then, Early-Bird, or ya fries'll get soggy." He hummed a couple of bars of The Chords' 'Sh-Boom', then licked his lips.

The rain and the others came together. First, it was just a sprinkling—wispy drips spattering onto my arm—but in less than a minute it had full-on changed gear, huge drops pelting onto my forehead and running in little rivulets down my nose. At the same time, there was the sound of footsteps and the ricochet of a whistle looping round the alley, as if they were somehow part of the same crazy onslaught, everything punctuated by the steady 'bop, bop' noise as the droplets hammered onto the rim of Taylor's baseball cap. Water was billowing out from a broken drainpipe somewhere, tires sloshing through puddles, far-off feet pattering along the sidewalks as folks scurried for shelter.

By now, the mist had thickened, and the sky had grown so dark that a lone streetlamp flickered into life. In the murk of the passageway, all it gave off was a faint, blurry glow, but it was enough for us to make out the silhouettes of two figures at the bottom of the alley, slowly making their way toward us. Taylor dropped from his roost and started in their direction, all the while squinting to see who was there. I pushed my wet quiff to one side and craned my neck. My heart was going like the clappers, my teeth were chattering non-stop, and my hands had turned a weird shade of purple from the cold. I breathed on them, rubbed them together, the rain still beating me about the face, the droplets drumming on the table like a million nervous fingers. And then there was the smooth, velvety jangle of Dakota's voice calling out, "Earl? Is that you?"

All I could do was stare down at my boots because Taylor was suddenly racing up to her, sweeping her into his arms, as Booker looked on. Don't get me wrong, I was glad Dakota was back, safe and well, but there was a full-on jealousy swimming around inside of me, too—a misbegotten shark frolicking with a dolphin, sinking its teeth into my bones, ripping away at my chest, teasing me with the wretched but undeniable truth that things could never be the same now that I was in love with her.

Earl got up to greet the girls, and I followed him, still in a daze, not really wanting to go through the motions of slapping everyone on the back, shaking their hands, and listening to a bunch of pointless jabbering. I remember Booker grabbing Taylor's Gazelles cap and putting it on backward, and Earl waving a corked bottle of hooch in front of everyone, then cracking it open and passing it round. Booker was the first to take a swig, and it somehow started her off sniggering.

"I kept seein' Elvis as this weird multicolored potato," she told us. "We were sailin' along in a floatin' car, and all the while he was tryin' to brainwash me with a radio... or was it an apple pie? I couldn't really tell. How 'bout you, Kotes? What did you see?"

Dakota was too busy staring at Taylor. She wasn't smiling, but her gaze was fixed on him so hard, it got me all choked up. I couldn't stand to see it anymore, so I focused on the rain instead: the droplets battering the sleeves of her baseball jacket, bouncing off in V-shapes like little see-through butterflies.

"We drove round a bunch lookin' for you, Kotes," Earl said. "Where were you?"

"Folks took me over to Hap Town in the jeep. Been out all day."

Booker was fussing over her Polaroid 95B. "Scrabble up onto the wall and pose for the camera," she urged. "I can set it to auto, and the dark won't matter; it's got a built-in flash."

There was the snap of the shutter, a glare, and then, just as the film quit whirring, a startled holler from Dakota.

"Someone's comin'!"

Another shadowy form at the end of the alley was weaving its way forward, so we jumped down, all five of us standing shoulder to shoulder, silently and defiantly, almost like we'd rehearsed it. And as the figure walked into the path of the streetlamp, a ringed pattern formed around it, masking its face, but tracing its shape in a scattered arc of light. I broke into a cold sweat.

"Pumble? You there?" The specter spoke sharply, his words slicing through the mist like a guillotine cutting paper. He was about ten feet away when his face was finally caught in the gleam of a passing car's sidelights, and I was able to make out the features. He was middle-aged, wrapped in a beige, knee-length trench coat—a brawny-looking guy with a dark, well-groomed beard and 'tache.

Taylor made a few strides forward. "Rider? What you doin' here?"

"Just came to tell you it's all over. Cops got Ranton about two hours ago. Guess he'll get sent down for good this time, maybe even shipped off to Magnatella. Anyway, you guys can rest easy; looks like you're off the hook."

Taylor tried to wipe his forehead with his sleeve, but the rain was pounding down so fierce it was useless. It reminded me of something Lucy said when I was seven years old and bellyaching because we'd driven over a hundred miles to the beach and the rain wouldn't stop.

"It's just the sky's way of cryin', Smoky, and that's good for the soul."

17

Strumpole

Sometimes when you sleep, you don't really dream; you just kick an idea about, or struggle with a never-ending chore that seems to have you beat. All last night I was trying to scale a brick wall, and every time I thought I'd made it to the top, more bricks would show up, stretching away into the shadows, so that whatever was on the other side was always out of reach.

It's a relief when the medics change shifts and there's enough cortisol floating about in my bloodstream to prod me into consciousness. But before I can give it any more thought, I catch sight of Weinberg dozing in the chair and almost freeze with shock.

"Man alive. How long you been sittin' there?" I scowl at him, but all that useless scrambling has worn me out, and I can't keep it up.

"I thought we'd begin early this morning, if that's alright?"

"Guess it's okay. I mean, my social schedule's pretty wide open these days."

Weinberg flashes a smile. "You're making jokes," he says. "I'm glad the tale's got your mind working on other things… besides your own predicament, that is." He flicks through the binder, careful to keep the writing under wraps. "We'll pick up the main thread in due course. But for now, we're going on a slight detour. What I mean to say is, I can't really tell you Doran's story without introducing you to his arch nemesis—a man called Torgon Strumpole."

DORAN'S STORY

Torgon Strumpole had never seen so many folks in uniforms shaking their heads all at once: three officers from the Porporrol Fire Department, two police on patrol bikes, and the Pin Lake County sheriff, who had him handcuffed to a lamp post, as plumes of black smoke wafted in front of their faces.

"Why couldn't it be something normal?" his father said quite calmly, once they got home. "Why not trainspotting, birdwatching… even stamp collecting? I mean, pyromania, of all things. I just don't get it. What's the attraction?"

"It was only a bus shelter," Torgon said, fighting to conceal his anger. As far as he was concerned, it was his mother's fault for being a raging alcoholic and ignoring him most of the time. Burning things helped him feel in control, but he wasn't about to tell anyone.

His father sighed. "This is the last time they'll let you off with a warning. The sheriff told me himself. You're fifteen now and it'll be jail next time, for sure. You do know what that means, Torgon? You'll be locked up."

Torgon laid off for a while, but just before he turned sixteen, he hit on the idea of stealing dictionaries from the school library and setting fire to them in the stationery cupboard after everyone went home. On the third run, he was caught red-handed, formally expelled, and told to wait in the principal's office while the police were called. However, rather than endure the retributions, he fled some hundred miles north to the town of Covell, spending close to eighteen months living in a trailer with other waifs and strays, gambling to earn his keep.

It was a visit to a mystic's tent at a fair in nearby Salpa that set him on the straight and narrow, albeit temporarily.

"Everyone thinks you'll wind up rotting away inside a louse-ridden prison, and that could well be your fate," the old crone rasped as she waved her spider-like hands over a collection of crystallized hop stones. "But coming here was the shrewdest move you ever made. I know what needs to change to stop you going down that path. All your life you've been fulfilling folks' expectations, but that ain't never enough. You hear me, boy? You need to do something that forces them to change what they expect of you."

The words somehow struck a chord with Strumpole, and within a week he'd packed up, left the trailer, and returned to his parents' house in Porporrol. Over the next two years, he worked part-time in one of the local ore mines to pay for past damages, finished high school, graduated, and applied to study for a Bachelor of Education in physics at the Comjenk Institute of Technology in Kantrololand, the northernmost island in the Nellic chain. Given his preoccupation with fire, we might have expected him to take up chemistry, but it seems he had been nurturing a fascination for all things nuclear.

You're probably already aware that the Nellic Islands sit south of Cassaforta in the Actuic Circle, and that they provide the continent's only seat of higher learning. At these colleges, Cassafortans can gain essential degrees such as teaching, law, and medical care before returning to their hometowns to practice their craft. And they're allowed back to Cassaforta because the old scientific theories are the only ones taught there. Even when it comes to medicine, these degrees acknowledge Dillingerian principles only from a historical perspective.

Once Strumpole was settled on the island, he proved to be quite the prodigy, graduating top of his class in 2297, impressing his tutors so much that he was encouraged to apply for a doctorate in nuclear physics to commence at the start of the next academic year. Scientific research degrees are extremely rare in Cassaforta, as the funding is limited to only one student per subject per annum and they are always education-focused because the governors must ensure that technology never advances in any way. Naturally, Strumpole was delighted to accept the funding and completed his thesis in a mere two and a half years, arriving triumphant in Porporrol in April 2300, a Bachelor of Education and a doctorate in physics sitting proudly under his belt, not to mention a respected position as head of science at the school that had once expelled him.

The man spent about eight trouble-free years as a physics tutor, but despite all his achievements, it just didn't seem enough. Perhaps he couldn't wrap his head around the fact that once people's expectations change, you're back to square one: simply fulfilling them. Thus, he found himself embroiled in a scandal that saw him exiled to Magnatella for an act of willful aggression.

You see, Porporrol is like any other Cassafortan town in its abhorrence of war, violence, and anything that assists them. And in this case, the town's governor discovered that Strumpole had provided his students with textbooks, smuggled in from a small port in Magnatella by his own arrangement. These books described the actual science underpinning the leptotronic bomb. Of course, they were immediately destroyed, but that was not enough. The entire population of Porporrol had to be expatriated following the incident. All the residents, adults and children alike, were hurriedly shipped off to various locations across Magnatella, and Strumpole himself was dispatched to the fourth-largest city, Tavon, which lies in the southeast Cottafarral territory.

We regret to inform you... Strumpole grew weary of the same old phrase. Every time he applied to teach science in Tavon, he was turned down flat, and for exactly the same reasons: no official training in Dillingerian principles, and the Cassafortan Aggressor (or CA) status being permanently recorded as part of his tagmesh data.

To his credit, he refused to give up, spending most of his days reading Dillingerian texts in an effort to compensate, meticulously building proof-of-concept gadgets based on the use of leptotronic circuitry to test the theories. He became obsessed with the technology, especially its use within the tagmesh. Every time a prestigious conference came up, he would gatecrash it, posing as a professor from the highly esteemed Skitolas College. There, he would befriend and socialize with researchers at the very vanguard of their field: physicists who were publishing papers on cutting-edge nano-leptotronics, and neuroscientists pioneering the groundbreaking technologies on which he was becoming increasingly fixated. I suppose, in his twisted mind, he felt he belonged with such a pantheon of greats, and he was not afraid to pick their brains to further his research endeavors. You see, his goal was to reverse-engineer the tagmesh so that he could override it—harness it to his own advantage. He even toyed with the creation of his own (albeit rather crude) implant devices, and gadgets to reprogram them.

Strumpole also began to teach himself the fine art of forgery. By June 2312, he had produced an intricate and expertly crafted counterfeit Skitolas College diploma that attested to one Diego C. Buchannan having completed a Bachelor of Education in physics. And, at almost the same time, his research efforts finally paid off. He found a way to change his name and erase the CA status recorded in his tagmesh data.

Thus, in July of the same year, he used his new identity and the bogus certificate to apply for the role of physics master at one of Tavon's more elite prep schools, and the selection panel were so taken with him that they offered him the job right there and then. But, as luck would have it, three days before the start date, a member of staff in human resources called up the education department in Skitolas, asking for his transcripts. The ruse was uncovered, and Strumpole was arrested, tried, and sentenced to four years' imprisonment in Califrod Penitentiary on the northwest coast of Magnatella. As you can imagine, the mystic's prediction festered away in his head from day one, so it's fair to say his escape was inevitable.

Strumpole absconded from prison after serving less than three months. He set fire to the laundry room and the blaze eventually spread over to the west wing, where it blew the main boiler, the resulting explosion killing three inmates and one of the wardens. In the chaos that ensued, he snuck out of the grounds in the back of one of the emergency vehicles, leaping out into a field when he was certain he would not be seen. Few have ever crossed the Disian Ocean westward for reasons I'll discuss in the next session, but Strumpole succeeded in returning to his native Cassaforta, settling in a run-of-the-mill manufacturing town called Tusslin Kantop, about four hundred miles southeast of Grade Glennings. He forged an impressive set of Nellic Islands diplomas in the name of Findal Hauntmead, and later used them to secure a coveted role as both principal and governor of the newly established Dover Plain Reform School for Boys.

It seems his Hauntmead persona gained quite a reputation among both staff and students alike. The words 'psychotic' and 'sadistic' were bandied about rather a lot when folks were questioned, although it could be an exaggeration; after all, it's human nature to embellish things. The simple truth is that the staff were reluctant to cross him because of his tendency to fire them for the most trivial of matters. He would think nothing of slapping their faces, and when they threatened to report him, he would unleash what he called his 'blackmail files'. He had a dossier on every one of them. Naturally, the boys in his care were scared witless most of the time. He meted out corporal punishment as if it were part of the curriculum, and by corporal punishment, I'm talking about his use of his fists on them.

THE PRESENT

"Thought the story was meant to be relatable. It's all a bit hard to swallow if you ask me."

Weinberg smiles again, but it's deadpan. "That's often the way with the best ones," he says. "We rack our brains for a long time after, asking ourselves if it can really be true. And such tales do a magnificent job of distracting us from the humdrum—the pain of everyday life. Anyway, Doran's the one I'm hoping you'll connect with. Strumpole was probably—how shall we put it? Ah, yes—completely detached from humanity."

"Are all your characters basket cases?"

He scratches slowly at the side of his neck, crossing his legs without answering, and then it dawns on me.

"Jeez! It's not him down the corridor, is it?"

"Heavens, no," he says, chuckling. "They wouldn't keep a guy like that here. Anyway, I told you not to worry about that fellow. It's none of your concern."

An orderly comes in pushing a squeaky metal cart with a canister on top, and the peppery smell of hot gulistan soup fills the room. I pull the wheeled table across the bed and watch as he ladles the broth into a dish before handing me a spoon. But after a couple of mouthfuls, I glimpse the eagle.

"Sorry, can't eat this no more. I need a Band-Aid for my wrist—somethin' to cover it up."

"Eh?"

I hold out my arm so the orderly can see. "My best buddy in the whole world's lyin' unconscious someplace, with an ink just like this. And I can't look at it no more 'cause it's all my fault; I committed aggravated assault."

"It's true," Weinberg says. "Please. Fetch the boy a Band-Aid. And another dose of Xenon 90 while you're at it."

After they jab me and Weinberg leaves, I turn to the past again: the time the Arch Angels painted an extra space in the school parking lot when we were fifteen. Earl's old man came to pick him up one afternoon, but he was turned away because it was jammed full. So, we climbed the gates after dark, marking out a new rectangle with bright yellow paint—even signing it by adding the letters 'AA' in the middle. Booker panicked after we did it, saying the stunt was a sure-fire way to get us expelled, but nothing came of it in the end. It just so happened that the big cheese on the school board was called Antonia Arden, and everyone figured it was a special space reserved for the pearl-gray Jaguar XK150 that she drove about town—the one the kids all hankered after. In fact, when the council repainted everything six months later, our dodgy space was given a shiny fresh coat along with all the others. Even the initials were treated to a makeover… hang on. It was 'AA' they painted, not 'HW'.

For cryin' out loud! Not again! "Get the hell outta my memory, Harvey."

He puts a finger to his lips. "You need me," he says. "I'm keepin' ya safe. It's Wallbanger you wanna watch out for."

"But you *are* Wallbanger. It's what everyone calls you. That's what you told me."

Harvey shakes his head. "Wallbanger's the other one. Wants to feed you a bunch of humbug that's all part of a major conspiracy. That's why he snuck into the bathroom and left you that tacky message. But I won't let him tell you; I promise." He looks fondly at the painted parking space, like he's just tickled pink to be seeing it again. "And another thing—don't go trustin' that old chiseler Weinberg. Ain't right what he's doin', usin' you as his goddamn guinea pig. Pretty soon, he'll start with the serum, and you gotta say no, ya hear me? Just say no, Caldwell. Your life depends on it."

18

King Neptune's Fountain

The rain eased off during the night, and finally dried up as I watched from my bedroom window. By the time the drops stopped plinking off the puddles, birds were already twittering in the trees, and the sky was shedding its ebony overcoat, a pale violet kimono quivering underneath. I guess I was avoiding my bed because I'd had so many weird and fitful dreams, always about Taylor and Dakota, her being swept up into his arms in some way or other. One time, he kept flinging her about, just wouldn't stop, and when I tried to step in, he went totally off the rails, punching me so hard in the gut, I think I yelled out loud. And it was all mixed up with robbing booze from the Curzons' store and getting caught red-handed by Kota's old man.

I spent all morning trying to make up for lost sleep, surfacing only when Leyland hollered up the stairs that it was time for lunch. Then, after I'd picked about with his mushroom gnocchi and not really eaten much, Earl called to tell me the Angels were meeting at four in Larchiment Square. I'd have been pumped about seeing them, all things being even, but because of the whole Dakota thing, I was dreading it. From now on, hanging out with the Angels was going to be rough as hell.

I hovered outside the living room doorway, still in my jammies, my heartbeat cranking up a couple of notches. "Leyland?"

He was curled up in the armchair by the window, reading glasses on a chain, a bulky medical tome in his hand, and a fat Regalbine cigar anchored between his teeth. He looked like a guy in his forties, but he was only twenty-five. "Hmm?" He peered at me over the top of the book.

"I've been doin' some thinkin'. It'd be the same if I went to Magnatella instead a' you. I'd send for you and Luce after three years, and then she could get her treatment." My throat tightened and I swallowed hard. "It's just, I don't wanna stay here in Hailey's."

Leyland closed the book, shoved it onto the coffee table, and sighed. "I checked the laws, Carney. There's only three ways you can get in." He puffed at the cigar a couple of times before leaning it at the side of the ashtray. "The first's a college place, but that's no good for Lucy."

Outside, Dol was breaking through the ripples in the stratus cloud, and somehow it spurred me on. "But the second is when kinfolk send for you, so it don't matter which of us goes."

Leyland sat forward. "That ain't exactly true," he told me. "There's a nigglin' technicality: the kin doin' the sendin' gotta be twenty-five or older." He sank back against the cushions, glum as an oyster. "If you went, it'd be seven years before you could even request it, and she needs sortin' soon as possible. I feel bad makin' ya wait for college, but… well, my hands are tied. You see that, right? I gotta do what's best for all of us."

His answer crushed me, even though I'd pretty much guessed it. I shrugged and smiled, telling him it was no big deal. He didn't mention the third option, but I knew well enough what it was: the only other way to get to Magnatella was to be kicked out of Cassaforta for being a non-pacifist.

It took some nerve and even more shoeshine to get me to Larchiment that afternoon. Before setting off, I swiped a bottle of double-strength Grimley's from Leyland's globe-shaped liquor cabinet and made sure to take plenty of swigs on the bus when no one was looking. As it turned out, I needn't have sweated because Dakota didn't even show.

"She called about an hour ago," Booker told us. "Still feels woozy. Ain't up to seein' no one."

Taylor huffed a bit, so Earl suggested hitting a few balls round the square to cheer him up. I was way too steamed, so I sat it out, using my battered leg as an excuse. They played for nearly an hour while I watched in silence from the town hall steps. And then everyone took a breather over by the fountain, me still hovering on the steps, giddy from the Grimley's, a Dime Chime dangling from my lips. The sun was in the west, skimming the top of the library block, bright little rays bouncing off the marble, making the Neptune statue gleam. Booker was dabbling her hands in the water, and Earl was circling the basin, daring her to scramble up the statue and jam Taylor's baseball cap over the crown. Of course, she was up there like a shot, leaping onto the trident and sliding down ninja-style once she was done. She took a bow when she landed, and everyone whistled and clapped. I flicked the ash from my Dimer, and when I looked up again, Earl was piggybacking her round the fountain, while Taylor spouted on about the cap costing him twenty-eight bans and how he wanted it back so bad he could taste it.

"I love the Triple Gees every bit as much as you, Pachello," he griped.

"You do? Prove it!"

Taylor shimmied up old Neptune to grab the cap, but he missed his footing on the way down and sprawled into the water on his backside. The others were in stitches, but I couldn't bring myself to join in because the skit seemed lame somehow, and, more than that, I felt an odd sense of detachment—as if one of those thick winter fogs had drifted down from the Bolars and lodged itself right in the core of me. All I could do was gulp down the Grimley's, my buddies too full of themselves to notice.

At first, I couldn't figure out why the whole fountain sketch felt like such a drag. And then it hit me; this was the other side of that day at the creek, the time we all jumped in—the flip side. It was trying to capture that same spark of wildness, but just couldn't cut it. It could only echo those memories sadly and weakly, and because it was fake, the only things that really stood out were the flaws. "It's like the B-side of a record tryin' to match up to the A-side," I mumbled, "but everyone knows it's feebler." I guess the Grimley's had pretty much waved a magic wand over inhibition, and once the words were out, they seemed to cement the truth of the idea, although I couldn't understand why it mattered so damn much.

Booker was the only one who picked up on how greased I was acting. She came over and sat beside me on the steps. "You're awful quiet," she said. "You okay?"

The question caught me off guard, and I was getting more crocked by the second. "Think I'm just comin' down with a chill after the rains last night," I managed to say.

"Look, Carney. If there's somethin' you wanna get off your chest…"

She was trying to be a buddy but, what with the liquor and everything going on in my head about B-sides and Dakota, it felt like prying, and I guess it just bugged the hell out of me. And it didn't help that last night she'd been sending up the rush, as if it was all some sort of game.

"If there was, I wouldn't tell you about it," I blurted out gruffly. "What? You think you're some kind of expert on life just 'cause you popped half a rush and conjured up a goddamn Elvis potato?"

It was like the liquor was remote controlling my mouth, and all I could do was sit there and listen to the bitterness oozing out of it, as Booker's puzzled expression slowly changed into a frosted one. She was wrinkling her face again, knitting her brows, and it made her nose crease up all cute and funny-looking.

I willed myself to pipe down, but it was useless; more hooch-powered hot air was on the way. "Man, I used to think so high of you—used to think you fell straight out the sky." I pointed over at the fountain where Earl was busy slugging it out in a spoof boxing match with Taylor. "And as for Earl, he ain't nothin' but a strait-laced fun sponge."

Without making a sound, her lips pressed firmly together, Booker slipped her arm inside my jacket, snatched the half-full, diamond-shaped Grimley's bottle, and twisted the lid off. I remember seeing the glass catch the light in a flood of little rainbow streaks, just before she lifted it over my head and poured what was left of it over me. Then she pushed the empty bottle hard against my ribcage. "Go home, Caldwell," she said, turning her head away. "Before you get me so mad, I'll…"

I shrugged, brushing my wet hair to one side. "I didn't mean nothin', Booker."

"Look. Ain't no one else knows what I'm gonna tell ya," Booker said. She looked up at Neptune, then gave a long sigh. "I had a twin sister called Irwin. She was born with a bone disease—died when she was just six weeks old. Maybe I'm borin' as hell with all my books and always goin' on about space and college and Magnatella… and I know kids laugh behind my back, call me a suck-up—I've heard 'em. But I don't give a rat's ass what anyone thinks, 'cause I'm doin' it all for her. I want the best chance I can get in life, 'cause she never had one."

"Gee, I'm sorry, Books. I dunno what to say." I tried to sound gracious, but I guess I was pretty close to passing out. "I'm starched is all," I told her. "Need to get me on home. Tell the others Leyland wanted me back for chores."

I staggered back to the bus stop, hiccupping, stumbling a few times, a nagging voice in my head telling me that if I hadn't rotated that box, Booker's sister would still be alive. And the more I thought about it, the more I saw the world as a kind of B-side—one that could never match up to the A-side. I started to fret that it was somehow a copy of reality—a fake existence that the Eastern Europeans were forced to make because I was too damn lily-livered to step inside that machine.

19

Nentoke

can't figure out why Weinberg lifted the lid on Cassaforta, and I wish he'd just let things be. It's like he's rammed the truth down my gullet without even asking—forced a pill on me that it chokes me to swallow. And I can't stop going over stuff in my head, driving myself crazy with it all. Last night, I kept tossing and turning—just couldn't sleep a wink because it hit me that Buddy Holly must be dead. I always dreamed I'd make it to Magnatella someday—see him play live. So many things I took for granted now have giant question marks hanging over them, and even though nobody I know got wise to it, I can't help feeling like a prize jackass.

They jabbed me with Xenon 90 again this morning, when I told them I was having trouble with the zees, and ever since then I've been seeing a bonsai tree in the space on the wall—a tiny shrub growing at the far end of an overhanging ledge. The backdrop is a starry evening sky complete with a thick yellowish full moon, and everything is tinted rosy at the bottom on account of Dol being just about to dip below the horizon. I can see a clear line where blue changes to pink, and it gets me thinking that, if you were somehow stuck in that bonsai world, Dol would never finish setting. And Cassaforta isn't so much a tectonic plate as a living art gallery, crammed full of landscapes that never seem to age.

Weinberg taps gently on the door, and I pipe up with, "Step right in, Nils. Just open up that binder and we'll get right down to business." There must have been some serious juice in that shot, because it's not the way I normally talk.

He strides over to the chair and makes himself comfortable. "That's great, Carney," he says. "I'm glad you're so enthusiastic this afternoon."

He has no idea.

DORAN'S STORY

"So, we live in a totalitarian society?"

Doran stumbled a little over the word 'totalitarian'. He shuffled his cards, first into one hand, then into the other, and cursed silently because his sleight of hand wasn't smooth enough. He was out on Novaturrell's notoriously edgy Mercedes Way, about to perform his first live card trick under the watchful eyes of Scout and Domino. He gazed around him. The place was full of seedy bars, tattoo parlors, and street hustlers looking to make a fast buck with their conjuring illusions, gambling booths, and bootleg liquor stands. His hands quivered.

"It's the tagmesh that makes it that way." Scout slipped the deck from his fingers and showed him, again, how to conceal the Ace of Diamonds without it poking out of his sleeve. "No one knows for sure how bad it is. I mean, there are so many theories about what it does, on the quiet, without ordinary folk being aware. Could just be conspiracy stuff, but I guess there's no smoke without fire."

Domino took over, almost seamlessly. "They say it secretes a synthetic hormone that makes you totally docile and submissive—satisfied with life, no matter what. I bet the government thinks they can stop crime and wars from happening that way." She sounded a little glum, perhaps from the realization that such a thing might actually be true.

"There are even rumors that it creates the illusion of a whole other identity," Scout went on, eyes wide, as if she was competing with Domino to garner the biggest shock factor. "I'm talking about a false reality that you're forced to accept as real. Maybe that's a bit over the top, but who's to say?" She slapped the deck back down onto Doran's palm. "It's weird, as well, that no one mentioned how the damn thing worked till fifth-grade social education class."

"They taught you that at school?" Doran was open-mouthed.

"Well, in a very matter-of-fact way. Everything we learned about the tagmesh was kind of drip-fed, slowly, probably so's we'd get used to it—so's we'd think it was normal. How about you?"

"They called it 'the insight,'" he replied, grimacing. "But I can see now that they hyped it up—got us actually looking forward to it." He gave the cards a fancy dovetail shuffle, and Scout applauded. "How does it work, anyway?"

"There's a forcefield they call Protson 13 that surrounds the whole of Magnatella," Scout explained. "It interacts with all the tagmeshes, stops them from sending certain signals to the brain. But beyond it, there's no such protection, so if you happen past it, the defector chip kicks in, completely wiping your memories."

Doran was scowling at the sheer horror of it all. "You musta been scared to death."

"Not scared exactly. Mr. Prichard told us not to worry. He said there's no reason at all to leave Magnatella, 'cause it's got everything a person could ever want." Scout sighed audibly, and Doran noticed how delicate her skin looked. "It made me angry, though, thinking how you had to have this thing in your head, and there was no choice about it. And then we learnt that it makes you infertile—that you have to apply to have a child."

By now, Doran was indignant. "Apply to have a child?"

"You didn't know? It's the Grand Models that get to decide, based on the latest population data and DNA profiling. You'd think folk wouldn't stand for it. But, according to Prichard, nobody since the original pacifists ever thought about crossing the Disian Ocean."

"But people must wonder about Cassaforta."

"It's like Barlin was saying," Domino told him, offering out a bag of candy to lighten the mood. "No one cares 'cause it's such a backward place. That's why they call it Podunkia. Here, have one of these—a gumball for luck."

Doran ran through the trick again, but the cards slid from his hand, scattering onto the sidewalk.

"Let's not talk about the tagmesh anymore," Scout said, and it was the first time he'd heard her talk so curtly. "It's giving Doran the jitters, and he needs to get this trick nailed."

THE PRESENT

Weinberg cocks an eyebrow at me. "Mr. Prichard was wrong on one count, wasn't he? Someone made it back to Cassaforta... and with his memories still intact, too."

"Strumpole?"

He nods, raising his brows. "You may recall that he settled in a manufacturing town by the name of Tusslin Kantop, over in the southeast."

I mesh my fingers, slowly rotating the thumbs round each other. I guess it's my way of hiding how caught up I've got in the story. "How'd he do it? Without losin' his memories, I mean."

Weinberg strokes the bridge of his nose, his eyes fixed on the ceiling as if some half-imagined painting is hanging there, too—a reminder of his instructions and the lines he shouldn't cross. Either he's admiring it, or he's taking some time out to heed the warning. "I can't give you a technical explanation," he says, after a while. "But he must have figured out how to override the defector chip, which is the part responsible for memory drain. Or perhaps he worked out how to remove the tagmesh altogether."

"Look, Nils. I know where all this is leadin'. You're tryin' to tell me I'm Doran—that I was tagged, and all my memories were somehow zapped—replaced with false ones. I mean, that's gotta be why you're so hung up on my case."

Weinberg frowns. "I'm implying nothing of the sort, Carney. Why do you think that?"

I gawk at the wall where a non-existent bonsai tree waits forever for the sun to go down. If I've learned anything this past year, it's that things can be beautiful even if they aren't necessarily real.

"I'm going to start you on a drug called Bovix 40 this evening," Weinberg says. "It'll complement your other treatments. Help you get through this... difficult time."

He's being so goddamn patronizing it makes me want to hurl.

20

Swapping Secrets

B ird's Nest was droning on and on about canyons, oases, and sand dunes, while I sat there, head bent down, nursing a bad case of barrel fever. I felt so delicate, it was like an electric fence had been wired tight round my body, and her prattling was really starting to grate on me. But it wasn't as bad as knowing that, in five minutes, the hands of the clock would hit twelve, and the lunch bell would ring. For one thing, I was bound to run into Booker, and I wasn't sure I could face her after mouthing off the way I did yesterday. Worst of all, it was the unwritten rule of the cafeteria that Taylor and Dakota would share a bench seat and get all cozied up with one another. How the hell was I going to deal with that? I kept wishing Dillinger had come up with a way to halt time instead of fiddling about with space.

"So, can anyone tell me the main cause of desertification?"

"Kinda fittin' that she's talkin' about deserts," Earl whispered, as he sketched the Appaloosa in his notebook. "Her classes are dry as dust."

"Do you have something to say, Earl?"

"No, Ms. Piper. Only that your hair looks particularly lovely today."

Bird's Nest frowned at him, and everyone giggled. She was round as a hoppity hop, was pushing sixty, and her hair—a scruffy gray bun that looked more like a bird's nest—was just about as far away from lovely as you could get. Earl carried on doodling, but he was careful to make it look like he was copying the map of the Regarafian desert plains that she'd chalked on the board. Two desks away, I could see Taylor poring over the latest copy of *Wipeout* magazine. Then, out of the blue, he shot his hand up.

"There must be deserts in Magnatella, too," he said. "How come there's nothin' about 'em in our textbooks?" He sounded pretty fired up, which probably had something to do with Mr. Addison swatting him with the blackboard cloth for dozing off when we were meant to be reading silently from *The Go-Between* in English.

Bird's Nest just brushed him off, telling the class to pack up because it was nearly time for lunch.

As we made our way over to the dining hall, kids kept coming up to Taylor, patting him on the back and shaking him by the hand for rattling old Piper's cage. And he was lapping up the attention, a massive grin daubed on his face that he was wearing like a medal. Then Booker spotted us and came striding over.

"Kota feelin' any better?"

"Didn't you talk to her in social studies?" Taylor asked, still beaming.

"No, she wasn't in class. Thought she stayed home today."

Taylor dropped the medal grin, his face turning pale as winter. "But she gave me a lift in the Hornet this mornin'."

And that was when it hit me that something weird was going

on. "I know where she's at," I told them. "But I think it's best I go alone."

Taylor was shaking his head. "Screw that—we're all goin'. You just lead the way, bud."

I didn't want the others tagging along. Something was telling me this was my call, and I was sure that, in some inexplicable way, it was all to do with the cantaboon boat trip, as if a small sliver of its mystery was lingering—reaching out to me. "Look, the way she's feelin' right now, she won't want folks crowdin' round her," I said, eager for them to back off. "And we can't all cut classes; Chalky'd throw a fit. Trust me, I know what I'm doin'."

"Alright," Taylor said, with a quick nod. "Just see to it she's okay. Y' hear?"

Earl gave me a thumbs up. "I'll tell old Chalky you went home with the bellyache."

There was a real sense of purpose in the way I was marching through the sea of giant cornstalks, but I felt oddly calm. It was like I knew I was meant to be there, so nothing could ruffle me. I scrambled over the fence, glimpsing two looth birds perched in an ulu. They were cooing such a sweet and mellow lullaby, yet somehow managing to sound super strong and sure of themselves.

I skidded down the bank, bringing down a landslide of tiny mottled stones, and there she was, sitting cross-legged at the end of the jetty, half-heartedly hurling pebbles out into the middle of the creek. She heard my footsteps when I was about three feet away, and spun round with a gasp, so I knelt down next to her, quiet as I could manage.

"Is everythin' okay? They're all frettin' about you at school."

Dakota looked away, just gaping out at the water. She didn't answer, didn't smile. And then I spotted her jacket floating in the splash pool under the falls, the Angels logo just about poking out above the surface.

"Your jacket…"

"I threw it in," she said casually, like it was something that happened every day, but her words were slurred, and she wouldn't look at me.

"Why?"

She stretched her legs out, slow and careful, dangling them over the edge of the walkway, and then just sat there, gawking at them. I couldn't see any empties lying around, but it seemed to me she'd gotten nearly as trammeled as I did at the fountain yesterday, so I dug inside my pocket and pulled out a wad of smokes with two Dimers left inside, offering out the packet.

"Smoke a cigarette with me?"

Dakota turned to face me then, her skin so washed out I could have been looking at one of those old-fashioned porcelain dolls. She slid one of the Dimers out and put it to her lips. "It's nice when someone offers you a light," she said, as I held out the flame. "It's like keepin' a promise. Makes you feel you matter in some small way."

I guess it boosted my mettle, hearing those words and having the smoke right there in my hand. "You wanna talk about the night we took the rush?"

She shook her head, dragging slowly on the Dimer. "You ain't meant to be here. Finish the cig if you want, but then you gotta go." She sounded tired, hollow, and deflated—like she couldn't care less whether I stayed or not.

"C'mon, Kotes, don't be blue. Whatever you saw, it wasn't real. It was just a crazy, screwed-up dream. You know that, right?"

Her glaring would have come across as frosty on anyone else, but because it was her, it somehow tore inside of me. I wanted just to fling my arms round her—tell her everything would be okay. "You wouldn't understand," she muttered after a while, scratching restlessly at the lichens on the slats with her fingernails. She forced a smile, but it only made her jaw quiver, and she had to draw on the Dimer again to cover it up. "Sorry, Caldwell," she said. "Guess I'm just tired a' myself—tired a' bein' halfway between an awkward mess and almost invisible. Wish I could be more like Booker."

"Don't matter that you're different," I said, hoping it would cheer her up. "Would be borin' if the world was full of Pachellos. I mean, I ain't nothin' like Early-Bird or Tayles, but it don't bother me none."

Dakota tossed her head back. "Probably for the best. We got enough clowns already."

Almost as if they'd been cued, the looth birds fluttered out their nest and sailed overhead. They circled a couple of times, then splashed down into the shallows and started wading through a patch of mud, all the while pecking round for worms. Water shrews were scurrying about near the hibut reeds, most likely on the hunt for mayfly larvae, and gorgonflies were hovering and whirring over by the lily pads—still one minute, flitting about like mad the next.

"You gotta remember this, Kotes. What some folks see as flaws in themselves, others might not. Take Booker, for example. She feels like a nerd most a' the time 'cause of all the studyin'. But she's doin' it all for her twin sister, who died as a baby. And you? Sure, you got a fragile side, and you're deeper than most, but some might see real beauty in that... Don't let on about Booker's sister, though. It's kind of a secret."

"If we're gettin' into secrets, how'd you like to hear one about Taylor?"

"Sure."

Kota rested her chin on her knees, drew in a breath, and there was a long pause while she exhaled. It sounded so resigned it was like she was holding herself in a state of limbo, not wanting to tell after all. And by then, the tip of the smoke was hovering so close to her shirt, I had to slip it from her, stub it out on one of the wood panels. "He went nuts with a kunai knife—him and that big fat maggot with all the scars. They were actin' so crazy, I just… Hell, I ain't gonna talk about it. All you need to know is I woke up in a ditch at four in the morning. Had to thumb a ride back to Hailey's."

"Jeez, Kote. Kunai knives? It wasn't real."

She scowled, so I changed the subject.

"Was I there? I mean, with Tayles and the knives an' all?"

"Don't recall… There was somebody, though: a stranger." Her words were getting so faint, so broken, it took me all my time just to figure them out. "He was trapped inside a giant bottle of Diamond Cut, just waitin' for his chance to get out, to shine. And in the end, I saw that it wasn't a bottle of Grimley's at all. It wasn't even glass… he was stuck fast—held tight in someone else's soul." She paused again, and for a moment looked right into my eyes, like she trusted me completely. "I think this world we're livin' in is fake—this goddamn ideal pacifist world, where the only things that matter are rock 'n' roll and hangin' out in coffee bars. It's all a lie. The rush takes you to reality—where violence and hatred are part of everyday life, and there's nothin' you can do about it, except fight back." She rubbed at those big, beautiful, cornflower-blue eyes. "You must think I'm crazy."

"Course not, Kota. It's just the plant; it gives you all these wacky notions. And the thing is, when we were walkin' home after, Taylor kept tellin' me how worried he was about you. It was a bum trip, that's all. They call it the shurbs when it goes that way. You want me to fish your jacket out the river?" I was scanning the banks for a loose branch—something I could use to hook it—but then I noticed Dakota was quaking so bad, the whole jetty was wobbling.

"No. Leave it where it is!" she said, spitting the words out as if they were poison. "Swear you won't touch it!" Her lips were trembling—soft little blossoms caught in the wind. It got me so stirred up I just wanted to lash out at Marshall and Taylor—tell them they had no damn right to push that plant on her, force her into such a messed-up, scared, and angry state.

"Okay, I swear. I mean, I totally get it. Those trips can bring out some pretty intense feelin's." A flood of adrenaline was thundering through my veins, each pulse pleading with me to tell her. Asking Leyland about college had been tough, but this was on a whole new level. I was going through with it, though. No power on the planet could stop me. "And while we're on the subject of secrets… you were part a' my trip. It's hard to explain but… it's like we were totally in tune with one another… and we were just sailin' down the creek in this beautiful white canoe. After that, I guess I…"

Dakota raised her brow, eyes round as an owl's, such a starry look in them that, just for a moment, she became the girl in the dream again, chasing after poppies and scarecrows, and I wished, for the second time that day, that I could freeze time, just hold it where it was, treasure it. I couldn't keep the secret any longer, though; I had to set it free.

"I'm… in love with you, Dakota." It dawned on me right away how lame it must have sounded. The girl needed someone to talk to, not to hear about some freaky, blissed-out fantasy. But it was like she was struggling to stay awake. Maybe she didn't even hear what I said.

"I see it now, clear as anythin'," she whispered after a while, eyelids all red and puffy. "You were that stranger. Things get jumbled up in dreams; you know how it is. People become almost… interchangeable." She glanced over at me again, and the sweetest, faintest of smiles had appeared on her lips. She closed her eyes and, little by little, eased her head onto my shoulder. It felt so light I had to slip my arm around her, just to prove I wasn't dreaming.

We sat there together on the jetty—an illusion made real, the sound of the current a delicate melody as it babbled and clattered over the boonstones, distant looth calls adding silver-toned harmonies every once in a while. I could feel the rise and fall of Dakota's lungs against my chest, her hair, warm from Dol's rays, brushing my neck as the soothing scent of gacia pollen wafted over from Beau Lily Fields. I gazed at the spangled ribbon of water tapering away into the far-off hills of Hap Town—watched as a tiny rye bird darted from a nest in the hibut reeds, its shrill cry echoing faintly before it dived into the hedgerow. But when I looked back at Kota, I knew right away that this was the B-side of the rush trip, because her breathing had gotten so shallow, her lips were turning blue.

"Kota!" I shook her, but she was limp as a dishcloth, and dark rings were spreading out under her eyes. "Wake up, Kota! Don't do this to me!"

I remember the tears running down my cheeks, the way they stung me as I carried her. I was stumbling through the cornfield in a panic, the salt from the tears trickling into my mouth, the cornstalks whipping me on the thighs as I sped past, Dakota dangling like a rag doll in my arms. I kept telling myself I just had to get to the roadside, just had to keep putting one foot in front of the other, no matter what, because after that, there would be a groundy and everything would be alright. *In the name of Gilbert Gowder, the founder, please let it be alright!* I stared down at my legs and feet, aware that their movement seemed separate from everything else going on in my body. I puffed, panted, sobbed, and ranted, my breath wheezing out like the last bursts of smoke from a useless, clapped-out old steam engine. And then, when I finally staggered onto the sidewalk, I flagged down the first car that passed, and the driver let us in. He took one look at Kota and floored the gas pedal.

Once we got to the emergency room, they put her on a crash cart and whisked her away so fast it made all the flyers on the wall flutter.

"You gotta pull through, Kota. You just gotta."

I thought about Booker's twin sister, about Lucy, and the dark rings under Dakota's eyes. In the real world, none of that bad stuff would have happened, but everyone was stuck in this B-side place, this copy of reality where everything was a mess because I didn't have the guts to go inside that machine.

Stop it with that shit, I told myself. *It was a goddamn dream.* But I could feel the guilt raging away inside of me, hot and heavy in my guts, spreading outward to the tips of my fingers, worming its way, inch by inch, into my psyche.

What the hell is wrong with me?

21

The Tome-Bots

A knock, even though it's soft, jolts me out of sleep, and I make out Langley's fuzzy form dithering in the doorway. "Just came to bring some news," he says. "A hearin' date's been set: three weeks today. An' anytime you need Trellaman, just let Dr. Weinberg know, and he'll pass on the message."

He nods to me, then swivels, just as the governor appears behind him. Their eyes meet as they pass in the doorway, but neither of them says anything. And there's something in the way Weinberg smiles at Langley. I can't decide if it's smugness, or if he's just pitying the old jake for being so gullible.

DORAN'S STORY

During the day, the Shadow Dwellers spent their time hustling out on the streets, trying to obtain money and provisions in whatever inventive way they could manage, and, despite their skills, that often meant having to scrobble. Doran found this quite hair-raising, because there was a thin line between being daring enough to pull it off and coming close to getting caught by the Tome-Bots—robot police whose primary goal was to locate and incapacitate untagged vagrants. But he was willing to endure the angst, because scrobbling meant being paired up with Domino. They would plot out their maneuvers in the mornings, put the plans into action in the afternoons, and more often than not, emerge victorious, returning to Nentoke with sufficient plunder to fill their bellies—sometimes plenty to spare as well.

Every other week, The Sergeant and Carina would visit Nentoke, or Doran and Domino would stay overnight on *The Dreamcatcher,* losing all notion of themselves as they narrated stories, both real and imagined, by the firelight. They would play endless rounds of Scrabble, dance away on the quayside to the spellbinding sounds crackling out over the barge's shaky old PA system, or they would simply talk, covering subjects as diverse as poetry, philosophy, and astrophysics.

"Tell us about the Big Freeze again, Sarge," Domino said once, shortly after Doran first joined the troupe. The dawn chorus had just broken out, and the sweet warbling reminded him that they really ought to stop their yakking and turn in for the night.

"Now, that's the scenario where the universe ends and all matter eventually finds its way into a black hole," Humbucker told them, the shiny white dots on his cravat catching the firelight. And, as he elaborated, Doran finally clicked.

"Until the stars turn black. I get it now. That's what you always say instead of goodbye."

Doran's lifestyle was a far cry from the luxury and comfort he had enjoyed at Maple Road, but he considered himself fortunate and, in all likelihood, he would have dwelt in that subterranean world indefinitely had it not been for a particular incident that occurred fifteen months after he first arrived.

It all began the day Barlin sprained his left ankle while descending the cellar stairs. Scout didn't want to go out scrobbling alone, so she went to the Widameer Mall in the Mulchaft district with Doran and Domino, while Catlow stayed behind to tend to Barlin's injury. The mall was home to one of the largest superstores in the capital, Hepton's, and Domino's plan was to lift some bedding from there.

It was about two o'clock in the afternoon when Doran strolled up to the exit with a fractal-design comforter stuffed inside his backpack. He had removed the security tag with wire cutters when visiting the bathroom, so he was not worried about the alarm sounding. In fact, he was feeling rather calm, because he'd taken items from Hepton's many times before and never been caught. However, when he passed the exit, he was immediately stopped in his tracks by a uniformed security guard.

"Open the backpack."

Doran fled at once, only just dodging the guard's grasp. His instinct was to head for the escalators, but in his panic, he jumped onto the wrong one and found himself going up instead of down. Glancing back, he saw that the guard was not in pursuit, so he allowed himself a small sigh of relief. The upper mall looked busiest, so he carried on to the top floor, shuffling quickly into the bathroom at Ponta Pisto's, where he stretched a beanie over his head, and ditched his jacket. Then he pulled the old hand-comp out of his pocket—the one that Catlow had given him—and called Domino.

"I almost got busted."

"Where are you?"

"Ponta Pisto's."

"Wait there. We'll come get you."

A fretful minute passed, and then he could see their faces bobbing toward him in the crowd. There was no sign of the guard, so he waited, quivering only slightly. But just as he was about to dash forward, blaring sirens started, the mall music was cut, and a monotone voice erupted over the PA system.

"Tome-Bot alert. This is a Tome-Bot alert. Please leave the mall by the nearest exit."

Folks began streaming out of the stores and down the escalators, muttering to each other about "damn vagrants" and the inconvenience of having their shopping pleasure disturbed.

"Calming gas is being dispersed," the voice said, as a gentle hissing sound filled the air. "It will not harm you if you are tagged."

Domino sidled up to Doran. "Just follow the crowd. Act like everything's cool."

And it was then that Doran noticed a giant, metallic Tome-Bot towering behind Scout, its telescopic arms curling out toward her.

"No tag detected. Initiating stun."

There was a flash of light, then Scout dropped to the floor like a withered leaf in fall, and all Doran could feel was his brain rattling non-stop against his skull—a white-hot agony beyond anything he had ever endured. Movement was impossible; he couldn't even cry out. And when, finally, the pain let up, all he could make out was a sea of heads clustered around Scout: paramedics, cops, Tome-Bots, and bewildered looking bystanders.

One of the paramedics was draping a blanket over Scout's face. "Time of death: 2.25." Doran just wanted to run to her, but he was in the grip of a Tome-Bot, its tentacle-like arms doubled tightly around him.

"Age estimated as thirteen. Untagged. Escort to nearest police facility for immediate tagging."

They kept Doran lingering in the dimness of a boxlike cell for three days solid, with nothing to do but fall prey to his own paranoia. The horror of witnessing Scout's death, coupled with the anguish of being separated from Domino, created a sickening disquiet that tore away at the pit of his belly, ruthlessly tormenting both body and mind. It was as if he were reliving the pain of Quin's departure all over again but magnified tenfold. He was fighting an urgent need to pace, but there was no room to do so in such a claustrophobic cell.

However, at the end of the third day, a medic dressed in a white coat appeared outside the door. Upon unlocking it, he found the boy just rocking back and forth, continuously repeating, "Where are you, my Astronomy Dominé?"

"Come with me. It's time you were tagged."

He led Doran out of the detention area, past the office, through the back entrance into a parking lot, and up the steps of a white trailer labeled 'Mobile Tagging Unit'. Inside, there was a reclining chair with a large Plexiglas dome angled above it.

"Lie down, please. I'll take some details, and then we'll get the tag implanted. Don't worry; you won't feel anything."

"The ones I was with," Doran said softly. "What happened to them?" He felt a peculiar jumble of fear about what would happen to him, shame at getting caught, and anger that the Tome-Bots had killed Scout. But the thought making his entire body shudder was that he might never see Domino again.

"Damn, we're out of rubber gloves. Sit here and relax for me. I'll be back in a minute." The medic got up, strode across to a security panel on the door, pulled a wire from it with a scanning card attached, and touched it against the side of his head.

When he returned, Doran was waiting, a hefty spanner clenched in his fist.

It was late in the evening when the boy returned to Nentoke, and his nerves were all over the place. He squeezed through the hole that led inside the main cave, shoulders drooping, hoping he could hold back his tears long enough to explain himself to Barlin and Catlow.

"Doran. Thank Dillinger." Domino bundled him straight into her arms, and the unbearable ache inside of him was immediately placated. "Are you sure no one followed you?"

"I'm sure. But... Scout."

"I know," Domino whispered, shaking her head.

"She was epileptic," Catlow told him, her voice hoarse with grief. "She never talked about it much—liked to keep it to herself. When the Tome-Bots scanned her, she must have gone into a seizure. The irony is, if she'd been tagged, she could have gotten treatment for it... Look, you lie down, Doran. I'll fix an iced latte for you."

She turned to go, and it struck Doran as out of place, as if the idea of drinking at a time like this was absurd.

"Best add a drop of Don Julio," Domino muttered. "If we got any left, that is."

Later, still inside the cave, sounds that were as familiar to Doran as breathing suddenly felt different, strange, more affecting. Water was trickling down the stalactites into the pool at the back, and he heard it as a lament, as though it were tears that were falling, cold and raw. He watched Catlow unfasten her rucksack, rummage inside, and take out a fresh dressing for Barlin's ankle. And then Domino was unraveling the old bandages, lightly bathing the swelling with a wet cotton ball.

"Are we sure she's... dead?" The word made Doran cringe, and he felt the urge to find a dictionary and hurl it out the nearest window for having such a cruel definition. "It's just, it doesn't seem real. I keep thinking she'll come strolling in here, giggling, telling us it's all been some huge prank."

"They covered her face, Dormouse." Domino pinned the binding, then sat on the floor in front of him, baseball cap clasped in her hands.

Doran thought about the iced latte with Don Julio, tears dripping down cold limestone, and a dictionary tumbling angrily out of a window somewhere. And it was like the sum of those things meant sadness and pain, but nothing as great as his relief that Domino had come back to him.

"We should be thankful you escaped the Tome-Bots, Dom," Barlin said, clutching his mandolin tight to his chest. "If you got busted, they'd most likely dump you on an Earth ship. Sometimes I hate living on the edge like this."

"There's nothing we can do about it." Domino swallowed hard, leaning back against the cave curtains that had always reminded Doran of an old-fashioned pump organ.

"There is one thing." Doran spoke so quietly, no one really heard, so he cleared his throat and pulled himself up. He thought that if he was standing at their level, they might at least take him a little more seriously. "As soon as Barlin's fit to travel, we can cross the Disian Ocean. We can go to Podunkia."

THE PRESENT

"Did the medic... bite the big one?"

The bile in my belly is churning, and all because some kid called Doran knocked seven bells out of a guy I never met. Is that what Wallbanger was alluding to when he wrote that freaky message?

"He was out for a while," Weinberg says. "Long enough for Doran to get away, but he only suffered a slight concussion." He checks his watch, then strides over to the door. "I need to get going. Next time we'll move on to Doran's plans for fleeing

Magnatella." He gives me a swift nod, then exits, just as a medic arrives bearing a tray.

One thing's for sure: Weinberg's determined to bug me with every little detail about Doran before he makes his big exposé, and there's not a lot I can do. If I split, I won't get far; Stringy and Lardy will see to that. And I can't go through the window—can't even reach to see out of it. But if Weinberg won't get to the point, maybe Harvey Wilder will.

"Roll your sleeve up for me, please."

Two vials of Bovix 40 and three Xenon 90s slide around on the tray as the medic pushes it onto the nightstand. It's time I did a bit of play-acting.

"Can't breathe."

I feign passing out, and by the time she's back with help, the Bovix 40s are hidden, unused, under my pillow, along with three empty Xenon 90 jars.

I'll start with the time Earl was called into Thackery's office for doing crude impressions of Mr. Jackson, the science teacher.

"You know what you are, Hunter? You're an attention-seeker. You'll do anything for a cheap laugh, even if it means throwing away your school career. What do you have to say for yourself?"

The rest of us had our ears pressed hard against the door.

Earl huffed, like he was resigned to his fate. "You got me pegged, sir. But there must be some way I can make it up to you. Let me sing you a song, just to show you how much you mean to me as a leader, a mentor, and a principal."

We heard him clear his throat, then looked at each other in total shock as he threw himself into a perfectly pitched and very sweet rendition of Perry Como's 'A - You're Adorable'.

"What the hell's goin' on?" Taylor whispered. "Is he actually singin' in there?"

Booker grinned. "He knows what he's doin'. Bet he's dancin', too. Sure wish we could see it."

"Stop that at once," Thackery began, but Booker hit the nail on the head; as well as flattering the pants off the principal, it tickled his funny bone in all the right places, and Earl only had to do a three-day detention for his crimes. I've often wondered which line in the song swung it for him. Earl reckoned it was the one about being light as a feather because that was when Thackery quit frowning and let out a quiet chuckle.

"Yep. That was the line." He's there, in his drainpipe jeans, winklepicker boots, and baseball jacket, dressed just like an Arch Angel. He's smoking a Dimer, even though they were banned at school on pain of a two-week expulsion.

"How'd you know, Harvey? Or are you Wallbanger this time?"

He shrugs, like he's getting a real kick out of keeping me guessing.

"Just tell me what I need to know."

"Ain't gonna do that," he says. "You'll have to talk to Wallbanger."

"Then bring it on, man. Let him come out."

Harvey stubs out the Dimer, fixes me with a lukewarm stare, his image fading into flimsy shapes that shift around silently, vaguely, and in snatching at them I blunder into deep sleep, wakefulness slapping me hard in the face at three in the morning.

I pad over to the door in my bare feet, peeking out into the corridor. Chances don't come often, but Lardy's chair is empty now. Maybe he overdosed on donuts and Stringy had to take him to the ER.

Quietly, I edge toward the crank's door, pushing down firmly on the handle, finally managing to pull the damn thing open. And then I'm standing in front of a tiny closet, gaping open-mouthed at a stack of neatly folded washcloths, boxes of toilet paper, freshly pressed sheets.

"What d' ya think yer doin'?" A medic with a flashlight

bangs the door shut, angrily steering me back to my room, the glow from the bulb stinging my eyes.

"Where the hell is he, then? Where you keepin' him?"

"Let's get you another shot of Xenon, Mr. Caldwell. Somethin' to help you sleep."

This time, Broughton Alley wanders into my head: winter nights in fifth grade, slam-dunking with Booker, Earl, and Taylor, a camping lamp balanced high on the wall so's we'd know which way to shoot. We'd have a basketball in one hand and a soda in the other, gangly shadows of us curling across the brickwork.

"That was before you met Dakota." Harvey drags on another Dimer from up on the wall, the heels of his boots kicking idly against the side.

"You're back? Not much use, though, are ya? You ain't tellin' me nothin'."

Harvey sighs. "Okay. I'll tell you somethin' about that goddamn Bovix stuff. It's experimental. It's for folks with Alzheimer's and senile dementia."

"Get real, Harvey."

I guess I'm sneering at him, but he springs off the wall and shuts me down with the warning jab of an index finger in my chest.

"You gotta get outta here, Caldwell," he says, not quite yelling. "I'm serious. Find a way, before the goddamn bastards turn you back into Doran."

22

The Cobweb

THE PAST

"Name's Colt," the medic told me as he shook my hand. "Dakota's folks are on their way."

"But what did…?"

"Don't you go frettin' now," he said. "She's gonna be fine. She swallowed a few pills back there, but we got 'em outta her in time. Any idea what coulda made her take 'em?"

I didn't want to land Dakota in a heap more trouble, so I kept things as vague as I could. "She moved here from Losterdinos 'bout seven years ago. Couple from The Willows adopted her 'cause her real folks were neglectful. Guess it coulda been somethin' to do with that."

"The Willows, eh?"

"Leyland says gossip is king."

"We'll be discreet." Colt jotted down some notes, then sat down next to me. "Well, physically there shouldn't be any long-term damage," he said. "It was Dimensadol she took—little pink sleepin' pills. Sure was lucky you were there with her down at Pettiworn."

He said it all kindly enough, but as soon as I heard the name of the meds, the hairs on my arms, back, and neck started to creep up, and I got all nauseous and dizzy.

"You seem a bit spooked, son. You alright?"

"Sure. I just wanna see her." I figured there was no point telling him about the message—about the 'Dol Dimension'. I mean, I didn't want him dragging me off to the psychiatric unit.

"Apart from her folks, there's no visitors till tomorrow," Colt said. "She needs her rest, and you look like you could do with some, too. There's a phone in the lobby if you wanna call someone."

I called Kepple's and Leyland came to pick me up.

Back at home, it was hard to focus on anything besides Dakota, the message, and the pills. I kept churning it over in my mind: the whole 'Dol Dimension' thing, and how eerie it was. The Curzons ran a pharmacy as well as a liquor store, so she most likely snatched the sleepers from there, but it was all so unsettling, it was easier just to convince myself that it was me who scrawled the message, on account of being squashed into two dimensions and dragged into the dazzling heat of Dol. Or maybe the rush was reaching out to us, linking us together in ways we had no hope of understanding. How else could I have known she'd be down by the creek, sitting on the jetty?

After dinner, I took to pacing up and down the living room carpet, dogged with thoughts that just wouldn't let up. It sounded crazier than a betsy bug, but it was like the trip—the part where Dakota sailed down the creek with me in the cantaboon boat—was a dimension in itself—a place you could get to only by swallowing a dumb old plant from the Pugnax system. But if that was the case, Dakota's trip was a dimension too, and it would have felt every bit as real to her as mine did to me. I guess that's why she flipped out so bad. And I kept coming back to what she said about living in a fake world, and the rush showing her a reality dominated by hate and violence. Was it all linked to the Eastern Europeans? Maybe shifting that box somehow pushed everyone into this phony existence.

For cryin' out loud, Carney. Just quit. Things are bad enough without harpin' back to that.

I went over to the phone to call Earl, but I had no idea how to explain any of it, so I went back into the living room and just sat on the couch with my head in my hands, listening to the sound of Leyland scrubbing away at the dishes. Then he came in, took one look at me, and poured out a brandy, shoving it into my hand.

"Drink up, Li'lbro," he said, nodding firmly after I'd gulped it down.

"Let's go to the movies, Ley. I don't much care what's on. Just need somethin' different to think about."

The sweaty theater manager stood in front of the curtains. "You're about to see the latest blockbuster." He always gave a speech before the lights went out, so's folks would get bored and buy more ice cream. "It's called *The Cobweb,* and it stars Richard Widmark and Lauren Bacall. What's it all about? Well, without wantin' to give too much away, I can tell you it's all about the private world of human emotions."

I laughed out loud, and all the folks in front turned round and glared at me.

The picture started with a headcase running through a cornfield, which kind of freaked me out, but after that, it was just about two shrinks and a bunch of inmates squabbling over who got to hang some drapes in a nuthouse library. One of the shrinks was acting all selfish and petty—I guess they all were, but the headcase couldn't hack it when they snubbed the drapes he'd made, so he threw himself in the river, although they managed to pull him out in time.

I guess it wasn't the smartest choice of movie, given what happened with Dakota, but the acting was too over-the-top for it to bother me much. What really grabbed me was the title, and the slogan under the poster about the characters spinning a human cobweb. It kind of played on my mind how the guy got so tangled up in it. It seemed as if fate, or the rush, or something I was struggling to grasp and could never hope to put into words, had been spinning its own sort of web, sending out subtle little strands of cryptic coincidence that were slowly and surely starting to reel me in.

"You can have the mornin' off school to go visit Dakota," Leyland told me as we were heading back home in the truck. "And I'll get someone to cover my shift so's I can bring you there myself."

"Thanks," I said, offering him the last of my popcorn and frowning. "Y' know, Leyland, life's a lot more complicated than it seems in pictures."

"What makes you say that?"

"I dunno. I guess it's just full of all these things that seem small and insignificant, but somehow they come together to trip you up. It's much stranger than anythin' a movie studio could ever dream up."

The brandy, and the thought of seeing Dakota in the morning must have helped me wind down some, because once I got home and my head touched the pillow, my brain managed to churn out enough delta waves to send me soundly to sleep. And I never once dreamt about cobwebs.

Tuesday, April 29th, 2324

We were in our jammies at the kitchen table, munching away on Sugar Jets, when the phone rang from out in the hallway. Leyland got up to answer it, and my heart started pounding like a printing press in overdrive. He was putting on his phone voice, but everything he was saying was vague and hard-headed, and it kind of shook me up.

"I see... Well, s'pose that's for the best... I'll tell him." He hung up, and I was forced to shove my bowl away.

"Carney—"

"Just tell me she's alright, Leyland."

"She's doin' fine, kiddo. But..." He pushed his hair out of his eyes and sat down again. "That was her pop. They've moved her to a place in Crosswinds Bridge: a mental health unit." He was speaking real gentle. "She'll get the proper help she needs there."

It was a weight off my shoulders but, at the same time, an awkward pang of disappointment was skulking in my stomach. I wouldn't get to see her. *Don't be so selfish,* I told myself. *Look what happened in the movie when folks thought only of themselves.*

Leyland emptied some more Sugar Jets into his dish and flicked through the pages of his anatomy book, the steady tock of the pendulum papering over the silence. It made me think about time, and how it's so damn pig-headed, just marching on with no regard for anyone who might want to stay behind for a while.

"Only seems like yesterday we were sittin' here with a hale-and-hearty Lucy, Clue pieces all spread out. You ever wish you could hit a button, Ley—just go back?"

He put the book down, and it struck me how much his eyes were like Lucy's. "Sometimes," he said, smearing a dollop of strawberry jelly onto his toast. "I mean, everythin' seemed so simple back then. Life felt easier. All that really mattered was figurin' out who broke into Mr. Boddy's mansion."

"An' tryin' not to get the stitch from laughin' too hard. Man, Lucy's bright remarks—all that banter. But good times don't hang round for long, do they?"

"Old 'uns go, but there's always new 'uns round the corner.

And the old 'uns, well, I like to think of 'em as little golden boxes you can dust off every once in a while. Nothin' wrong with a bit a' nostalgia."

"Golden boxes?"

"Yeah. Why not?"

Leyland's words brought on the jitters so fast, I couldn't keep my legs still. What if all those golden boxes in the dream were memories? What if I messed up the whole universe by moving one? *Jeez, just quit with that!*

"I'm gonna get dressed—get myself off to school. Feels like I'm playin' hooky."

"You sure, Li'lbro?"

"Yeah. If I stay here, I'll only end up broodin'."

I walked to school instead of taking the bus because Dol was breaking through the clouds, and it heartened me to meet the warmth of its eager little sunbeams. By the time I got to Mindow Fields Lane, it was half past ten, and Earl and Booker were lying under the big beech tree near the memorial benches. Booker spotted me sauntering across the tarmac and came jogging over.

"We heard about Crosswinds Bridge," she said, when she was a couple of feet away. "Kota'll get what she needs there."

She offered me a stick of Beemans, and all I could say was, "Thanks."

"Well, you missed all the drama this mornin'," Booker went on. "Taylor quit the Angels. He was so damn guilt-ridden, he just upped and left town."

She was looking at me all weirdly, and when I just stood there without replying, her cheeks flushed up the color of rose petals. At first, I figured it was down to all that shameful stuff I said to her over at the fountain, but there was also a quiet, almost childlike awe in her eyes that told me it had more to do with Dakota and the cornfield than anything else. I bit at my lip, not knowing if it would be wrong of me to smile, given all the bad shit going on.

In the end, I just mumbled, "Jeez. Seems like everyone's goin' away just lately."

"Yeah, tell me about it," Booker said. "Kota's folks said I could fetch the Hornet, so I guess she's not comin' back anytime soon. I promised 'em I'd take good care of it."

We were strolling through the quad toward the beech tree, and I was frowning. There'd be a barrage of questions, no doubt about it, and some of them just plain had no answers.

Over at the benches, I managed a thin and wavering smile, greeting Earl in the usual way with backslaps, high fives, and handshakes. But all afternoon, I couldn't stop staring at Taylor's empty desk and chair. And I kept thinking about that time in junior year when Mr. Addison had us all write poems about loss, and how Earl wrote about his cat getting run over, and then Addison scribbled a list of adjectives on the board. And I realized you don't need words and descriptions to feel anything. Taylor's chair was empty whether the word existed or not. The only real statement you could make was the seat itself, over by the window where light was shining down on bare, lifeless wood.

The events of the day left me so deflated that, instead of hanging out with Booker and Earl after baseball practice, I made excuses and went downtown alone. I'd been toying with the idea of catching the forty-two from Larchiment out to Sorley Ridge. I guess I thought it might help to hear what The Rooster had to say. If he was spinning a similar yarn to Dakota, then maybe I should worry.

I got off the bus just outside the gates in front of Sorley Ridge House, suddenly hesitant about going in. The place was starting to look real creepy in the dwindling light, especially since some of the downstairs windows were boarded up. And the flaky white paint on the brickwork, coupled with the huge, pointed tower in the middle, made it look like some spooky Gothic nightmare.

Inside, it stank of high-grade disinfectant, and a heated vocal exchange was going on behind closed doors: a woman screaming, "No" over and over as unduly serene voices tried to hush her. It was nothing like the nuthouse in the movie.

"I've come to see Rufus Lester. He's an old friend."

The man at the front desk showed me to a table in the visitors' room. "Wait here."

I bit at my fingernails, wondering why the hell I'd come, a dingy light flickering all the while above a scuffed metal floor. I thought about all the poor lost souls whose boots must have trodden it, pangs of dread coursing through my veins like mighty rivers at the height of a monsoon. And then, before I had a chance to hightail it out of there, Rufus appeared in the doorway. I didn't recognize him at first. His face looked fuller—red and blotchy, sore with open acne wounds that he never used to have. He sat down in the chair opposite me, stroking a hand over his matted mess of thick dark curls.

"Do I know you, man?"

"Don't matter," I said kindly. "I'm just here to ask about the rush."

A spark of something flitted across his bloodshot eyes, and he smiled, knowingly. "I'm not who you think I am," he said, winking at me. "They want you to go on believing all the lies, but I met Gilbert Gowder ten years ago. He doesn't exist. He's a machine, a nobody."

"What's the Dol Dimension? You know anythin' about it?"

The Rooster gestured to the middle of his chest, raising his head like he was super proud, eyes fixed on me. "They chose me to execute the plan. They chose *me*. *I'm* the one."

"What plan?"

"To rebuild the universe, atom by atom."

I never told anyone about going to see Rufus. I mean, I expected weirdness but nothing on that scale. I guess it was something I just wanted to forget.

The next day, after school, I called Leyland from the payphone at Dawn's Diner and told him I'd be sleeping over at Earl's. Then, after stuffing ourselves full of hot fudge sundae, we took the long route back through Jade Walk Park, along its winding, tree-lined footpaths. When we passed the sunken kids' playground, Earl sprang up onto one of the self-push carousels, and I scooted it round a few times before hopping on next to him.

"Sure is gonna be strange round here without Tayles," I said. "Okay, he shoved that rotten plant on Kota, but there's no way he coulda known how things would turn out. Can't believe we won't see him no more."

"Things change. No point bein' down in the mouth about it." Earl plucked a pack of Dime Chimes from his pocket, offering me one.

"Was there a scene?"

"No. Wasn't like that night at Buddy's; it was his idea to go. Reckon he couldn't face the rest of us after what he did. Left for Nefamincle before you showed up. Said he was gonna bum a ride there, meet up with Marsh, and look for work on one of them wind farms. Then he set off for the freeway."

"Musta figured you don't need a high-school diploma to be a drifter."

"They'll do just fine, both of 'em. Lots a' great surf spots in those parts." Earl dragged on the Dimer and then, when the ride had slowed some, he lay back and looked up at me, the cigarette bobbing up and down in the corner of his mouth as he spoke. "How'd you know Kotes would be down at the creek?"

I leaned on my elbow so that I was facing him. "You want the truth?"

"You trust me, don'cha?"

A pang of guilt swept over me for not having the guts to tell him in the first place. "I just knew," I said, hoping it wasn't too late to make up for it. "It was kind of a sixth sense, if you believe in that shit."

Earl shrugged. "I only believe in rational explanations," he said. "Anyway, didn't know you and Kota…"

"It was after I popped the rush. She was with me on this far-out trip, that's all. It's hard to describe the feelin', but I guess it was all about connectedness and peace. Seems like this massive deal now, though—like I'm intertwined with her in some way, and that's how I knew where she'd be." I yawned and rubbed at my eyes, drained by everything that had gone down in the last few days. "You probably think I got rocks in my head."

Earl was busy drawing on his cigarette, and every time he snatched it from his lips, he would study it, like an artist inspecting the clay before making a profound and beautiful sculpture. I guess that's why I was expecting him to come out with something deep, but in the end, all he did was lecture me. "If wantin' the feelin' back is top a' your agenda, don't be tempted," he said. "That rush is bad shit. If you take enough, it can rot the brain—get a guy so's he can't even tell what's real no more."

"You're preachin' to the converted," I said, trying to get the image of The Rooster out of my head. "Wish I'd never set eyes on that good-for-nothin' plant."

I stared up at the sky. The curls of cloud had floated off to the west, and Dol was riding high, warming the wood on the carousel. And over by the swing bars, I could hear the leaves of an old cinnabar tree rustling in the wind, like tiny messengers urging a fretful boy to calm his troubled heart.

Earl stubbed out the Dimer and sat up. Then he turned to me, the start of a roguish smile sneaking onto his lips. "So, about me bein' a strait-laced fun sponge…"

"Man, I'm so ashamed a' that. Was hopin' it wouldn't get out. You know it was the booze talkin', right?"

Earl nodded and was about to open his mouth, but I got in first with, "Anyway, it's okay, Hunter; I ain't sweet on Mackenzie no more. You can ask her out if that's what you're after. I don't mind at all."

"Gee, thanks, Carney," he said, giving my shoulder a friendly squeeze. "You think she'll go for me, though? I heard she's got big dreams about gettin' into some kinda super league over in Magnatella. And I'm just a small-town hick, happy to grease engines for the rest a' my days."

I tried to look kindly but couldn't keep from sniggering and ended up taking in a lungful of smoke. Then Earl started snickering too, thumping me hard on the back as I coughed and spluttered.

"Bring it up," he said. "Might be another gold watch. And if the akka-dials are bigger and fancier than the one you got already, I got dibs."

I wiped away the tears, putting on my best serious face so as he'd know I was talking plain and wished only the best for him. "Look, you go for it, Early-Bird. They say opposites attract. And anyways, maybe you ain't so different. Baseball's a sport and so's drag racin'. And don't forget what we overheard them girls sayin' after you played Brick in sophomore year."

Earl's face was suddenly glowing. "Damn it, Caldwell, you're a genius. So, my eyes really smolder when I narrow them, huh?"

"Well, not for me, bud. But maybe you could show up at the record store, perched on the 'Loosa or somethin'… maybe even have a bottle of bubbly ready in your hand. I could lend you twenty bans for it. Leyland gave me two weeks' allowance in advance. Musta felt bad for me."

Back at Earl's place, we hung out in the cellar, listening to the

Jamie Jenkins show on the radio, guzzling his old lady's jungle juice, and cheating the hell out of each other in a crazy game of Monopoly that brought impressions, wisecracks, and forfeits into the bargaining. It felt just like being a kid again.

"Rattle them bones," Earl said, as he shook the dice. "The baby needs shoes."

I tried to think about the last few days, but the memories seemed shriveled and distant, like I was looking at a bunch of dusty black-and-white photos no one had bothered with for years. "Y' know, Earl, all that shit about the rush, and Kota, and the pills; it seems kinda lost now—like it ain't part a' my life no more."

"Best keep it that way. Live for the moment; that's what I do... Hey, what d' ya know? Boxcars! Don't tell me you own Javapod Street."

"I got a big fat hotel there, and it's gonna set you back four thousand bandols."

"Jeez. That's some racket you're runnin'." Earl flicked through his deeds and scratched his head. "Don't wanna sell Larchiment back to the bank. Everythin' I got is a money-spinner. I guess all I can do is take a forfeit." He pulled a card from the pile. "Oh, glory. I ain't goin' to no all-night gas station in my boxers with six rubber ducks taped to my butt."

"You wrote out the cards. I think on some level, you musta wanted to."

Earl huffed. "Okay, I'll go," he said, acting like it was a major dilemma. "But only if you say you'll still respect me in the mornin.'"

I grinned. "Sure. All that matters is I got closure. And Kota'll be back in Hailey's before too long, anyways. Everythin's lookin' peachy."

"Not so sure about that," Earl said, taking another swill of corn liquor. "My butt ain't gonna look too peachy, dressed up in all them bath ducks."

And so, for a while at least, I forgot all about the rush, Dakota, and B-side worlds. I quit thinking about pills, machines, boxes, and cobwebs, and I lightened up. I guess I had no way of knowing that the web would be putting out its feelers again come the end of summer, or that they'd be digging in so deep by then, nothing would ever be the same.

23

Ballino Heights

The amber lights from the tavern wiggled gently in the canal's stagnant sheen, illuminating the wooden hull of *The Dreamcatcher* as it pitched up and down like an old man nodding off to sleep. Doran and Domino stood under the swing sign, the muffled sounds of music, chatter, and laughter drifting over from the bar.

"Should we go over or wait for him to come out?" Doran kicked at a lamppost. He was tense, and it showed on his face.

"Hey, take a chill pill," Domino said. "You know The Sarge'll do all he can to help."

"Sure, but what if he tells us we're bound to get caught?"

"Don't be so downbeat." Domino strode over to the barge, Doran trudging behind her. Then, before they'd reached the edge of the towpath, he saw a spindly figure emerge from the cabin, and his doubts gave way to optimism and gladness.

Inside, the galley was lit only by a small peach-colored salt lamp on the windowsill, and by the glow of two marigold flames that were licking and hissing at the top of the grate, casting flickering shadows onto the walls. In the background, Doran could hear the familiar, blues-soaked riffs of Pink Floyd's 'Shine On You Crazy Diamond'.

"We need to get to Cassaforta," he explained, as he spread out by the fireside next to Domino. "But there's things we still don't understand. Why have a Disian run at all when everyone's forced to stay here?"

"For the movement of goods. And so that folk from Cassaforta can come to live here." Humbucker was preparing *boisenbois* again, whistling as he ground up pungent-smelling herbs with a mottled pestle and mortar made from coconut wood.

Doran held out his arm so that Carina could waddle onto it from the table. "They really do that? Can't see why they'd be interested in a land ruled by the tagmesh." He tousled the raven's neck feathers, whispering, "Pretty girl."

"They come because the Cassafortans don't want them. Either they're too bright, or they're not peaceful enough. Some are sent here to study; others are incarcerated or permanently marked as aggressors." Humbucker stirred some oat milk into the *boisenbois,* then passed down two piping-hot mugs before sounding a palatal click to Carina, who strutted rather grandly over to her food bowl to drink her share of it.

"And they know about the tagmesh?" Domino asked.

"They understand that they can never return once they get here. But most arrive full of hopes and dreams, wishing only to leave their old lives behind them. They think that banishment from Cassaforta is a small price to pay for the benefits of settling in high-tech cities such as this." Humbucker poured a measure of absinthe into a crystalline tumbler, watered it down a little, and then knelt down beside them.

"The real question is… can you help us stow away on one of

the Disian freighters? After all, you're the expert in making the run. You did it for more than twenty years."

Domino had a way of smiling with her eyes as well as her mouth. She would look down and then back up at people, the gesture so full of charm and confidence that Doran almost forgot the reason they had come. He afforded himself a chuckle because it was reassuring to see her putting her teachings into practice. She'd told him always to end with flattery when you wanted something from someone. "You gotta be a real apple-polisher," she would say every time the lesson came up. "Make lots of eye contact, and act like you're just as happy as a clam, never glum or desperate."

The Sergeant sighed a little, placing a palm on each of their shoulders. "My advice is not to risk such a thing. The ships never sail without a crew in case the auto-nav fails, and they're not allowed to carry westbound passengers. You wouldn't be able to hide in one of the cargo crates either, because they're always scanned on arrival in Cassaforta. If you were found, the punishments would be severe."

Doran felt his heart sink vacantly to his boots. "There's no other way for us to get across?" He tried to bury his disappointment, but he knew he was failing badly at it. Hot tears were welling up and fighting them back was making his jaws ache.

"What about the Selfraic Ocean?" Domino said, focusing on the galley ceiling where The Sergeant had hand-painted every planet in the Dolon system.

"I'm afraid there are no ferries at all on the east side, only naval ships."

The girl simply shrugged, but Doran's feelings had gotten the better of him. He rose and, not wishing his friends to see him weep, retreated silently from the galley. Domino started after him, but Humbucker gestured for her to return, and from out on the deck, Doran just about caught his words.

"Give the boy a moment. He sees you sitting there, wielding your self-control like some mystical talisman, and he is filled with shame because he wants to be just like you. He'll be back when he is ready."

When Doran returned, they were stretched out by the hearth, just listening to the crackle of the fire, and the echoes of soul-wrenching string bends that were made nearly four hundred years ago. And, as he watched from the stairway, Domino suddenly turned to Humbucker.

"There's something I always wondered about, C-POD. The sailors on the Disian runs—when they pass Protson 13, don't they lose their memories too?"

"Don't ask me; I can't remember." Humbucker's eyes were like huge blue harvest moons, his smile more bewitching than Doran had ever seen.

"Sarge. Quit winding me up." Domino elbowed him in the ribs.

"You really want that? You don't like my jokes?"

"Come on, I'm curious. I wanna know."

"Alright, I'll tell you. There are two main operational modes for the tagmesh. Most are implanted with the standard type one program: the kind with the potential to eradicate memories. But if you join the navy, or work on the Disian ships…" Humbucker rolled his eyes, "or become an interplanetary explorer—any profession where you're required to pass outside the Protson field—the mesh program is downgraded to a type two, turning it into a simple data storage and tracking device. Magnatellan sailors are monitored in this way, once they reach the Cassafortan shores, to make sure they go no further."

He held his glass up to the firelight, swished the drink around a few times, and then took a sip, just as Domino's face brightened.

"I have an idea."

"Well, don't keep it to yourself."

"You can take us over in *The Dreamcatcher.* If you stay aboard, they won't come after you, right?" There was a pleading in her voice that Doran had seldom heard.

But Humbucker, recognizing that he could not fulfill the girl's wishes, exhaled dismally, clasping her hand in his. "I am so sorry, my dear friend. *The Dreamcatcher* is a tiny barge, an old-time vessel. She's not built for maritime endeavors, especially not the Disian Ocean... and it's more than four thousand miles to Cassaforta. Look, if she were made for the sea, I would whisk you across in a heartbeat, you know that. The truth is, a journey of such great distance requires a modern oceanic craft—one that is capable of sub-leptotronic speeds." The Sergeant looked despondent, and it saddened Doran. Eyes like Humbucker's, he thought, were meant always to be dazzling and impish.

"It doesn't matter," Domino told him, but Humbucker was gazing at the curling shapes in the hearth, lost in a meditative silence.

He took another nip of absinthe and then whispered, "I see how much it means to you to be free from the threat of the tagmesh—from being sent back to Earth. But worry not, child. We will travel to Port Isoboon. There, I will find a ship that can take you to Cassaforta."

THE PRESENT
Wednesday, January 28th, 2325

"Shoulda just flown there in one a' them floaties."

"Think about it," Weinberg says, all guru-like. "It wouldn't do for Cassafortans to spot one of those futuristic-looking things up there in the sky, would it? That's why the machines cease to function within a sixty-mile radius of Magnatella's coastline."

He twirls his pen for a while, waiting for me to comment, but getting words out seems more trouble than it's worth, somehow.

"Anyway, it was a point well made," he says. "It's about two thousand miles to the west coast from Banunus City, and high-end air-cars can be switched into sub-lepto mode—Barbastelles, Goshawks, brands like those. They can clock up to six thousand miles an hour, depending on wind speeds, of course, and how well tuned the engines are. Pretty handy things to have around when you're faced with a long-haul journey. The only problem was getting hold of one."

"So, how'd they manage it?"

DORAN'S STORY

"Buying tickets just isn't an option," Domino muttered, thinking out loud as she sat by the waterfront, tossing bread to the gulls. "There's five of us, and they cost way too much."

Humbucker was quiet, and Doran imagined he could hear the sailor's brain ticking over as he worked out a plan.

"We could borrow an air-car," Humbucker said at last. "We could take one, fly it over to Creoloone, then program it to return before it would ever be missed. That way, no one would come looking for us."

Doran opened his notebook and began to scribble ideas down. "What if we lifted one from the parking lot at Ballino Heights?"

"Good thinking," The Sergeant said, clicking his fingers. "Folks spend all day there, and the parking receipts always show the time of return. We'd know precisely when the owner was coming back." He paused, smiling at a small catamaran that was waiting in the lock. Then he tapped on Doran's notepad. "Pencil it in for the last Saturday in September. There's a naval parade that takes place every year in Port Donnelly. If anyone asks, we can say we have an invitation to join the main procession. Of course, I'll have to rip the NASA patches off my naval coat, but it's all in a good cause."

"Don't forget the caterpillar buttons," Domino added, her cheeks dimpling. "And that earring'll have to come out." She pointed to the silver Akkasine charm dangling from Humbucker's ear.

Doran passed his notebook to Domino. "I gotta go. Said I'd meet Barlin in Tierramont Square for a busking session, and I'm already running late."

After a short stroll through the Asternus district, mandolin tucked under his arm, he passed the grassy part of the square where two larger-than-life Dillinger statues were gazing down on everyone, and he could already hear his friend's cries.

"Get ya raffle tickets! Only two bans! Lovely mandolin up for grabs!" Barlin was sitting on the steps that led up to the Colonization Museum, his hat upturned. He was polishing the body of the much-cherished instrument that he liked to call Uma.

"You're not going to part with her, are you?" Doran sat down beside him, shuffling the deck of cards that Scout had given him on his first day out hustling. The smooth feel of the cotton-paper in his hands always calmed his nerves.

"No, course not. It's a scam. But no one's gonna come after us in Podunkia."

Barlin plucked at Uma's strings, and a few bars in, Doran recognized the tune as 'Man of Constant Sorrow', so he joined in on the old spruce mandolin that Barlin had helped him scrobble from a dusty old antique store. Then, when they got to the end of the number, two punters came up to them wanting tickets.

"Do you think Domino likes me?" Doran asked, once they'd

gone. "I mean, in a romantic kind of way? Sometimes I think she treats me more like a kid brother, but I'm only a year younger than her."

Barlin rattled the coins in his hat. "Hard to know," he said, doing his best not to grin too much. "Girls tend to like older guys; it's true. But don't be in too much of a hurry to grow up, Doran. It can be hard. Just enjoy being a kid for now. Things'll even out in time, you'll see."

He gestured over to the courthouse, where a patrol of three spider-like Tome-Bots were stalking the streets in the distance, the clatter of their metal feet echoing chillingly through the square.

"We better get out of here."

The last Saturday in September came around far too quickly for Doran, and, as they were packing to leave, he was dismayed to learn that Catlow had chosen to stay behind.

"You're really not coming?" He exhaled heavily, disheartened to be parting from her, but no more so than when he left the other children at Maple Road in search of Quin. That's just the way it was with him; provided his closest ally was present in his life, he was, more or less, mentally steadfast.

Catlow straightened his jacket collar, lean fingers pressing on his shoulders. She was much thinner now, as though the ghost of Scout was hiding in her bones somewhere—a slip of a girl. "The fight is here in Magnatella," she told him. "And going to Podunkia is like... running away. It's not what Scout would have wanted."

The old tavern's sign creaked slowly in the wind, and Doran thought it was like a protest, like the crescent moons were signaling their disagreement. "But once we get to Podunkia, we won't always be looking over our shoulders. We'll be safe there."

Catlow smiled at him, the way Amber used to sometimes when she was proud. "You're like a cactus, Doran. You grow without anyone needing to water you. I remember the first day you came here, and you talked about the people rising up against the tagmesh. I laughed to myself then, just like Barlin. But since we lost Scout, it's all I can think about." The smile faded and there was a sadness in her eyes. "Anyway, I'm going to do something," she said. "I don't know what exactly—not yet. But I feel the calling."

"What we're doing is risky, too. It's gonna take real guts," Domino said, noticing that Catlow's words had dampened Doran's spirits.

"Of course. But I've every faith in you. Your courage knows no bounds." Catlow embraced each of them, and when it got to Doran's turn, he felt like a fraud because she'd called him brave when, truth be told, fear was the only thing motivating him. He thought about Domino and how she could so easily be caught by the Tome-Bots, sent back to Earth, lost to him forever.

"All my hopes go with you," Catlow was saying. "Until the stars turn black."

Then, after a slick display of secret handshaking that Doran had never quite got to grips with, Domino slung her rucksack over her shoulder.

"Let's get going then, troops," she said. "Podunkia or bust."

By the time they found themselves in the grassy picnic area at Ballino Heights waiting for the operations to commence, Doran's stomach was practically turning somersaults. Stealing a car seemed markedly more serious than scrobbling for food, and far too much was riding on the outcome. All he could do was hover impatiently by one of the oak tables, while Domino sat cross-legged on top of it, studying The Sergeant's battered old map. He could see where she'd circled a coastal region to the southwest of Magnatella, and that it was labeled 'Port Isoboon' in small, swirly print.

When, at last, they were ready to select and seize the vehicle, The Sergeant first raised his flute to his lips, and Doran felt the knots in his stomach walls instantly unravel. The sounds, to his ears at least, seemed to be telling the story of a waterfall trickling lazily over rocks, everything gilded in mist and sunlight.

The music stopped and he saw that Carina had glided down from an enot tree, landing lithely on The Sergeant's forearm, but he was speaking to her so softly, Doran could only catch the final part: "... watch over them, *petit plumes de nuit.*" Humbucker set her down on the picnic table, then turned to Barlin, who had been tasked with bumping the locks.

Doran gazed at the two shrinking figures as they strode off toward the parking lot, Dol climbing slowly west across the windy morning sky. And all he could think was that he was spending his last moments in Banunus City—the vibrant, glittering metropolis that was the only place he'd ever called home.

THE PRESENT

The medic is detached and silent as usual while getting the happy juice ready—no Bovix vials rattling around on the tray this time. I guess there's no rule against talking first, though, and Weinberg left an hour ago, so I'm free to say whatever takes my fancy.

"There's stuff I could tell you about Cassaforta that would knock your socks off—Magnatella too."

The medic doesn't bat an eyelid. "That a fact?" she asks, cool as anything. She's chubby, freckled, and fresh-faced. And she smells so much of Cuticura Soap, I feel like I'm in a drugstore.

"You bet. But only town governors get to know about it."

The girl swabs a cotton ball over my thigh and dispenses the jab, wholly underwhelmed.

"You ain't gonna ask?"

She shrugs, as if getting back to the gossip in the staffroom is way more important, and a thorny wave of anger stabs me harder than the needle.

"You don't even care!"

"Look, Mr. Caldwell," she says, her gaze finally meeting mine. "You're Dr. Weinberg's mental patient, and he warned me this might happen. You live in your own little fantasy world. Whatever you might claim, it ain't gonna shock me. I'm just here to make sure you get your medication."

Somehow, the words wash over me. It's just like Harvey figured, and it sets me off chuckling softly to myself. "Well, you ain't doin' a very good job. You forgot the Bovix."

"That's comin' soon, honey," is all she says, and when she leaves, she bolts the door behind her.

Some three hours later, nobody's announcing anything. There's no, "This is your Bovix shot, Mr. Caldwell", but I know that's why they're here because at least five of the assholes are pinning me down. I struggle, fight so hard against them that I slide onto the floor, catching a glimpse of one of those manic Magnatellans bending over me—the ones with the weird voodoo masks. I try to raise my arm to grab at it, to see who's under there, but my limbs feel too heavy to move.

I'm aware of just one thing now: vibrations coming from the floorboards, tweeting sounds like birdsong speeded up, noises in full four-dimensional color, the fourth being time. It's beautiful in a trippy kind of way, but real creepy too. I'm just lying here, all thoughts and ideas stripped back, like I can't remember the right words for things. And all these indescribable notions I have in my head keep repeating, orchestrated by those bird sounds—by the fourth dimension in the images of them, the color representation of time, which passes in alternate beats of silence and terror. I can't count them. Numbers don't exist here.

I don't know if any of this is real, but I'm outside in a parking lot now, somewhere in the dead of night. I'm still in my jammies, goosebumps all over my arms. I sit up slowly, wearily, noticing someone who looks like Harvey lying next to me. He's totally zonked out, so I shake him.

"We escaped," he mumbles, stretching out his arms, scratching at his head.

"They gave me the Bovix, Harv. Just like you said."

"Damn. You know what that means?"

"No."

"It means I ain't Harvey."

"Shit!"

I tear across the lot, scooting over an old brick wall, landing in a heap of grassy compost in someone's backyard. Heart in my mouth, I creep over to the garden gate and peer out warily. Wallbanger's still stalking about, limping on his right leg, the sword dangling from his hand.

"Ain't no gettin' away from the truth, Caldwell," he hollers. "You'd better brace yerself."

A groundy passes, the light from its headlamps flashing over the sign facing the highway at the front of the lot, the words 'Sorley Ridge House' jumping out at me like something from a horror flick. And when I glance back at the building behind the yard, a silhouette stares out at me from a downstairs window. It's The Rooster. I just know it.

Then someone takes a slug at me, knocking me to the ground, and when I come around, I'm wrestled out of bed again, jabbed over and over with needles by a faceless voodoo Magnatellan, three others gripping me by the arms and legs.

"Rufus! Help me, man!"

"Rufus can't hear you," a male voice says from behind the mask. "He's already been sedated. It's best if you don't fight with us. We only want what's best for you, Doran."

"I ain't Doran!"

"Damn straight," Wallbanger says. "Don't let 'em fool ya, bud."

I didn't even know he was here. And he's so laid-back about it, I'd grab him by the collar if the shitheads weren't holding me down so tight.

"Bud? You were houndin' me with a goddamn blade out in the lot."

"Ain't no blade, Carney," he whispers. "You're just seein' it that way, 'cause a' the way things are. I can make 'em stop if you want—if you'll listen to what I gotta say."

But all their heads are planets now, orbiting gracefully around mine. I'm Dol, and my world is a blissful silent one because I have no ears.

24

Cobone Hill

I pushed another window open in the living room, then spun the dial on Lucy's Zenith F-510, the humidity clinging to me tighter than a mussel clamped on beach rock.

"Today, we're joined by climatology expert Cal Cassidy from the National Weather Service. So, Cal, can you tell us why July always brings a subtropical heatwave to Hap County?"

"Sure thing, Archer. It's all down to high pressure in the north comin' in from the Pleasian Ocean, pushin' warm air onto the ground…"

"Leyland, what's for dinner?"

"Salad. Too damn hot to cook." He came in with a half-sliced tomato still in his hand. "There's a fan in the attic. Why don'cha bring it down? Lucy'll be glad of it."

I started for the stairs, but then the phone rang, so I picked it up.

"Hi, Carney."

"What's up, Books? You 'bout ready to wilt, same as the rest of us?"

"Just callin' to say we're gettin' together on Cobone Hill tonight."

Cobone was one of the Bolar Hills, just a short walk from The Willows, where the Curzons and the Pachellos lived. Meeting there was a stroke of genius because the trees offered more than enough shade, and the old water tower at the top had a small redbrick building at the side of the shaft, which was real cool and airy inside.

Earl and I rolled in just after seven. Dol hadn't let up, so our mouths were dry as chalk dust by the time we got there, and Earl didn't waste a second. He plucked one of the beers from the duffel bag, pried the lid off, and took a long, hard slug.

"Lay it on me, man," he said, flopping down onto the quilt next to Mackenzie.

He dubbed her an Arch Angel the day she agreed to go out with him, but I was finding it hard to accept her. She spoke like some wannabe actress, droning on endlessly about the Gazelles, and I hated that she was taking Dakota's place in the gang. I didn't let on how rattled she got me, though. I mean, Earl was my best buddy, and I guess that was just the way Lucy raised me. *Think it, but don't say it. Never bad-mouth anyone.*

"Can't believe we'll be graduatin' Monday." Booker tried to smile, but she looked so blue I could tell her mind was on bigger things than quaffing ale. I guess the thought of going to college was bittersweet for her. She was eager to get to Magnatella, but that meant leaving Hailey's Town behind—permanently.

"It's a huge deal for you, what with headin' off to Amchuda an' all," Earl said. "But for me 'n' Carney, I guess it don't matter so much. We're stayin' put."

"End of an era, though, bud." I nabbed a Wild Bandit, downed a few swigs, and then rolled the bottle slowly across my forehead. "There's still a month before you set sail, right, Books?"

"I'll be leavin' August twenty-first."

Mackenzie lit a Dimer and leant against Earl's chest. "I'll be cheerin' loud as I do for the Triple Gees when you lot get your diplomas," she said, overdoing the melodrama as usual. "Might even end up bawlin', what with havin' to move away an' all."

"What you sayin'?" Earl looked at her all bug-eyed and open-mouthed, pretending like he was shocked to the core, but he was just playing it for laughs.

"Sorry to spring it on y'all like this," Mackenzie went on, "but I only just found out. My folks applied for jobs in Lope Horn Town a while back. Got the offer letters this mornin'."

Lope Horn was more than eight hundred miles out of Hailey's. I remembered it from geography. It was back east in the Placops belt, famous for all the jooba fruit. Part of me felt like punching the air, but the shame of that made the whole thing seem thorny.

"It's so far from Grade Glennin's, it might as well be on Akkasine," Mackenzie said, as beads of sweat formed on her Egyptian-goddess-like nose and cheeks. "That's the worst of it. Won't get to be with Earl, and I won't get to see the Gazelles play no more, neither."

I was full-on expecting Earl to act out in some way, but all he did was wink at her. "We'll see," he said, beaming like he'd just found a twenty-ban note stuffed under a couch cushion.

We played Candy Land for a while, and then, when it was getting on for dusk and a light wind had drifted in from the east, we left the tower and sat under one of the enot trees, a festival of downy little dandelion seeds floating randomly through the air like drunken fairies.

"If you catch one in your left hand, you can make a wish," Mackenzie said.

"I told you to stop all that. I ain't gonna turn into Henshaw in the middle a' the night, no matter how many you grab." Earl was grinning so much he was probably getting a jaw-ache, and

Mackenzie was forced to beat up on him. "She still carries that cut-out round with her," Earl said, as he tried to fight her off.

"Ain't true. Anyway, you can talk. You wrote to Jeanne Crain in Magnatella and asked for a lock of hair."

"Shut up, Mackenzie. Let Earl alone." I filled my lungs with the sweet smell of freshly cut ryegrass. It was good to feel some energy flowing through my bones again. The sky was turning the color of mulberry wine and Dol was slipping down like a sinking ship, drowsy from swilling it. I snatched at a passing fairy and caught it in my left hand.

"Make a wish, then," Booker said. "Somethin' that just might come true."

I gazed across the hills, and it struck me that, from up here, the town didn't just look miniature and far away, but tired, old, and weak—as if it had been planted in the middle of nowhere for no good reason, and it was crying out from its roots for a purpose—a link with something other than itself. To the west, I could see the creek snaking through a score of patchwork fields on its way up north to Hap Town—a vein in the flesh of Hailey's, carrying its very lifeblood. And seeing it on a night so sweet and warm brought a stab of mental pain—an aching in the core of me that was hard to shoulder. I sighed, flopping backward onto the grass for a while, wishing only that it was last summer instead.

Booker prodded me. "Well? Ain't you gonna share?"

"Just wish it would cool down some."

"It will. Just needs to get a bit darker is all."

We sat quiet for a while, and I didn't dare look back at Hailey's until Dol sank down altogether, and a web of tiny orange lights was all you could see—a shiny citrine necklace draped across the landscape. There was something real noble about those distant streetlamps—the way they were just sitting there, silently heralding the coming of night-time.

"Damn it. Let's go on a long hike—bring some tents and stuff." I plonked my beer down so hard on the grass, some of it splashed out. "It'd be like a vacation—somethin' to celebrate our last days together. Gowder knows, we need to blow off steam after all them goddamn exams we've suffered just lately."

Earl's eyes were gleaming. "That's an awesome idea," he said, giving me an almighty high five. "I've got an old tunnel tent in the attic. Sleeps four, I reckon."

Booker screwed her face up, the somber peep of giddyback birds echoing over from the woods. "Graduation's happenin' Monday, Caldwell. Don't tell me you forgot already."

"We'll be back by then, Books," I said, beaming. "We'll follow the Ditania Trail out to Bajenco. You've walked it a ton a' times. Hell, we could even hitch a ride over to Tennacia Bay."

Mackenzie shook her head. "That's miles away. Booker's right—we'd never make it back in time."

"We would if we left tonight." I stood up and began gathering up the empties, stuffing them one by one into the duffel bag, then zipping it shut. "Who's in?"

"Let's make it interestin'," Earl said, raising his eyebrows. "Betcha fifty bans we miss the ceremony. Me an' Kenzie versus you and Books."

"You're on."

Booker parked the Hornet at the foot of the hill, and we fetched the cookout nosh and camping gear from the trunk. Then Earl let Bear out the back seat, and we started up the steps on the west of the slope, Booker leading the way, the pampas grass at the sides rippling gently like the waves of a long-forgotten ocean. There was a stillness about the mountainside at night that kind of made my spine tingle. It was as if Cobone had an actual soul—an ancient presence that seemed to be watching out for anyone brave enough to tackle it in the darkness. And as we pushed on further to the top, I started to wonder what it was like to be a critter out there, relying on the Bolars for warmth, shelter, and food. I could hear the woof-like whoop of spotted owls above us in the trees, and every so often, the wavering yips of coyotes prowling across the scrubland on the hunt for prey.

When we got to the gateway in front of Ditania Country Park, Booker spread out the map, the cone from her flashlight drawing in a couple of lulite moths that kept fluttering round it. "Been hikin' out here with my folks so many times I lost count," she said. "Two or three weeks solid, just campin' out under the stars. You'd think I'd know the way by now."

"Well, there's a bunch a' different trails. Easy to get mixed up." I glanced over my shoulder. Earl and Mackenzie were straggling behind with Bear, so I figured it was a good time to ask about Dakota. "Been nearly six weeks since Kota left Crosswinds," I said. "Have you heard from her?" Her folks had sent her to spend the summer with an aunt and uncle who ran a vineyard and brewery over in Barraleah—one of those rustic towns tucked away in the Gellatirran Plains, some fifty miles inland from the southwest coast.

"She called me once or twice," Booker said, trying to smile. "Think she's made a few friends out there. And her aunt pays her a decent wage for workin' in the vineyard. She's learnin' so much about how a brewery works… how to run a business too, I dare say. It's been real good for her, spendin' summer there."

I pointed my beam at the big acacia sign nailed to the gate, so that Booker could see which footpath was which. What I was planning to say next took some pluck, so I dithered a while, just breathing in the warm cedar-scented air. "Sure would be great to have her Barraleah number, Books—if she's up to talkin' with the old gang again."

Booker was looking down, still trying to figure out the routes on the map. "She ain't quite there yet, Carney," she said quietly.

Then she glanced up at me, her face solemn. "Don't mention any a' this to the others, but I was ear-hustlin' once, when my old man was on the phone to hers. I reckon Kota thought she killed Ranton, Taylor was gonna rat her out, and her jacket was evidence for the whole damn thing."

The words made me swallow so hard and so sudden my eyes started to bulge. "Jeez, that's heavy stuff," I mumbled, hoping Booker didn't notice how gawky I was sounding. "Did she say anythin' about comin' back?"

"Oh, she'll be back, bud, come September when school starts again." Booker flicked off the flashlight and shook her head. "Can't help worryin', though. I ain't gonna be here."

A cloud slid past the oat-yellow crust of Akkasine as it waxed gibbous high up in the north, while Akkasom waned, poking out a powder-blue crescent just above the horizon. I checked my watch and couldn't help but smile when I saw the akka-dials were spot on.

"It'll be alright, Books," I said, stuffing the flashlight back inside my pocket. "I'll keep an eye on her. It's maybe a good thing I ain't goin' away to college this year, after all."

Sunday, July 20th, 2324

At dawn, I unzipped the pop-up tent's storm flaps and peered out. Mist was crawling over sun-yellowed countryside, Dol easing up from its lazy coral bed, and in the distance, you could just about make out the pointed shapes of marble foxes stealing across the plains. There was a real sense of the world stirring from slumber. Even the hills pushing up through the fog seemed to be yawning and stretching.

Last night, we hiked non-stop until we stumbled on Mallanbury Moor in the dark, about five miles shy of Bajenco.

Then we had to pitch the tents by flashlight, so by the time we got our heads down it was about two in the morning. Now that I was up, I guessed the others wouldn't thank me for waking them, so I dressed real quiet and wandered over to the other side of the field to get my bearings, suddenly feeling Bear's warm breath as he panted at my heels. I knelt down to pet him, smoothing out his ears and running my fingers through his neck fur.

"You're up early, boy. Guess you're excited to be out in the country, huh?" He trotted in the other direction a few yards, then stopped in his tracks, turning to look back at me, tongue hanging out. "You wanna go that way? Come on, then."

He led me down through a ragbag of hayfields and heather meadows, past a beat-up old outhouse that looked uncannily like a sad old face. The windows, high up in the eaves, were the eyes, and the shadows of alder branches, winding over the whitewashed stone, were its wrinkles. A few hundred yards further down, we found ourselves in a moor-grass pasture bordering the roadside and, just as I was planning to turn back, I saw Bear pawing at something in the undergrowth.

"What's up, buddy?" He was pulling at a thick plastic sack jammed under a privet hedge, and when I caught up to him, he unclamped his jaws from it and just sat there, wagging his tail, proud as punch. "Good boy. Yup, you did great." I ruffled the fur along his spine, and then bent down to see what he'd found.

The bag was waterproof but had been tied up with rotted string that fell apart just as soon as I tugged at it, the whole thing sagging open, spilling out a wad of faded paper packets. I tore into one, my stomach lurching when I glimpsed the clutch of little lime-green cubes tangled up in leaves. Without a second thought, I crammed everything back inside, refastened the bag, and shoved it under the hedge again.

"It was great work findin' it, Bear, but it's gotta stay put."

When I got back to camp, Dol was ripe like a tangerine, and the glorious smell of barbecues was wafting everywhere. Mackenzie was buttering bread rolls on the fold-up table, and Earl was busy frying plant rashers on the portable stove.

"Just in time for breakfast," he said, winking, as he watched them sizzle and pop.

"Say, is there a disused railroad anywhere near here?"

"You mean the Tundles line?" Booker was all sprawled out in the clovers, sipping from a can of soda as she tucked into one of Earl's hoagies. She fished the map from her rucksack and studied it, wiping breadcrumbs from it every now and then. "Yeah, down in the valley on the north side. Not far away at all. Why?"

"No reason. Just thought I could see it from up on the moor when I was walkin' with Bear." I didn't want to bring up the rush. It didn't seem right, given that this was meant to be the Arch Angels' last great fling before graduation.

In any case, all eyes were on Earl because he was busy juggling three bread rolls in the air. Then he caught one in his teeth, tossing another to Mackenzie, who sliced it in two, almost like they'd rehearsed the whole skit. The Marcels' 'Blue Moon' was purring out the radio, and Mackenzie started singing along, all the while working the two roll halves up and down. Then everyone was joining in, bopping round the hob with pieces of warbling bread, me included. There was so much craziness going on, Mackenzie knocked the lighter fuel over, and the stove blew up, setting the grass alight, singeing both her eyebrows and Earl's hair on the right-hand side. Booker flung her soda at the hob, but she missed and ended up dousing me, so Earl lobbed a wet cloth over the stove, and then we were all stomping on the grass, beating wildly at it with dish towels until the flames finally fizzled out.

"Good mornin', campers," Earl said, deadpan as he could manage, using a wooden spoon in place of a mic. "We're sorry to inform you there will be no breakfast service this mornin'. Unfortunately, the chef got skunked and can't get his pants on. I repeat: no pants, no pancakes."

By ten o'clock, we were squashed onto a wooden bench outside a tiny post office in picturesque Bajenco. The temperature was creeping up, the haversacks were weighing us down like lead cannons, and reaching Tennacia Bay was starting to feel like an impossible dream. The plan had been to cadge a ride on one of the big farm trucks that passed through on the way to Grade Glennings, but we had to wait another two hours before Earl spotted a gleam of silver way off in the distance.

"Is that a truck?"

"Probably a mirage." I loped into the center of the road, waving my arms about as the wagon got closer.

Booker giggled. "Look. It's Windy."

Earl's eyes lit up like skyrockets. He dashed over to where I was standing, launching himself into the same old schtick, arms in full swing. "Sorry, Mr. Thackery. I didn't mean to draw them diagrams. I get muddled up sometimes 'cause of all that wind blowin' through m' belly." It seemed all the wackier, what with his hair all frazzled up like that. He carried on, only quitting when the ten-ton diesel truck pulled over and a burly-looking driver stuck his head out the window.

"You kids need a ride? There's room for one in the cab, but the rest of you'll have to pitch in with the cargo."

I scanned the payload. The cab was hooked up to a steel trailer full to the brim with industrial-sized garbage containers.

"I call shotgun," Booker yelled.

Earl just scowled. "Damn it, Caldwell. Looks like you're gonna clean up after all."

25

The Barbastelle

"It's quite a capricious little machine," Weinberg says, placing a steaming-hot beaker of coffee in front of me. "But I managed to wrangle these from it." He settles himself into the floral chair, then takes a few sips from his own.

I've been biding my time, waiting for him to stroll in so's I can fly off the handle, vent all the anger that's been festering away since I talked with the medic. But now that he's here, the only urge I have is to fling the cup against the wall—slam it so hard it'll splash clean across the empty rectangle. I'd have a real painting to gape at then. But somehow, I can't bring myself to do it.

"I'm your mental patient, am I? Livin' in some fantasy world?" My voice comes out softer than I thought, but my legs have turned to jelly, and my breath's so jerky I'm forced to break off. "It was me those janitors were on about, first night I was here. It was me all along. I'm Doran. You oughta just fess up now, asshole. You're tryin' to drug me with that Bovix stuff—to turn me back into him. And while we're on the subject, why'd you lie about the goddamn diary?"

Weinberg makes a slow blink, sighs real heavy, his shoulders slumping forward. I can see this is a moment he secretly hoped would never come. "Look, Carney," he says. "You must understand that this 'mental patient' business was all just a cover—a precaution, let's call it. I had to say those things for your own protection—in fact, for the good of everyone on the planet. The people who work here can't be exposed to the truth. It's best they believe your blathering to be nothing more than a crazy man's delusion." He nudges the beaker in my direction, waits for me to talk, but my arms are folded tight across my chest. "And, yes, you took my diary. But I didn't know what you read, so I made out it was a dream—again, for your own good. Mental health isn't just about being sane or crazy, you know. You're in no fit state to hear all these truths at once."

I'm still glaring at him.

"Look. If you really don't want it, I'll make sure you're taken off the Bovix."

"Damn right you will."

"Come on," he urges. "Don't fall out with me. In the end, you'll see that I made all the right choices, and in the meantime, we'll carry on with the story." He turns a page in the binder, purses his lips, and looks over at me for a while. "You know, a major concern for our intrepid absconders was the mismatch between vehicle owner and driver. They were painfully aware that scans of the car's ID chip and Humbucker's type two tagmesh would quickly bring that to light."

DORAN'S STORY

They got away with a Barbastelle Luxfloat SL-H7 in the end. It was only two years old, very sleek and stylish, but I guess you don't need all the details.

Despite stowing away on a leptotronic spaceship, Domino had never traveled in an air-car before, not even for short journeys, so she insisted on riding up front next to The Sergeant. Doran, of course, recalled his days at the orphanage, and the frequent visits to the Palderboon district, which always ended with an air-ride back home. But, fascinated as he was by the vehicles, he didn't want to argue with the seating plan. He was content just to sit in the back, Carina nestled sleepily on his knee, the tickle of her feathers soothing his disquiet.

"What's he doing?" he whispered, nodding at the twenty-something flight technician, who was sitting in the driver's seat, busily tapping away at the navicom's keypad.

"He's programming the lepto trajectory," Barlin explained.

Doran stared at the complex assortment of blinking lights, digital gauges, and manual switches arranged on the dashboard. Then he peered through the window, marveling at the mélange of miniscule streets and buildings down below them. He let his eyes wander to the edge of the horizon, and wondered, momentarily, if it was possible to see Maple Road, but the landscape appeared so small and confusing, he couldn't recognize anything. He ruffled Carina's neck plumes and then, when he remembered how big a risk they were taking, silently wished for the mellowness of Humbucker's flute music, so his mind could return once more to the tranquility of the waterfall.

The technician stepped out onto the sky-ledge where Humbucker was waiting. Then he scanned the vehicle's chip, keyed some data into a handheld device, and waited. You see, any mistakes in the sub-lepto calculation can prove disastrous. That's why the routes need to be verified by Sky Control; vehicles can only be punched into sub-lepto mode once they've been granted a code of sanction, or COS code.

"Just need to check your tagmesh," the engineer said, waving the same contraption over the sailor's forehead, but he frowned when he saw the readings. "Your name's D'Argent?"

"Yes, that's correct."

The vehicle behind them hooted in impatience, and it startled Doran so much that, on pure reflex, he pushed his fingers deep into the foam of the seat in front.

"You're a type two?"

"That's right. I'm a naval officer and this vehicle is government property. I'm taking part in the grand parade tomorrow over at Port Donnelly, along with my sea-scouts." Humbucker spoke with such authority, Doran found himself almost swallowing the tale, but the attendant's brows were still knitted tightly together.

"I see you're licensed to drive a sub-lepto, but this one's registered to a Mason Edwards."

"He's the admiral over at Hattersley Base. If you zap him, he'll confirm everything."

The other car sounded its horn again, forcing Doran's heart almost to leap from his body. And all the while, the technician kept swapping his gaze between his readouts, the license plate, and Humbucker, a bewildered look on his face.

"Why's the vehicle coming straight back unattended?"

"To collect another party."

"Okay. Wait while I zap the admiral."

By now, Doran's nerves had reached breaking point. He flung the car door open and hurled himself out onto the sky-ledge on his belly. "The admiral's my father," he wailed. "Please don't call him. He banned me from the parade, but all I want is to take part. Please."

"Let him do his job, Doran," Humbucker said, but the young man's puzzled look faded, and he nodded casually, winking at the pair of them. Doran got up, smiling gratefully, as the technician printed out the COS code and handed it to Humbucker. Then he went into the standard patter.

"Your route's been approved by Sky Control. I guess you know the drill, but I'm obliged to repeat it. Enter the digits into the flight computer, pull up to the jitter screen, punch her into SL, and as soon as I have final clearance, I'll release the hatch and you'll be on your way. Have a safe trip."

Humbucker thanked him, opened the back door for Doran, and scooched back into the cabin, snapping his safety belt into place. He keyed the COS code into the navicom, released a catch between the two front seats, and then tapped the gas pedal, the vehicle coasting forward a couple of feet until the bumper was butting up against a metal sheet about the size of a garage door. Next, he thumped a button on the steering wheel, the car hissing and juddering so violently Doran had to grab onto the handle above the door. He watched as the technician jerked a lever upward, and then, for a split second only, he was aware of feeling nauseous, weightless, and breathless all at once, before slipping out of consciousness altogether.

When he came to, he found himself staring up at the roof upholstery. He was still in the back, but his head was resting on Domino's lap, and Barlin was in the front, seemingly oblivious to the mighty whooshing sound that was making all the windows rattle. The air smelled strangely acidic, like soldering iron, but everyone was calm, so Doran allowed himself to relax a little, smiling dizzily at Domino.

"I dreamed I was one of Carina's feathers."

Humbucker glanced over at him. "I knew you wouldn't be out for too long," he said. "And don't worry, Doran; it's perfectly normal to pass out the first time you go sub-lepto."

Twenty minutes later, the cabin fell almost silent. There was just a faint whine from the navicom, followed by the determined click of the locking system, and then a motorized whirring sound as the doors slid slowly open. Doran heard the succession of noises almost as a poem—a musical interlude that was hinting at something simultaneously awe-inspiring and terrifying, but he pushed all doubts aside and told himself they were doing the right thing. Carina was the first one out, scuttling down from the dashboard onto the seat and then half-hopping, half-flapping onto the sky-ledge.

The docking station was virtually identical to the one from which they'd come, except that the flight controller was a somewhat gangly-looking service bot with large, round camera lenses for eyes. Humbucker approached it, explaining that the vehicle was returning directly to the point of origin with no passengers.

"Roger that," the robot said, and once they'd retrieved their backpacks from the trunk, it extended a spindly arm toward the elevator, gesturing for them to climb inside.

When they strode out of the lift shaft at ground level and into the bustle of the arrivals lounge, Doran was struck by the vastness of a Plexiglas sign that ran the full width of the exit, the writing flashing across it so fast, it seemed to be shrieking at them:

WELCOME TO CREOLOONE SKYPORT.

THE PRESENT

The ceiling has eyes, watching me, frowning, judging. I draw on the last of Weinberg's amber-scented Oakwood Milds, thinking how it's just a trick of the smoke and the moonlight.

I guess it's all falling into place now. Doran's set to cross the Disian Ocean, and at some point he'll be tagged and forget everything. Maybe it's a blessing if my own story is a pack of lies; it means I didn't beat up on my best buddy. But then, who is it lying unconscious someplace, and why did they run me in?

Cuticura Soap comes in bang on midnight. I watch her fingers ballet-dance across my arm, feel the sharp scratch of the needle, but the past seems too out of reach tonight, like there's no point wallowing in someone else's thoughts.

Who am I? Maybe a more fitting question is: *What* am I?

"You there, Wallbanger? We gotta talk, man. I saw the message. Who else did I fry?"

And then I'm out in the corridor, like I've slipped into some weird ethereal time loop, where I discover the crank's room is nothing more than a closet, over and over. The lights are dimmed and no one's around, so I tap twice on the door.

"Come in, Carney. We've been expectin' you."

The room is identical to mine, except that there are two beds, two high-up windows with bars, and two patches on the wall where paintings must have hung. Harvey and Wallbanger are chained to their beds, both grinning at me, but in totally different ways. Wallbanger's jeering; Harvey just looks stoked to see me. I can only tell them apart because their names are written on whiteboards above the beds.

"Don't fret," Harvey says. "He can't hurt you while I'm here."

"They got you all chained up, huh?"

"So's we don't rip each other to shreds," Wallbanger says, and Harvey snorts with laughter, then frowns at me.

"Don't tell the medics what you saw in here. They'll move you to Sorley Ridge, for sure."

Wallbanger wrinkles his nose. "I don't care what you tell 'em. It's a battle of wills at the end a' the day. And I'm gonna win. There's no way to stop it. Doran's real, and he's important—"

"Shut your goddamn mouth," Harvey yells. "Don't listen to his lies, Carney. Remember all that shit with the mirror? How can you trust a guy like that? Just focus on the past. It's all you got left. You said it yerself."

He gestures to the empty rectangle above his bed, where

something's taking shape: a forest of pine trees spilling down into the Great Hap Water Hide, mainstem of Pettiworn Creek. Lucy used to take us camping out there every summer before the stroke, and the last time was when I was fourteen and Earl came along. I remember we were bombing along the dirt roads of the Old Kandal Valley in Lucy's trusty Ford F1, and Earl just wouldn't shut up about Elvis. It was driving Lucy nuts.

"If you mention that man one more time, I swear, I'll sling ya goddamn sneakers out the window."

"Well, thank you very much."

That night, while we were huddled round the campfire, the carp started jumping up out the hide. We'd throw them a piece of sourdough bread and they'd catch it in their mouths before plopping right back in.

"Fifteen years ago, I sat right here with Dolly," Lucy told us. "We saw a shootin' star, and your ma wished the night would last forever."

"Look at the picture," Harvey says, his eyes pleading with me. "Are fish leapin' up out the canvas? Are shootin' stars blazin' by? Is Earl harpin' on endlessly about Elvis? If you focus real hard, maybe you can actually hear them."

"He's so full of crap," Wallbanger says, the image evaporating instantly. "You gotta let go of the past, Caldwell. Move on, for cryin' out loud."

"Okay, but what's the deal with that goddamn dream I had when I was six years old? What was the machine? What did I change by movin' that box, by runnin' away? Is it all just paranoia? Or is it somethin' to do with Doran and the tagmesh?"

Harvey's tutting. "Sweet irony," he says. "There's Weinberg, tryin' to convince folks you're nuts, an' all the time you really are. I mean, you can't think for a minute that either of us is real."

I march over to his bed, heart thumping wildly, legs so wobbly it's like the bones have just plain dissolved. "You shut yer trap, Harvey Wilder. You're like a goddamn B-side—the part nobody wants."

"Guess that makes me the A-side," Wallbanger says, smirking just a bit. "But Harvey does have a point. You're sufferin' from mild schizophrenia, brought on by the rush. I mean, that's when you first started obsessin' about the dream, about B-sides, cobwebs, and the like. Correct me if I'm wrong."

"No, you ain't wrong, Wallbanger. Sorry I yelled."

"You better get gone while I'm bitin' my tongue," he says. "Next time we meet, it'll be the showdown."

I turn to leave, suddenly aware that the room has shrunk, gotten darker. I fumble for the handle, stepping out into the blandness of the corridor. And when I turn back to look, there's nothing but wooden shelves stuffed full of toilet paper, sheets, and towels.

26

Tennacia Bay

THE PAST

Tennacia Bay was part of the Jigdips, a geologically old and rugged coastline that sank a fifty-mile-wide bite into the granite bedrock of Northern Cassaforta, churning up a string of secluded little coves with calm turquoise waters, all of them tucked away under towering cliff faces.

"Sure feels good to see old Tufty again, eh, Carney?" Earl took the lead as we wove down the steps to the bay, the sweeping curve of the pearly-blue Bochartinian Sea stretching away in front of us.

"Yup, almost wanted to throw a stick for him."

Mackenzie frowned. "Who's Tufty?"

"It's the headland," Earl told her, as Bear trotted at his heels, his tail swishing so fast it was like a fan cooling my shins and ankles. "It's made a' welded tuff. Looks just like a lazy red dog."

Tufty's rump and tail were on the seaward side, and on the landward side a knoll that was the spitting image of a canine head was propped against a thin limestone outcrop, as if he was busy guarding an old, dry bone.

I gestured toward the row of spiky basalt pillars over on the east side. The first time I saw them, Lucy said they were like a band of giant sentries, forever watching over the bay. "Wonder what turned those poor grunts to stone."

Booker caught up to us, pausing on the steps to get a good look. "Reckon it was moonlight magic. There was a battle, a thousand years ago, and Akkasine punished 'em for fallin' asleep when they were s'posed to be on guard duty." She wrinkled her nose and scowled. "You lot don't smell so great."

"You wouldn't, neither, if you'd been ridin' in the back with all those rotten-smellin' trash cans," Mackenzie said sharply. "It was four hours, an' Dol was beatin' down so hard, we thought we'd pass out. Tell her, Earl."

"Everythin'll be hunky-dory once we get down to the beach," Earl said. "Just you wait 'n' see."

We quickened our pace and ended up galloping down the steps like a herd of wild mustangs. And when I threw myself into the ocean's glorious lukewarm waters, it felt better than Disneyland.

"This is what it's all about."

I lay on my back and floated, letting the waves steer me gently out toward the small rocky islet that Earl and I had dubbed Angel's Point, almost ten years ago. The water was so calm and shallow, Earl and Mackenzie had already waded out to it, and now they were sunning themselves at the edge, Bear at the side of them.

"You remember that time we got lost up on the cliffs, Hunter? Ended up seein' all those nestin' puffins?"

"Sure do. It was when we found that upturned rowin' boat in the sand, and we sculled out past Tufty, usin' shovels as oars."

"It was one hell of a walk back to the cottage," I said, chuckling. "Lucy got so mad, I got sent to bed with no supper."

"My folks got pretty boiled an' all, but it was totally worth it. Never seen so many birds all in one place." Earl sat up, gazing out at the peninsula, his eyes squinting in the sunlight, his hand flattened out just below his brow.

"How old were you?" Mackenzie was dangling her legs in the ocean, swirling them about, but not so hard that it made a splash; she was just enjoying stirring up the water.

"About ten, I reckon," Earl said. "Woulda been the year before we met Kota."

At first, her name cropping up out the blue felt like the biting sting of jellyfish venom. But then I remembered she was coming back, that Earl knew all about it, and I loosened up again, thinking about the sound of her name for the first time in a long while. There was a calmness about those syllables—the cadence of them—and if you whispered the word in the right way, it was almost like a poem—a flurry of sighing blown across deserts by some ageless Aeolian wind. And there in the bay, a hair's breadth from Angel's Point, hearing it seemed not only apt and heartening, but strangely poignant and prophetic.

I didn't get to muse over it for long, though, because a bout of cussing was echoing over from the bluff.

"What's goin' on back there?"

We splashed our way over to see what all the fuss was about. It turned out Booker had been puffing away at a massive inflatable beach chair, but it'd burst on a rock when she went scurrying out to the ocean, and now she was busy booting it round the cove in a hot and sweaty rage.

"Damn you, you no-good piece of shit!" She gave it a final kick that sent it spinning into the crags, bouncing down across lumps of scree, and finally settling in a rock pool.

Earl tapped her on the shoulder. "What's up, Books? You're lookin' kinda deflated."

"Left the goddamn pump at home," she said, her face all red, sweat trickling down it. "Blew it up with my own breath."

"Chill out, man," I said. "It's only a chair."

And then Booker saw the funny side, and we took turns booting it down the beach, until it glided out into the sea.

"These're the moments you'll remember all ya life," Earl called out, as he charged in after it.

We spent the rest of the afternoon either swimming in the ocean, sitting by the shoreline, or exploring the rock pools. We talked, goofed around, waded, skimmed stones, and hunted for bochart shells, stringing them together with twine to make necklaces, and Earl thought it would be a neat prank if we all wore them to graduation.

"No one'll know why we got 'em danglin' round our necks," he said. "They'll be scratchin' their heads so hard, everyone'll think they got fleas."

As the evening wore on, Dol started to sink behind the headland, tinting the rippling waters flamingo, and I thought how strange and beautiful it was: the union of an orb of fire a hundred million miles away, and the shiny mirror of an ocean where I was standing at the shoreline, just watching it happen.

We unpacked the bags and started rigging the tents again, and all the while I felt moved, mindful that a whole chapter of my life was drawing to a close. I wondered if my schooldays would slip away as dreamily as Dol, and what the horizon might look like without them. And then I realized we hadn't been drawn here on any kind of whim. It was more to do with craving a rubber stamp—something that could mark the transition from one phase of our lives to the next. Coming here was like a living rite of passage—a treasure to grasp onto whatever time, in its dutiful and detached way, might foist upon us.

We lit a fire just outside the tepee so as we could roast wild hoshoo nuts and corn on the cobs, and then settled ourselves on the slabs under one of the basalt soldiers. Mackenzie flicked the radio on, and we played pontoon with different-colored pebbles, while Bear dozed next to Earl, and The Dells belted out

'Oh What a Night'. By the time we'd done feasting, the station was spinning The Spaniels' 'Goodnight, Sweetheart, Goodnight', and Earl got up to slow-dance with Mackenzie, barefoot, in one of the little rock pools that the tide had left behind. The sun had dragged a blue-black blanket in its wake, but it was filled with stars, and the sky seemed almost like a proclamation—a promise of Dakota on the jetty come fall, a bottle of Grimley's clasped in her hand, and a smile as broad as an oak tree. And so, I watched them, and in the shapes of their dancing I saw the shapes of our dancing—Dakota swaying gracefully to the rhythm of the music, her head pressed lightly against my shoulder.

"Would you do me the honor?" Booker was offering me her hand, bursting the little bubble of bliss I'd dreamed up. I didn't like turning her down, but it seemed kind of hinky to swap the idea of Dakota for the reality of a different girl.

"No, thanks. I'm gonna take an evenin' dip. You can come if you want." We kicked off our shoes and padded out to the ocean, the sand cool against the soles of our feet.

"Gotta be in our sleepin' bags well before midnight," Booker said. "Need to set my alarm for five, so's we can get back in time. And not just for some lame bet. I worked damn hard for this, Carney."

"I know, Books."

When my eyes jarred open, my watch was reading half past seven, so I wandered out my tent. Dol had already claimed its throne, the ocean a diamond-studded cloak shimmering in front of it. I cussed silently and quickly roused the others.

"Never went off," Booker mumbled, snatching at her Mickey Mouse alarm clock, shaking it violently. "Sand got inside. Damn hands are stuck."

I went to check mine, and it was the same story. Circling gulls shrieked loud as banshees as we ran around the beach, scooping everything up and squashing it all, bit by bit, into the backpacks. Booker was in such a frenzy, she didn't look where she was going, and ended up tripping over a lump of slippery driftwood, spraining her ankle so bad she had to hop everywhere.

"Still think we'll make graduation, Caldwell? Reckon me 'n' Earl got the action all sewed up." There was something real weaselly about the look in Mackenzie's eye, and I twigged right away.

"*You* put the sand in our alarm clocks." Suddenly, I couldn't stand to look at her. "Did you know about this, Hunter?"

"Not me, man."

"Okay," Mackenzie said, still grinning like a moron. "It was me. But all's fair in love 'n' war. Snuck into yer tent at about two in the mornin'."

"Love?" Earl glared, first at her, then at me. "You sure it wasn't just the clock you were messin' with?"

"You take that back, Hunter." I was so hacked off with him for coming out with such a crackbrained notion, I fixed him with the meanest scowl I could pull. I was so damn mad, I was shaking, but Mackenzie still had that same dumb expression on her face. She was giggling.

"Don't fight over me, boys."

"Why, I wouldn't fight over you if you were the last girl alive. You're a goddamn embarrassment; that's what you are—an annoyin', self-centered little shithead."

We didn't talk much the whole ride back, except to agree that the bet was null and void. To make matters worse, Bear stank of horse manure, a can of orange paint spilled out over us in the back of the truck, and one of my rucksacks blew away when a juggernaut cruised past us at seventy on the Longboon Highway.

27

The Rattling Skeleton

There's a watercolor in the rectangle: an empty vase shaped something like a pineapple, but smoother. It must have fallen and smashed at some point, because you can see the lines where the shards have been glued back into place. I wish some dahlias or lilies would appear inside it—anything to make it brighter—but it's just a blob of jagged jade-green chunks, set against the drabness of the wall.

I've been thinking a lot about Lucy, too—all those little pearls of wisdom she used to come up with, way back when, before she was mostly mute, and how she was so tough, funny, smart, deep, and cool. Maybe that's why I dreamed up the painting. It could be I'm just trying to build something out of what I remember about her—piece her back together like the shattered pineapple pot.

DORAN'S STORY

"Three singles to Port Isoboon and one round trip, please."

"Twenty bans each for the singles and thirty for the round trip; that's ninety in total."

Doran smiled quietly to himself as The Sergeant handed over the money. It was satisfying, knowing they'd raised the funds entirely by their own efforts, and that this part of the journey would be wholly legitimate.

The eighty-five road miles between Creoloone and Port Isoboon passed quickly and pleasantly, and soon the troupe were stepping off the bus at the port's main harbor, where auto-cranes were busy hoisting giant containers onto cargo ships. The sheer commotion of it all made Doran feel a little uncomfortable, but Humbucker led them away from the seafront, through a couple of narrow backstreets, to a grassy square called Turntide Point, bordered on one side by a towering granite rock face. Looking up, Doran saw that the shaft of a lighthouse was built into the escarpment and, at the very top, a wooden pub sign, 'The Rattling Skeleton', was bolted onto it.

"Carina's going to meet us here?" he asked, biting anxiously at his lip.

"Yes, she knows this tavern so well, she has a special sound for it," The Sergeant told him. "That, and a way of shaking her feathers. She will come to us here on the topmost floor."

"All the same, I wish we could've taken her with us on the shuttle."

After the mammoth climb up narrow flights of twisting stairs, the troupe were thankful for a seat and a beer, but Doran couldn't help gazing out longingly at the sea. He'd never encountered such a massive stretch of water before, and yet there it was below them: the Disian Ocean, tossing about wildly, like there was some great plan or purpose behind its movements.

"When will Carina get here?"

"Soon, Dormouse. Don't you worry." Domino sprang down

from the bar stool, ambled over to the window, and perched on the ledge with one knee raised, looking out at the ocean.

"But there's a wind on. What if she loses her way or takes too long to get here?" Doran stared at the thin white clouds skulking eastward. The sky was the color of periwinkles, but so blustery he couldn't stop wringing his hands.

"The wind is her map," The Sergeant said from over at the bar. "And as for getting lost, that's impossible; the landmarks here are imprinted on her soul." He fetched one of the comfy armchairs from the corner of the room, wheeled it up to the table, and allowed himself to sink back into it. Then he picked up his flute box. "Would you like for me to play a little something while we wait?"

Doran was about to nod vigorously when he spotted the mischievous grin of a uniformed sailor who was approaching them. The man was about forty or so, with fair, shoulder-length hair, 'Waders Ferries' embroidered in brown along the top of his cap next to the corporation's famous curlew logo. Humbucker rose and greeted him warmly, patting him on the back, shaking him firmly by the hand. Then he leaned in so close, Doran could make out the tiny hazel-colored flecks in his eyes.

"This is Kadon," he whispered. "He will see you onto the *Telanthera* when it is time."

Kadon was one of those people who never stopped smiling. With a pint of Guinness in one hand and a cigar in the other, he began to reel off tale after tale about his escapades with Humbucker out on the open seas, each one captivating Doran so much, he forgot all about his troubles.

"We were caught red-handed one time, and by the boss, no less. It was about three in the morning, after we'd spent the best part of an hour down in the mess getting barreled up. And I'm telling you, this was no ordinary stash of booze. It was meant for the corporate bash Waders throws every summer when they announce their profits. We were busy helping ourselves to the munchies, too: brownies, pecan pie, cheesecake, you name it."

"Sheesh, what happened when the boss came?" Barlin asked, eager for the payoff.

"The Sarge just turns to him and says, 'Got any more of that Pusser's Rum? It's the best I've ever tasted.' And the boss, well, he's so damn flattered, he tells us, 'Wait here, guys; there's two more bottles over in the galley.'"

While everyone was busy chuckling, Carina sailed in through the window, landed on the table, and made a kind of guttural rasping sound that Doran had never heard before.

"She'll tell you," Kadon said. "She was there too, pecking away at the strawberries."

Down at the wharf, the wind was whipping at the water, a roller coaster of vertical little wavelets plopping and swishing below them. The air smelled of salt and seaweed, and Doran could hear the harried squawks of gulls fighting over scraps. They followed Kadon, who escorted them through the doors of a gigantic concrete silo into a small, windowless office at the rear.

"Be so kind as to walk us through the plans again," The Sergeant said, once the door was firmly closed.

"I'm rostered onto the *Telanthera* tonight," Kadon told them, speaking very quietly. He was referring to the huge floating container painted royal yellow that they had passed in the cargo quay: a ten-year-old sub-lepto Disian freight ship. "And as you know already," Kadon continued, "cargo ships don't carry passengers, so you're gonna have to pretend like you're payload. You'll be hiding in crates that I'll stash in the lifeboat before the rest of the crew gets onboard."

The Sergeant continued with the instructions. "Domino and Doran will ride in one dinghy, Barlin in the other, and Kadon will jettison the boats very discreetly about a hundred miles after cutting the sub-lepto engines. By then, the *Telanthera* will be about thirty miles from Port Rohume in Cassaforta. Pay attention now, because this part is crucial to your success. The lifeboats will be set to autopilot twenty-five miles south to the Isley Banna estuary, and then another fifteen miles down the river to the ferry point in a small town called Addonite's Gate. Once there, you will need to key the code one-zero-one into the dinghy's navicom to return it to the *Telanthera*. It will be dark when you arrive, and you must disembark as silently and as quickly as you possibly can. Are we clear on this?"

"We got it covered, Sarge," Domino said. "When the dinghies stop, we type one-oh-one, then bail. Right, Barlin?"

Barlin grinned and saluted. "Podunkia or bust."

With that, Kadon and Humbucker marched out into the storage area and dragged three empty packing crates, the size of large treasure chests, into the office.

"Just imagine you're in your alcoves back at Nentoke," The Sergeant told them. "You'll be cooped up for more than nine hours, and such thoughts will help keep claustrophobia at bay."

The word induced a mild panic attack in Doran. "I'll need a flashlight," he stammered. Then, while Kadon was fetching one from the store cupboard, he added, "If you've got a spare pair of airphones, maybe you could set them to play *Tubular Bells* on repeat as well."

Domino embraced the old sailor, and if there was any hint of grief gnawing away at her heart, she concealed it well. They shook hands for the last time, parting with the words that Doran had come to view as uniquely theirs:

"Until the stars turn black."

Images of *The Dreamcatcher* crept into his mind: the cozy evenings spent curled up by the fireside, discussing the fate of the universe, making up tales. And suddenly he was gripped with a desire to cry out in pain, to announce that they should turn around at once and hasten back to Nentoke. It wasn't easy for him, but he managed to stifle the impulse.

The Sergeant was clasping Barlin to his side, telling him, "Perhaps one day—who knows?—the tagmesh will become a thing of the past… and we shall meet again." And then he turned to Doran, observing that tears had begun to trickle down the young boy's cheeks. "Why so sad, little Dormouse?" he said, his forehead wrinkled, his eyes full of empathy. "You are going on a great adventure."

"You… and Carina," was all Doran could burble between smothered sobs and gulps for air. He brushed his elbow over his face, ashamed of what he saw as weak and childish weeping.

"Have cheer, dear friend." Humbucker reached for his flute case, then held it up in front of the boy. "This is for you, Doran. Whenever you need me, you have only to play, and it will be as though I am standing before you. And as for Carina, there is no want for sadness. She'll be traveling with you, in your crate."

"But… she's yours."

"Hush. You know that she belongs to no one. She decided to accompany you last night and notified me early this morning. Indeed, she has journeyed between the continents more times than I care to count. Her spirit walks in both those worlds."

THE PRESENT

I'm dwelling on A-sides and B-sides again, thinking how Weinberg's tale is neither. It's more like there's a hidden side to the record—one that plays a hauntingly familiar tune no one bothered to write, as if the music somehow folded in on itself and a parallel universe dropped right out. It's past midnight and the painting's still there, flecked with tiny icicles of light from the window, and the more I stare at the vase, the more that otherworldly song seems trapped inside of it, desperate to break free. Maybe it's me who's holding it there, refusing to release it, clinging to a past I can never hope to recapture. And all the while, Wallbanger's words sit somewhere in the folds of my cerebral cortex, niggling me harder than thoughts about the dream.

After all that Sorley Ridge crap, I thought he was the one ready to thrust the dagger into my heart. But I'm starting to think it's Harvey who shouldn't be trusted. I mean, he's the one keeping stuff from me.

I won't be laying the past to rest any time soon, though. Maybe it's just a bunch of sentimental crap, but for me, huckleberry dreams have nothing to do with psychedelic delirium brought on by a weird-looking plant. My huckleberry dreams are my memories, and just like Leyland said, I can dust them off whenever I want. I can chuckle at the funny parts— laugh my butt off if that's where it takes me. I can roll on the floor like it's happening right here, right now. My story matters, goddamn it— more than some random tale about an orphan kid on the other side of the planet.

28

Graduation

The pickup pulled up sharp by the school gates. Earl had been dozing, his head cradled between a sack of potatoes and a crate full of beets, but when the brakes squealed, he shot upright, eyes bulging like a startled bushbaby.

"Graduation!" he yelled, leaping over the side of the truck. "Come on. We might still make it."

"You lot go ahead," Booker said, moving real careful on account of her ankle. "I'll catch up to you."

I hopped out after Earl and Mackenzie, the three of us tearing off in the direction of the sports field, Bear galloping along at the side of us. We raced through the yard, passed the library annex, and rounded the corner, where familiar names were echoing out of a massive PA system, bouts of applause rippling steadily across the pitch.

Thackery was standing on a makeshift stage behind a big wooden lectern, flaunting his neatly pressed academic gown and mortarboard. He was calling out the roll of honor, the

Hailey's Town mayoress waiting on the far left, all decked out in white-and-navy robes and a regal-looking livery collar. She was shaking the students' hands, offering out the diplomas as they crossed the stage in their equally crisp, maroon-colored gowns.

Once we got to the steel pipes at the back of the bleachers, the principal called out, "Earl Hunter", and I gave my buddy a quick once-over. He was wearing the same old faded shorts and paint-stained shirt he'd used for swimming in the bay, his hair was scraggy and singed, and he was streaked all over with mud and oil. And as if that wasn't enough, the guy reeked so bad of manure it was hard to keep from hurling.

"How's that for timin'?" Earl said, beaming from ear to ear.

"You ain't seriously goin' up there, are ya?"

The audience were gawking about them, muttering to each other, and you could tell old Thackery was getting prickly because he was gripping the lectern and pursing his lips so tight you couldn't even see them. He read out the name again, eyelids shut, chin lifted as if he was meditating. I chuckled to myself as I thought of him quietly praying for the sight of Earl Hunter. He must have thought it would sway his cause, conjure up the image he was longing for. But when he caught sight of Earl sauntering down the aisle between the two sets of seats, his mouth gaped open so wide, you could have parked a Chevy 4990 in it. If Earl had spent a week in a dumpster, he couldn't have looked any rougher, but there he was, marching up the steps, grinning like there was no tomorrow. And once he was up on stage, he turned to face the crowd, a look of pure childlike wonder glittering away in his eyes.

Folks were giggling, whispering, and tutting. In the end, Thackery had to raise a hand just to shut them up. Then he cleared his throat. "I'm sorry, Mr. Hunter," he said. "I simply cannot allow you to graduate dressed… like that."

Suddenly, Mackenzie snatched a mic from a stand, scurried over to the stage, and swung herself up onto it next to Earl. She tapped the grille a couple of times to check it was working. "The way Earl's dressed don't matter," she said, doing her best to sound dignified. "I mean, he's here, ain't he? That's all that counts."

At that point, the crowd gave up being namby-pamby about it and started laughing out loud, and I mean big, proper belly laughs. But it wasn't Mackenzie's words tickling them; it was what she couldn't see. Bird's Nest and Chalky Hobart, the math teacher, were slinking up behind her. They grabbed her by the shoulders, snatched the mic away, and set about bundling her down the steps, but she struggled free, dashing over to the lectern where Thackery was probably having a mild heart attack. And then she knocked the mortarboard clean off his head. It was like watching some half-baked comedy sketch that the audience were going nuts for.

After that, Mackenzie was led away into a big marquee at the side, but Earl was still facing forward, the bochart shells glinting away in the haze of the sunlight. I guess the on-stage antics were Mackenzie's way of apologizing for the cheap alarm clock stunt, and even if I was sore at Earl for what he said, he was still my best buddy, so I marched into the middle of the aisle and drew a long breath.

"Let him graduate!"

For a while, there was just the embarrassing echo of those three small words bouncing off the wall at the bottom of the field. I was about to scuttle out of sight, crushed by the double whammy of being banned from my own ceremony and the plan totally bombing, when Booker started with the same phrase, and it wasn't long before most of our classmates were in full chorus, too. They were cranking the volume so high it was drowning out Thackery's words, and then everyone was chanting. They started stamping their feet, jumping on the chairs, yelling, screaming, wolf-whistling. Things were getting more frenzied by the second.

"Let him graduate! Let him graduate!"

And just when it seemed like it had peaked, Earl took a small step forward, slowly raising his arm, fist clenched in a kind of triumphant salute. I guess, for me, it was one of those watershed moments you never forget. He stood there, all proud and noble-looking, like the captain of some cobbled-together sports team that had just snatched a victory by the skin of its teeth. He strode over to the lectern, shook Thackery by the hand, and then went up to the mayoress to claim the diploma, the crowd bellowing out their approval, clapping and cheering even louder than before. I guess only Earl could have gone up there, rank as anything, and come down the other side smelling of roses. Poor old Thackery was so shocked, he just didn't know what the hell to do with himself. Booker was next and, as class valedictorian, hobbling across the stage so humbly, the ruckus for her was biggest of all, but I could tell she was bummed out by not being properly dressed for the occasion.

"And now," Thackery said, "we come, as always, to the final presentation of the ceremony: the award of the annual Santa Sasoonia Medal of Honor. And I'm delighted to tell you that this year's winner is… Mr. Carney Redmond Caldwell."

I panicked so bad I almost froze on the spot. But I couldn't back out of graduating, not after we'd fought so hard for the right and won, so I pulled myself together and strode over toward Thackery, telling myself over and over that if Earl could do it with his hair looking like that, anyone could. I mounted the stairs and stepped onto the stage, everything lapsing into slow motion—an astronaut out on some exploratory moon walk, floating specter-like over the dusty landscape of Akkasom, the sounds—the clapping, hollering, and whistling—all muffled and far away. Thackery waffled on about how I'd made a sacrifice, put off college for Lucy, but it was like listening to the static on an S-band radio, the words just garbled snatches from a million miles away, meant for some other person in another time and place. He handed me a silver medal with an eagle on one side and Gilbert Gowder's head on the other, but once I'd accepted it and come down the steps, reality kicked in so fast, I freaked out big time. I got to the edge of the bleachers, but I was gasping for air, wrestling with the fact that high school, a part of my life that truly mattered, was over, and there was nothing at all I could do about it. Things would change now for sure, and I didn't want them to change. I clutched at the medal, willing myself to calm down, but then Thackery was into the closing speech, and it had me more antsy and panicked than ever.

"Students often ask me how they can be sure of making the right decisions, and this is a very important question. After all, what is life but a series of choices played out against the backdrop of randomness? Today, I will share with you the wisdom I impart: if we uphold what's decent, what's noble, the very things that people expect of us, we can always trust the outcome."

Somehow, in my mind, he was sending us out into a world full of doubt and confusion, and it got me so blue, so hopeless, I got to thinking about cobwebs and B-sides again, and how, when things start to close in, you have no control over life at all. I just couldn't face anyone, so, when folks started filing out, I hung back, hoping it would be long enough to give the others the slip. It kind of worked, but I didn't figure on running into Leyland in the parking lot. He'd been watching the whole thing from the front row.

"Boy, that was some spectacle," he said. "I'm proud of you, though, kiddo. No one was shoutin' louder than me back there. You wanna ride home?"

"No, I'm gonna walk. Need to get me some air, clear my head."

After he'd gone, I crawled through the hole in the fence behind the science block, taking the shortcut home through the mustard field at the back of the canning factory. It was good to be alone, but still, nothing felt right. I couldn't stop thinking how everything was coming to an end. Taylor, Marshall, and Kota were gone, Booker would be next, and Earl and I were pretty much drifting apart because of Mackenzie. And now, to top everything, I'd been given a goddamn medal that I didn't even deserve.

29

The Westward Crossing

THE PRESENT
Saturday, January 31st, 2325

Weinberg presses his fingers together, forming a pyramid shape. "I did my fellow governors a bit of a disservice when I called Cassaforta a sham. Okay, it's a land with controls, but we've cherry-picked the best of everything—dispensed with all that we consider hostile or obscene. Effectively, we have obliterated the unwanted parts of Earth's past—removed from history that which we deem 'inappropriate' for our people."

"Real noble of ya."

He nods, dismissing my scorn with a kind of gracious squint. "Okay, we chose that wonderfully sublime 1950s era as our base model, but we took only what was good and wholesome about it, eradicating anything remotely offensive. Do you know what the term 'discrimination' means, Carney?"

"You serious?"

"Humor me," he says, shrugging.

"The dweebs got picked on at high school… and the fat kids. Folks judged 'em on stuff that shouldn't matter—didn't care who they really were."

"That's true enough. But you might be surprised to learn that, during the 1950s and for many years after, people were judged on demographics such as the color of their skin and their gender. Torment and harassment, lower pay for the same work as others, and denial of opportunities were just the tip of the iceberg. Earth history is littered with atrocities so terrible that I'll not speak of them any further. I'll just state that here in Cassaforta, we have embraced a snapshot of life from Earth's past, but we have stamped out these vile and antiquated prejudices, so that people can experience first-hand the simplicity of the time, but also exist peacefully and harmoniously with one another. Animals are respected and left alone, too. It wasn't always that way on Earth; sheep, cattle, pigs, and countless other species were legally slaughtered for their hides and flesh well into the twenty-first century."

His ideas are so far out, all I can do is snigger like a lamebrain. "I'm s'posed to believe all that?"

"I'm glad you think it's so absurd," he says. "It validates the Cassaforta way. But I promise you, everything I've told you is the truth. And truth is the cornerstone of what we do as governors." He starts with a cocky smile, but my frown takes the starch right out of it.

"Jeez. You're the biggest hypocrite this side a' the Disian Ocean." I'm not yelling, but I guess he knows from the tone how pissed he's got me. "The truth's just for your kind; everyone else gets a bunch a' crap. And the lies are so big now, you can't even take 'em away—not without pullin' everyone's goddamn rug out from under them. Your society's curled, no matter how you whitewash over it."

Weinberg's eyes start to twinkle with a newfound respect.

"You have it exactly right, Carney. As I said before, ordinary Cassafortans must be shielded from the truth."

"Then why ya tellin' me?"

He folds his arms. "Because of this incident and its wider implications, you're no longer regarded as ordinary. Whatever happens, you'll be shipped off to Magnatella. You probably worked that out already."

I shrug my shoulders, and for the life of me can't see why I got so riled up. The guy's on my side. So what if he goes around kidding everyone that they're living in some bygone age? No one's perfect. "Mighta been some denial in it, but yeah, I figured."

"Anyway," Weinberg says, "most of the time, what we believe becomes our truth, not the other way around. We tell ourselves a narrative to make sense of things, or to bring about comfort, even when the information we have is incomplete or inaccurate."

"Shouldn't you be gettin' on with the story?"

DORAN'S STORY

The *Telanthera's* sub-lepto engines were duly cut after two and a half hours, when the liner was about 130 miles from the Cassafortan coast. Following another five hours of somewhat turbulent twenty-knot cruising, at about ten at night Cassaforta East Time, Kadon made his excuses to the crew, slinking down to the cargo deck to program the dinghy navicoms and initiate the release. He had to go through with the plan, even though he was cursing their rotten luck for coming out of sub-lepto into the full onslaught of a northwesterly gale. Still, it wasn't a tornado, or worse, one of those Pleasian hurricanes that had been known to capsize the smaller passenger ships. He was confident the rafts would hold their own. At least, he told himself, he'd be able to pass them off as having been ejected accidentally by the impact of the waves.

Once the navicoms were set, Kadon rolled the lifeboat hatches open, only to be greeted by a gust of wind so ferocious it nearly knocked him off his feet. He clutched at the iron pipework, the gale snatching so hard at his shirtsleeves he thought he'd be dragged overboard. Salty spray was whisking through the air, drenching him, stinging his eyes, and out in the darkness he could see great swirling waves smashing brutally into the sides of the *Telanthera*. He unlocked the crates, and then lurched over to the control panel, where his fingers hesitated for a few seconds. Then he flicked the release switch and watched the boats, crates and all, glide down the ramps into the howling frenzy of the storm.

Doran was still dozing when he heard Carina squealing over the top of 'The Sailor's Hornpipe', so he switched off the airphones. The crate was sliding about chaotically, and he could feel the raven's beak jabbing bluntly into his ribs as icy water seeped in through the gaps in the wood. Panicked, he punched the lid off the basket and clambered out, blinking in disbelief.

Domino was at the helm, clutching at the ropes with one hand, a single paddle in the other. She was drenched and shivering, the rain coming down in twisting sheets, lashing at her. And waves the color of tar were surging over the dinghy, forcing it in a fit of different directions, almost sending it under. Doran glanced up, the mist-draped discs of two full moons glaring down at him between the thunderheads, like evil, voyeuristic eyes savoring the horror of it all.

Domino saw that he was out of the crate and scrabbled over, reaching for him as the vessel plunged, bow first, into the depths. Doran clung desperately to the sides, dizzied with confusion as the raft was tossed into the air before smashing onto the foam so hard that he lost his balance. He toppled overboard into the might of the swell, gulping down great mouthfuls of seawater. Then he surfaced, coughing and spluttering, treading water until he managed to grab onto the upper buoyancy tube and, with Domino's help, scramble back inside. They huddled tightly to one another, Domino doing her best to whisper uplifting words to him.

"Are we going to die?" Doran asked, his face buried tight against her shoulder. Then his eyes happened on Carina, the movement of her wings. He watched as she launched herself into the bleakness of the sky and, in that moment, a flash of the Barbastelle dream came to him: the one in which he'd become a feather. "Water can't get to them," he murmured. He pressed his eyelids together, pushed every other thought aside—every horrific, wrathful sound—and just imagined he was back in the air-car, wrapped in the bliss of that beautifully sweet delusion.

When, eventually, the winds had quietened to nothing more than a chill and the waters were calm enough that they could stand in the dinghy, Dol was already rising behind them—a hazy golden lion, unraveling a warm mane of sunbeams. They were cast adrift not far from the mouth of a vast estuary that looked almost white in the dawn mist but, with each passing minute, an obstinate rip current was driving them ever further seaward. The storm had completely wrecked the navicom, but they guessed they were close to the Isley Banna delta, about fifteen miles east of their intended destination of Addonite's Gate.

"We'll have to paddle," Domino said with a shrug. "There's only one oar, so we'll take it in turns."

It was grueling work, wrestling the might of the undertow, which seemed to push them two strokes back for every three they took, and much of their strength had already been expended. But as the fog cleared a little, the angular protrusions of buildings began to appear in the distance—groups of clay-brick warehouses arranged in threes, rows of townhouses with little smoking-boxes stacked on the roofs. Dol was tinting the bricks with a pale salmon blush, the slates shining like silver. It strengthened their resolve to know that land was within their reach, and that this was their final hurdle, so they struggled on.

When Doran grappled at the reeds on the riverbank and hoisted himself out onto marshland, all he could do was lie there on his front, motionless, with Domino stretched out beside him, the Cassafortan sunlight tenderly warming the backs of their necks. And it was not long before they drifted away into a mutual wave of deep, re-energizing slumber.

Several hours later, a voice woke him, as if someone had just walked straight into his dream. "Just tell us who you are and what you're doin' with this lifeboat."

Two uniformed police officers were rifling through his backpack, while a third busied himself taking snapshots of the battered dinghy.

"You with them travelin' folk that passed through here last week?" the older one said.

Domino sat upright and gave them a stony glare. "That's right. We're brother and sister—Doran and Domino D'Argent."

"Any ID? Nothin' in the backpack."

"Don't carry any," Doran said.

"You'll have to talk to the crime squad."

They were driven to Borcole Stubbs police precinct, where, at just after three in the afternoon, they were arrested for the theft and partial destruction of a Waders Ferries lifeboat. After that, the officers locked them up in separate cells, and they were not allowed to see each other or communicate in any way. Doran remained optimistic, though, consoling himself with the fact that, during the questioning, Magnatella had never once been mentioned. Indeed, Domino had lost her backpack to the savageness of the sea, and there was nothing in his to suggest they'd come from there. In any case, it was such an outlandish idea, the crime squad probably never even considered it.

Incidentally, when the police liaised with Waders about the

Telanthera, the lifeboats were counted and only one was missing, so we can safely assume that Barlin's dinghy was undamaged, and that he made it all the way to the ferry's anchor point at Addonite's Gate.

A trial was held in late October 2320 at Borcole Stubbs Courthouse, Doran still convinced that the offense would be classed as a minor misdemeanor, and that they would simply be issued a fine and released. However, after a brief deliberation from the jury, Domino was told to stand.

"Domino D'Argent," the judge said, the gavel poised in her hand. "You have been found guilty of theft and willful damage to property. I hereby sentence you to serve five years in the Linnestone Juvenile Correction Center in Drayborn Fells." She brought the gavel down hard against the sound block, and then told Doran to rise.

"Doran D'Argent," she began. "You have been found guilty as an accomplice to the crimes of theft and willful damage to property. However, your attorney has asked that your age be taken into consideration when deciding on the punishment. Thus, the court hereby files a recommendation that you be sent to the Dover Plain Reform School for Boys in Tusslin Kantop for a period of not less than two years."

After the hearing, the authorities bundled them out of the courtroom so fast they didn't even get a chance to say goodbye. Doran could only watch silently as Domino was handcuffed to a policewoman and led away. She winked at him, though, smiling mutinously, and everything he needed to know was in that gesture; no prison on the planet could hold his beloved Astronomy Dominé.

30

The Eastward Departure

L eyland saw an ad on Kepple's bulletin board, back in July. It was posted by Garlan-Woodfin, a company that churned out groundy parts at a sweatshop over in Gravelbeck, about ten miles north of Hap Town. I called the same day, and the HR guy couldn't get his words out fast enough.

"Major order's come in from Mercury," he said. "We need QC shift-work temps, and plenty of 'em. When can you start?"

Garlin-Woodfin sure pulled the plug on all that post-graduation-day moping. I had to get up at five, take a bus out to Larchiment, and then hop onto the old GW shuttle just as the sun was coming up. They put me on days first, non-stop testing headlights from seven in the morning till seven at night. After a week of that, it was two back-to-back rotations on the graveyard shift—real grunt work, measuring and weighing camshafts and the like, which burned me out so bad I just didn't have time to fret about anything else.

And all the while, Leyland was counting down to August

twenty-first, when he'd finally set sail for Magnatella. He'd been offered a place at the Yantrista Medical School in a district of Banunus City called Nustosternus. I had no clue how to pronounce it, but he was pretty much over the moons about starting because the brochures all said it was the most scientifically advanced hospital on the globe, and it boasted a world-class research group specializing in cerebrovascular accident. "That's the proper medical term for a stroke," Leyland kept saying in the weeks leading up to the big day. "They'll sort her out no problem." It didn't really sink in with me that he was going, though, not even when he gave the rented pickup back to Kepple's.

Dol seemed to be splintering out of the sky from every angle when we bailed out the cab in front of the old station building. It wasn't much to shout about, just a big brown wooden hut at the junction between Low Road and Planter's Lane, and there were only two platforms, both so shabby they looked like they'd been closed down years ago.

We worked up quite a sweat dragging Leyland's four cases up the steps, over the bridge, and down again onto platform two. He was bound for Port Allinhoe, and Booker was going to cross over from Anthelion's Rock much further north, but they were going to share a train as far as Grade Glennings.

"Now, listen up, Carney—" Leyland slumped onto a bench, snatching some of his shirt buttons open.

"I know the score, Ley. We've been over it a million times already. Home help sits with Luce every weekday. They come at ten and stay till two, so I gotta call at three and four. If she picks up that means everythin's okay." I joined him on the bench, putting my feet up on one of the bags, mopping my brow with my scrunched-up Garlan-Woodfin cap. "And I gotta collect the pension from the post office every other Friday."

"Sorry, can't stop frettin' 'bout leavin' the pair a' ya, but it won't be long till we're all together again. Three years'll whiz by so fast you'll hardly notice, and then you can sign up for whatever course you want."

The marigolds in the hanging baskets had all but wilted, and I was busy feeling bad for them when I spotted the Arch Angels striding over the bridge. I hadn't seen Earl and Mackenzie since graduation, and I still wasn't sure if we were cool or not.

"Jeez, Booker. You takin' the kitchen sink?" I yelled, as the biggest trunk I'd ever set eyes on came thudding down onto the concrete.

"Knock it off, Caldwell." She lumbered over, lugging the suitcase. "Sure hope it's cooler in Amchuda."

Earl wrapped his arms round the big old crate, made like he was struggling to lift it. "Must be some sort a' baby elephant in there."

"They sell stuff in Magnatella. You do know that, Pachello?" Mackenzie kicked her boot against it.

"Look, you lot. You should be nice to me. I got somethin' for ya—somethin' real neat." Booker sat down in front of the bench, grinning up at Leyland. "Don't mind us. We were born delinquent."

Leyland pretended to scowl. "Are they always like this?"

"Pretty much, Bigbro, but you get used to 'em after a while."

Booker started raking through her pockets. "For the remainin' Arch Angels, I proudly present... the keys to the Hornet. May you drive her safely and share her wisely... until Kota gets back." She pressed the keys into my hand, looking me in the eye for as long as it took to signal, silently and finally, her thanks for getting Dakota safely across the cornfield. "She's over on Low Road by the drugstore. Tank's full too."

"We'll take good care of her, Books. Don't you worry."

"And here's somethin' just for you, Carney." She flipped the top compartment of her rucksack open and plucked out the Polaroid—the one she'd snapped that night in Broughton Alley, when the rain drenched us to the bone. "Her number's on the back. She told me this mornin' she's wantin' to talk to the old gang again."

I slipped it from her hand. Dakota was on the left about a foot from Taylor, her lips turned up in a kind of sweet faux smile that made her eyes look weary from the effort. She was staring down at the wall, her hair pasted to her face from the rain, hands clasped tight together. And in the space between her and the others, you could just about make out an old theater poster for the play *Kodachrome,* tacked to the door of the phone booth. I turned the picture over and saw that Booker had scribbled the Barraleah number in red marker pen in the top-right corner.

"Gosh," was all I could think to say, and it made me feel kind of lame.

When it got to half past two, the Grade Glennings train rumbled into the station and ground to a halt, the three carriages hissing and wheezing. Guards started bustling about, and a muffled announcement came over the loudspeaker, listing all the stops it would be making. Folks were boarding, so I helped Leyland with the bags, then jumped back down onto the platform as he dallied in the gangway, neither of us knowing quite what to say. Then the doors beeped, and he had to stand clear, so he just grinned, winked at me, and went to find his seat.

I stood next to the window, peering blankly through the pane, Earl hollering as he hammered on the glass. "Stay loose now, Booker. Y' hear me?"

Mackenzie blew a kiss, a whistle blasted, and then the train jolted away, clunking and rattling, before disappearing into Planter's Tunnel, a site famed for the long-eared bats that roosted there every summer.

We stared down at the empty tracks, a full minute passing

before I could get any words out. "Man, they won't get to watch the bats take off at dusk no more."

Mackenzie just shrugged. "Who's drivin'?" she said, digging her hand into my jeans pocket, snatching out the Hornet keys. She was waving them in front of me, but Earl seemed quieter than usual. He glanced at her, a glimmer of awkwardness in his eyes.

"I guess Carney oughta," he said. "I mean, he'll be the one..."

"Earl, we've been best buds since kindergarten. Somethin's wrong, I know it."

He sighed. "Didn't wanna bring this up, what with Booker and Leyland leavin' an' all, but I guess you've seen right through me."

"Don't tell him, Earl," Mackenzie said. "Not today. It'll be too much." She was biting at her bottom lip, all the while looking at me like I was some cute stray dog she'd found on the sidewalk, but I couldn't find it in me to fret. I knew I'd be talking with Dakota soon, and that was all that mattered.

"It's okay," I said, shielding my eyes from the sunlight. "I can take it."

"Mackenzie's old lady found me a job." Earl parked himself on the bench where Leyland had been sitting. "Trainee mechanic, workin' with dirt bikes at a racetrack over in Lope Horn. I'll be livin' with the Mulhoones."

"Earl, man. Way to go an' all, but I thought you was hell-bent on stayin' here in Hailey's."

"Yeah, but you gotta run with whatever fate slings at you sometimes. And it won't be forever. Who knows? I'll most likely be back after a year." Earl grinned sneakily. "Come now, dear boy," he said, taking on the blood-and-thunder voice Thackery always put on in assembly. "Let's head over to Buddy's for a game of pool. And with any luck, I'll wipe the goddamn floor with both of you."

I chuckled, stuffing my hands into my pockets. "We're cool, right? I mean, you don't really think me 'n' Kenzie..."

"Forget about it," Earl said. "I was bein' a total jerk."

31

Dover Plain Reform School

DORAN'S STORY

You were probably expecting to hear that Doran went to pieces once the trial was over. After all, protecting Domino had been his primary motive for making the long and arduous journey to Cassaforta. Escaping the tagmesh, noble a cause as it was, had very much played second fiddle. But the truth is, as he was driven away from the courthouse in an unmarked police van, his mind was so preoccupied with devising a plan to find her, he had no time at all to pamper his grief.

Still engrossed in the logistics of obtaining a map to Drayborn Fells, he arrived in Tusslin Kantop late on a Friday afternoon, accompanied by a lone police officer, who ushered him, manacled, up the five foot-worn steps of the Dover Plain Reform School for Boys. The street seemed quiet enough, but the building was exceedingly drab, the bricks all blackened with soot. The officer buzzed the intercom once, and when the door scraped open, he shoved Doran inside.

The first thing the boy noticed was the overpowering stench of burnt food. And then he caught sight of the faded carpet which, he thought, would probably disappear if it lost any more of its thread. He gazed about, grimacing when he saw that the hallway was covered in brown, gaudy-looking wallpaper, big patches of it soiled and torn.

"Doran D'Argent," the police officer said, addressing a middle-aged woman who was sitting behind the front desk. "You're expecting him." He held out a large duffel bag. "This is his stuff."

"You'll need to empty that out, over there on the table." The woman didn't smile. She wore too much rouge, and her eyebrows were just thin black half-circles, drawn on with a pencil.

The officer obliged, turning out some clothing, a photo-booth picture of Domino, The Sergeant's flute case, and the plush crimson octopus that the boy had carried since birth. His playing cards had been in the backpack too but, in all likelihood, were now at the bottom of the Disian Ocean.

"Hauntmead'll be along soon. Just keep him cuffed till then."

A door snapped shut in the corridor, and then the principal appeared in the lobby, towering over everyone else, his robes overlaying an expensive, tailor-made three-piece suit. Doran had never seen anyone with such a prominent chin, and the dark, horseshoe-shaped mustache served only to accentuate it. Hauntmead glanced briefly at the boy before turning his attention to the items on the table, but it was sufficient time for Doran to see that the hickory-colored eyes lacked any kind of soul. It was unnerving; Hauntmead regarded the child as if he were a dead fly that he'd just fished out of his soup.

"We'll take it from here," he said, dismissing the officer with a hasty wave of his hand. Then, when Doran was free of the cuffs, he led him across the hall into an office that had 'Dr. Findal Hauntmead, B. Ed, PhD, Principal' stenciled on the door in shiny gold paint. The principal held up the flute halves, dangling them at arm's length. "And what, may I ask, are these?"

"It's a flute," Doran said chirpily. "You have to push the two halves together."

Hauntmead glowered at the boy without saying a word, then fetched a steel mallet from his top drawer, bringing it down repeatedly on the flute barrels until the instrument was reduced to a flattened pile of splinters. "Don't look at me like that," he said. "I run a tight ship here, and you gave up all rights to sentimentality the moment you broke the law."

Doran watched, scarcely able to believe his eyes, as Hauntmead flung Domino's photograph and the remnants of the flute onto a fire that was hissing away in the marble hearth at the side of his desk. The boy felt curiously rigid, as if the horror of it all had somehow triggered a natural mummification of his limbs. All he could do was gaze at the flames as they licked greedily at the paper and the broken shards of rosewood. He'd reckoned on staying maybe two or three days before he made his bid for freedom, but he understood then that he should leave right away.

Hauntmead sat at his bureau, rifling hurriedly through the rest of the belongings. "You won't need the clothes; we have a strict uniform here. I'll burn those later." Then his hand strayed toward the octopus. "I'm going to let you keep this, for the sake of good discipline. In other words, if you disobey me, you know what'll happen to it." He gestured for Doran to take it from his desk. "Right, I'll get someone to show you around."

As an older boy marched in, Doran was drawn to a small oil painting of a swan above the witherwood bookcase. He pictured Hauntmead choosing it, deciding that a swan would look elegant there, just right for an office such as this. *Somewhere inside the man there must be a soul,* he thought.

Doran's guide led him up a wooden staircase, past giant prints of famous bygone Earth scientists, all the pictures sealed in dusty frames that had not been hung straight. Doran wanted to level them out, but he knew it wasn't his place.

"I'm Todd Tremlin," the boy told him, once they got to the dormitory on the third floor, but it was nothing like the cozy little bedroom that overlooked the orchard at Maple Road; it was just a cold, sterile corridor full of iron bed frames, each with the thinnest of mattresses and a single, worn-out blanket.

"Right, stuff ya need to know," Tremlin said curtly. "First off, don't go thinkin' I'm yer buddy; no one likes newbies round here." He dumped a parcel onto one of the beds. "This is yer uniform—a boilersuit, 'cause we do menial chores in the mornin's, startin' at seven: moppin' floors, laundry, washin' dishes. You get the picture. Lessons are in the afternoons, one till six. And supper's at seven downstairs in the mess hall, but it's nothin' to get excited about. Cook burns the food on purpose, by order of The Reaper." Then, just before he went out, he glanced across at Doran again. "One more thing: the cellar's outta bounds to the likes of us."

"Why, what's down there?"

"The Reaper's lab, that's what. And don't let on that's what we call Hauntmead behind his back." With that, Tremlin turned and went clattering down the wobbly old staircase.

Doran was glad to be alone because it meant he could start looking for ways to get out, but before he had a chance to think where he might begin, he heard a sharp tap at the window and, wandering over, was thrilled to see Carina flouncing up and down the sill on her beautiful, wiry little legs. He slid the lower pane up, and she hopped in, chirruping with delight.

"Shh, little one. We don't want anybody knowing you're here." He picked her up and ran his palm down her back feathers as she clicked away, her articulated talons curled tightly round his forearm.

It was while admiring them that he spotted a small scroll attached to a ring that had been loosely fastened to her left leg. When he slipped it out and saw that it was signed by Domino in rich black ink, his heart skipped a beat, and he found himself smiling. Although there was limited space, the note contained the mailing address of the institution in Drayborn Fells which, Domino assured him, they could use to communicate their tactics for escape and rendezvous. *It'd be dumb of me to head down to Tusslin Kantop,* she wrote, *if you're planning to travel all the way up here. But when you write about the plans, use the Shadow Dwellers' code; prison letters always get read.*

Immediately, having resolved to remain where he was until their arrangements were finalized, Doran composed a heartfelt letter to Domino, expressing in code how desperate he was to get away from Dover Plain. His letter was far too long to fit into Carina's leg band, so he sealed it in an envelope and placed it in the outgoing mail rack by the front desk, praying that a response would come swiftly.

THE PRESENT

Cuticura Soap stalks in, like it's a real pain in the butt. "You buzzed me?"

"Yeah. Need the bathroom, and this damn thing's blocked."

She frowns suspiciously when she sees the john rammed full of paper. "I'll go with you."

Inside the cubicle, there's no window, no way out. If I was Doran, I guess I'd have the backbone to club her over the head with something hard enough to knock her out, and then I'd make a hasty exit through the window above the basins. Is it in me? If we're one and the same, it must be. I stare at the cistern lid, not flinching. I was never one for upsetting the apple cart, but I need to get out of here, and fast.

"You done in there? I got things to do."

"Two more minutes." The lid is in my hands, the bright orange ball valve bobbing at the top of the tank along with dark spores of mold, a line of limescale, all these things laid bare in front of me. They're crying out in their foulness. *Imagine her face—the gut-wrenching pain, the trauma. Could you live with yourself? Don't you have enough damn guilt to carry?* "Okay. I'm done."

Cuticura Soap has her back to me when I exit the cubicle, but she sees my reflection in the mirror, and then she turns. "Let's get you back to bed."

"Say, is there a medic here called Colt? I met him once, a while back."

"Colt Rivers?"

"Dunno his last name."

"He works in the ER, but I'll get him to look in on you."

We walk side by side, back to the little room with the high-up window, the roots of something ancient tugging at my soul, the quietness, the stillness of the Bolars not far from my thoughts, and for a moment, it feels almost like Lucy is with me—like, just for an instant, I know who I am.

32

Long Distance to Barraleah

THE PAST
Friday, August 22nd, 2324

The minibus bumbled over the old sandstone bridge at Caters Mead on its way to Larchiment Square, and with every mile I was getting more and more skittish. I'd gotten way too wrecked last night to risk calling Dakota, and it was the first evening at home without Leyland, so I figured I'd just set up a game of fake Lucy poker and talk to her tomorrow. But now that it was getting so close to crunch time, the thought of calling her just wouldn't let up. I could almost hear the purr of the dial spinning back into place, the soothing hum as the lines connected and long-distance crackles gamboled along the wires between Hailey's Town and far-off Barraleah.

By the time the bus dropped me in the square, my face was sweating, and my legs were shaking so bad people kept staring at me. Even my hands were starting with the tremors, and when I got onto the second bus, I ended up dropping the fare and cussing.

The twenty-minute ride from Larchiment felt more like an hour. I guess that's the way when you're all psyched up for something. Even when I got back home and kicked my boots off, I still had to fix dinner, and then sit and eat with Lucy in the kitchen before doing the dishes. After that, Lucy shuffled into the living room with *The Call of the Wild,* so I tucked her up in the window chair, closed the door, and then finally bounded over to the handset in the hall, where Booker's Polaroid was waiting on the table.

I sat on the stairs, my thighs still juddering as I dialed the number. There was a short hissing sound, and then I heard the peep of the ringtone on the other end.

"Hello? Barraleah 296486." It was a lady's voice, but real gruff-sounding.

"Is Dakota there?"

"Who is this?"

My palms were so clammy, the receiver almost slipped from my grasp. "It's Carney Caldwell—a friend of hers from Hailey's." It was pretty hard to act cool, what with my legs quaking and her being all blunt with me, but her tone totally changed when she heard my name. It was like I'd uttered a secret code word that automatically poked her into meek mode.

"Oh, hi there, Carney. I'm Dakota's aunt, Cora Curzon." She sounded so sweet there was only one way to explain it: my part in getting Kota to the medical center on time. "Dakota has mentioned you, but she's not here at the moment," she went on. "She's gone on a weeklong camping trip with Silas and the others, but she'll be back on the twenty-ninth. Shall I get her to call you then?"

"No, it's fine, Ms. Curzon. I'll call back next week. Bye now." I hung up, feeling a bit shameful about how bummed out I must have sounded, and about my voice cracking a couple of times. It was just a setback, though; I could manage another seven days without talking to Dakota, even if the twenty-ninth was my last stint at the factory, and the morning that Earl would be setting off for Lope Horn.

Thursday, August 28th, 2324

Garlan-Woodfin told me that if I cut the last day, they'd dock a whole week's money from my paycheck, so Earl and Mackenzie said they'd come over the night before they left. Earl turned up first at about half past eight, four bottles of semi-fermented grog jammed into his pockets.

"Chateau Hunter, 2324. An elegant little angular wine with real backbone." He uncorked one with his teeth, poured out a glassful of the murky stuff, and then just stood in the kitchen, sniffing at it.

I frowned and reached for the bottle. "You ain't gonna fix one for me?"

"Patience, patience," Earl said, slapping me on the wrist. "Half the taste is in the smell."

We heard the clatter of an engine, and then a car door slammed, so I lifted the sheer curtain in the living room. Mackenzie was waltzing up the garden path, cradling six cans of pale ale.

"Budget Buster's finest," she told me, plonking them into my arms once I'd let her in.

"Carney's too cultured for that kinda shit," Earl said, pretending to scowl at her. "My gift was homemade—sweated and toiled for. Well, my old lady did most a' the work, but I watched her pick the apricots."

Mackenzie just poked him in the chest. "Probably tastes like paint stripper," she said, handing me the Hornet keys. We'd agreed the groundy would stay here with me, because Earl had the Appaloosa, and Mackenzie's folks had promised her a decent second-hand Chevy as soon as they got to Lope Horn—no doubt a guilt gift for dragging her halfway across the continent, away from the Gazelles.

Lucy had already turned in for the night, so we spread out on the living room carpet, the Zenith turned down low.

"You all packed then, Early-Bird?"

"I'll do it in the mornin'; there's no big hurry. I travel light anyways." He propped his back against the sofa, stretched out his legs, and sat there, chugging at the ale.

"Old lady says we gotta have our asses in gear by ten."

"Got it, Kenzie. Say, don't forget to pack that Henshaw cut-out." Earl sniggered and Mackenzie clobbered him, then looked at me like she expected me to grin or something, but I just sat there, guzzling down the Chateau Hunter.

"Man, this is sharp. And I swear it's got a kick that could rival a double Diamond Cut."

"You're s'posed to sip the damn stuff, Caldwell. It ain't soda." Earl topped me up, just as the opening bars of 'Blue Moon' started on the radio, but it didn't set me off thinking about the zany lip-syncing, and the stove flaring up on Mallanbury Moor. The song was conjuring up saccharine thoughts about the cantaboon boat, and how time had stood so still with Dakota the night we took the rush. And by the time Roy Orbison's 'In Dreams' came on, I was practically floating on air.

It was odd; it didn't really register with me that Earl was going away. For one thing, it seemed too crazy to be possible, and for another, the thought of talking to Dakota somehow made it all feel bearable. It was like there was an invisible layer of chain mail stuffed under my shirt that could take the sting out of anything, even Mackenzie's non-stop jabbering about the Gazelles.

We spent the rest of evening playing Earl's crazy version of Traffic Jam, until finally, at about a quarter past one, he yawned, mumbling, "Time we were off. Don't wanna keep you up all night."

We strolled down the garden path, pausing by the front gate, Mackenzie shivering because she'd left her jacket at home, Earl buffing at her arms to warm them. The sky was velvety and plum-colored, spattered all over with milky little stars that looked just like moondust shaken from Akkasom rising in the west. And a pair of gawd warblers were clicking away in next door's pear tree, all proud and pompous, bowing their heads in unison as Earl scribbled down the Lope Horn Town address on the back of his empty Dime Chime box.

"Boy," Mackenzie said, the corners of her mouth twitching a little, as if she wasn't quite sure whether to smile. "Akkasom's so big tonight you could almost put a ladder up to it."

I gazed at the sky, awestruck by how round and fat the moon looked. "Yeah, but when you got so far up, you'd suddenly start fallin'."

Earl slipped the Dime box into my shirt pocket and patted it. "Come out and see us whenever you want," he told me. "You got the Hornet, after all."

The smile never quite made it onto Mackenzie's lips. Instead, she drew her arms around me, and I could feel her words vibrating softly against my ribcage. "Bye, Carney Caldwell. And thanks for puttin' up with me all this time. I know it can'ta been easy."

Earl rolled his eyes, then, once she let go of me, shook me by the hand. "Listen, you sure you're gonna be okay?"

"You bet. Ain't like I'll be all on my lonesome. Kota'll be back real soon."

"Right, then. Hope it all works out for you." He beamed at me, all childlike and cheeky-looking—my best friend, Earl Hunter—so damn cocksure of himself, always ready with a prank and a wisecrack, but all of that at odds with the way his soul was wired: ancient and noble like a mountain.

It was time for them to go, and I wanted to come out with something fancy—to send Earl on his way with wise and whimsical words that would let him know just how much he meant to me—but my mind was so full of daydreams and what the future might bring, it drew a total blank. In the end, I just raised my hand in a lame goodbye gesture, and mumbled, "Get outta here, you punks." And then they turned, striding arm in arm down Captain's Way. I watched until all I could see were the Bolars washed in moonlight, peeking out over the rooftops in the distance.

Friday, August 29th, 2324

I snatched at the dial, feeling way more calm than last time because I knew the ropes.

"Could I talk to Dakota, please? It's Carney Caldwell."

"Hi, Carney. Wait just a tick; I'll get her for you." There was a muffled shout, some scrabbling noises, and then a sound that, even though it was made only from electrical energy flowing down a wire, was as sweet as honeysuckle.

"Is that really you, Carney?"

"Yeah, it's me. It's… so good to talk to you, Kota. Seems so long since…"

I cussed silently, wishing I could start over and not be such a goddamn klutz, but she brushed it off.

"Guess you wanna know when I'll be back, huh?"

"School starts on the third, so it'll be in the next coupla days, right?"

She breathed in deep, as if it was something she'd spent a long while thinking about—done her darndest to prepare for mentally—yet somehow it had still managed to trip her up. "Sorry I ain't been in touch. It's just… well, there's somethin' you should know. I only decided a week ago, but the thing is… I ain't comin' back to Hailey's. I'm gonna finish my last year of school here in Barraleah."

I felt the words like a physical pain, as if a huge medicine ball had suddenly dropped onto my chest. "But why, Kota? I mean, Barraleah's out there in the sticks, and your folks are over here, after all." A burst of static fizzled down the line, but it couldn't cover up how bad my voice was quaking.

"Look, Carney. I'll always be grateful for what you did," Dakota said. But she sounded so desperate to wrap things up and go, the soft soap fell way short of the mark. "The truth is, I've met someone here: my cousin's friend, Wyatt. We've... kinda fallen in love. That's why I'm stayin' here."

The second medicine ball was much heftier than the first. I guess you could call it the killer blow—the sort that puts an end not just to the battle, but to the whole godforsaken war. And when it landed, the whole world felt suddenly different: bitter and empty, like nothing had any meaning anymore. I wished her well with whatever the hell the guy's name was, told her I hoped she'd enjoy her new school. It was pretty hard to keep it together, all things considered, but I think I just about pulled it off.

"That message in the dust at the warehouse—the one about Dol and dimensions and stuff. Was it you who wrote it?" I should have just said my farewells and hung up, but the words were floating out my voice box, like some ghostly alter ego was sitting cross-legged in front of me, charming the damn things out of me with a flute.

"Dunno what you're talkin' about, Carney. Look, I gotta go."

What happened after the phone call is kind of fuzzy—a bunch of hollered words I've done my best to forget, all of them aimed at Lucy. I guess it went something like this:

"You don't remember nothin'! What use are you? All those summers we spent campin' out on the Great Hap Water Hide! I mean, that time Leyland thought you were in the shower and threw cold water over the top, and it turned out to be some old man. How could you forget about that? You must be dumb as a rock. All these memories I got, but in your screwed-up world, it's like none of 'em happened. As far as you're concerned, all of it's gone!"

"Comin' back."

"You crazy old mare! She ain't comin' back; she just told me!"

In the end, the neighbors knocked on the wall to shut me up, and all I could see was the muddled, frightened shell of someone I once knew, her hands quivering, a pain lodged deep at the backs of her eyes.

I thundered up the stairs, threw myself onto the bed, and crawled under the covers like some old brooding reptile, even though it was only twenty past eight. I didn't even bother to get undressed; I just lay there without moving, listening to the silence, the air seeping deep into my lungs, stinging me as though it was toxic. The room was so quiet I couldn't stand it. I dug my nails into the mattress, and the springs felt hard and mean.

"Where you hidin', Lucy? Where?"

33

The Reaper

THE PRESENT
Sunday, February 1st, 2325

"Ain't got long, but Narla said you wanted to see me?" Colt looks different. He's shaved off his stubble, cut his hair real short.

"You remember me? I came here with a girl called Dakota Curzon, last April. She took a bunch a' sleepin' pills?"

Colt shakes his head, flushing a little. "Sorry. I see so many patients."

"Then give my records a once-over; tell me why I'm in this place."

"Sure," Colt says. "I got 'em right here." He backs into the floral chair, sits down, then flicks through the file. "So, I see Dr. Weinberg is your psychiatrist."

"That's the thing. He ain't a psychiatrist or a psychologist or nothin'. He's the governor of Hailey's Town. He told me Cassaforta's a fake world."

"Says here, he's treatin' you for a psychotic condition called delusional disorder. People who have it can't tell what's real from

240

what's imagined. They suffer delusions—beliefs in scenarios they've invented."

"He made that up to protect me—to protect the whole planet." Despite sailing so close to the wind, I find myself chuckling; it's like something The Rooster would say. "Look. I just wanna know who I am. What's my name? Is it written on the folder?"

He raises his eyebrows, as if he can't quite believe what I've asked. "Of course," he says. "Your name's Carney Caldwell."

"Does it say anythin' about a kid called Doran, or a guy named Harvey Wilder?"

Colt checks the pages again, shakes his head. "No, nothin'. Just says you're to be given two hundred milligrams of Xenon 90 three times daily, and that your therapy is ongoing." He drums his fingers on the arm of the chair. "Hmmm."

"What?"

"Ain't my specialty, but Xenon 90 seems an odd choice of drug for a condition like yours. One of the documented side effects is hallucination. Think I need to have a word or two with Weinberg."

"No, man. Best let things alone. I got unfinished business with a couple of my delusions."

DORAN'S STORY

I wish I could tell you that things went smoothly for Doran at the reform school—that he settled in well, came to terms with his predicament—but sadly, that was not the case. The other boys were hostile to him from day one. When he came down to supper at seven on the first evening, Tremlin and his cronies were waiting for him. They denied him a seat at the table, and when he returned from the serving area with his plate of burnt offerings, they poured salt onto the food so that he couldn't eat it. After the boys retired to the dormitory, Doran was left alone on a stool in the corner, hungry, thirsty, and miserable. It was then that the cook came over to him.

"I'll fetch you some bread 'n' butter," he said, smiling warmly, "and a nice mug of hot chocolate. You can sit with me in the kitchen while I do the dishes. My name's Jenson."

"Are they like that to all the newbies?" Doran asked.

"Let me tell you somethin' about human nature," Jenson said, winking. "If you stand out as different from the crowd, they don't like it. And you, my friend, stand out a mile. I sense a good heart in you, and most a' the lowlifes in here ain't got a decent vein or artery to share between 'em." He laughed vigorously, and Doran saw a little of Humbucker in him, although the cook was stout and red-faced.

"And what about Hauntmead?"

Jenson dropped his smile. "The guy has issues. He's a control freak and obsessed with fire. You think old Jenson wants to burn the food? Folks came from as far away as Unsworth to taste my caponata when I worked at Camfort's over in Grade Glennin's." His eyes lit up at the memory of it, and then he led Doran through into the kitchen. "Don't cross Hauntmead and you'll be okay. And get to know everyone's routine," he said, nodding, "then you can keep well outta their way. If you need a friendly ear, just come see old Jenson. Skip supper at seven. Eat with me after everyone else has gone."

Doran took the cook's advice, keeping himself very much apart from the other boys, devoting most of his energies to figuring out the best way to abscond when the time came. The windows on the ground floor were all barred, the front door was always securely locked and guarded, and he no longer carried one of Barlin's custom-made rapping keys. The only other exit was the one that led out onto the exercise yard at the rear, but the surrounding wall was much too high for him to scale, and there were no footholds. The only method of escape, he reasoned, was to climb out of one of the upper windows and abseil down, but he'd need some sturdy ropes for that. He spoke with Jenson every evening in the kitchen, but he never mentioned his plans for escape, Carina, Domino, or his origins. He thought it was all a little too risky.

Carina would visit every afternoon at precisely four o'clock, when the other inmates were running about in the quadrangle, as was customary. Having her there certainly raised Doran's spirits. In fact, he began to regard her as his marvelous little secret. But two weeks after his arrival, when she was tapping on the pane with her bill at the usual time, Doran heard what sounded like a gunshot ricocheting off the brickwork. He let Carina in, frantically checking her for wounds, but she was unharmed. And then he felt someone dig a finger, hard, into the small of his back. It was Todd Tremlin.

"The Reaper wants to see you," he said, smirking. "Reckon it's about that old buzzard you're so fond of. He thinks it'll make a real tasty pie."

Hauntmead's words were not much different. "If I see that bird again, I'll not only shoot it; I'll wring its neck with my bare hands."

That night, very solemnly, Doran tucked a tiny rolled-up message into Carina's leg band, explaining to Domino that their cherished corvid friend was not at all safe in Tusslin Kantop. And then he whispered his instructions very carefully into the raven's quills. "Take to the air right away, Carina; bring this message to Domino. And once you get there, don't ever come back to this miserable place." He kissed her on the neck. "I'll miss you," he said, certain she'd understand. Indeed, stretched out by the fireside on *The Dreamcatcher*, Humbucker had often regaled him with jaw-dropping tales about the raven's remarkable intellectual gifts. He just wished he could fly to Drayborn Fells too—sweep sublimely through sprawling skies with Carina by his side.

THE PRESENT

"This is grim, Nils. Just cut to the part where he bails from that shithole."

"I'll get to that, but for now, there's more that is rather unpalatable. I can water it down a little if you're finding it too distressing." Weinberg rests his chin on his knuckles, stares at me, all the while clicking the nib of a pen in and out.

"No. Tell it how it was. And quit with the clickin', will ya?"

DORAN'S STORY

After four weeks of waiting for a response from Domino, Doran's nerves were becoming increasingly frayed. He checked the incoming mail racks daily, but there was never anything for him. It was bad enough that he'd been forced to send Carina away, but now he couldn't help worrying that his letter had gotten lost.

Soul-draining as it was, he composed another, delving more deeply into his plans for escape. He found a pastel he'd made in art class: a sketch of some oak trees sheathed in thick coats of ivy. *The oaks are dressed for their afternoon stroll. I wish I was going with them,* he wrote underneath. Then he stuffed it all into an envelope and dropped it in the outgoing mail rack, resolving to give it three weeks. If by then there was no response, he would break out anyway.

However, by the end of the first week Doran had begun to dread his trips downstairs to check the mail. Each time he stood beside the pile of newly arrived letters, he would almost pass out from anticipation, his hopes invariably swallowed in despair when he saw that there was nothing bearing his name. The absence of any contact from the outside world seemed to bore into the very essence of him, deflating and devastating him, cultivating within him a sense of worthlessness. I suppose, in a way, he felt invisible even to himself. Worse, just as the second week was coming to an end, something very frightening happened—an incident that convinced him he must flee at once.

It was past midnight, and Doran had been dreaming he was back on Humbucker's barge, lush peals of flute music transporting him to dreamlike landscapes as Carina bobbed about in the shadows of his consciousness, rotating her head, robot-like, in perfect synchronization. But when he stretched his arm out to pet her, the vision dissolved, snatched away by a noise so close it had his ear buzzing. It was as if a rubber band had been snapped hard against the inside of his skull, leaving a sharp pain shooting through it. Irritated and confused, he slowly opened his eyes, and there, at the foot of the bed, bathed in the ashen light of a streetlamp, a wraithlike silhouette was pulling a pair of latex gloves onto its fingers. It was Hauntmead.

A scream caught in Doran's throat, his heart thumping so fiercely he was sure the whole dormitory could hear it. He buried his face deep under the blanket, keeping his limbs as still as he could manage. But then, his eyes tight shut, he felt himself being scooped up and carried out of the dorm, down the stairs, and further down into the cellar. He risked peering out, observing that he was about to enter a small room that looked like some kind of bygone surgical theater. There was a large metal dome suspended above the operating table, just about large enough to fit over someone's head, but he lost consciousness before he crossed the threshold.

He woke at five in the morning, back in his dorm bed, hardly daring to move, the bedclothes covering his face. Then, after what felt like an eternity, fearing to breathe too loudly and dreading to think what might be lurking in the shadows, he threw back the covers, but there was nobody there.

34

Little White Jug

THE PAST

It wasn't easy dragging my ass out of bed the day after the call, but a job wasn't magically going to land on the doorstep, so I bit the bullet and drove downtown, parking the Hornet in the big multistory opposite the library. As soon as I hit Javapod, though, a sickly wave of nostalgia came over me, and I had to turn down a side street. I just couldn't bear the thought of being anywhere near Buddy's. In the end, I spent most of the morning wandering aimlessly from store to store, not talking to anyone and not buying anything. I guess I was angry with myself for being so wet behind the ears—for thinking friends were a right, not a luxury. And I totally got what Dakota meant about feeling invisible.

It became an everyday thing, seeing the places without the people: Jade Walk Park, the alley, the Bolars. Every time I passed them, I got a huge lump in my throat. They seemed so goddamn lifeless, tainted with an emptiness that was echoed, hollowly and hopelessly, inside of me. And when I got home, it would run through my head that my life had somehow turned into the B-side of what it was meant to be, and I didn't know what the hell to do about it. The cobweb was the cause and the B-side the effect, but in my messed-up way of thinking I saw them as one almighty beast that I had to crush in some way, so's I could get back to the A-side of everything.

And that's when I figured the sack of crinkles up on the moors might hold the key. With them, maybe serenity was mine for the taking, and I could waste the creature once and for all. Finding the field would be a breeze, because the whitewashed outhouse with the long, sad eyes was a dead giveaway. I could follow the same route I took with Bear, then snatch the bag from under the hedgerow. Then I'd only have to drag the plunder down to the roadside, fetch the Hornet, and dump it in the trunk.

Thursday, September 4th, 2324

Everything went exactly to plan. The only part that threw me was setting eyes on the campsite again. The grass was still black and charred near where the stove caught fire, but apart from that, there were no visible signs that a bunch of kids had ever camped there.

Once I got back to Captain's Way, I checked that Lucy was out of sight, then hauled the grimy container up to the front door, bumped it up the stairs, and lugged it into my room. But when I tore into the packets, there were only hard, shriveled lumps inside them. The wily little plants must have withered and died in the height of the July heatwave, so I called AJ and asked him to come over.

"You gotta look at the leaves, Carney," he said. "If they're wilted, ain't no hope. But if they still got the fur on, and they're all shiny and bright…" He was working his way through the sack, plucking out the crumpled bags, peering at the contents through a magnifying glass.

"Found any decent ones yet?" I was pacing the aisle between the bed and the closet, but I quit when I remembered Taylor in the corridor outside Marshall's apartment. I didn't want this to end up as the B-side of all that.

"No. But there'll be some at the bottom, for sure. Heat won't a' gotten to those. We'll have to stash 'em in the icebox, soon as we find 'em." A pile of discarded crinkles was forming in front of the nightstand.

"What'll we do with the bad 'uns?"

Alpin-Joe snatched at another tatty packet, ripping it open with his teeth. "Best if we burn 'em."

When we got down to the creek it was about eleven at night, and the sky was charcoal black. A few days ago, coming here would have felt like pulling teeth, but now my eagerness for the rush, and the fact that we had a job to do, was somehow numbing the pain.

"You got the lighter fuel?"

"Sure thing, AJ."

He lobbed a matchbox at me, and I caught it in both hands. I doused the sack, dropped the lighted match, and stood back a couple of feet, watching as it swelled into a fully rampant pyre, the flames projecting eerie, twisted shadows of us onto the ulus over on the other side.

"Shame you waited so long before fetchin' it. We coulda saved a whole lot more." Alpin-Joe was stoking the blaze with an old pool cue, his eyes watering from all the smoke. "Trouble is, they won't last forever," he went on, trying to waft it all away. "What you gonna do when you've sunk 'em all?"

"Didn't think about that." I shivered, then moved a little closer to the bonfire.

"Now that Ranton's out the picture, me 'n' Rider Partridge... you know him? Tall guy—'tache and beard."

"He showed up in Broughton Alley once." I warmed my hands on the grasping flames. There was something wholly soothing about them—not just the heat, but the way they were eating everything up, slowly and methodically, as they swayed and popped in the darkness. The sack was starting to collapse in on itself, the packets crumpling up, turning first to cinder-edged sheets, then into glowing-hot ashes that spun up into the smoke like newly hatched spiders.

"Well, me 'n' him, we're in touch with some a' Yale Cuthbert's lot over in the Troccas. This Cuthbert fella, I tell ya, he's the man. Can hook you up with whatever y' need."

"I'll bear that in mind."

Alpin-Joe chuckled to himself. "He ain't cheap, though, no siree. Anyways, seein' as you're a bit stuck an' all, we could maybe put the word out—set you up workin' for the guy. After all, you wouldn't wanna be blowin' all a' Lucy's pension on the green lady now, would ya?"

I tossed Booker's Polaroid onto the fire and watched it bubble up, the flames latching onto the edges, curling them inward as they frazzled. The *Kodachrome* poster was the last to disappear, and when it went, I expected to feel some sort of relief, but none came. I guess I figured torching it would wipe out the memories, erase the past, and it would all just melt away. But staring down at the embers, the grief bit deeper than ever. And then a flurry of wind laced through the pyre, sending the cinders twirling out toward the creek, and I thought about everything that had happened: the baseball jacket in the middle of the splash-pool, Dakota's lips turning blue, her head slumped on my shoulder, eyelids closed, like there was only so much blue her face could hold. Then it hit me that some guy in Barraleah would get to spend a lifetime gazing into those eyes, all because they managed to get the pills out of her in time. And the thought lingered—a shard of glass in my throat—all my words held hostage until finally I managed to swallow it down.

"Let's go back, AJ. I wanna see if this goddamn shit still works."

I figured it made sense to do everything just the same as before, even factoring in the liquor—what, when, and how much. Before AJ drove us down to the creek, I gave him a few bans and had him stop by Parapine Street to pick up some Grimley's and six bottles of Hoffman's—the same beer Dakota fetched after we jumped in the creek. Then I had him call into Buddy's for a Dutch spice to go. We sat swilling the ale on the rocks just before we torched the rush, and I downed a mouthful of Grimley's in the groundy on the way home.

When I got back, I cracked another beer open, warmed the coffee on the stove, then laced it with a bonus double shot of Grimley's for luck. There were no clean pots, so I poured it into a little white milk jug that had always sat in the window as an ornament. By the time I got everything sorted, Henry Aldrich was playing 'A Summer Song' by Chad and Jeremy, so I took the radio upstairs with me and got into bed, all the while staring at the tiny green shrub in the palm of my hand. Then, when the song was done, I turned the radio off and set the crinkle down on my tongue, the leaves tickling the roof of my mouth, the tang of the aniseed forcing me to lick my lips. I guess it was kind of corny to be doing this after listening to a song about summer ending and losing some girl, but the Grimley's got me thinking there was something altogether deep and tender about it. Grappling for the jug on the nightstand, I gulped the plant down, telling myself that nothing could go wrong: I was safe in my bed, Lucy was calling hogs two doors down the landing, and there was no place I had to be in the morning.

I must have dozed off after the Dutch spice, but a feeling of time being warped inside of me woke me up. I glanced down at my wrist to see how long I'd been asleep, but ended up chuckling because my arm was covered all over in multicolored scales. They were shimmering, rippling up and down it in slow, wave-like sweeps, first pointing one way, then the other. The colors were changing so subtly and so hypnotically, I could have lain there all night just watching them, but I wanted to see how far it had gone, so I threw off the bedclothes.

Man! I was fully decked out in them, but surprisingly, they were light as a feather, and I found myself floating up, drifting over to the door, and sailing right through it. I glided down to the bottom of the stairs, where I hovered over the phone table, the handset growing bigger by the second. Or was I shrinking? I guess it didn't matter much. Pretty soon I was the size of an ant in comparison, and then I was sucked headfirst into the mouthpiece, space warping and twisting, wrenching at my body, stretching me out so long and thin, consciousness seemed to fly out my brain like a pea being popped from a pod. I was just a pattern of magnetic vibrations—a little buzzing thing of energy, part of a much bigger thing that, if you strung all the parts together, might add up to something huge. I tried to talk, but I had no clue whether I'd said the words or just imagined them.

"I'm consciousness. Just a little pocket of it, but it's everywhere. Everythin's made of it, not the other way round."

"So, you're back again, eagle-boy?"

I was balanced on the deck of the pirate ship, the morning wind blasting clean through the bones of me, tugging at the scores of soot-laden ropes in the rigging. The sails were flapping, and the hull kept lurching and creaking as waves of olive green thrashed against its sides. I forgot all about the little pockets of consciousness and the fun I'd had being one.

"Boy," I said, "I was hopin' you'd show up. I got so many questions, I could burst."

"One question, one answer, then on yer way." The tone of the ship was so low it made my fingertips tingle.

"Okay. Why'd they all up and leave me?"

It laughed, long and hard, the sound rumbling across the cove like the distant boom of a monsoon thunder. "You sure as hell ain't alone, eagle-boy, you know that. In any case, fate ain't static. Maybe there's somethin' hidin' up its sleeve—somethin' well worth diggin' for."

An almighty crack toppled me as the rotten panels of the deck splintered open, and I found myself tumbling wildly through the chasm of space, racing past a thousand swirling galaxies. I yelled, huddling myself tight into a ball as I plunged on down through the blackness, images flashing in front of me. There was a young girl with long hair tied high on her head in twin tails. She was wearing a Gazelles shirt and frayed denim shorts, just like Booker the day she aced it in the biggest tube race the Arch Angels had ever staged. We were standing by the waterfall down at the creek, and Earl was just about to hand her the wooden trophy he'd carved in shop class. Then she was prancing about, holding it on her head. But I wasn't sure if the girl I was seeing here was Booker or Dakota. And the crazy thing was that it didn't seem to matter. It was like there were two different versions of reality, both equally valid.

"Take your pick," Thackery said from far away. "After all, what is life but a series of choices played out against the backdrop of randomness?"

I opened my eyes. It was late, and I was knelt on the floor of the tower building on Cobone Hill, a dusty light from a third-quarter Akkasine streaming in through a broken window. And in front of me, the little white jug was giving off a faint, kind of ultraviolet glow.

"Dakota? You here?" I rummaged through my pockets for a flashlight.

"No. But you can hear my voice." She sounded calm, and so clear I was sure she was only a couple of inches away. I scrabbled about in the darkness, scraping up nothing but moldy leaves and moss.

"It's okay, Kota. Your voice'll do just fine. Only don't leave me this time. Swear you won't."

"You gotta make it on your own now, Carney." She was getting fainter. "When I slip away, it'll be just like the other time, 'cept I won't be there."

"No, please, Kotes. Ain't no good on my own. Dunno what the hell I'm s'posed to do."

A waterfall of thistle-colored smoke was spilling out the jug. Then some of the plumes floated up, turning into flimsy little hummingbirds that were fluttering and hovering about level with my nose. I giggled, swatting at them to see if they'd disappear, but every time I swiped at one, it just split into two.

There was a perfect silence—a stillness that was transcending everything. It was as if the birds had forged a pathway through my consciousness, a golden thread of lucidity dangling in their beaks. I tried to tap into my memories, but there was nothing there to latch onto, nothing at all: no past, no future, no endings, no beginnings, no order, no chaos—just a seamless singularity where extremes were absorbed into each other, canceling them out, turning them to dust. And the guy everyone knew as Carney Caldwell, he just wasn't there anymore, didn't exist. But, totally at odds with all that, a beautiful, defiant, and strangely humbling truth was making itself known.

I was everything.

35

The Pinnacle

Marble-sized paint blobs were dripping from the ceiling, splashing into a gooey pool on the bedroom floor. It always started out that way, with movement and color. I watched from the bed as the goop climbed higher, slopping onto the quilt, pockets of it gurgling, plopping, and spewing out slush like miniature mud volcanoes. Then I jumped down into the middle of it, scooping up dollops of the gunk in my hands and lobbing it everywhere. It smelled of bayberry candle wax, and every time it splattered onto the walls, it would mold itself into shocked and angry-looking face shapes, including Windy's, which appeared on top of an extra-large blob stuck to the mirror.

"Sometimes there are side effects," he said, "when space curves in on itself. Have you ever thought about that?"

"I ain't talkin' to you. You're just a figment of my imagination."

Windy hardened his gaze. "Maybe that's true," he said, "but it doesn't prove a thing. If I'm real to me, it makes me real, and no one can say otherwise, not even my creator."

He fizzled away, and I sank down into the pool, floating on the skin of it, sculling my arms up and down. Then I got it into my head that, if I eased the door open, it would all go flooding down the stairs, maybe even rise up like a great muggy freak wave. That would be fun to watch. I paddled over, reaching for the handle, but as soon as I touched it, the giant snail on the other side started blasting out 'Walk Right Back' by the Everly Brothers, everything hip and swinging.

I hung around outside Buddy's, kids bustling past me, all of them wired and wild, yakking non-stop in a bid to be the loudest, the flashiest. The air smelled of ale, horns were blasting, and groundies were zooming past me so fast all I could see was a trail of psychedelic dust. And then the music, the babble, the horns, the heaving walls of Buddy's all seemed to be throbbing away inside of me, and I could feel the blood of the place surging through my veins, as feet plodded noisily along the sidewalk above.

Somehow, I had become Javapod Street, and prying was what I lived for: listening in on folks' conversations, catching the banter as they passed on through me. It was like I was a giant satellite dish, tuning in to the sounds and deciding where to put them. And every snatch of gossip mattered because I knew that if I pieced it all together in the right order, I'd solve the puzzle—the huge, cosmic one that held the key to everything.

Time felt weird, like sometimes it was running backward, or forward extra slow, and sometimes it looped, skipped, or just plain stood still, but after a while I figured out how to control it—bend it so that I'd always be able to work out what they were saying, and fit that part of the puzzle into the right slot. It seemed to take hours, just collecting and sorting, collecting and sorting, over and over. But once it was all in place, I was back to the pinnacle: that seamless singularity where I was nothing and yet, beautifully, brilliantly, in the same breath, I was everything.

Reality grabbed me by the scruff at five in the morning,

jeering at me, ramming it down my throat that I was all alone and useless. I was sweating from head to toe, quivering worse than a rickety old rope bridge, but I couldn't really argue with it, even though Lucy was only just down the landing because, in a way, she'd been the first to go.

"Get a grip," I told myself. "And don't even think about gettin' stoned durin' the day. Lucy needs you."

And so, September passed in a bleary-eyed muddle of daytime misery that I watered down with beer and pinch, and nightly Grimley's-fueled rush benders that would always find me waking at dawn, dead beat, shivering, and longing for Dol to go down so's I could do it all over again.

Thursday, October 2nd, 2324

"I hate this part, but have you got the gowder?" Alpin-Joe sat at the bench tables in Broughton Alley, cradling a package to his chest as if it were a tiny, unweaned pup.

"Sure, I got it." I dropped my wallet on the table and counted out the bans for AJ. It was the last of my savings, but money well spent as far as I was concerned. Paranoia about the machine and twisting the little gold box had come back with a vengeance since the end of summer, and the rush was the only thing that could stifle it.

Alpin-Joe slid the parcel across the benchtop. "You're Leyland's little brother," he said, "so I'm gonna give you a piece of advice: let me bend Cuthbert's ear. I mean, you're a crinklehead now, good 'n' proper, and your next fix ain't gonna pay for itself."

I shoved the gear inside my jacket, zipping it up real hasty. "I don't wanna be a felon, AJ. Don't even like that I take the stuff, but I guess I'm saddled with it."

There was a nip in the air, and he kept buffing his hands and breathing on them, sending out curls of vapor that had me hankering after those wispy hummingbirds I'd dreamed up last month when I thought I was inside Cobone Tower.

AJ shrugged. "You do know buyin' it's a crime too?"

"Sure, but I ain't hurtin' no one."

That night, for the first time, I sunk a rush and only saw swirling patterns of color and, sweet as it was, I felt mad at AJ for palming me off with a dud batch. So, in the morning I swigged a shot of Grimley's and marched over to Kepple's, where I found him out the back with his overalled legs sticking out from under a picotee-blue Mercury Montclair, swearing under his breath every once in a while.

I knelt down near where he was working. "AJ, we gotta have words, man."

Alpin-Joe slid out, frowning at me. "Carney? What's up?"

"That package you sold me—reckon I was scabbed. It did jack shit for me."

"Ah." Alpin-Joe rinsed the oil from his hands and tossed me a soda from the workbench. Then his eyes darted from side to side. "There's somethin' I shoulda told ya."

"What?"

AJ was whispering. "Well, it's like anythin', I guess. Remember when you first had a beer… or a smoke? Probably made you sick or somethin', right? But you got used to it in the end, eh?"

"You're sayin' it gets… weaker." I thought about what that meant in terms of the gowder, and my legs started trembling.

"The more you take, the more your body adapts." AJ leaned over the hood of an old blue Skylark, tightening a nut. "I'm guessin' where you're at now, if you wanna get a real high you gotta double the dose."

I groaned, and Alpin-Joe gestured for me to sit down.

"Look, I was thinkin' last night about your situation," he

said, calm as anything. "And I've come up with a plan: you could sell the Hornet. I mean, a nifty little runner like her, she'd fetch some serious dough. And Troy, he'd snap her up. You just bet ya boots he would."

36

Pladen Craggs

THE PRESENT
Monday, February 2nd, 2325

"We're stumblin' about in the dark."

Lucy's words strike such a chord, my eyes ping open purely on reflex. It's almost like she was here, but it was just a catnap's dream. She'd say that sometimes, late in the evening, when Uncle Boo came round with his vodka. They'd sit there supping it, getting into long debates about the nature of consciousness, and Lucy would always start on about how folks live the whole of their lives without really understanding what it means. I wonder if she's blundering about, more blind than ever now. Or, by being in this almost non-existent state, unaware of self and lacking any kind of ego, has she finally twigged?

The jury's still out when Weinberg comes in, but all the while he's talking, I see a painting of an old-time galleon on the wall, constantly fading in and out of focus. Maybe for Lucy there's a ghost ship just like this one, forever fighting wind and waves, stubbornly sailing through the sea of spaces that the damage left behind.

DORAN'S STORY

Taking advantage of being alone in the dorm while the others were at breakfast, Doran tied several bedsheets together, attaching one end of his makeshift rope to the hot-water pipe by the side of his bed, and hastily slinging the other out of the window. He stuffed the octopus into his pocket, and then, very warily, his body shaking more violently than a rattlesnake's tail, he clambered out onto the ledge, and grabbed hold.

He clung to the fabric like an infant marsupial, aware that if he slipped, or if the knots came undone, he might not survive the fall. However, by alternating the grip of his hands, he was able to edge his way down until at last he felt the bliss of his feet scraping against the paving stones below him.

Doran had no map, no knowledge of the town, and Dol had not yet risen, but an illuminated sign pointing north at the top of the street caught his eye. It read, 'Pladen Craggs, 31 miles'. He plodded toward it, the streetlamp reflections like hazy yellow pathways at the side of the wet road. Then, feeling somewhat guided by them, he took to his heels all at once, fleeing in that direction until there was no breath left in his body.

It was about three hours after dawn when he found himself strolling briskly across a large hayfield flanked on one side by old stone cottages. A sheet of gray cloud was dimming Dol's light, but the air felt warm, so he sat by a drystone wall that was sheltered all round by a cluster of gangly enot trees, their trunks shining silver where sirus snails had slithered across them in the night. A patch of the bark was sparkling so bright, Doran had to squint, and just for a moment, his soul felt joyful, like he had some business being alive.

"We're away from that place," he whispered to the octopus. "We just need food and somewhere to sleep. Soon we'll be on our way to Drayborn Fells."

He scanned the surroundings, spotting a long line of washing dancing in the breeze in the back garden of one of the cottages. He had packed nothing in his haste to get away, so the blanket in the middle would be a blessing if he could take it without being seen.

"Good thing I was taught by the best," he said, thinking rather sadly about Catlow all alone in the caves back at Nentoke.

Doran arrived in front of the Pladen Craggs sign some eight hours later, his belly filled with cawt fungus that he'd found growing in the woods, and honku berries that he'd plucked from hedgerows in the meadows adjacent to the Ollius River.

"We won't look for the library yet," he told the octopus. "We need to rest up." He'd spied a large concrete pipe tucked under a bridge in a field on the left side of the road. The area was deserted, and the pipe seemed sturdy enough to protect him from whatever the night might have in store. He lined the end of it with dead leaves, then wrapped himself in the blanket he'd pilfered, idly watching buna bees scoop nectar from the strings of pinder flowers tangled in the weeds. Jackrabbits were bounding from bush to bush, nibbling daintily at clumps of ducas grass, and on the horizon, a range of rolling, rouge-colored hills seemed to wrap themselves around his cold, aching body. Doran closed his eyes, breathing deeply for the first time in a long while, and soon he was slumbering.

Was he dreaming? It seemed as though, momentarily, he had slipped back in time. There was that same sound—a snap—and a hot stinging pain inside his head, as if his brain had just been burned with an iron. And then he was pulled from the pipe, coarse fabric brushing against his skin. He had not properly woken, but he could sense an overwhelming fatigue in his muscles as consciousness slowly ebbed away. The last things he remembered were being tossed inside a small space, a clicking sound like a trunk being locked, and then darkness.

Doran recalled nothing of the journey back to the Dover Plain Reform School, only the moment when the six o'clock bell sounded for breakfast, and he opened his eyes. The other boys were dressing, laughing, joking, flicking wet towels at one another.

"You stay put," Tremlin ordered, kicking at Doran's shin when he tried to get out of bed. "The Reaper wants a word."

Once they'd rattled down the stairs, Doran dressed himself, pulling the octopus from his pants pocket, hurriedly jamming it between his mattress and the headboard. And then Hauntmead sauntered in, eyes narrowed, lips pursed tightly.

"Hand over the toy."

Doran stuttered. "I-I lost it. Sorry, it's gone."

Hauntmead shook his head. "Then I'll have to punish you some other way. I simply can't have disobedient boys in my care. It reflects very badly on me." He gestured for Doran to follow him, leading him down to the basement, past his lab, and into a tiny box room with no light and no windows. There, he chained Doran's wrist to a wall.

"There will be no meals," he said. "You'll be locked in here, alone, for two days. Cross me again, and it'll be four."

37

Jack of Spades

"Gimme a break."

Every damn station was churning out love songs, and it didn't matter if they were slow and soppy or fast and chirpy; they were grating on me big time. I turned the dial and downed another Aglo.

"It's 12.45, this is Archer Hanton, and you're listenin' to Radio Hailstrom broadcasting live from cozy downtown Hailey's. And to take your mind off all that rain and sleet out there tonight, we've got Percy Faith and 'Theme from *A Summer Place*.'"

"Thank you!"

The sound of violins quivered through the ether in a burst of broken-heartedness, but the trumpets were making the whole thing soar so high you couldn't help but feel uplifted. I reached for the Grimley's, sank a couple of shots, then poured out a Wild Bandit, but instead of flowing into the glass, the ale was rising up and then swirling about the room in a kind of vortex. And the more I stared at it, the more it seemed to be a gateway to the summer place. I wanted to jump right in there so's I could get to it. Colors were flying out the speaker like water pouring from a showerhead, so I switched off the radio and staggered up to bed.

The trip was intense this time. Color was something that lived in your brain, but it could leak out your eyes, and you could travel around on it—just jump aboard a light beam and go whirling through the galaxy. And sound was something you could see—something that seemed to yank every emotion clean out of your endocrine system, roll it all into a ball, and send it hurtling through the cosmos. At one point, I think I made it to the summer place, and it was like being back at Tennacia Bay, only I was a wave, and the ocean, the water between land and sky, was my blood.

I guess it must have lasted a good six hours, because I woke up shivering at seven in the morning, curled near the foot of the walnut burl dresser—the beauty, the weirdness, the final bliss of it all just a memory, wrenched away as always by the crushing realization that it was over. I was back in the copy world I'd created by refusing to climb inside the machine, and the only way to counter the pain of that existence, the agonizing responsibility for it, was to take more rush so's I could reach the pinnacle—that wonderful state where all notion of self was tossed clean out the window. It was a vacuum pump for the mind alright, but at the same time, the perfect remedy for the vacuum of loneliness tearing away at my soul.

I wobbled over to the drapes and peeked through the gap, stung by the sight of the empty space where the Hornet used to be. I'd sold her to Kepple's for five hundred bans about a month ago, and now most of the money was gone. I was all set to bolt down the stairs, raid the liquor cabinet, and fill a glass with something sharp and strong to take the edge off it, but then I remembered Lucy, and climbed back into bed, wriggling deep under the covers.

"Glad I'm rid of it anyway. No point clingin' to the past."

It was about one in the afternoon when a battering at the front door finally nudged me out of sleep, so I stumbled back to the window, forced the frame up, and jerked my head out. Alpin-Joe and a familiar-looking older guy were skulking behind the oil tank, breathing so loud and quick they might have just run a marathon.

"Wait there, I'm comin'."

I thudded down the stairs, opened the door, and they tumbled in, damp from the drizzle.

"Carney, man. You gotta hide us." Alpin-Joe was struggling to catch his breath. He seemed real fraught, all flushed and sweaty-looking, and he couldn't stand still for more than a second. And then I placed his sidekick; it was Rider Partridge, the guy who showed up in Broughton Alley the night of the rains.

AJ wiped his brow with his shirtsleeve. "We were seen doin' a deal over on West Shields," he told me. "Cops tailed us as far as Brindle, but we managed to shake 'em. Reckon we'll be okay, long as we wait here till the heat's off. Fuzz don't know who we are or where we live."

"Best come into the kitchen, AJ. You look like you could use a drink."

"Sure," Alpin-Joe said. "Game a' poker wouldn't come amiss, neither. What d' ya say?"

"Okay, I'll get Lucy. But you gotta play along and make out like she knows what she's doin'. Leyland told you about that, right?"

On the third hand, Rider folded, and I was just about to raise the stakes when there was another almighty thud at the door. It scared AJ so bad, he tossed his cards clean into the air.

"It's them. I know it!"

"Cool it," I said. "I'll get rid of 'em. You two stay here, and don't move."

The two cops flashed their badges at me so fast, they could have been tickets to the circus for all I knew.

"Carney Caldwell?" The lady cop was hamster-like—short and podgy—and I could tell she was the one calling the shots because she kept peering into the hallway, craning her neck.

"Yeah?"

"Sorry to bother you at home, but we're makin' some routine inquiries. Do you know an Alpin-Joe Steele or a Clyde Partridge?"

She frowned at me, hands on her hips, her lips all thin and mean-looking. I guess something in her stance told me she was a badass—someone you wouldn't want to mess with—so I just mumbled, "AJ comes round sometimes. My brother used to work with him."

"Your brother in?" The other one was a dead ringer for Roy Orbison. If things hadn't been so bad, I guess I'd have sniggered.

"Don't live here no more," I told him, my voice turning suddenly croaky.

Roy pulled a notebook from his top pocket and frowned. The rain had steamed up his shades, so he took them off and rubbed at them. "When was the last time you saw Alpin-Joe?"

"Coupla days ago, I think. Why? He in trouble?"

The badass folded her arms. "Okay if we come inside and take a look around?"

The clang of a trash can falling over out the back sent them ramming past me so hard, I stumbled backward into the wall, and when I got outside AJ and Rider were all set to scale the gate. They never made it over, though; they were grabbed, wrestled face down into the dirt, and cuffed with their hands behind their backs, Roy urging them over and over to, "Relax; take it easy."

Then, in a flash, they were dragged to their feet and marched, all mud-cloaked and wet, back through the kitchen and out the front onto the street. Rider went first with the badass, and Alpin-

Joe was led out by Roy, tinny-sounding messages echoing out over the squad-car radio: *"Mountain Quail to Supernova, come in, Supernova. Respond, please. We've got a possible 11-8-5 over at the drugstore between Anchors and Main."*

They were thrust in the back, Rider with a kind of fatalistic look on his face, AJ frowning like a fourth-grader struggling to solve some complex math problem. And then, just before the doors slammed, he hollered at me, "Jack a' Spades, Carney. Jack a' Spades", as if that was the answer.

The wagon pulled away, and all I could do was traipse back into the dining room where Lucy was sitting pie-eyed, clutching the Jack of Spades under the table in her left fist. When I tried to tug it out her hand, she let out a gravelly wail and clenched her fingers so tight, it ended up crumpling.

"It's okay, Luce. You can keep it. I don't want it anyways."

I guess it was a stroke of luck, the fuzz not ransacking the place, but a twist of anger was bristling away inside of me. Alpin-Joe was the last guy in Hailey's I could truly call a friend, and now he might be sent away too. The more I thought about it, the more I saw it as the B-side of Broughton Alley. Rider Partridge, the rain—most of the elements were there, but they were weaker, and everything had been warped into something altogether worrisome. Instead of folks coming back, they were slowly and systematically being removed.

Shoulda gone inside that damn machine. You ruined everythin'.

I don't really remember how I got through the rest of the day, except that pinch, Grimley's, and passing out had a lot to do with it. And when I came to, it was late, so I got Lucy settled for the night, then trudged into the dining room, eager to kick-start another swill-up and get things underway. But before I got to the liquor cabinet, I spotted the Jack of Spades poking out from under the hearthrug, 'That'll Be the Day' scrawled at the bottom in spidery blue ink. I strode over to the pine bureau where I kept my forty-fives, plucked out the single, and saw right away that someone had jammed a hastily scribbled note inside the sleeve. It was a name and address: 'Yale Cuthbert, The Holdings, Troccapago'.

38

Pellaman Town

DORAN'S STORY

"Eat up, son. Ya must be starvin.'" Jenson held out a warm bowl of leek and potato soup, then offered Doran a crusty bread roll smeared with olive butter. "Can't believe you climbed out the goddamn window."

"I had to get away," Doran stammered between mouthfuls of broth. "Hauntmead… did things to me—in his lab. I dunno what. Do you know what he does in there?"

Jenson shrugged. "He's a physics master. I guess he plans out his classes in there—the old pendulum experiment. That's all I remember from high school."

Doran shook his head. "I can't stay here, Jenson. Hauntmead's put bars across the dorm window frames. I need to find another way out. Can you help me?"

The old cook's eyes widened, and he scratched at his beard. "You remember what I told you about Hauntmead? Don't rattle him and you'll be okay. He likes to feel he's in control of everythin.' And, between you and me…" Jenson lowered his voice. "I think he's some kinda sociopath. Cares more about what folks think of him than people's feelin's. You wanna just toe the line, be polite, never complain. Hell, that's what I do."

"Please, Jenson. You must have a key. You work here."

Jenson sighed, patting Doran on the shoulder. "The only way out is the front door. And it's guarded night and day. I need to buzz in and out, same as everyone else."

"Then smuggle me out in a suitcase. Tell them you're having a weekend away."

The luggage plan was executed three weeks after the first escape attempt. Jenson purchased a massive trunk, and Doran practiced huddling himself into a tight ball, so that he would be able to fit inside it. A week before, Jenson applied for leave, telling everyone he was heading off to San Breccia in the Nellics for a well-earned break. The plan was for the cook to drive to the rail station, buy a one-way ticket to Pellaman Town—about ninety-five miles north of Tusslin Kantop—and then see Doran safely onto the ten o'clock train.

"Night, Jenson," the guard said, as he buzzed him out of the building. "Have a great vacation."

"Will do," the cook replied.

Doran felt the case bumping down the steps, sensed a sudden drop in temperature. He was out, but the part he'd been dreading most was being locked in the trunk of the car, still inside the suitcase. They'd agreed not to talk until he was out of it, to avoid suspicion, so all he could do was close his eyes and imagine that he could hear Humbucker's soul-elevating flute music, the roar of a mighty waterfall as it cascaded down rocks into the waiting mists below.

His breath was coming out in panicked bursts by the time Jenson opened the trunk and pulled him out. But the cook was smiling, holding out the train ticket, and a plastic bag crammed full of clothes, food, and blankets.

"Fifteen minutes till it pulls out," he said, embracing Doran genially. "Best get on board, little buddy."

During the journey, Doran studied the map of Cassaforta that Jenson had given him. Drayborn Fells was a further 460 miles north of Pellaman Town, but the cook knew of a hydro plant in Pellaman that was taking on casual laborers, providing free accommodation and meals. Doran figured it would take him at least a week to save up enough for a ticket to Drayborn, but he was content just knowing that every little clatter of the engine was taking him closer to Domino. He wrapped his fingers tightly around the crimson octopus and smiled.

The hydro plant had been hard to find. It was four miles from Pellaman Station, way out in the back of beyond, and he'd had to ask several people for directions. However, once he heard gushing water, and saw six wooden silos looming in the distance, Doran's hopes were restored. He passed the mossy man-made watercourses, being careful not to slip, the huge waterwheels paddling and churning behind him. The air felt crisp, and he breathed it long and hard.

He was sweating a little when, at last, he entered a small hut in front of the main silo, where a gray-haired man in his early sixties was sitting behind a desk.

"I've heard you're taking on casual laborers."

"That's right. Name and age, please."

"Quin Oakley. I'm sixteen."

The man looked Doran up and down a few times, then squinted, his hand reaching for the phone. "Wait there," he said to Doran, flatly. Then, into the mouthpiece, "Come over to number four."

Presently, two stocky police sergeants strode into the building. All Doran could do was stand there, silently wishing the ground would swallow him up.

THE PRESENT

It's late at night, the Xenon's buzzing through my veins, and I'm harking back to the time Earl and I played baseball with some younger kids in Jade Walk Park when we were thirteen. I noticed him throw our game a couple of times, and when I quizzed him about it later, he said he let them win so's they'd head home feeling good about themselves.

"He was like that, Earl: always puttin' others first. Never went round mollycoddlin' an ego. Guess he was pretty damn close to perfect, that best bud of yours." Harvey's on the push-along carousel, hand gripping an Aglo Stout, his face coasting past me every twenty seconds or so as the merry-go-round creaks under a frosty, star-filled sky.

"Can't do it no more, Harv—hide behind these memories. Wallbanger was right. I gotta face up to the here and now, take responsibility for whatever it is Weinberg wants to tell me."

Harvey's lips tremble a little, and he stops the carousel by dragging his heels on the tarmac. "Then I can't protect you no more," he says, slumping down opposite me onto the grass. "And that means I got no business bein' here." Already he's getting paler, flickering, and I can't tell if I'm looking at his outline or the dark shapes of the bushes as they bend in the wind.

"Harvey? Don't go, man. I didn't mean what I said." I'm bawling good and proper now, beating my fists on the ground, burying my head in a sea of white daisies, their petals tickling my tear-soaked cheeks. "Jeez. I don't wanna be Doran."

"Little golden boxes, Carney," Harvey whispers before his voice fades completely. "We dug every one of 'em. We dug 'em all."

39

Troccapago

One of Cuthbert's heavies whacked me on the jaw and then just stood there, smirking about it. He looked so smug it crossed my mind that the move was probably something he'd practiced ad nauseum in his bedroom with one of those punchbags on a stick. Then he took a potshot at my chest that sent me sprawling onto the floor.

"He's only playin' with ya!"

Cuthbert was a human blimp: beer-bellied, short, and bald save for a few straggly grays at the side that he'd smeared with moly grease, judging by the smell, and then scraped across his scalp as an apology for hair. The guy was pug-ugly too, covered all over in these tacky, washed-out tattoos. He was a prize slimeball, no doubt about it, and the thought of him made me squirm, but AJ got sent down for six months, so I had no place else to go.

"It's a warnin'," Cuthbert said. "You buy from the Sherman Tanks from now on—just us, no one else. If we find out you've been sniffin' round Kellerman or any of his lot, then there'll be more a' this to come. *Comprendo?*"

I didn't much care about his beef with other gangs, so I just rubbed my face where it was sore and nodded at him. I guess it did the trick because he hurled the packet at me, and as soon as I had it zipped into my jacket, I couldn't help grinning. I'd actually pulled it off. The first time I came to this hellhole, I didn't have enough. The graduation medal only fetched two hundred at Shancey's, and they wanted nine, so I had to go back to Hailey's, hock my mom's gold wedding ring, and then hitch all the way back. They even made me give them the pawn ticket to prove the gowder was good.

"Can I go now?"

Outside, the sky was gray as lead, and a smattering of thunderclouds were sweeping in from the west. Hailey's was just over an hour's drive north, and I wanted to get to the freeway before the downpour started, as it would be harder to thumb a ride after that. I scurried down the embankment, relieved to be away from the junkyard and Cuthbert's rancid old crib. Then, once I got under a streetlamp, I pulled out the map, figuring it would be quicker to cut through the playing field that ran at the side of the railroad.

And that was where they sprung me.

I think there were two of them, but I couldn't say for sure because they clubbed me on the head from behind, and I slumped to the floor before I had a chance to turn round. My nose was down in the dirt, and I was dazed as hell, but I could still hear them. They were frisking me, digging their hands into my pockets.

"Must be our lucky day!"

"What is it?"

"Some sort a' drug!"

"Best wallop him again."

There was only blackness, as if the void had rightly swallowed me up and I'd gone into it willingly, grateful for the release. But then my eyelids started quivering, and I could make out a face looking down at me, all fuzzy and jumbled, cloaked in a delicate veil of greenish-colored mist. A cool palm was resting on my forehead, and it reminded me of home, of Lucy and Leyland, the way they used to tend me when I was a little kid off sick from school. And then someone was quietly calling my name, as if it were a question.

"Carney?"

I lifted my head, a wall of pain searing through the back of it, but as my eyes got used to the light, he started to take shape: a dude in a dusty old fedora. Was this some kind of dream? "Marshall? What the hell're you doin' here?" My head and torso ached something chronic, and when I tried to sit up, it smarted so bad, I felt nauseous.

"Is that any way to greet an old friend?" He was kneeling over me, dragging on one of those sweet-smelling ebbies, with a calmness about him that seemed almost mystical.

"But… those assholes."

"Don't worry; I chased 'em off." He pulled the parcel out from one of his pockets and laid it on my chest. "Y' know, you really oughta take better care of the P. W."

"Eh?"

"Pugnacian wildflower. Come on, man. I'm parked over by the bridge."

He helped me up, and it wasn't long before I found myself riding shotgun in a shabby old Kaiser Manhattan, the seat springs digging into my thighs as it burned along the freeway at a law-breaking eighty-five miles an hour.

"What happened to the Dodge?"

"Rolled it in a drag race 'bout three months ago. Sold it for scrap."

The rain was coming down thick and fast, and the Manhattan's engine was rattling louder than a bulldozer, but Marshall seemed to have a way with the old girl.

"And you live in Troccapago now?"

"I work for Diesel Kellerman. You heard of him?" He cranked the window open, sending the butt of the ebby spinning out onto the road.

"Cuthbert mentioned the guy. Said not to have dealin's with him, or else."

Marshall raised his thick black eyebrows, took a slug from a bottle of liquor. "Your choice, Caldwell, but I'd bat for our team if I were you. Diesel's a thoroughbred—knows what's what when it comes to the pug-flower, and he only takes *el primo*. Can't say the same for the Shermans."

"Jeez. Wish I'd run into you before AJ put me onto Cuthbert."

He threw me a withering look.

Once we got over to Captain's Way, I thought it only right to offer Marshall a beer, but one just didn't seem enough. You know how it is.

"I'm way too tanked to drive back," Marshall said, about five hours later. "Mind if I crash here for the night?"

"It would be my honor," I told him. "There's a sleepin' bag in the closet somewhere. Come on up and I'll dig it out."

Upstairs in my room, I spread the bedroll alongside the window, smoothing it out with my hands. "Last time I had this baby out we were down on the beach in good ole Tennacia Bay. You shoulda stayed with us, Marsh, instead a' runnin' off like ya did. We had such a gas over the summer, before we all went our separate ways, that is. And graduation was a riot. You shoulda seen us."

"You talk too much, Caldwell." Marshall downed another swig of Aglo Stout, then fired up a Dimer.

"Can't help it; been alone too long. And maybe it's that crack on the head, but I feel wired as a plugboard. Say, you collect baseball cards? I got two Steadmans if you want the duplicate. They're rare as hen's teeth, but I guess I got lucky."

"I'll take it off your hands if you don't want it." Marshall pulled off his baseball boots and stretched himself out on the sleeping bag, arms behind his head. "Well, one thing you'll be glad to know: took me a while to get round to it, but I got the Angels tattoo."

I swung myself up onto the bed. "How come? Thought you reckoned it was dumb?"

"Oh, I dunno. Guess it was... just somethin' I had to do."

"Why? Can you explain?"

A pack of Dime Chimes and a matchbox rattled onto the pillow, and then Marshall shuffled over to the window on his knees. He gazed out, elbows balanced on the ledge. "You chase the green lady, so you know the deal, right?"

"Sure. It can be intense as hell sometimes. But most of it's beautiful. Didn't lapse into the shurbs, not once."

"Yeah. Them huckleberry dreams." He chuckled, shaking his head. "You ever feel like you're tryin' to solve a puzzle, though? And all it does is tease you—offer you the barest snatches of what it is you're searchin' for?"

The rain was slicking down the panes, and I could hear the angry grumble of thunderheads somewhere out past the Bolars. I lit a Dimer and tossed the box back down to him. "I know wha'cha mean. At the start, there was this big ole ship that kept on talkin' in riddles. But after a while, I stopped seein' it. I was pretty crushed when it went. Guess I was wantin' answers about why everyone wound up someplace else. Just never thought I'd end up all lonesome like this."

Marshall looked over at me, the glare from the streetlamp caught in his gaze, and for a fleeting second it was like that time down at the creek, all those months ago, when something was there, burning away in his eyes—something nebulous, but powerful and real—a feeling he was desperate to hide. It seemed like an age had passed since then, but, as he pressed his fingers to the glass and stared out at the dimness of Hailey's Town, I finally realized that it wasn't fear at all; it was just an aching, hollow emptiness, exactly like my own.

"Never talk to pushers about loneliness," he said. "Most of 'em wrote the book."

I'd been chewing on the question all night, so I let my guard down for a while and forced it out. "There was a message scraped in dust at that old warehouse—the one where Ranton dumped us. Was it you who scrawled it?"

Marshall slid inside the sleep-sack and drew on the Dimer, watching the smoke curl away in front of him. "That's my point exact. It was all part a' the trip, but I dunno what it means. Just remember there was someplace I had to get, whatever the cost. But in the cold light of day, I couldn't figure it out, so I just headed west." He glanced at the ash on the Dimer, frowned a little. "That's how I wound up in the Troccas, sellin' for Diesel."

"What about your old man?"

"Called him once I got there and he upped sticks and came with me. We're both dyin' to get back to Hailey's, though. No place like it, and that's where we belong." He pushed up his shirtsleeve and held out his wrist, but it wasn't an Angels ink he was showing me; it was an expandable, sterling-silver bracelet that bore the inscription, 'Marshall Bexley, Hailey's Town'.

"Wow, you've worn that all your life?"

"Damn straight. The old man had it engraved and everythin' before I was even born. He was that made up I was comin'."

"And your mom?"

"Ran off with a bank teller when I was two. Don't hear from her no more."

"Sorry, man. Never knew my mom, neither."

Marshall stubbed out the Dimer and yawned. "Y' know, Caldwell, we should be out dancin' on a night like this. We should be out chasin' girls, not some dumbass plant."

"You could go—out dancin', I mean—but I can't leave Lucy on her own."

"Bring her along. No law against old-timers goin' out after dark. Tell ya what; I'll come over Saturday night an' we'll hit the dance floor over at Buddy's."

The next morning, I thought he'd left early, but as I was bounding down the stairs, I heard the distant pulse of a bass guitar coming from the dining room. And when I peered in through the gap in the door, I saw that he was in there, slow-dancing with Lucy as the honey-coated croon of Sam Cooke's 'You Send Me' crackled through the speaker of Leyland's old wind-up gramophone. They were stepping across a square of dappled winter sunlight that Dol had happened to carve out for them on the carpet. And, as shadows from the mahonia bush glided daintily over Lucy's face, I realized I'd never seen her look so proud, so joyful. I could scarcely believe what I was witnessing. It was just so unexpected, so mind-blowingly beautiful.

40

Lucy Dancing

I was dodging the ice puddles at the front of Kepple's, feeling kind of smug because I'd bagged myself an interview for an apprentice mechanic job. Oddly, setting it up had been a real cinch, and weirdest of all, I had Marshall to thank.

His visit changed everything—not because I was made up that one of the Angels had finally set foot in Hailey's again. It was more to do with how cool he'd been about Lucy, offering to bring her to Buddy's with us, dancing with her so sweetly in the dining room. I guess it opened my eyes, reminded me she was worthy of moments like that. He was just some half-crazy, dope-peddling hood that I barely knew, but somehow, he made me see how lousy I'd been acting ever since Leyland and the others left town. He gave me the proverbial kick up the ass I needed, and now all I wanted was to fix everything: to quit the green stuff, find some work, and save up enough gowder to buy back the wedding ring.

There was something else besides all that, though—something to do with the sight of Lucy dancing and the way it brought me hope for the first time since summer ended. It was a fleck of light in a darkened world, a little ray of joy that life had flung at me when I was least expecting it. And most important of all, the grace, the sheer perfection of it was very slowly unraveling the cobweb, shrinking the vacuum just that little bit more every time I pictured it. I knew, as sure as anything, that the wheels were set in motion, that it had somehow carved out a path—a blueprint for my sense of who I wanted to be. I guess, sometimes, the smallest of acts can have as much sway as a life-changing decision to take up medicine or something.

All this stuff was going through my head when I spotted a Manhattan, just like Marshall's, parked outside the drugstore on the other side of the street. Then I saw him strolling out of Fenmart, dropping a bag of groceries into the trunk. He was just about to jump in the driver's seat, so I crossed over and waved.

"I can get you a discount, y' know, once I land the Kepple's job." I poked at the flakes of rust on the hood, and Marshall grinned.

"Hey, Caldwell," he said. "We're back in Hailey's permanent now, me an' the ole man. How's about you and I head over to Buddy's to celebrate? We could shoot some pool, if you're up for it."

It was strangely quiet inside, as if the chaos of Buddy's in the evening was some feisty feral that they only dared let out after dark. Some tradesfolk were smoking at a table near the dance hall where 'Poor Little Fool' by Ricky Nelson was playing, but no one else was around, and Tamzin had turned the jukebox down real low. She was stretched out on the bar, her back leaned against a pillar as she mouthed the words, a bottle of ale in one hand and a half-smoked Camel in the other.

She beamed when she saw us. "Ain't seen you two around for a while," she said, jumping down behind the beer taps. "What can I get you?"

"Marshall's been outta town, and I guess I've been too busy just lately. I'll take a Pepsi." I pushed a ten-ban note across the counter.

"A Wild Bandit for me and a token for the pool table." Marshall pulled out a bar stool and sat himself down.

"Comin' right up. So, what brings you back to Hailey's then, Marsh?"

He took his hat off, twirled it in his hands a couple of times, and then ran his hand over his quiff. "Oh, I was just thinkin' the other night as I lay in my bed—how we're born and then we die, and all anyone ever really does is try to make sense of the bit in the middle." He smiled at her winsomely, as if that was all part of the explanation.

"Well, I'll be. Never heard anythin' profound as that at ten o'clock in the mornin'." Tamzin squeezed the button at the end of the soda gun, and a frothy stream of cola hissed into a tumbler. "So, did you? Make any sense out of it, I mean?" She grabbed a beer from the icebox and jimmied the lid off. "Don't let on you're too young to be drinkin' this, okay?"

Marshall downed a few short gulps. "The way I figure it, folks are always chasin' after what they see as beautiful. Don't matter if it's a girl, a dip in the ocean, or a brand-new Plymouth Fury. They want to own it, become one with it, just to keep from thinkin' too hard about death and how it's unavoidable. You could call it escapin' by proxy if you like. But holdin' onto anythin' just ain't possible, no matter what. Best you can do in this crazy world is dance."

Tamzin stared at him, kind of thunderstruck. Then she said, "Don't explain why you came back. They got dance halls everywhere."

Marshall plonked the fedora on his head. "Well, there's a lot to be said for comin' back. It's a noble thing, 'specially when it's done in style." He winked at her. "Between you and me, I'm startin' at The Apex tomorrow. Monday to Wednesday I'll be chief projectionist, and on Thursdays and Fridays I'll be handin' out the ice creams at intermission."

Saturday, December 20th, 2324

True to his word, Marshall pulled up in the Manhattan at about eight on Saturday and, after we'd spent half an hour or so preening ourselves, and helping Lucy do the same, we guided her over to the old groundy. It was still slippery on the sidewalk, so we had to stride either side of her, arms linked together. Then we sped off, fresh air fluttering through the dash vents, grizzled moonbeams pirouetting over the fenders.

When we got to Buddy's, things were already buzzing. The only table up for grabs was the one by the window—the same place the Angels squabbled back in April, before Shap Ranton showed up. I was down to just two pugs every other night and I'd kicked the Grimley's altogether, but somehow, being in Buddy's and thinking about the past was okay. It didn't get me feeling all jittery and blue. We ordered some coffee, yakked while we supped it, and then settled ourselves by the jukebox over in the dance hall. The Chordettes' 'Lollipop' was jangling out of it, and Lucy was smiling so wide it was almost like she'd reached up to the sky and snatched down one of those moonbeams.

I'm not one for bragging, but I danced with so many girls that night, I lost count. And more to the point, I never once thought about B-sides, cobwebs, pug-flowers, or Dakota. It was like all that bad stuff happened to a whole other person—like the sweetness had melted it down to a bunch of foggy, half-forgotten shapes that no longer meant anything. And then, when the giant snail spun up Roy Orbison's 'Only the Lonely', I knew it was time. I marched over to Lucy and led her out onto the dance floor. I remembered her face flecked with sunlight as she flitted across the dining room floor, her hands resting lightly on Marshall's shoulders. I thought it was a one-off—something so rare, so far out it could never happen again—but now the self-same look was there in her eyes. It was like time had stopped being something linear and fixed, and she'd stepped inside of its brand-new shape, free of her broken mind and body. I swayed to the music, Lucy clutched at my side, and I was struck by a sense of harmony—a rejuvenating balance that seemed to be setting everything back to its rightful place.

Taking the P. W. had been a kind of one-man civil war, but I knew then, without a shadow of a doubt, that there'd be no more gunshots. The battle was over and there was no denying the victor. Carney the junkie, the weak, self-centered jerk I'd been fighting against, had been rightly crushed—slain by the proud and decent man he'd always wanted to become.

Ten days later, Marshall turned up on the doorstep, late in the evening, a tatty cardboard box under his arm and an apologetic grin on his face. "Old man's gonna be outta town for a while," he told me. "Needs another back op, but they can't do it here. I had to drive him all the way to Stockton Grange this mornin'. Mind if I crash here for a coupla weeks? I sure could use some company."

"Shouldn't you be at The Apex?" I said, and when he looked at me all sheepish, I realized the combined chief projectionist/ice cream seller thing had been a total wind-up. But I didn't hold it against him. Seeing how colorful he could make a tale and still have folks believe it was just one of his ways. Anyway, I knew he was good for Lucy, and seeing her so chirpy kept me on the wagon, so I invited him in. "You can have Leyland's old room," I told him.

Later that night, we played fake Lucy poker, taking turns to spin the records on the old gramophone, and when Bobby Vee's

'The Night Has a Thousand Eyes' breezed out of the speaker, an unbelievable feeling of gladness swept over me. The fire was sputtering away in the hearth, the rain was drumming on the roof tiles, and every pulse of Grandpa's pendulum clock seemed mollifying—like it was secretly pumping out some bliss-inducing elixir.

After Lucy went to bed, we downed a few root beers in the living room, me lounging in the comfy chair by the window, Marshall sprawled out on the couch.

"Y' know, Marsh, you seem so different. You used to be so…"

His eyes met mine head-on, and I half-expected that yearning, empty look to be there—the one I'd somehow mixed up with fear—but it was gone. "What?"

I shrugged. "Well… sullen, I guess. I dunno; it's like you swapped your lead for gold or somethin'. Just wonderin' if there's a reason for it?"

Marshall didn't answer me then, at least, not directly. He was full of his thoughts, and all I could hear was the sizzle of the fire, the even beat of the clock. Then he said, "I'm gonna do the same as you, Caldwell. No more for me. I'll even quit sellin' it."

"What's brought all this on?"

He looked up at the ceiling, then plumped the cushion, laying his head back against it. "It's like I told Tamzin," he said. "I'm done with chasin' round for things."

41

Long Distance to Drayborn Fells

DORAN'S STORY

"Thank you, gentlemen. I'll deal with Doran now," Hauntmead said, feigning warmth. Then, once the police were gone, he sat back in his chair, seething, his face so red Doran thought a blood vessel might pop open. The man kept tugging at his graying hair, slowly shaking his head and sighing. Then, at last, he spoke.

"I promised you a longer stretch in solitary if it happened again." His voice was surprisingly calm and quiet, but Doran found it more terrifying than if he'd yelled. "And you can forget about your friend, Jenson. I fired him as soon as I found out about your plot. He'll most likely be expelled to Magnatella after what I told the authorities about him."

He escorted Doran down to the cellar again, shoving him into the cooler room, chaining his wrist to the wall as before. Then he held up a bony finger, shaking it just under Doran's nose. "You'll have five days alone in here with no meals. That's plenty of time to think about what you've done and how much trouble you've caused me." With that, he exited, locking the door tightly behind him, and all Doran could do was curl into a fetal position, willing himself to sleep, despite the cold, the lack of any blankets, the hardness of the floor.

When he wasn't sleeping, Doran passed the time by dreaming things up in his mind, vowing to bring his creations to life just as soon as he had pen and paper in his hands. He designed drawings, composed poems, wrote stories, letters to Domino—everything committed to memory. And when the stint was finally over, he set about keeping his pledge. Indeed, he poured his heart out to Domino in a series of about seven letters spanning five weeks. He described his escapes in detail: the running, how far he got, the moments he was apprehended, the punishments. And he would always include some form of artwork with his correspondence: pencil sketches of the caves at Nentoke, stylized images of *The Dreamcatcher,* or detailed watercolors of Maple Road's apple blossoms budding into bloom at the start of spring. Sometimes he would send bird drawings, writing prose alongside them to provide some context. For example, beneath a large charcoal dated January 24th, 2321, he supplied the following annotation: *Timid little rook in cage. He's been fighting every day of his life to get out. And one day, by some twist of fate, he'll find a way. And then he'll launch himself, wings trembling, into a vast and undiscovered sky.* His messages were never answered, but he told himself he had to keep trying. After all, what else did he possess besides his hope?

February was winding to a close when his spirit, battered and bruised as it had been, was finally broken. He was attending a literature class, listening diligently to Ms. Godfrey as she read aloud from *The Third Man.* Just as she was coming to the part about the Wiener Riesenrad, there was an urgent rap at the door.

Then one of the senior boys was marching over to her desk, lowering his head to speak with her. Doran sat up with a start when he heard his name.

"Doran D'Argent. You're wanted on the phone at the front desk."

They let him go downstairs unaccompanied, and when he got into the lobby, Miss Glut was waiting by the telephone, holding out the receiver.

"It's Doran speaking." It was the first time he had used a Cassafortan handset, and he was unaccustomed to the weight and clumsiness of it in his hand.

The voice at the other end was relaxed but assertive. "This is Ben Truscott, chief warden over at Linnestone Juvenile Correction Center in Drayborn Fells. It's about your sister, Domino. We gather you've been writing to her."

Doran couldn't tell from the tone whether it was going to be good or bad news, but his pulse was galloping, he couldn't stop quaking, and his mouth was becoming dry as cracked mud. "Is she doing alright?"

The chief warden certainly didn't beat about the bush. "I'm sorry to have to break it to you like this, but your sister was assaulted by another prisoner back in October, shortly after she arrived here. She suffered a massive head injury. She remained comatose and critical for a few months, but unfortunately, she passed away early this morning at about a quarter past eight."

THE PRESENT
Tuesday, February 3rd, 2325

Weinberg gives me another pack of Oakwood Milds after finishing the chapter—not much consolation for such a glum ending. It's weird. I can't help feeling like I did last summer when everyone jumped ship and I found out Dakota wasn't coming back. Luckily, Narla gets here with the tray not long after the governor leaves, and I figure there's not much to lose—no smart tricks; I'll just ask her straight.

"I want two shots tonight."

"Okay, Mr. Caldwell."

I'm going to fight off all thoughts about the past, force myself to focus on the present—to accept whatever's happened, even if it kills me. But before I can start, I'm acutely aware of someone else in the room. I can't see him, but he's here, no doubt about it.

"Wallbanger?"

My voice is soft, serene. I don't want to drive him away. And slowly, in that empty rectangle on the wall, a face starts to appear: flaxen curls, Buddy Holly specs, the whole double-edged sword thing still glinting in his eyes.

"Yeah, it's me," is all he says.

"Harvey's gone?"

"Yep."

"Then I'm ready. I ain't scared a' ya no more."

He fades a little, fuzzy edges, and then I'm somehow in the picture with him, back in the parking lot at Sorley Ridge House, the groundies all rusted, burnt out, or smashed up and scavenged for parts. It's late at night, and the air smells strangely of freesias and catmint as we stare into each other's eyes. We're so close, I can count the freckles on his cheekbones.

"Come on then, bud. Show me the blade."

"Ain't a blade. I told ya. But that don't mean it ain't gonna hurt. Truth cuts harder sometimes. How you gonna live with what you did?"

"That bad, huh?"

"Yep. That bad. Maybe I should just take a swing at you?" His right fist lands at the side of my jaw, and then his left catches me under the chin, forcing my tongue to tatter against my teeth, blood dripping down onto the concrete. Then he thrusts me over the hood of a wrecked old Cadillac, pulls out some kind of pistol, and aims it at my temple. "That's right," he says. "This is who we are. Nothin' but mindless thugs. I sent Harvey packin', and I'm gonna waste you, too."

"Look, man. I know you ain't gonna hurt me, 'cause we're two parts of the same. Take me out, and you go with me. Right?"

Despite the words, we're both trying to hide how bad we're shaking. I can sense the anger swirling in his belly as the gun grip rattles against the ring on his index finger, my breath a burst of fits and gulps. Wallbanger's sweating so fierce his hair and shirt are totally soaked.

"You ain't wrong," he snarls. "Can't kill you exactly, but once I pull the trigger, you'll be me. You'll know everythin' I know."

"Then do it, Wallbanger. It's what I want. No point puttin' it off any longer."

I'm aware of something trickling down onto my neck. At first, I figure it's the sweat from his brow, but then he lowers the weapon, breaks down sobbing, head bent between his knees.

"I can't go on with this, bud."

I crouch down quietly beside him, and he looks up at me with eyes red raw, buries his face against my shoulder. "It's okay," I whisper. "Whatever the truth is, we can face it. I mean, it doesn't have to be this way. It's just the pills—the head trips. I know I sent my best bud into a coma, and I know it's worse than I thought at the start. That's why I conjured you up. But it's like we've switched places. Now I wanna know, you don't wanna tell me."

Wallbanger sits up, drags his shirtsleeve across his eyes. "Let's get outta this shithole," he says, glancing round at the wrecked groundies. "We're buzzed up, after all. We can be wherever we want."

As soon as his words are out, we find ourselves sitting on the hood of a khaki Chrysler New Yorker in Kepple's workshop, the hands of the old banjo clock about to hit midnight. I offer the guy a Dime Chime, Stephen Sanchez's 'Send My Heart with a Kiss' ringing out blissfully from the old groundy's radio as moonlight seeps in through the back window, wrapping everything in a soft blue haze.

"Never thought it would end like this."

"Me neither," he says, lighting up. "Thought there'd be a real brawl, but you never fought back."

"Was never gonna happen. Just ain't me."

There's a silence, an unspoken understanding between us that I'm not what he thought—that I'm still a pacifist, in spite of everything that's gone on.

"Y' know, I was glad, in a way, when Leyland stopped me goin' to college. Guess I wasn't ready to grow up, to find out whether all the scuttlebutt about Magnatella was true. But I ain't scared now."

My alter ego smiles back at me like Uncle Boo used to when he was winning at poker: a mellow, lopsided grin.

"I was thinkin', Walls. When they throw me in the poke, reckon I'll ask 'em if I can be a gardener. I'd be alright doin' that. I could plan out what to write in my books while I'm prunin' the hedgerows. Whether I'm Doran or Carney or a goddamn reincarnation of Gilbert Gowder, I can take the truth, however bad it is. I can write about it. I'll be okay in jail. I know it."

Wallbanger's frowning sadly now, eyes narrowed in the smoke. "The truth's Weinberg's responsibility," he says. "He knows what he's doin', and I won't interfere. The story's almost done." He pauses for a while, dragging on the Dimer like it's his last, and I guess it really is. His face is little more than a silhouette, silvered by the glow of AJ's old lava lamp behind him. But before he disappears, he turns to me, a wayward sparkle in what's left of his eyes. "That Weinberg's a crafty old son of a gun. All that stuff about *The Third Man*. It was a dead giveaway. I mean, how could he know that was the book? He was tryin' to tell ya."

"Come back, Wallbanger. You can't just bail. Not you, of all people."

A cloud slides over the moon, and the lamp trips out, plunging everything into darkness. And there's an eerie sense of something familiar, like the past is well and truly here with me now because I've dared to let it go. It's like something alive, breathing softly against the side of my neck. I jump down from the hood, move toward where the lamp should be, but there's no table, only emptiness.

"Wallbanger?"

A clock strikes behind me—a grandfather clock—twelve tolls in quick succession, echoing, booming back and forth as if I'm in some kind of tunnel.

"Don't be afraid, Carney Caldwell. The doors have opened. Step inside."

I thought if I ever heard those accents again, I'd freak out big time, but somehow they're comforting, like I've secretly been aching to hear them.

"Everythin's gonna be set right?" I shuffle forward in the blackness: five steps, six, then seven. I wait, tiny specks of color jumping about: no dread, no panic. Is time travel real? Have I really gone back? It's just that it was exactly like this, being six years old. I remember the way the air tasted, how every second felt like a spark of something wild, something precious.

"Carney?" It's Lucy's voice.

"Am I in the machine now, Luce? Is everythin' fixed? Am I in a world where you never got sick? Where Dakota didn't take all those pills?"

"No need to worry 'bout that," she says kindly. "It's over now. And if you ever feel lost again, just remember; no one knows who you are. Only you can know that. And when your time's done, there'll be nothin' at all to link you and your consciousness together. What greater freedom is there than that?"

"But the copy world—it's gone for good?"

Lucy laughs, like she used to with Uncle Boo when he was spouting crap after downing too much vodka. "Every heart has a cradle," she says. "And you're restin' in mine from now till the end of eternity. You're ready now, Smoky—ready to hear the truth."

When I wake, there's a note at the foot of the bed saying my medication will be changed to Stalabatim due to a shortage of supplies.

42

The Black Ink Message

Somehow, Doran found the strength to carry himself up that precarious old staircase back to the dormitory, but, late in the afternoon when the other boys discovered him there on his bed, it was as if he'd retreated permanently into a silent world of vacantness. Ostensibly, he was out for the count and, no matter how hard they tried, it was impossible to stir him.

Of course, Hauntmead was summoned, but according to eyewitness accounts, both of his tactics—slapping the boy and dousing him in freezing-cold water—failed to have any effect. Doran's body responded only as an empty shell. In the end, the tutor conceded, resigning the child to his "fate in the realm of the undead". At least, those were the words he used when he called the medics, but it was probably not out of concern for the boy's welfare. He was most likely worried that a death might instigate a full-blown investigation into the school's affairs, and he didn't want people snooping around, getting wind of his checkered past and all the skullduggery he'd thus far managed to conceal. As a result, Doran was transported by ambulance to Tusslin Kantop Medical Center that same evening, so that he could be monitored and fitted with a nasogastric tube. This proved to be the best course of action, because he remained in this semi-comatose state until mid-March.

It was early, and washed-out sunbeams were sparkling through the ward's east-facing windows when his eyelids, like the buds of spring's first snowdrops, slowly unfolded to the incoming light. Soon after, he was able to take in his surroundings and, although unable to speak, he gradually began to feed and wash himself. There was some debate about where he should be sent after discharge, but, because of the sheer volume of red tape and the lack of coordination on the part of social services, he ended up being escorted back to the Dover Plain Reform School at the beginning of April.

When he returned, he was deathly pale about the face and still wouldn't utter a word. It seemed he was animated only by the faintest, frailest trace of life force, and only because some kind-hearted medical staff had willed it so. It was as if the very essence had been sucked right out of him. Yes, he complied— showing up for lessons, completing his chores, staying out of trouble, and all the rest—but only because the fight was gone from him.

It was about eight in the evening, April 14th, 2321, a day that had endured non-stop rain since the small hours, and Doran was almost nodding off when a familiar squawk outside the window startled him out of it. At first, he thought he was imagining things, but then a mop of raisin-colored quills pressed up close against the glass, and Carina began to tap vigorously at the pane with her beak.

Doran tottered over, and when he lifted the frame, she leapt straight onto his forearm, shook her wet feathers, and clung to him, weaving her talons into the fibers of his tatty Dover Plain uniform. Gleefully, he skimmed his fingers over her plumes, kissing her on the crown. The bird was just like a miniature car-wash brush, all shaggy after the final rinse, and he was so overjoyed to see her that, at first, he failed to notice the tiny parchment slotted into her foot band. When at last he spotted it, he plucked it out and unrolled it, staring wide-eyed at the black-inked words elegantly inscribed in the curl of a hand he knew as well as his own.

April 9th, 2321

Dear Doran,

Carina came to me back in November with the message you sent. She stayed by my side, just like you wanted, but I'm taking a chance with her now because I wrote you several times by mail, but never got anything back. Security here has been hell, but there's an outing coming up soon—a real chance for me to slip away unseen. With any luck I'll be on my way to you in the next few days. Please wait for me.

Until the stars turn black,
Domino

Tears of happiness dribbled from Doran's chin, landing on the fluff of Carina's neck. Then he pressed his face into his pillow, unashamedly sobbing out loud. He felt revitalized, exhilarated, as if his heart had suddenly been fortified with galvanized steel. He could feel it thumping away of its own free will now, rather than out of a sense of duty to those that had nursed him back to health.

THE PRESENT

The relief makes me smile, and it's not something I can hide from Weinberg. Maybe I'm starting to care for these characters after all, just like he wanted.

"But the call?"

"It was faked. Strumpole bullied the geography teacher into impersonating the warden. He wanted to put an end to the boy's scarpering." Weinberg starts rifling through his briefcase, takes out a small rolled-up document all yellowed with age, and places it in the palm of my hand.

"This is the actual note?" I feel oddly humbled, like I'm touching some sacrosanct relic that's been stuffed away in a museum for thousands of years. But at the same time, my hands start to shake because it points to the truth of everything he's told me.

DORAN'S STORY

Unfortunately, Doran's euphoria was very short-lived. Just as he was setting Carina down onto the mattress, the door swung wide open, and Hauntmead stalked in.

"I told you I'd wring its neck!"

He strode over to Doran, making a swipe at the bird, but she was too fast and too smart for him. She stepped back, beating her wings to get airborne, and then she was lunging at him, pecking at his face, stabbing her bill into it as she hovered above him, just out of reach.

"I know she's alive!" Doran yelled. "So, who made the call? And what happened to the letters?"

Hauntmead was swatting at Carina like a clumsy old giant, but he couldn't get near her, and his face was quickly becoming bruised and bloodied. "Call it off and I'll tell you!" he stammered, Carina still flapping relentlessly.

"Carina!"

She swerved in mid-air, swooped, and then fluttered dutifully onto Doran's shoulder.

Hauntmead plopped himself down onto one of the beds, puffing, smoothing out his ruffled gray hair. "Your letters never left this building. I have them all in my bureau drawer downstairs, along with the ones the prison girl sent you." He paused, dabbing at his forehead with a handkerchief. "And one day, I'll crack that ridiculous code of yours. I can promise you that."

"What about the phone call?"

The tutor squinted at Doran, clutching the handkerchief tight in his fist. It seemed the assault had shaken him badly. "It was Mr. Leeward on the phone that morning. I couldn't have you running out on me again. After all, I have my reputation to consider."

"So, you made me believe Domino was dead?" Carina was nuzzled close to Doran's chest, the steady pulse of her heart giving him courage. He rumpled the scrag of down under her beak, and then stared at her, astonished by the smallness of Hauntmead's reflection in her eyes. "I'll make sure somebody hears about this," he said, his tone firm and steady. "I'll go to the cops next time I get out. You'll be finished then."

I guess no one had stood up to Hauntmead like that before. He rose, straightened his robes, and marched over to the door, his hand poised just above the handle. And when he spoke there was a hint of anguish in his tone. "Alright. I swear I won't harm the bird. I'll even give you the letters. I'm sure we can strike up a deal that'll give us both exactly what we want. Let's work together and not fight anymore. Send it on its way, and then come down to my study. We'll discuss this matter as equals." He looked properly into the boy's eyes then, perhaps for the first time. "You know, I see so much of myself in you." With that, he turned and walked briskly away, his gown flowing out behind him.

Doran tried, but he just couldn't picture Hauntmead as a fourteen-year-old child. And then he remembered the oil painting of the swan. Maybe there was hope for the tutor after all. Perhaps Carina's battering had rekindled something in him—unearthed a soul buried deep in the rubble of all that hatred. "I'm going to hear him out, Carina—give him one last chance to come good. He might even let me leave tonight." He set her down on the window ledge and watched admiringly as she jiggled her tail feathers, leaned downward so that her head was level with them, and then, with only a gentle rustle of her wings, disappeared into the freshness of the sky.

"Wait for me in the trees," he called after her. Then he trooped down the stairs, knocking loudly on Hauntmead's door.

"Come in."

Doran had only just stepped inside when a twine-bound wad of envelopes hit him in the chest.

"Here are the letters. If nothing else, I'm a man of my word."

The boy stooped to pick them up, slipping Carina's scroll inside the top one. But when he glanced up, he was somewhat alarmed to see the tutor waltzing over to the door, locking it with one of the keys that he kept dangling from his belt.

"Why are you locking the door?" Doran stepped sideways toward the window, panic setting in when he saw that there were no latches.

"Because I neglected to tell you something important up there in the dorm." An acrid smirk was dancing on Hauntmead's lips. "Didn't you ever wonder how I knew precisely where to find you when you got away?"

Doran didn't answer; he just inched closer to the windowpanes, trembling. Maybe, if push came to shove, he could smash one of them with his fist and get out that way.

"I planted a chip in your brain one night while you were off in the land of nod—a tracking device. Magnatellans call it a type two tagmesh, but I constructed yours myself. That's probably why you blacked out; damn thing must've become unstable."

"What about our deal?"

"Oh, there won't be any deal, boy, not today. I have other, much more convenient ways of keeping you silent. And you needn't look so horrified. I'm not talking about snuffing you out. The police would be flocking round me like a kettle of vultures, and that wouldn't do at all. You see, that tagmesh of yours can be altered at the touch of a button. I can make you forget you were ever even born."

Doran clenched the pile of envelopes tight in his hand, his fingers sweating so badly it was difficult to keep a grip. "All I want is to read what she wrote," he whispered. "I won't say anything about you, not ever, not to anyone. I promise."

"Too risky." Hauntmead edged forward, drawing a rectangular gadget the size of a matchbox from his pocket. Then, before Doran had a chance to do anything, he thrust it against the boy's temple. It made no discernible sound. When Doran fell, there was just the crackle of flames in the old marble hearth.

From out in the hallway, one of the janitors heard a noise like an almighty firecracker exploding, and it sent him scurrying straight into the principal's office. And not long after, all four resident tutors came dashing down the stairs, their mouths gaping as soon as they entered. The sulfuric reek of gunpowder was everywhere, and Hauntmead's lower left arm was gushing so much blood they thought at first it had been severed.

"The ghastly child shot me," the man was bleating. "How the hell did he get hold of a firearm? Someone better call the police."

Doran was lying by the windows, his arms extended above his head, a large revolver not far from his right hand. He was mostly still, but his eyes were open, and he was quivering a little.

"I think he's lapsed into another one of his blackouts," Hauntmead told them, deliberately forcing his voice to crack. "I'm afraid we can't have him here anymore. He's just too much of a danger to everyone."

THE PRESENT

"It happened April fourteenth. That's my birthday, y' know."

Weinberg shrugs. "You're right about that. Just a coincidence, I suppose."

"Guess so, but I ain't sure I follow. How did Doran manage to shoot the asshole?"

"He didn't. Strumpole shot himself. He reckoned no one would suspect that." Weinberg is nibbling at the end of a stubby blue pencil, and when he stops, I see flecks of the paint lodged between his teeth.

"So, Doran was innocent?"

"Innocent and, to all intents and purposes, no more. You see, Strumpole's self-made device successfully updated the program in the tagmesh, and when that happened, the latent type one capability was primed. Thus, as there were no waves from the Protson field to stop it, the defector chip kicked in, forcing all the boy's memories to slip silently into oblivion."

43

The Shurbs

I t's kind of amusing the way I've come to see the floral chair as wholly Weinberg's. Uncle Boo looks so out of place sitting there, clutching his clunky, chrome-plated microphone.

"Just think of it as prep for the hearin'," he says. "They want an audio statement, just in case you…"

"Pass out?"

Bewick shrugs, relaxes into a grin, then lays the bulky tape machine on the bed cover, level with my knees. "Well, let's just say they're aware of what went down over at the precinct." He jams the record and play buttons down, hovering the mic just below my chin. "I know we've been through this already, but can you tell me again what happened on January twelfth?"

"I guess it's ironic in a way, 'cause we quit the P. W."

"You and Marshall Bexley?"

"Yeah. We didn't need it no more, though we never figured out why." My voice gives out, and he's about to thump the stop switch, but I manage to pull myself together. "We were doin' the sensible thing, cuttin' it down. Early that mornin', Marsh went over to the Troccas to take the last of his gear back to Kellerman, but we kept enough for ourselves, just so's we could drive the shakes away. Lucy was out seein' *Singin' in the Rain* over at the Grayhide Center with some other folk from the film club, and when Marshall got back from droppin' her off, we split one. We were down to halves by then. We'd just see swirls of color, movin' shapes—nothin' to write home about."

"And what time was that?"

"Just past seven. I'd been offered a job at Kepple's, so I was pretty stoked, and we were plannin' to go chill over at Buddy's… maybe even pick up a couple of girls if we could manage it. Musta been gettin' on for eight when we got there, 'cause we left the Manhattan at home."

"And how long did you stay at Buddy's?"

"Only an hour or so. The jukebox packed up halfway through 'Smoke Gets in Your Eyes', so Tamzin closed the dance hall. And Marshall'd heard about this new joint over on Fiddler's Row, so we thought we'd check it out. We never got there, though. We stopped off in Broughton Alley on the way over. We lit up a Dimer at one of the tables. That's when…"

"It's okay, Carney. Take your time."

THE PAST
Monday, January 12th, 2325

It's crazy how a half could do it—and after all this time. At first, it was just like before; colors would melt, bleed into each other, go whirling through the air, appearing and disappearing like a mob of mischievous genies. I was pretty blasé about it really. I just sat back and let them get on with it, but after a while they vanished altogether, and everything went dark. Then this noise started up, as if an almighty engine was thundering to life, and I felt my body spinning. It was kind of cool at the start—like being on some weird, trippy carnival ride—but after a couple of minutes, I kept passing these grisly, elongated faces with no bodies. They were screaming at me, all the while yelling my name as if it was something vile and shameful. And there were hands with long, spindly fingers reaching for me. I thought if any of them touched me the world would end.

"You feelin' alright, Caldwell?"

"Marsh, we gotta get outta here. The hands—they're comin' for us. Think we've ended up in a B-side world somehow. And I can't get off this goddamn gramophone."

"Jeez. How many'd you take?"

"Oh, glory! I don't wanna be back here—anywhere but here." I was face down on the jetty, listening to my teeth rattle together in the bitterness of the wind, a mirror of frost the only thing visible between the slats. Hailey's Town had been destroyed—annihilated in a neo-apocalyptic war, along with almost everyone in it—and the creek was all that was left. I clung to the wood, scared that if I looked up, the hands would be there, waiting to grab me. I knew there was something out there because I could hear it whispering in my ears.

"Void's comin' back, boy. Gonna be stronger an' more cripplin' than ever; you mark my words."

A muffled thud came from underneath the walkway. I peered over the edge, real cautious, but ended up reeling back in horror. There was a human face trapped beneath the ice, and it was staring at me, the eyes wide and wild, the cheeks all pallid and bloated. She was pounding frantically, little bubbles trailing from her lips, her hair rippling behind her. It was Dakota, and suddenly the hands didn't matter anymore. Everything became panicked and urgent, my one mission in life just to get her out of there.

"Stay calm! I'll smash the ice!"

I blundered over to the west bank, desperate to find a rock heavy enough, but it was so dark all I could do was fumble about in the undergrowth. And then my fingers caught on something hard and lumpy, roughly the size of a football, so I snatched it up and scooted out onto the swampy ice rink. I slid over to the jetty and knelt, the mist rising from the surface, mingling with my breath so that I couldn't even tell which was which. I thrust the stone down hard, but the ice wouldn't break. All I could feel was the impact of it stinging me on the hand. I tried again—just kept lobbing it down, and every time the pain chafed so bad, I had to yelp out loud. Finally, echoing over from the crags, a crunching sound, like boots on snow, told me the whole of the lake was about to blow. I half-ran, half-skidded back to dry land, tripping over a tangle of lily pads and rolling head over heels into the reeds. Then I peered out at the pool of ice shards bobbing about in the fog and shadows. I could see Dakota's arms floundering for the jetty, so I tore across, slithering onto my belly, stretching out to her as far as I could reach.

"Over here! Grab hold!"

Her hand caught mine, and I hauled her up onto the walkway. She was coughing and shaking so fierce, I thought it would give way altogether.

"He's down there!"

"Who?"

A fist burst out from the splinters, snatching her by the hair and ripping her from me. She was teetering backward and, for an agonizing few seconds, she almost plunged back in, but I managed to pry the guy's fingers apart and pull her back. Her skin was cold as a tomb against mine, and when I glanced up, I saw that the night was black as tar, starless and moonless, as if its emptiness was some sort of warning—a reflection of the aching chill of holding her.

"Can you run?"

Dakota was in my arms, but it was Marshall's voice I could hear, drifting faintly over the rock tors behind me. "Just put the goddamn rock down."

"Is that you, Marsh? I can't see you. Where are we? What the hell's goin' on?"

Time and space were dilating so bad, it was like looking through a creepy, fogged-up fisheye lens, everything hazy and unreal. It was hard to make out, but a guy, dripping wet and holding a knife, seemed to be peering at me, his face lopsided, covered all over in scars. He had Kota's baseball jacket slung over his shoulder, and he was sniggering and pointing at it. Then there were sounds: witches' fingernails raking across a chalkboard.

"Hand her over, deadbeat, or I'll cut you in two."

I planted my knuckles square on Ranton's nose, no hesitation about it at all. I'd never belted anyone before, so it must have been pure instinct, the way I packed my full body weight behind it. Anyway, it turned out to be one hell of a blow because I heard the bone crunch, and he was forced to stagger back a few steps. He tried to regain his balance, but his guard was down, and that gave me enough time to pluck the knife from his hand, toss it into the ice pool, and deal out another Sunday punch that knocked the color clean out his cheeks. It sent him toppling sideways onto the grass. I risked a look over my shoulder at Dakota. She was face down on the bank, not moving.

"Don't slip away, Kotes, not again. I couldn't stand it."

"Relax, bud," she said, rolling onto her side. I thought she would smile, but instead she just wrinkled her face up like she meant business. She was pulling at the Inca dove etched on her wrist, all the while gritting her teeth, until a live bird slipped out of it and fluttered away into the trees.

One minute I was right beside her, the next I was perched in the big ulu tree, just propped against the trunk, my bones so leaden I couldn't move. All I could do was sit there as blades of grass shot up around Ranton, growing right through his limbs, sprouting out of him like some crazy speeded-up nature film. And then the silky strands of a giant cobweb were hauling him to his feet, and he was marching in Dakota's direction—a life-sized marionette, gossamer fibers draped across his torso, a train of tentacle-like leaves sweeping along behind him.

Once he got close enough, Dakota scrambled to her feet. "Time to pay the piper." She balled her fist, throwing punch after punch, and at such a speed the beast was doomed from the start. I think it went down after about five strikes. And then she was covering its head with her baseball jacket, slowly and solemnly, as if pronouncing it dead, but it felt like she was partly doing it for me as well—like something in me had croaked along with it—a childlike part that had been foolishly clinging to hope, full of misplaced dreams and innocence. She scattered the petals from three red poppies on top of the jacket, and I could hear her humming 'Sh-Boom', as though it was the saddest song in the world.

I don't know how long I spent in the tree after the creature took the pummeling. I remember a sense of respite for a while—a spell of sleeping, believing wholeheartedly that my soul was housed in the body of a humpback whale, somewhere deep in the Disian Ocean. But when I came out of it, I was back on the grass, bent over the fallen beast, the skin of my fingers streaked in dark, syrupy blood, just like the jacket. Dakota was gone, but her little pink Dimensadol pills were raining down everywhere in a stinging assault. I watched them fall as the scenery wrinkled away in front of me, a swarm of flickering blue lights taking its place, sirens yelping from all directions. The trip was winding down, but I didn't get why my hand was still bleeding, and why Marshall was slumped motionless on the tarmac, his right hand curled round a golden wedding band. The sight of it sent the blood draining from my head, made me buckle at the knees. Then my arms were forced behind my back, the cold steel of handcuffs biting into my wrists.

44

Incarceration

"What's the matter, Carney?"

Either Weinberg's got a bad bout of empathy or it's obvious I'm in bits. Maybe he knows the sheriff was in here earlier with his tape recorder, forcing me to go through all that shit again.

My jaw quivers. "Can't stop thinkin' about that goddamn weddin' ring."

"Ah, yes. Found in the victim's hand. That was meant to be the motive, or so I gather." He's shuffling through his papers again. "They're claiming you fought over it."

"Didn't even know he had it. I told 'em that." Thinking about the pug-flower is getting me all het up. "If I had a box a' those goddamn plants, I'd stomp all over 'em."

"Oh? Why is that?"

"Them and their cunnin' way of reelin' you in with the pinnacle. But all the while they're strippin' away reality—gettin' you so's you can't say for sure what's true and what ain't." It hits me that I'm opening up to Weinberg, but I guess it's okay now I know he's not a shrink. "Anyway, so much for your goddamn '50s dream—your little model of peace and perfection. If Cassaforta's so great, how come there's drug-dealin', and poor folk who have nothin' but the clothes they stand up in? I saw what it was like on that Ambinas Estate. Marsh pretty much had to deal 'cause his old man couldn't work."

Weinberg breathes in slowly, but it's only to hide his embarrassment. "I'll be honest with you, Carney," he says. "Some of the governors indulge, so they allow the drug cartels to prosper, although they'd never actually legalize the stuff. They want it to be available only to the elite that can afford it. All I can do is offer you my apologies and tell you that there's no such thing as a perfect society." He holds out a bag of mint humbugs, jiggles the packet in front of me, and tries to smile. "But we were talking about the ring."

"Wish I hadn't brought it up. Don't wanna think about it."

"Maybe it's a red herring," he says. "Some might suggest you blamed Marshall for the plight of your friend, Dakota. Is there any truth in that?"

Of all the questions he's asked, this is the easiest to answer. "No, not at all."

Weinberg leans back in the chair. "Perhaps we'll put the storytelling aside until tomorrow. I can see you're a little unhinged this afternoon."

"You're kiddin' me! We got this far, so you might as well spit it out. You left on such a cliff-hanger last time, after all."

DORAN'S STORY

When a police cruiser pulled up outside the Dover Plain building, Doran was being held near the front desk by Mr. Wiggins, the history master, the boy's wrists bound tight with parcel string to the arms of a chair.

"What's your name, son?"

"Not sure."

"Can you tell me where you are?"

"A building. Smells of… burnt food. Is it a hospital?"

"Did you shoot Dr. Hauntmead?"

"Who?"

"Okay." One of the officers freed Doran's right hand, then passed him some paper and a pencil. "Write the date here for me, if you would be so kind."

Doran wrote *January 1st, 2316,* and handed it back. "Just a guess," he said.

The officers turned to one another and began whispering.

"Seems placid enough, but kinda confused. You think he's just puttin' it on? A sneaky way of pleadin' the Fifth?"

"Reckon so. Let's get him outta here. He'll crack soon enough."

Of course, Doran didn't crack—he couldn't; he had no knowledge of the shooting at all—but unfortunately, the evidence against him was overwhelming. There was no denying the gunshot wound to Hauntmead's arm, and five witnesses had seen the suspect lying on the floor with the revolver next to his hand. More importantly, there was only one set of prints on the gun, and it matched exactly with Doran's. Thus, he was charged later that evening on two counts: illegal use of a firearm and aggravated assault.

The trial took place in May, and Doran was found guilty of both offenses. He was sentenced to seven years' detention in the juvenile wing of the Kakovellie Rehabilitation Center in Western Roe-Fotherguild, although there was some debate about shipping him off to Magnatella because of his previous conviction and the gravity of the crime. His age prevented such action, though. He was, after all, only fourteen years old.

The same day that Doran arrived at Kakovellie, the prison office contacted Dover Plain, asking them to forward his belongings for safekeeping until such time as he was released. Mr. Wiggins was duly appointed to carry out their instructions, but all he could find in the dormitory was a plush red octopus that had been stuffed between the headboard and the mattress of Doran's bed.

In the end, Doran D'Argent served only two years and three months of his sentence, but it was by no means on account of good behavior. Apparently, he became quite the hard case of the prison west wing, gaining something of a reputation for antagonizing the guards and general hostility toward any kind of authority. I suppose the only thing he knew about himself was that he was meant to have shot someone, and that was too much of a burden, so he walked around with a massive chip on his shoulder. Of course, we know now that he was innocent, but it should have been discovered much sooner. As a Cassafortan town governor, I'm ashamed to say that the system failed him entirely.

In the very beginning, his lack of any memory regarding the crime, and indeed his past life, should have raised alarm bells with social services. His condition clearly suggested a mental health problem, and commitment to a psychiatric unit would have been a much more fitting sentence. There, at least, he could have received the kind of help he so desperately needed. But there was never any follow-through with his case. The sad fact is, at Kakovellie he was more or less left to his own devices. No counseling appointments were made for him, no attorney was allocated to arrange an appeal, and social services did not visit him at any point.

As luck would have it, a new chief warden was transferred to the penitentiary in June of 2323. She was burdened with the unenviable task of whipping their affairs into shape ahead of the regional audit they were obliged to conduct every ten years. During this time, she slowly began to dust off a lot of the paperwork that had previously been filed away in the vaults and ignored. Of course, realizing how badly the establishment had let the boy down, she pushed for his early release, though it was wholly for self-serving reasons. There was a chance the auditors might select him for an interview, and prisons had been fined hefty sums in the past for negligence. Discharging him, she reasoned, meant that there was no proof of misconduct on their part.

Consequently, Doran was fetched from his cell on August 21st, 2323, and led out of the west wing, across the exercise yard, and into the main office complex, where he was asked to sign several discharge papers.

"As you're only sixteen and we've been unable to trace any family, we're sending you to a children's home," the deputy custodial officer informed him. Then he passed Doran a transparent zipper bag crammed with crimson-colored fur fabric. "Here are your things."

They gave him a token few bans and drove him as far as Tandorn Town, where they'd arranged a meeting with a social worker who was going to take over his case and deliver him to the facility in Grade Glennings. However, when the driver dropped him off at about three o'clock in the afternoon, in front of Tandorn's rather grand-looking Burwood House, Doran was understandably hesitant about entering. Instead, he sat on the surrounding limestone wall and emptied the contents of the plastic bag onto his lap.

There were just two articles inside. The first was a toy octopus the color of ripe strawberries, beautifully fashioned in the plushest acrylic with a head about the size of a grapefruit, and eight curly tentacles made from cream-colored corduroy on the underside. The creature had two glossy black beads as eyes, and a single curve, tenderly stitched beneath them, for a smile. The second item was an expandable sterling-silver bracelet— the type that a parent might buy for a newborn infant. When Doran inspected it closely, he observed that it bore a very simple inscription: 'Marshall Bexley, Hailey's Town'.

He'd already decided that he didn't want to wind up in another institution, but choosing somewhere to go had been a problem. Now that he had the enigmatic little bangle in his possession, it was just a matter of hopping onto the right train.

THE PRESENT

It's like I was listening to an outdoor symphony, straining my ears as it surged wildly to the kind of crescendo it had been gearing you up for all along. But just before it hit that final swell, the conductor threw his baton down, forcing the band to change the tempo, the pitch, the key—everything.

"You're wrong about this one, Nils; Marshall had a pop. He lived with him in Hailey's Town… and in the Troccas too. Last I heard, he was over in Stockton Grange gettin' his back fixed."

Weinberg is studying me like a naturalist, eyeing me up as if I'm some species that's never been cataloged before. "Did you ever see him?"

"No, but—"

"There you are, then. He most likely invented a father so that no one would be suspicious and report him to the authorities. That apartment he was living in—the one on the Ambinas Estate—it was never legally let. The council closed it off due to faulty wiring a month before he arrived in Hailey's Town. And he never attended school there, either. He wasn't even a senior."

It was a mean trick, springing the Cassaforta sham on me, but somehow, laughing like a demented drunk seemed to soften the blow. It's different now, though. I'm shaking my head like a spoiled brat, a tidal wave of rage swelling in my chest. I'm gripping the sheets with both hands, trying to beat down the urge to surf it, but it's useless; the floodgates have been rammed wide open.

"So, knowin' all this is meant to help me?! This is the climax of your goddamn story?!" I'm yelling so loud I'm freaking myself out. I kick the covers off the bed and leap out, and for once I'm standing over Weinberg, physically looking down on him. "I was dead on the inside. Yeah, that's right: dead! Everyone bailed on me and there was nothin' left at all—nothin' but a dumb, crazy-lookin' plant that somehow stopped reality... at least for a while. And then I stumbled on Lucy in the dinin' room, dancin'. Her, an elderly stroke victim, barely able to move, dancin' with all the lightness of an angel. And with him: this foul-tempered drug-dealer kid I never even liked. But somehow, everythin' changed when I saw it. It blew me away: her and him, and the way the misery of it all was lost, just for a moment—like the world'd somehow stepped outta time." The demented drunk is back, chuckling wildly at the thought of Lucy flitting about in the sunlight, but sobbing fitfully about the way things have worked out. The heat of the tears is stinging my face, making me gulp and splutter, but now that I've started, there's no shutting me up. "It dragged me out the quagmire. I was sinkin' fast, but he pulled me out: Marshall!"

"Simmer down, Carney." Weinberg is aloof as ever. Maybe he figures it's time for a quick hands-on lesson in practicing what you preach.

"No! You listen to me! I was headed for burnout, the point of no return, the point where I'd end up as the kind of spineless, selfish schmuck I'd always despised. But Marsh, jeez... he gave me back my soul. It was bad enough before, tryin' to live with all the sufferin' I've caused him, but now..."

"Carney, I think that—"

"Don't give a toss what you think. You hear me out! I've been rottin' away in here, listenin' to tales I didn't take to at first, but after a while I started rootin' for the little orphan boy. I buried my guilt in the craziness of his tales—made a connection, just like you wanted. I bore his sorrows, marveled at his dreams. And for what? You've used a crane to crush me, Nils—a goddamn crane!"

Weinberg opens his mouth, but I cough out a final epitaph before he has a chance to form any words at all.

"Marshall was… that huckleberry friend, the likes of which you find maybe once, twice in a lifetime."

"You got that right, but please, don't use the past tense."

I whirl round. A girl in a khaki Marines jacket is leaning in the doorway, a matching beret angled on her head. How long has she been lurking there, snooping? When our eyes lock, she frowns at me, but then her features seem to soften, and Weinberg says rather flatly, "Carney, I'd like you to meet Harper Daniels. A lot of what you heard in the stories came directly from her."

I'm lying down again now, looking across at a character from a story, who's crouched at the bottom of the bed. I knew Weinberg would find some sly old way to put my fire out, but this is something else. I guess this must be what it's like to be star-struck.

"You seem more relaxed now, Carney," he says, with more than a hint of smugness.

Domino is just how I imagined her: a light dusting of freckles over a button-like nose, deep chestnut-brown eyes that it's hard to tear yourself away from. Yup, you could lose yourself in those babies, alright. But there's something wild and willful about them too—a stubbornness that tells you it's a bad idea to rattle her cage, even though her face is bursting with how much fun she'd be if you could only get on her good side. And somehow, trying to square away those opposites gets you all worked up, makes you want to start writing secret schmaltzy poems late at night, or something just as lame. No wonder Doran got so hung up on her.

"I don't get it," I tell them. "No one mentioned the bracelet before."

"The toy was scanned as a matter of routine when it was first delivered to the prison site." Weinberg wriggles his shoulders against the back of the chair, as if he's trying to mold himself into it. He's probably glad the tale is over, and he can finally move on.

"They found the bracelet lodged inside the stuffing," the girl chimes in, her accent lacking the familiar Hap County drawl.

Weinberg is leafing through the binder again, and I wonder why he hasn't filed it away someplace. Then it occurs to me that there might be more. I mean, how did the bracelet get there? And what did he say down at the precinct that turned all my lights out? Marshall was born in Magnatella? He lost his memories when he was fourteen? That would hardly do it.

"Okay. I'll buy that. But what made me swoon over in the slammer?"

Before anyone can answer, a medic swings by, asking Weinberg to follow him. And as soon as they're out of sight, the girl bounds over to the doorway and peers out cautiously. Then she turns to me, thrusting a jacket and some baseball boots into my arms.

"Let's get out of here, Caldwell," she says. "Cops are busy with a fake brawl on the second floor."

We're past the coffee machine in the corridor now, skirting a waiting area where two old-timers in checked robes are battling it out in a coughing contest. It's the furthest I've been since they brought me here. We circle right, heading down a long, airy passageway, me always just a couple of paces behind the girl from the story. I alternate, one minute gazing down, watching her boots meet the polished red tiles as she marches forward, the next looking up as her hair flies away from her shoulders. Then, halfway down, she stops in front of a narrow elevator door, thumps at the button.

"He's getting to the crux of it now," she whispers, as we wait for the cage to come down. "But I don't think he should be the one to tell you."

45

The Crimson Octopus

pictured monitors, tubes, ventilators wheezing up and down. I thought his face would look kind of different too—maybe older or scarred in some way—but it's not like that at all. You'd think he was in the middle of a nap if it weren't for the hospital bed, the cannula scratched in his hand, the drip.

"This is my cousin," Domino tells the medic. "Can you give us a couple of hours?"

Once the medic's out the way, we crouch either side of the bed, and it's then that I catch sight of the blue-black corvid inked onto Marshall's wrist. The wings are fully opened, the letters 'AA' jumping right out at me in the middle of the chest—everything just like Earl set out in the blueprint.

"Jeez. He told me 'bout a tattoo, but I never thought to ask what kinda bird it was. It's a goddamn raven. It's gotta be."

"I saw it yesterday," the girl says, brushing Marshall's hair out of his eyes. "Memories must be in there somewhere."

"He was poppin' pug-flower, y' know. Said that's what made him get it. Said it was somethin' he just had to do."

"Musta been helping him remember—stuff from way back, I mean."

"And there was me, takin' it to forget. Kind of ironic, huh?" I have to stare real hard at the artwork just to keep from full-on bawling. "What became of Carina, anyway?"

Domino gets up, strolls over to the window, and slowly slides the frame up with both hands. "She used to live with me in Linstock, over on the Nellic Islands, but right now…"

A dark ball of plumes steps onto the ledge and prances proudly onto the girl's forearm. The sight of the critter makes me gasp out loud, gets me all giddy. The legs are like the puffed-up pants of an Arabian knight at the top, but thin as pipe cleaners at the bottom. And the feet are all ringed and gnarly, talons shaped like miniature sickles.

"Boy, this is a lot to take in."

Domino brings Carina over to the bed, lets her settle on Marshall's chest, and as the bird busies herself pecking at his pajamas, I reach out, my palm gliding over the quills.

"Man, feels just like silk."

Carina wiggles her tail feathers up and down awhile, then fans them out into a glossy midnight-blue oyster shell.

"So, it's true. All of it."

"Every word," Domino says. "Although I left out some of the details. Catlow was planning to move to the caves in Pabowimble after we left the city. Didn't want the authorities coming after her, so I didn't mention it."

"And you escaped from Drayborn?"

"Yep. Made it all the way to… Tusslin Kantop." Domino mouths the name, as if saying it out loud would be the worst kind of blasphemy. "But I was too late. Doran was gone and no one would tell me anything. Only found out what happened when Nils called me. It took a week to get here from the Nellics, and even then, they wouldn't let me see him right away."

"Musta been hard."

Domino takes Marshall's hand, wraps her fingers round his. "Nils said he'd see to it that I got full citizenship if I helped with the inquiries. And once I agreed, he let me have the letters— the drawings too. Gave me them for keeps." She smiles, but there's an ache inside of it that you can see, plain as anything. "There's one of Carina that's just like the tattoo: all fluffed up with the wings ready for flight. And underneath he wrote how desperate he was to get away from that hellhole—go someplace secret where no one could find him. The words he wrote were like poetry—a desperate intention, he called it. I'm glad I got to read those letters."

Hearing the phrase has an oddly calming effect. I know now, for sure, I was never a card short of a full deck. "Was there anythin' in the poem about a Dol Dimension?"

She looks over at me, knitting her brows, so much empathy there in her eyes it's like staring into a deep, silent lake. It's uncanny—makes me feel as though I've known her all my life. "That was part of it," she says. "And he wrote it on the back too, in big uppercase letters—colored it in and everything. I couldn't figure out what it meant at first, but then I realized it was just the scrambled letters of my name: Domino Daniels. How'd you know about it?"

After I've told her about the warehouse and the message, we sit quietly for a while. "Guess Doran came to the surface that night," I say eventually. "Anyway, why you bein' so nice to me? It's my fault Marshall's in this mess."

"Don't be too sure about that. Folks aren't meant to have wires in their brains."

Domino leans down, pulls something out of the bedside locker, and a character that was just a wispy notion in my head is suddenly brought to life. I'm face to face with the unsung hero from Weinberg's tale: the crimson octopus.

"They took me to Captain's Way, showed me his room. And this little guy was hiding in a box under the bed. He took it everywhere with him when he was a kid, y' know. Used to sleep with it next to him in the alcoves at Nentoke."

She pushes the toy into my hand, telling me without words how much she trusts me. My fingers dig into the worn-out fabric, trace the stitching of the sweet, innocent smile. And just by holding it, having it so close to me, I'm peeling back the layers of time, gazing into a gateway: the moment when he turned up at Maple Road, a fleecy mantle and a tangle of tentacles snuggled up beside him.

"Ain't gonna fester in here no more. Not without doin' somethin' to help. Look. Go back to Captain's Way. There's a key under the big boonstone in the backyard. You'll find a tin in the drawer under the kitchen sink. Get a pug-flower an' crush it. Bring me the juice. I'll stay here with Marsh. It's a long shot, but I gotta do somethin'."

I guess ninety-nine percent of the population would have called the nuthouse already, but not Domino. Maybe she was thinking the same thing. She checks her watch and bites at her bottom lip. "Okay. I'll be back before you can say 'Gilbert Gowder.'"

"Come on, man," I whisper, once she's out the door. "I know you can make it. And I ain't just sayin' that so's we can get to the bottom of everythin'. Ain't bothered what happens to me no more. I just want you to wake up. And I'll tell you right here, right now what I told lanky old Weinberg: I had you figured all wrong. Truth is, I never had a buddy quite like you. And if I could trade places with you, I would—no question."

I'm welling up, and all the while Carina nestles against Marshall's neck, her head stretched out over his jaw, her beak all bristly at the bottom, not smooth like you'd expect.

About forty minutes later, the door squeaks open and Domino steps in, but there's a weird clomping sound trailing behind her in the corridor—low, lopsided footfalls echoing against the brickwork. It gets louder, and I brace myself for trouble. If Weinberg wants me back in that room, he'll have a problem on his hands. There's no way I'm leaving Marshall now. They'll have to drag me there, kicking and screaming. Domino is holding the door, and I'm drenched in adrenaline, ready to give them hell, but it's not Weinberg who comes in—it's not even a medic; it's Lucy, frail as confetti in a rainstorm. The girl flicks the lock across, draws a chair up to the bed, and slowly steers Lucy into it.

"Lucy. Man, am I glad to see…"

Her eyes are glazed over, totally detached, like the last shreds of sanity have been drowned right there in the sockets. She doesn't recognize me at all.

"I sent a cab to fetch her," Domino says, passing me an old aspirin bottle with a green-colored liquid inside. "She needs to hear this, too."

"Hear what?"

"I swiped some pages from the binder while Nils wasn't looking. And when you're ready, I'm gonna tell a little story."

"Alright. But let's put some drops on his tongue first."

46

Kohoutek Scrub

When the sled came to a standstill in the small desert village of Kohoutek Scrub, Dolores noticed that there were no shadows.

"Don't be too long. And use the sunshade. The well's in front of the post office, on the left." Shillaker hated playing the overbearing medic, but he'd dealt with too many cases of heatstroke to give in to his inhibitions. He didn't want another, and it would be his fault anyway for not bringing enough hip flasks out with him.

Dolores stepped down onto the garnet-colored sands, squinting into the heat shimmer as she extended the white lace parasol that she'd carried in her backpack for the last five days. This probably passed as the focal point of the village, she thought, but it was just a handful of dusty market shacks with faded wooden signs announcing what was for sale, everything closed until three. There wasn't a soul in sight. She drew a drink from the well, but gulped it down so eagerly it started her with a coughing fit. In the end, Shillaker had to come over and carry her back to the wagon.

"You alright back there?" he asked, after a while.

"Yeah. Sorry 'bout that. Journey was a rough one, I guess, 'specially once I got to Ikeda Bennet. Big locomotives don't go any further south, so I had to get the little trains. Lots a' waitin' round on baking-hot stations. Nothing but cacti and tumbleweed everywhere."

"That's Regarafia for you. What did you think to the underground hotel at Norinko?"

"The idea—buildin' it outta clay, I mean—that was a stroke a' genius. It was so cool inside. And the guide couldn't do enough. Drove me there in the evenin' an' then out to the caves just before the sun came up. Even waited with me near the owl statue till he saw you comin' over." Dolores leaned against the window, taking in the sea of windswept mounds and ridges that dominated the route between the caves and the Rohart Center. "So, you can't travel by jeep out here?"

"No, not once you get past the Bunukuko Caves. Dunes are way too thick, so it's gotta be a sand-sled. Don't worry, though; I'm an expert in handling kuschada beasts."

When the buildings finally came into view, Dolores was pleased to see that they were much grander than the hovels they'd passed in the village. The main annex was a lengthy, single-story cabin made of dark-stained ulu wood, partially built into a towering sandstone outcrop at the rear.

"That's Tethton Rock," Shillaker explained, as he slowed the kuschada with a click of his tongue. "It's why we chose this site. Shades us real well. You'll be staying in the big hut over on the right. We call it the Homefell."

Dolores dragged her sleeve over her brow, scanning the rest of the encampment as the faraway bay of doster dogs echoed across from the canyons. There were six smaller cabins of the same design, all clustered around a central quadrangle that contained a large, hand-pumped well with a circular boonstone wall. "There ain't no faucets?"

Shillaker climbed down from the sled and opened the back door. "You'll get used to how we do things out here."

"Hope it was the right call—comin' all this way, I mean."

"Can't offer no guarantees. But it's like I said on the phone: I've been running this place nine and a half years, so the figures don't lie. Sixty-four percent of the patients who pass through these doors make a full recovery."

Adjusting to the climate was challenging at first, but after a month of resting, absorbing the bone-dry heat at the right times of day, avoiding it at others, and breathing in the sweet juniper-scented air, Dolores was beginning to feel less constricted by tight and aching lungs. If the test results were encouraging enough, they might even agree to send her back to Hailey's Town.

Shillaker skimmed through the notes and bit at his nails. "The bacteria are still present, and you're probably wondering why we dispensed with the chest X-ray."

"That's easy. It's 'cause I'm doin' so well, right?"

The medical officer glanced down at his records and scratched his head. He wasn't sure why, but he felt especially disappointed that the news wasn't better—more so than with any other patient. He pushed the feeling aside and focused on delivering the prognosis as gently as he could, just as he'd been taught all those years ago when he was a student on the Nellic Islands. "Look, Dolores, it's like this. Nunal consumption can persist for months, sometimes even years. Based on the lab results, I can't send you home, not even to visit. I know you're longing to get back to Chase and the kids, but the north can be so cold in winter. And on the upside, it's encouraging that you can do a lot more."

She was all set to return to the Homefell building, but Shillaker raised an index finger, signaling for her to remain.

"We picked up something else when we ran the tests. In fact, it's the reason no X-ray was performed."

Dolores frowned. "I don't understand."

"You're carrying a child."

Shillaker put in a request to the medical center at Ikeda Bennet for someone specializing in obstetrics, and in mid-December he found himself hitching up the kuschada again to go out and meet the medic at the Bunukuko Caves. She was very easy for him to spot; the young woman was carrying a portable ultrasound machine that had been carefully covered in plastic to keep all the dust out. An hour later, through warped and foggy images composed wholly of pulses and echoes, the fetus was identified as a healthy male of nineteen weeks.

"Bad timin', eh, Mr. Shillaker?"

"Maybe. But there's very little risk to the fetus," the medical officer told her. "You can carry on with your treatment, just as before. And you can call me Hillban, if you wish."

Two weeks after the scan, a parcel arrived for Dolores in the lobby of the Rohart Center, and Hillban took it upon himself to deliver it to her quarters. He watched as she untied the string, peered into the packaging, and pulled out two boxes: one large, one small.

"Chloe had a catalog from a boutique in Hubble's Town," she said. "Everythin's handmade, and there were ten whole pages of baby gifts. I couldn't resist."

The boxes had been neatly wrapped in gold-colored tissue paper, and as she carefully removed the layers and lifted the lids, Dolores was beaming. First, she showed Hillban a bright red fleecy octopus with a head the size of a coconut, elasticated tentacles coiled loosely around the body. Next was a silver baby bracelet that she was holding up to the light.

"It's perfect—just what I ordered. Didn't tell you I chose the names, did I? He's gonna be called Marshall Bexley. And I had Hailey's Town engraved there, too. Why, when you hear that wind singin' over from the Bolars in the springtime, and you see all those gorgeous purple-colored hills, you just know you're in the best little town in the world."

"Marshall Bexley Caldwell," Hillban said, smiling kindly. "It has a wonderful ring to it."

THE PRESENT

This time there's no nosedive to the floor, no Harvey Wallbanger shenanigans. I guess it's all down to Weinberg and the way he played his hand. I see it clear as anything now: that he was a goddamn conjuror all along, and I was just a kid at his magic show, waiting for him to pull a rabbit out of a hat.

"My mom's name was Dolly. That's what Lucy told me… Leyland, too."

"Guess they called her Dolly for short." Domino folds the pages in two and places them on the blanket. "There's a couple more sheets. It's about how the baby ends up in Magnatella." She leans over, squeezes another drop of pug juice onto Marshall's tongue.

I turn to Lucy. Her eyes are just like before: blank as the emptiness that swamped me after the Barraleah call. But in the dining room, when she danced with Marshall, they were vibrant as a field full of mountain laurels, and the spark of that remained, all the while he was with us.

I make a beeline for the window, pressing my hand against the coldness of the glass. Outside, ordinary people are going about their normal everyday lives: walking dogs, parking cars, playing baseball in the park. Right now, I can't help but envy them.

47

Full Circle

There must have been something about the way Dolores opened the parcel. Or perhaps it was how sweetly she talked about the wind singing over from the Bolars as she lifted the bracelet up to the light and smiled, much more to herself than to him. He tried to deny it at first, but when Hillban Shillaker went back to his office, he couldn't stop thinking about her. Over the next few weeks, his feelings persisted, and the more he saw of her, the more certain he became that it was not just a simple case of infatuation.

These days, Hillban is a man racked with guilt. He wears it like an invisible second skin that he just can't seem to pull off, no matter how hard he tries. He knows the choice he should have made, and if he could somehow reverse time, go down a different path, he wouldn't hesitate. They arrested him as soon as it was all pieced together, about sixteen days ago, and he sank to his knees in the main examination room at the Rohart Center, confessing it all.

You see, her symptoms got much worse at the beginning of March that year, and her health declined so rapidly that, by the middle of April, Dolores was bedbound and completely incapacitated. Hillban's duty was to provide the best care possible for his patients given the resources at his disposal, but he knew that, unless he could get her to Magnatella, she would not last much longer.

He went over the alternatives so many times that, in his own words, he almost lost his mind. "I never admitted my feelings to her," he told the police when it became evident that he could no longer cover things up. "But I couldn't stand by and watch her slip away. Making the decision was the hardest thing I've ever had to do."

The first option was for his patient to remain in Cassaforta and pass away in a matter of weeks. He might be able to save the child, but Hillban just couldn't shake the image of Dolores holding up the silver bracelet, her face the perfect picture of hope and delight. He wanted more than anything for her to live, to bestow the gifts, to watch the infant grow. The second (and only viable) choice for the despairing medic was to smuggle her to Magnatella as fast as he could arrange it, and he was running out of time. She would not be able to return from there, but in his eyes, it was a crime that a leptotronic cure existed and yet here, in the barren wastes of Regarafia, she was denied it.

It's the same for the family either way, he assured himself repeatedly. *If she dies in Cassaforta they'll be without her. And if my plan succeeds, they'll be parted forever, but at least she'll survive.* As a qualified medical officer, he was fully authorized to sign death certificates and even to cremate bodies if they were deemed a health risk to others, so it would be relatively easy for him to complete fake paperwork accounting for the deaths of Dolores Caldwell and her unborn child.

It was April 27th, 2307, and just after dawn when Hillban

removed Dolores' wedding ring and dropped it into an envelope, along with the phony death certificate he'd just typed out, and a handwritten letter of condolence for the family. Minutes later, he was draping Dolores across the rear seat of the sand-sled, buckling her in so that she wouldn't fall. Then he swung himself up front and clicked his tongue, urging the snorting kuschada to make haste to the caves, where a guide and a jeep were waiting.

Hillban could only watch nervously from the quayside as the unconscious Dolores, swathed in a blue cotton blanket, was carried up the gangway of the cargo ship *Prosperity*, moored in the solitary wharf at Port Helix, about eighty miles northeast of Ikeda Bennet. Crickets were chirping away from the scrubby yume bushes dotted around the seafront, and a gentle, dusty ocean breeze was lifting the tarpaulins.

"Make sure these go with her. Please. It's important." Hillban pressed a rounded parcel against the chest of the young deckhand who had agreed to sneak Dolores aboard in exchange for five thousand bans.

To his surprise, the boy delved inside the package and removed the contents, raising the little bracelet toward the veiled light of the two quarter-moons rising in the east. He squinted at the legend. "Hailey's Town, eh? That won't do. It's best if there's nothing whatsoever to identify her when she's found." He offered Hillban the trinket, but when he saw how deflated the medic had become, he shrugged. "Tell you what I'll do. For another hundred, I'll sew it inside the toy. That way, she can have the inscription altered once she's settled."

"And you say you can avoid the scanning on the other side?" Hillban was so fretful he couldn't stop his teeth from chattering, despite the balminess of the air. He felt like he was teetering dangerously close to the edge of some mighty metaphorical precipice. "That's crucial. Not just because it would give her away. I told you of her condition."

"Don't worry, sir. All the incoming crates get loaded onto lorries before inspection. I can sign that one off as defective, stash it in the trunk of my floaty while they're changing shifts. I'll get her to the park unseen, then call an ambulance anonymously, just like we planned. She'll be safely in the hospital before anyone has a chance to ask questions."

Hillban returned to the Rohart Center in the dead of night, a small beige candle in his hand. Solemnly, he lit it, placing it in the center of his work desk. It was tough, accepting that the consequence of his actions would always be unknown. If fortune was smiling down, and Dolores and her baby survived, then the joy of that knowledge would never be his.

"I'll trust them to the hand of fate," he whispered. "And by the time this candle burns out, I will have convinced myself of their safety."

The deckhand kept his promise, carrying out Hillban's instructions to the letter. He watched from a distance as the ambulance trundled across the grass at Port Quadroon's Golden Gable Park in the subtropical Mackalonian region of Magnatella, walking away only when the paramedics knelt down beside Dolores. She was still clinging to life, lying on her side in a patch of sun-bleached clovers by Gables Lake, the crimson-colored octopus snug to her chest, held firm by the blanket he had swaddled around her.

Within minutes, a sub-lepto air ambulance was rushing her to Arnabule Municipal Infirmary about two hundred miles east of Banunus City but, regrettably, she went into labor and slipped away during the journey. She was pronounced dead on arrival at about eleven o'clock in the morning on April 29th, 2307, just as Hillban's candle was releasing its last tired curls of smoke. The tagmesh scan showed a blank, so the staff assumed Dolores was one of the vagrants reported three days ago in the vicinity of the old Quadmack Bridge.

The child, however, was safely delivered by Cesarean section about two minutes before his mother's death. He remained at the hospital for six more weeks in accordance with accepted practices, so that they could get him up to a healthy weight and be certain he was free of infection before discharge. As the authorities failed to trace any identity for the mother, he was surrendered to Banunus City social services, and temporarily placed in a foster home, awaiting a decision from City Hall about where best to send him.

THE PRESENT

"Then it's come full circle." I'm leaning on the window ledge, watching elongated raindrops spatter against the pane. And outside, a jigsaw of ebony clouds with little silver veins are sweeping listlessly over the sky.

"I guess Shillaker meant well," Domino says, hooking her fingers over the edge of Marshall's bracelet. "He was just too late. It coulda worked out differently."

"They sent him to jail, though?"

"Hasn't been tried yet, but I guess that's where he'll end up."

"And Strumpole? I hope they throw the goddamn book at him."

"Nils told me he was jailed about three years ago for beating a kid in his care. They sent him to Delmagado 'cause no one knew about his past and his other identity. The bad news is he busted out. Never been heard of since."

The door handle rattles, and someone thuds loudly on the wood. "Open up in there! It's Weinberg! The police are here!"

48

Weinberg's Request

When Domino unbolts the door, Weinberg, Bewick, Stringy, and Lardy file slowly into the room.

"You gotta come back down, son," Bewick says, his face all troubled and weary. "This place is outta bounds."

"No. I ain't leavin' Marsh 'n' Lucy—not now."

"You have to come with us," Weinberg says, firmly but gently. "You're not through with the therapy yet."

Domino waves the desert pages under his nose. "I took the liberty, Nils. Guess you can have these back now."

At first, he acts kind of put out, but then he just nods and smiles, slipping the papers from her. "Maybe it was better coming from you after all," he says. "Look, Harper, you take Lucy down to the lobby. Bewick can order a cab for you both. I'll deal with Carney."

They troop out, Weinberg holding the door for them, and then the bolt makes a thwack sound as he draws it across the catch.

"Why you lockin' the door? It's over. I know now he's my

brother, and I didn't collapse or nothin'. I'm totally fine and dandy: no more Wallbanger, no frettin' about Eastern Europeans."

"Please, sit down."

Weinberg gestures toward the chair. A minute ago, Lucy was hunched there, and now all I can cling to is the fact that the seat's still warm, evidence she was here in this godforsaken place. Weinberg settles himself at the end of Marshall's bed.

"I was put in charge of the wider investigation," he says. "I thought, at first, telling you straight was the best way to deal with what we found out. But after what happened at the precinct, I was told to make amends. They said it was inconsiderate of me to break it to you the way I did: without any context, without any backstory."

"Well, if we're talkin' about makin' amends, you gave it your best shot. Whoever 'they' are, they ain't gonna argue with that."

Weinberg suddenly looks twitchier than I've ever seen him. "You're right. All they asked of me was a page or two—for me to make a couple of visits to your bedside, to fill you in on Doran's background in the mellowest of ways." He's staring down at his hands, picking at the fingernails. "But once the details started to emerge, I just couldn't stop writing. I couldn't stop asking Harper for more information."

"Why?"

There's an awkward smile. "I asked myself the same question. Of course, the answer was staring me in the face all along, but I suppose I was in denial about it. It was only when you stood there today, yelling at me, telling me how wrong I'd got things— about the crane I used to crush you—that I finally understood. I'd never seen such passion, so much fire in a man." He raises his brow, like he doesn't want to be the one to say it—like he expects me to figure it out all by myself.

"Come on, Nils. Just get it off yer chest, once and for all."

He inhales deeply, the smile softening, the ice in his eyes

breaking apart, finally melting. Or maybe I just imagined it all along. "Alright," he says, talking so hushed I have to lean in close, "but you must know that I speak in the strictest of confidence, that I act in the most earnest, the solemnest of ways. My instructions were clear. I was to tell the story, but without divulging any secrets. I was not to mention the tagmesh—not even hint at the Cassaforta sham. But the tale makes no sense if you take away the corruption that drove it." He pulls the front of his store coat away from his chest, as if he needs air, all the while trying to hide from me that his hands are trembling. "And regardless of that, I told you the truth because, once you get to Magnatella, I want you to do something. In Doran's words, and with Harper's help, I want you to rise up: to defeat the tagmesh, put an end to the Tome-Bots."

"Me? Jeez! You must have a head full a' stump water. What the hell can I do? They'll put me in the tank, for sure. And they'll tag me anyways, once I get there. Won't be nothin' I can do to stop 'em."

"Carney, your situation makes you the perfect choice. Don't you see? For one thing, you have absolutely nothing to lose. But more importantly, you possess the traits: the ones necessary for such a role. I sensed a gentleness in your heart from the very beginning. And that's essential for devotion to a cause like this. Yes, it's a common quality in Cassaforta; you could say we're bred that way. But rarely is it coupled with a willingness to fight. I know you regret what you did, but you *can* do it. It's a part of you. It's in your soul."

"No, it ain't. You go off to Magnatella and start some half-assed war against the Tome-Bots. Leave me out of it."

Weinberg shakes his head, his forehead crinkling as he smiles. "Oh, but I can't do it, Carney. Yes, I have power, but you must understand that I sit within a hierarchy. If I were to step out of line, challenge the norm in even the smallest of ways, those above me would snatch it all from my grasp. Besides, you'll find a way to fight them." He nods over at Marshall. "You'll do it for him because he deserves no less."

"You can't do that! You can't say it! You can't put the goddamn burden on my shoulders. Don't you think they're heavy enough?" I'm standing again now, like this is all some crazy re-enactment of the last time I lost it with him. "You ain't got the right!"

I shake my head, wipe away a tear that I hoped wouldn't fall. I'm all set to beat it out of there, but halfway to the door, out the corner of my eye I see it: Marshall flinches, the muscles of his mouth, cheeks, and nose twitching, fingers stretching open. He clutches weakly at the sheets, eyes closed.

"Marsh?! He moved!"

Weinberg is leaning over the bed. "Marshall. Who did this to you?"

And then, with just a single word mumbled in sleep-talk, lips quivering, the kid from the Ambinas saves me yet again. "Yale."

"Carney, fetch a medic. Hurry!"

Down in the lobby, Bewick has my clothes bundled to his chest—the ones I was wearing when they first brought me in. "Guess you're free to go now, Carney," he says. "Squad over in the Troccas is onto 'em already. Just came over the radio, not five minutes ago. They wrung a full confession out the scumbags."

"I'm free to go?" All I can do is stare into space like some tripped-out nutjob.

Lardy holds out a plastic bag with a wedding band inside. "We don't need this no more," he tells me, but somehow I can't bring myself to take it, so he slides it onto the table.

"What's gonna happen to Marshall now?"

"Seems it was just a glitch," Bewick says hoarsely. He lifts his hat off, scratches at the wisps of hair above his ears, then coughs a couple of times. "Medics say he blacked out again, soon as they got there."

Weinberg glances sideways at me. "We need to get the four of you over to Magnatella without delay. Only there can things be dealt with properly."

Before I can read too much into it, Domino is beside me, pressing a cup of hot espresso into my hand. "Here, drink this, Carney. There's a lot going on, and you gotta keep your strength up."

"Sure. But maybe we can start with what really went down in the alley that night."

The sheriff nods slowly, plonks the clothes down on top of the bag. "Look, son. Get yourself dressed and meet us back here in a couple of hours. We'll have the full report by then." He winks across at Weinberg. "And I'm sure, once we've been debriefed, your learned friend over there'll be good for one final story."

"The rivalry is legendary, stretching back at least thirty years. When you entered Cuthbert's lair back in December, as far as the Sherman Tanks were concerned, you had a contract with them. And so, when you failed to offer repeat business, they became suspicious—assumed you were dealing with the Ghetto Destroyers, and in a way, they were right. Marshall worked for Kellerman, who'd taken over the running of the Ghettos three months prior.

"The Tanks began to spy on the Ghettos, and you may remember that Cuthbert still had that receipt of yours from Shancey's. Thus, when his spies reported that Marshall had relocated to Hailey's Town, he put two and two together, ended up with five, and sent some scouts out. They were watching when the two of you sauntered into Buddy's Deck for an afternoon coffee on January eighth, and they stalked you all the way home. Observing that Marshall had moved in with you, they concluded that the Ghettos had expanded their operations and that you were both working for Kellerman from the new base.

"Of course, Cuthbert was furious when they reported back to him, so he began to orchestrate a plan—a stitch-up that would send a clear message to Kellerman never to mess with the Sherman Tanks. He ordered the scouts over to Hailey's again, instructing them to purchase your mother's wedding ring from the pawnbrokers, to lie low until opportunity was ripe. You see, Cuthbert's been in the drug trade almost all his life, so he knows a thing or two about spiking a drink. The stuff they slipped into your coffee was tailor-made for bringing on the shurbs.

"Their original idea was to have you black out in Buddy's and carry you away, posing as medics, but when you succumbed in Broughton Alley, things panned out even better than they'd hoped. The alley is so narrow, anything that goes on down there is largely concealed from view. I guess that's why it's so popular with minors. But in this case, its blind spots played against you, turned you into sitting ducks. They thumped your knuckles repeatedly with a rock until they bled, and then they beat up Marshall, placing the ring in his hand as soon as he lost consciousness. After that, all they had to do was get you into position, alert the police, and wait for you to take the fall."

"Why'd it take so long to figure all this out?" Domino sure has a way with folk. The way she asks isn't pushy at all, but it probably has them feeling as guilty as they ought to be.

"Probably because they were meticulous, both in the planning and in the execution of the crime." Weinberg is clipping all the paperwork together before filing it away in the briefcase, and it strikes me that we'll be parting ways for good now. He nods to me, shakes me by the hand as if it's graduation day all over again, but this time there's no medal. I guess it's only right. "Wait for a call from Lansdown Ferries," he says. "I'll make the arrangements. Good luck with everything, Carney. I really mean that."

Outside, I taste fresh air for the first time since the arrest, but the sight of Marshall's Manhattan already has me in pieces.

"I'll drive," the girl says.

We cruise along Main Street, bound for Captain's Way, Domino behind the wheel, me in the passenger seat, and Lucy sleeping upright in the back. And all the while, Carina parades up and down the dashboard like some kooky fashion model, preening her feathers whenever we stop at a red light. She wobbles every now and then, and I cup my palms underneath her in case she falls, but she always manages to hang on.

When we pass by the station, I start to fiddle with the ring in my pocket, pressing my fingertips hard against the edges, feeling the coolness of the metal against my skin. It's back where it belongs now, but after hearing about the desert, the idea of pawning it seems downright criminal. *Just ride with it, Carney. This is all gonna take some gettin' used to.*

Finally, I step inside the hall at Captain's Way, feeling weirdly out of place, as if the essence of that medical room has somehow tethered itself to my psyche. The house seems bigger than I remember, stuffed full of ghosts and relics from the past.

"Y'all get comfortable in the livin' room. I gotta change outta these goddamn clothes."

In the shower, thoughts drift in and out of focus, but they're chaotic and random, at odds with one another. My head, neck, and shoulders seem lighter, as if the albatross I was carrying around was a physical bird that's suddenly upped and flown away. It means I can look at the eagle ink without being racked by guilt, but I can't seem to feel any kind of relief at all. There's just a sense of numbness, like I've been wedged inside the foot of a Pleasian iceberg with not so much as a chisel to fight my way out of it. Maybe I need some sort of road map to tell me how to act now that I finally know the truth about everything. I guess at the heart of it all, I'm just struggling with the fact that

Marshall's been left behind, and the grief of that is too much to bear.

I dress, hurry down the stairs, hoping the girl is still here. "Domino?"

Lucy's nodded off again on the sofa, and Domino's slouched in the big comfy chair, the corvid rattling her quills and scuttling about on top of the backrest.

"So, what do we do now?" I'm crouched on the living room hearthrug, a Hoffmans Lite in my hand. "I mean, literally, I'm clueless."

"We wait for the call, just like Nils told us. We know too much, so they won't drag their heels when it comes to shipping us outta here." Domino reaches over and scoops up Carina, who wriggles onto her shoulder with a funny kind of croaking sound.

"Look, did he ask you to do anythin' once you got to Magnatella? Shady stuff, I mean?"

"No, why?"

"He was on about risin' up—doin' somethin' about all the goddamn corruption over there. He thought I was off to jail, had nothin' to lose."

"There'll be a time," Domino says. "But first we gotta do right by Marsh and Lucy. And then you gotta pick a college, claim all the things fate denied you."

"And after that?"

"After that, there's a world of possibilities." She shuffles over to the fireplace on her knees, Carina with her. "I was majoring in politics over in Linstock. If Nils keeps his word and grants me citizenship, I can finish my degree in Banunus City. Reckon I can shake things up from the inside, once I graduate. And you could sign up for the Marines, get the tag downgraded to type two. Maybe we could even find some lepto-techs, get them on our side. I mean, Strumpole figured out how to deactivate the damn things, so we know it's possible. But all that's a long way off. For now, we just gotta take one day at a time. Mind if we light the fire? It's awful cold in here."

Once the flames are roaring in the grate, Domino hunches beside them, calmly stoking the coals. Carina is fanning her wings at them, like a set of huge, feathery bellows. It's just after nine, and I can hear the gawd warblers scurrying about on the porch.

The girl glances over at Lucy. "You know, when we get across, there's every chance that…"

"They couldn't save Dolly. Sorry, didn't mean that to come out so cranky. Guess I'm just whipped."

Domino doesn't answer. She's gazing into the fire as it sputters and spits, and I wonder if she's making up some tale, just like all those years ago, back on *The Dreamcatcher*. Then, out the blue, she asks, "You want me to help with Lucy's packing?"

"Sure," I say kindly as I can, eager to make up for being so crabby. "After all, you're the expert on Magnatella and what folk might need over there. Just hope they let me bring my Buddy Holly records."

49

Duality

'm slipping into that whimsical realm between wakefulness and sleep. There, *The Dreamcatcher* and the pirate ship drift slowly downstream in deep, semi-tidal waters, gently shunting into each other every now and then, as if some weird undercurrent is silently nudging them toward the same fate, determined to synchronize everything.

Leyland elbows me and my eyes jar open.

"Have a mint, Carney. Might steady your nerves." He still looks dazed, just like he did when we got to the end of the story, late yesterday evening. It was the short version, but I guess it's not every day you gain a brother.

Domino has been left holding the crimson octopus, so to speak. She keeps winding the tentacles round her fingers and then unraveling them, all the while gazing down at Marshall's artwork spread out on her lap.

"He'll be okay," I tell her, doing my best to smile, but I'm not sure who I'm trying to convince, and she doesn't quit with the twiddling.

"This is the finest hospital on the planet," Leyland says, for about the fifth time since he watched the porters trundle Lucy's bed down the blindingly white corridor.

"You already said that, Leyland."

I click the fastener open and lay the akka-dial watch flat in the palm of my hand, where I can feel its weight, follow the sweep of the slim little second hand. I guess, in our own way, we're all grasping onto something.

"How you findin' the zipper?" Leyland asks after a while, trying to fill the silence.

"Didn't feel a thing when they did it. Can't get used to havin' a phone in my head, though… and Magnatellan music, well, there just ain't no soul to it. The Cassaforta sound was way more classy."

Leyland turns to the girl, his eyes settling on the faded pastel sketch. "How 'bout you, Domino? I hear you used to be anti-tagmesh."

"Still am. I just did what I had to, so's I could be here for Marshall. It's not the end of the road, though. I'm biding my time."

They tagmeshed us almost as soon as we came ashore in Port Crompton, at about nine o'clock yesterday morning. I must admit, despite what she told me, I half-expected Domino to hoof it out of there, but she just sat in the chair and let them bring that big silver dome down over her head. Anyway, Weinberg kept his part of the deal. The paperwork granting Banunal citizenship to one Harper Perkin Daniels was fully signed, sealed, and delivered in the Magnatella consulate room on board the ocean liner *Papillon* while we were still in transit. She won't have to worry about being dumped on an Earth ship anymore. They also made out a birth certificate for a Marshall Bexley Caldwell, born April 29th, 2307, stamping it with the official Magnatellan crest, and trusting it to my safekeeping along with a signed letter of consent from the government for the removal of his makeshift tagmesh.

Domino passes me the picture—the one of Carina with the poem underneath—and when I flip it over, I'm hit by the starkness of thirteen uppercase characters that were drawn in yellow pastel and bordered with black, more than six years ago: 'A DOL DIMENSION'. Having this here with me, being able to see and touch it, is like being granted a peculiar kind of validation. It's proof that someone lived, and that they laughed, loved, lost, suffered, and yet somehow survived. But more than that, it points to a rare and secret truth—one that even wily old Weinberg never managed to fathom. I'm holding a miracle in my hands, and it gives me the nerve to trust, more than ever, that they'll be coming back—both of them.

At about a quarter past six, a resident surgeon strides into the waiting room, all pea-green scrubs and shiny skin. I shake Leyland lightly by the arm to wake him.

"Right," the surgeon says. "You're here with Lucy and Marshall Caldwell."

Leyland sits up with a start, his face pale as the decor, but somehow, I know everything's going to be okay.

"Both operations went well," the resident tells us. "We removed the rogue zipper from Marshall's brain, and unlike a standard tag, there was no permanent connection to the hippocampus. My bet is, he'll get his memories back right away. As for Lucy, it was a textbook case—a real success for us, because we were able to reverse so much of the stroke damage. I'd estimate about ninety-eight percent for speech, and eighty-five for movement. She'll likely need some long-term therapy to get properly mobile and conversant again, but the prognosis is excellent."

"When can we see them?" Domino asks, head held high. She's smiling so much she looks fit to burst.

"Best leave it till morning. Oh, and just so as you aren't fretting about it, they're both officially exempt from the zipper on account of their medical history. It'll just be a tracker in the ankle, once they're ready for that."

"Come on then, Carney," Domino says. "There's someone I'd like you to meet."

The air smells moist and earthy as we duck through a sinkhole into the cavern, every trace of light swallowed whole. Carina flutters between columns, her squawk a question, like she's calling out for someone—a girl who lived here once, in the shadows.

Domino skirts the cave wall until she finds a small crevice, pulls out an oil lamp, then strikes at a match. "Catlow? You here? It's Domino." The words echo back at her, beads of water plopping steadily into a gour on the other side—a pool that ancient tides must have gouged, millions of years ago. It's like standing in a mausoleum.

"Maybe she's out scrobblin'."

"Look at all the cobwebs, though, Carney. No one's been here, not in a long time." Domino troops forward, the beam from the lamp curling, quivering as she walks.

"I'll wait here, Dom. It's kinda spooky."

In a ruckus of wings, Carina is suddenly on Domino's shoulder, puffing herself up, a noise in her throat like a car blinker gone crazy.

"Carney! Over here, on the wall. It's a message, written in the Shadow Dwellers' code."

I move closer, feeling my way with my hands, careful not to stumble. Then I see symbols flickering, swirly white glyphs etched onto a flat part of the crag where Domino waits with the lantern.

"Looks like the Rosetta Stone or somethin'. You can read it, though?"

It's murky as hell, but when the rays fall on her face, there's a stifled kind of dread in her eyes that sets me off shuddering.

"For pity's sake, Domino, tell me what the damn thing says. I'm hittin' the panic button big time over here."

"She went north about six months ago. Went to join up with a group of anti-tagmesh militants she'd heard rumors about. The message talks about taking down the lepto servers—the ones that host the Grand Models."

"You'll be leavin' us, then." My words are rough and sour, laced with a disappointment it's too late to hide. Shamefaced, I try to get a hold, talk to her kindly, but it's hard to cover up how burned I'm feeling. "Look, you can't just go tearin' off. Marshall needs you right now."

Domino shakes her head, the shadow of it spreading out across the rock face as the lamp bobs to and fro in her hand. "I won't go," she says, her eyes in the dimness like dark ships gliding silently through fog. "If the fight was more important than him, I never woulda let them tag me."

"Sorry for assumin'. Guess I'm just used to folks bailin' on me. Goddamn it, you've restored my faith in humanity, Domino Daniels. You know that?"

I'm expecting a smile, maybe a wink, or a quick thump on the shoulder, but she's frowning, my reflection just a passenger on those dark, misty ships.

"I meant what I said about college," she says. "Life owes us that much. And everything we learn there, we can use against the system." Still, there's no smile, and I figure there's got to be a reason.

We pick our way back to the sinkhole, arm in arm, the warm velvet of Carina's feathers brushing my cheek.

"You gonna tell me what's up?"

"Okay, but you're not gonna like it."

"Tell me anyway."

"At the end of the message, Catlow wrote about the group's leader." The girl turns to face me, Carina still gripping her shoulder, a low moaning coming from the back of the raven's gullet. "It's a man called Torgon."

A solitary caw ricochets through the emptiness, clean as a gunshot. *So much fire in a man!* And Weinberg must have known it was the exact same feeling when Ranton stood there, knife in hand: the fist, the blow, the Sunday punch.

"The urge is there, Dom. Just wanna track the scumbag down, give his ass a kickin' he'll never forget. Musta been why Nils singled me out. Guess I'm nothin' but a lowlife after all."

For a while, she acts like I'm some crazy, surrealist painting hung in a gallery—something folk are meant to gawk at as they try to figure out what the hell it all means. But then the smile I was waiting for appears—not on her mouth, but in her eyes—a smile that has the air of an old mulled wine.

"Wait till tomorrow before you decide anything," she says. "Just wait till then."

Friday, February 13th, 2325

You'd better get down here, the chief of surgery wrote when he zapped Leyland at about seven in the morning. *We've never seen anything like it.*

Out on the ward, an orderly points to a side room with ivory-colored swing doors. Domino pushes them open, and next thing I know, I'm doing a double take. Marshall is slouched in the chair next to Lucy's bed, reading aloud from *The Call of the Wild* like he's just another visitor. If he wasn't lost in an oversize hospital gown, I'd probably have been totally fooled. But when he catches sight of us, he just sits there, stiff as a ramrod, as if three phantoms just strolled in. Then he gets up real slow.

"Careful," Lucy says. "You were under the knife not s' long ago. Mind you, if that intern comes back—the one with the Mars tattoo and the silver earring—I might get up just so's I can keel over in front of him."

"Jeez, Luce." Leyland marches over to the bed. "Resident said you'd need therapy."

"Didn't figure on a Caldwell for a patient."

"But it's been so long since I heard you talk that way. Feels kinda like… I dunno… what d' ya reckon, Carney? You're the buddin' writer."

"Dunno either, Ley. Guess I could make somethin' up, but you know as well as I do there ain't no words good enough." It's true. Right now, the only words that matter are the ones coming out of Lucy's mouth, each one a sublime little time capsule that the genius of Dillinger somehow managed to unearth. "Your right arm—can you…?"

"If you ain't brought cards, I'll clout you with it," she says with a quirky kind of grin I'd totally forgotten about. Then she frowns a little. "Look, I can feel it. That's more than I could do before."

"Sorry 'bout the cards, Luce. We got you some flowers, though." Leyland lays the pink peonies down on the bed, along with the white apple blossoms we picked out for Marshall. It's how we imagined the ones out the back at Maple Road.

"Well, glory be. Where the hell we gonna find a vase big enough for those?"

Marshall stares across at the Earth girl, and this time there's no mistaking the look in his eyes. Maybe once, for the longest while, there was a kind of brooding emptiness, a hole wide enough to make you think the stars had fizzled out. But now they're misted over, draped in the dew of his unborn tears. "Probably shoulda ditched that lifeboat," he says, with a wink. He breathes in deep, swallows hard, but there are too many tears now, and nothing can stop them from falling.

"Maybe it was just the way things were meant to be," Domino tells him. "You'll get what I mean, once you've heard the story." She holds out the crimson octopus, and it's like she's standing at the waterfront again, all those years ago, moon-dimples in full bloom. "I brought him," she says.

"And Carina? The Sergeant?"

"They're waiting for you."

Marshall reaches for her, and I can't help but hear Weinberg's vaporous voice spinning dizzily through time and space. It's talking about violins and Irish jigs, about folks rising out of their seats, driven to dance purely from the joy of being alive.

Domino was trying to tell me something in the cave last night, and I think that's what it was. I close my eyes, and Lucy and Marshall are there again, where, within the very bones of me, they always will be, swaying to and fro in the dining room at Captain's Way, with Sam Cooke, the gramophone, the little patch of sunlight, golden on the floor. It's what they're made of, and what I'm made of too.

How could I forget?

Epilogue

Back in Cassaforta, I'd never have known The Sergeant was playing Mozart's 'Flute Concerto Number Two in D Major'. Maybe that's the thing about college: you suddenly become all cultured without realizing it. Anyway, the music's only part of what's in store. There's a brand-new rosewood flute on the table as well, all boxed up and wrapped in silver ribbons. There's even an octopus-shaped cake that Leyland had specially made.

Carina lets out a sharp croak—no doubt her way of telling Marshall to hurry up and open the next package—and at first it looks like he's going for the big flute box, but then he reaches for the one that Lucy and I ordered from Tilbury's.

Tanith grips my hand. "This is the moment," she says.

Time, I've come to appreciate, is made up of these mysterious little things called moments, and they can be a real mixed bag. But when you string them all together and start to pick out the gems, you understand that, even though we're stumbling about in the dark, life can be wonderful. That's why I like to dabble my feet in the past every now and again, as an exercise in sifting out the diamonds, large and small. The most rare and precious could be something as simple as gathering round a campfire in the Old Kandal Valley, summer's wind warm on your face, or leaping into a stretch of clear, babbling water just for the hell of it. And it's wondering about the next one that, for me, keeps the beasts, cobwebs, and B-sides at bay—stops me from fussing and fretting about the future. In any case, it seems to be shaping up pretty well.

I'm studying to be a psychologist at Hordsparn College in Banunus City, and for the past three months I've been dating a very classy lady called Tanith, who works at the planetarium there. Marshall's majoring in art and literature, Domino's taking politics, and we all live in the same hall on campus, near a big lake where we go canoeing twice a week. And now that we're here in Magnatella, it's almost like the good old days are back because Booker gets to travel down from Amchuda some weekends to visit with us. When she zaps me about it, she calls it an Arch Angels reunion, and that's how I've come to think of it—with Dom and Tan as honorary members, of course.

We also ran into Mackenzie Mulhoone back in December at a careers fair in Palderboon. She told us that when she left Lope Horn for sports college last September, Earl went back to Hailey's with the intention of setting up his own motorcycle repair store. I often wonder how he's doing back there, and whether he's missing the old gang, but then I remember how tough and easy-going he is, and I figure he'll always be winning, no matter what he chooses to do. I guess Taylor must be out there somewhere too, wandering from town to town on that never-ending journey he was so hell-bent on chasing. Or maybe he's moved on to those 'more wholesome pursuits', whatever they might be.

I rarely think about Dakota these days. Sometimes it crosses my mind whether she ended up with that guy from Barraleah, but it's no great shakes; if she did, I'm happy for her.

You're probably wondering about Weinberg, though, and how I can bask in all this newfound serenity when his request that I 'rise up' is dangling in front of me like the sword of Damocles. I mean, college days won't last forever, and that guy Strumpole is still at large, spearheading the goddamn campaign I'm supposed to up and join. But I think part of being able to stay cool about the whole crazy business comes from knowing how hard-fought the last battle was. I mean, conquering the pug-flower. And against all the odds, I nailed it—after Marshall gave my moral compass a swift kick in the right direction.

In any case, as well as studying full-time and going steady with Marshall, Domino's also plotting out a whole revolution in the lined pages of a pocket-size notebook that Humbucker gave her from his old-time Earth collection. "We can't afford to get complacent," she reminds me every once in a while. "If we don't push for freedom of movement, for uniting the continents, people are gonna carry on dying in Cassaforta from lack of medical care. And we'll never see the place again—never catch up with the ones we left behind."

So, yeah, Domino's plans and Weinberg's request are always at the back of my mind, but the more I think about it, the more convinced I am that Strumpole was wrong. It's not about whether you fulfill folks' expectations or surpass them; it's about staying true to your own. And now that the dust has settled on everything, I'm just as sure that, when the time comes, I won't be scared to stand up and be counted, to speak out against the corruption that's rife on this continent—spell out what needs to be done. Or, rather, even if I'm quaking in my boots, I'll do it anyway—because, in Catlow's words, there'll always be someone covering my back.

Marshall tears into the paper, pulling out the box and then the watch, and Lucy leans in close, whispering, "That's from me 'n' Carney, and it's all been set. If you look up at the sky, Marsh, you'll see just how beautifully it works."

He takes a slug from the beer bottle. "Well, we got Akkasine up there, waxin' crescent, and Akkasom's the same shape, but wanin'. Lemme check… She's right, y' know, Dom. That's just what the dials say."

Everyone is gazing up at the heavens, the moons about the same height above the horizon, a handspan apart, like a pair of wise, silvery eyes glittering down on us.

Lucy's in her element. "Wish I'd brought the ole telescope now. Never seen the stars shine so bright. But what the hell. Let's get our priorities right. Who wants another beer? Leyland? Domino?"

"She's fond of this little tavern, your Lucy," Humbucker says.

"Yup. It's one of her all-time favorite places."

I glance across at the stillness of the canal, where mottled ripples of light are playing on the shadows. And just for a moment, the hull of *The Dreamcatcher* seems to break into a smile.

Acknowledgments

I should like to thank the following people for their contribution toward making this project a reality: my editor, Faye L. Booth; Lauren Bailey, Hannah Cather, Jonathan White, Lauren Stenning, Stephanie Carr, Katy Hare, and Jessica Woodward at Troubador; my beta readers, Nadene du Plooy, Julia Spano, and Julia Chevalier; and Lucija Dupliak and Mariana Costa for their helpful insights.